BATTLEWOLFE

A Medieval Romance

By Kathryn Le Veque

Part of the original de Wolfe Pack Series

De Wolfe Motto: *Fortis in arduis*

Strength in times of trouble

A knight with a de Wolfe pedigree… as the bastard son of England's greatest knight, William de Wolfe.

But he doesn't know it.

Yet.

Warwick "War" Herringthorpe was born of a Northumberland de Percy daughter and the Wolfe of the Border, William de Wolfe, back in the days when William was a rising hero, unencumbered by marriage, free to do, and love, whom he so chose. A brief relationship with Jane de Percy left Jane pregnant and William unaware of the situation. Jane's father had bigger aspirations for his daughter than a mere knight and quickly married her to a much older, titled husband who was willing to overlook her indiscretion.

Years later, War has returned to Northumberland as a royal knight, the garrison commander of mighty Bamburgh Castle as Simon de Montfort creates havoc throughout England. Heir to a minor barony, War has made a name for himself as one of Henry's fiercest knights. In a battle against de Monfort's loyalists, the garrison at Bamburgh is joined by some of the most powerful families in the north – de Wolfe included.

De Wolfe allies who see Herringthorpe fight, including de Wolfe sons, swear there is a new force to be reckoned with in Northumberland. His gestures, movements, and appearance are reminiscent of a young William de Wolfe.

And the rumors begin.

When War ends up in a battle against opportunistic Scots, he is gravely wounded and crawls from the battlefield to stay clear of deadly Scots. He is saved by a young Scotswoman he never expects to see again.

He was wrong.

Upon his mother's death, War's true father is revealed, plunging War into a world he doesn't want to be part of. He comes to resent the Wolfe of the Border, who left his mother when she was pregnant, and so begins War's intention to meet the greatest knight in England. Perhaps he might even intimidate and dominate him. But there's only one catch…

The lovely Scotswoman who saved his life happens to be William's kin.

Join War and Annaleigh as they navigate a romance that is as complex as it is beautiful, where family ties will be tried – and tested – and love is the ultimate glory.

These are the original de Wolfe Pack in their prime in this story of secrets, redemption, and sacrifice.

THE DE WOLFE PACK CIRCA 1267 A.D.

(Issue = children)

Scott (married to Lady Athena de Norville, has issue)

Troy (married to Lady Helene de Norville, has issue)

Patrick

James

Katheryn (James' twin) – (married to Sir Alec Hage, has issue)

Evelyn (married to Sir Hector de Norville, has issue)

Baby de Wolfe – died same day. Christened Madeleine.

Edward

Thomas

Penelope

Kieran and Jemma Scott Hage

Mary Alys (adopted) – (married, has issue)

Baby Hage, died same day. Christened Bridget.

Alec (married to Lady Katheryn de Wolfe, has issue)

Christian

Moira

Kevin

Rose

Nathaniel

Paris and Caladora Scott de Norville

Hector (married to Lady Evelyn de Wolfe, has issue)

Apollo

Helene (married to Sir Troy de Wolfe, has issue)

Athena (married to Sir Scott de Wolfe, has issue)

Adonis

Cassiopeia

AUTHOR'S NOTE

This is something I never, ever thought I would be able to do again.

Write about the original "OG" de Wolfe Pack. William, Kieran, Paris and the rest – here I am again. And I'm thrilled!

Better still, we've got the (older) sons of William and Jordan in this tale as adults. Full-fledged adult knights, fighting alongside William, Kieran, Paris and the group. Super rare. We've seen it in a few novels (*DarkWolfe* comes to mind), but it's oh-so-rare. You're in for a treat – at least for the first chapter!

So, we've got a lot of complexities here, not the least of which is that this book is set in a time period where William and Jordan's sons – Scott, Troy, Patrick, James – are new knights. Scott and Troy are married and have very young children, but Patrick hasn't married yet. Their sisters, however – Katheryn and Evelyn – are married with young children (married to Hage and de Norville sons). Some siblings aren't in the story at all because the action mostly takes place at Castle Questing and the de Wolfe offspring are spread out and living in other places; as a source of context, this book is set right before *Nighthawk*.

A du Reims knight plays a secondary role in this story and so you understand his relationship to the rest of the du Reims family, he is the grandson of Dashiell du Reims from *Godspeed*. There are subtle hints as to his lineage, but to make it clear, that's where he comes from. His great-great-grandfather is Tevin du Reims. There is also a d'Vant, but no specific lineage for him. I do that often – the reader will just assume that he's part of that family, a cousin or otherwise.

Something else revisited in this novel is the chieftainship of Clan Scott. In the novel *The Wolfe*, that position was held by Thomas Scott, Jordan's father. When he died without a male heir, the position passed to his next brother, Matthew Scott, who was Jemma Scott Hage's father. When he passed away, the position went to his eldest living son, Ian – who is our heroine's father. If you've read *The Wolfe* (and it's a must for this series), then you know that Jemma had four older brothers, but two were lost during the course of the novel.

Now, let's visit the hero briefly, the bastard son of William de Wolfe. Of course, he's an overachiever. You'll see just how much. He's about three years older than Scott and Troy, so technically, he's William's eldest son. War is a man of dedication, intelligence, and skill, something that is in the man's DNA. You can't help but like the guy because he's very much like William in many ways. I think he's pretty spectacular.

Now, the usual pronunciation guide:

- The heroine's name – Annaleigh – is a variation on an old Celtic name. It's pronounced AH-NAH-lee. Say it fast a few times and you'll see how it flows. It's a genuinely lovely name.
- The hero's name – for the Americans and others who may not be familiar with English spellings and pronunciations – is Warwick but pronounced *Warrick*. The second "w" is silent.

And with that, I really hope you enjoy *BattleWolfe*. It has some truly touching moments in it, and humorous moments in it, as you would expect from the de Wolfe Pack. It's difficult to write a book like this and not feature William and Jordan heavily, so I run the risk of it becoming "their" book with my intended hero and heroine as supporting characters. But I believe War and Annaleigh really shine in this novel. I think you're going to love them.

Happy Reading!

THE MAN KNOWN AS WAR

13th Century Chronicle
Author unknown

In days of old
When men were bold
A warrior rose in the north

His time had come
This man, this son
To rise and show his force

War was his name
His skill, his domain
An abundance of courage had he

A cub, some said
His father, not dead
But shadowed by the greatness to be

All shadows found their way to he

War… they said,
it was thee.

PROLOGUE

January
Year of Our Lord 1267
The Scots border

I T HAD BEEN a horrific skirmish.

Unfortunately, it hadn't been for love or money or even territory. It had been a revenge attack, with Clan Scott and Clan Johnstone leading the charge, heading for Etal Castle because two drunken Etal soldiers had found a Scott lass tending a flock of young sheep just over the Scotland border near Coldstream and they'd attacked her. The girl had managed to get away with torn clothing and nothing more, but the drunken soldiers had stolen her flock and sold them off to unsuspecting English farmers.

That had lit a fuse to the powder keg that was the Scots border.

It was a mess from the start. Because Clan Scott was involved, Castle Questing and the empire of Baron Kilham, William de Wolfe, abstained from supporting Etal. When the request for support had been sent from Lord Manners of Etal

Castle, William had calmly replied why he could not defend Etal against his wife's kin and went so far as to call the men who had assaulted the Scott lass idiots. He further asserted that they were lucky he wasn't joining Clan Scott considering his wife was a Scott and directly related to the clan chief.

Etal hadn't taken that news kindly.

With the biggest warlord in Northumberland abstaining, they were in trouble. Etal had been forced to call upon the royal garrison at Bamburgh with their newly appointed commander because Berwick and Alnwick, with ties to de Wolfe, had also abstained. The only help Etal could get was from Bamburgh because no one else in the north wanted to involve themselves in what was essentially a revenge plot. Involving themselves would not only enrage de Wolfe, but it would put them in the sights of most of the border clans. When everyone was trying so hard to keep the peace on the rough and ready hills of the borderland between Scotland and England, Etal would have to fight this battle alone.

Except for Bamburgh Castle.

Enormous and well-staffed with about two thousand royal troops, Bamburgh answered the call. Since it was a royal garrison, it didn't have the family ties or loyalty ties that most of the fortresses did in the north. Because the king's troops were inherently against the Scots whatever the situation, Bamburgh agreed to support Etal when Clan Scott and Clan Johnstone crossed the River Tweed east of Coldstream and headed south, through lands belonging to de Wolfe and his close ally, Northwood Castle.

De Wolfe didn't stop them.

The Scots eventually came to a field with no name, only knowing it was north of Etal Castle, which could be easily seen in the distance. There were quite a few hills and dales in the area and the Scots came over a rise with Etal Castle laid out before them in the distance. The only problem, as they saw it, were the thousands of English that were on the field between them and the castle, but they forged forward anyway. Them, their support groups, and even the women who came along to steal from the dead.

It was simply the way of things.

The battle was nasty from the start. The English, mostly those in the crimson and gold of Bamburgh, were resistant to letting the Scots near Etal, so the fight was brutal from the outset and throughout the day, which turned into a very long day and an even longer night. Men didn't usually fight at night, as those battles were rare especially if there was no light of the moon but, in this case, the battle waged into the night. The moon was full and bright, illuminating the land and the killing below.

And the next morning came.

For a battle that had expected to be nothing more than a skirmish, it had become quite deadly. The Scots were incensed, the English were angry, and the entire situation grew out of hand. As dawn broke over the glistening fields, the English and the Scots were slugging it out in meadows that had turned from grass to mud to slicks of bloody mud mixed with mashed grass. Both sides were extremely weary and even the English were considering retreating to Etal and locking it up to wait out the Scots, who still had to make it back across the River Tweed.

The number of wounded was great. Because the Scots had been shadowed by gangs of women preparing to scavenge what they could from the dead or dying enemy, the English had made sure to collect their wounded and dead, hauling them back to Etal. Unfortunately, there had been several English who had separated from the main body, including the commander of Bamburgh's army and several elite soldiers. They'd gone off chasing what seemed to be the command of the Scots army and as dawn broke, no one had seen them for quite some time but no patrols were sent out. It was safer, for the moment, to stay in Etal until the Scots retreated. They couldn't open the gatehouse to send out patrols and risk the Scots somehow making a last surge for the castle.

What the bulk of the English didn't know is that the splintered faction of Bamburgh men had ended up in their own vicious battle with some of the Scots' commanders, off to the northeast where the River Till cut a swath through the countryside. That had taken place during the night and even though there had been a full moon, they had been fighting in the heavy foliage that surrounded the river for most of the night.

And that's where she found herself now.

By the river.

Her mother had told her to go to the river where her father and uncle and older brothers had been fighting. The carnage was heavy there, she'd been told. The women had been watching everything from a rise to the north and when they saw men finally moving away from the trees as the purple dawn began to break, indicating that the fighting was over, her mother told her to head in that direction. She'd even sent a couple of young women with her so she wouldn't be completely alone.

Get what ye can from the Sassenach, her mother had said. *Tend yer kin should ye find them.*

Annaleigh Desdemona Scott simply didn't have the stomach for the brutality that went along with warfare. Her mother and some of the other older women had no hesitation when it came to cutting off a finger to get to a gold ring or even an entire hand if a man was wearing precious metal around his wrist and they couldn't get it off. In the past, she'd seen full hands in baskets.

But Annaleigh wasn't as ruthless as they were.

The two young women who had followed her towards the thicket were hiding, cowering like fools. She could hear them sniffling. They didn't want to collect valuables and they didn't want to cut off fingers. The fighting in the foliage had gone on for much of the night but when day broke, she'd seen the Scots ride off north, at least those who had survived, and she'd also seen the English head back towards the south, some of them carrying wounded or dead.

She didn't expect she'd find much in the thicket.

She was wrong.

As the slender fingers of dawn began to penetrate the canopy, creating streams of light, she saw a boot. An enormous boot. But the rest of the body was in the shadow, tucked up underneath the bank that was crowned by the trunk of a tree. Half of the earth had fallen away, revealing the roots and creating a cave of sorts. The body that belonged to that boot was tucked up inside the cave.

Annaleigh could see everything but his face, shrouded in shadow.

"Well?" he said, his voice weak. "If you've come to rob me, I shan't give you much of a fight."

His voice was deep and rich, even in his weakened state. He rumbled like thunder. She could tell by his accent that he was English and her heart began to race. She had a dirk with her, but the size of the man's body was enormous. He was three times her size and then some. If he tried to charge her, even in his weakened state, she probably couldn't have given him much of a fight herself. It would be an odd battle – a tiny woman against an enormous, but wounded, knight.

"Ye're hurt?" she asked.

"I'm not sitting here to enjoy the sunrise, my lady."

"How bad?"

"Bad enough."

She heard him sigh, heavily. So far, he hadn't moved a muscle. He'd only spoken. Fingering the hilt of her dirk, she debated about what to do. She could have turned the other way and disappeared or she could try to take something of value from him. He had told her to, after all.

Or, she could help him.

Annaleigh wasn't unmerciful by nature. In fact, that sense of compassion is what had gotten her into trouble in the first place, the same sense of compassion and decency that had started this entire battle. She'd been the lass who had been accosted by the English soldiers because one of them had seemed ill and she meant to help. As it turned out, he was only drunk and he took her offer of help to mean something else.

So here they all were.

And this English knight was dying because of her.

So, perhaps she simply couldn't turn away, after all.

"What happened tae ye?" she finally asked. "Where are ye wounded?"

He didn't say anything for a moment. "I'll not give you any more help," he said. "You know I am weak. Take what you want and leave me to die in peace."

Those words brought Annaleigh closer, to within a few feet of his boots. As she drew near, she could see both of his legs now. She could also see the way he was sitting, sort of on his right side. It took her a moment to realize he was keeping the weight off his buttocks and lower back because she could see copious amounts of blood on the earth beneath him.

No wonder he was so weak.

The man was bleeding to death right in front of her.

"I'll not take anything from ye," she said. "But ye're injured badly."

"I know."

"Willna ye tell me what happened?"

He grunted, shifting slightly, and she caught a glimpse of his face. Straight nose, square jaw, and well-shaped features. Handsome features, in fact.

Very handsome.

"I took a pike to the back," he muttered. "And a short blade to the back of my left knee. Is there anything else you wish to know?"

She regarded him a moment. "Ye're a knight."

"Brilliant observation."

It was a derisive comment, one that left her feeling the least bit offended. But she'd been around men and women in pain and she knew that, sometimes, great pain made people behave in ways they wouldn't normally behave.

She could hear the anguish in his voice.

Anguish she had caused.

Feeling the least bit guilty that this man, this knight, had been forced to fight against her angry kin for something she had inadvertently caused gave her more patience than she would usually have. She had no great love for the English even though her father's cousin was married to the greatest English warlord in all the north. She had many English cousins as a result. She hoped that if one of her English kin had been badly wounded on the borders, that a Scotswoman might give him a bit of kindness.

Truly, it was all she could do.

Her mother *had* sent her to tend the wounded, after all.

"Let me see what they've done tae ye," she said, throwing caution to the wind and moving forward. "Mayhap I can help."

He held up a hand that was as big in circumference as her head. "Stop," he commanded quietly. "Come no closer."

She came to a halt. "Why not?"

"I do not need or want your help."

She sighed sharply. "So ye would rather bleed tae death?" she said. "I mean ye no harm, Sassenach, I swear it. Will ye not let me help ye?"

"Nay."

She cocked her head, frustration on her face. "I swore tae ye that I willna hurt ye," she said. "Not every Scot is out tae kill ye, ye know. Certainly not me."

He seemed to be growing weaker. He'd been propping himself up with his right arm but she could see that he was trembling. He simply shook his head, but the effort was too much. He lost his balance and his right arm gave way. With a grunt, he fell to the earth, his head resting on the dirt.

"Just… go," he muttered. "Leave me in peace."

Annaleigh was more determined to stay than ever. She had no idea why she was set on helping this stubborn knight, but she was. Perhaps it was her way of doing penitence for the battle she'd caused. Whatever the reason, she felt the need to do something.

Anything.

Or he would die.

"What will yer wife think when ye dunna return from battle?" she said, trying to reason with him. "What will yer mother and father think? Do ye truly feel that 'tis glorious tae die in a foolish border skirmish? 'Tis an ignoble way tae leave this life, Sassenach."

She was trying to provoke him a little, to force him to think. English knights were always so arrogant. So perhaps if she reminded him that he was about to die in a worthless battle, it might provoke him into letting her help.

But he simply lay there, an enormous lump of flesh and bone and armor on the ground.

"I have no wife," he mumbled. "No one who will mourn me other than my father and friends and king. I'd always thought… well, it does not matter now."

Annaleigh threw caution to the wind. She went to him, setting her basket down beside him and peeling away his tunic. When he felt her, he put a big hand back to swat her, but he only succeeded in shoving her a little. She pushed his arm away and continued working.

"Stop yer foolishness," she commanded softly. "Let me see if I can help ye. It may be too late, but let me see."

He couldn't fight back. He mumbled something, probably an insult, but she didn't hear him. He wasn't making any sense, anyway. Carefully, she peeled back layers of tunic and pushed aside mail, finally seeing the puncture wound in his lower back. The pike must have penetrated something vital because it was still bleeding, oozing out dark, red blood that was trying to clot.

It was difficult to get to the wound because of the layers of protection he was wearing, but the dirk she'd brought with her served a purpose. She cut through the wool and linen and leather, pushing the mail aside enough that she was able to finally get to the puncture wound on his lower back.

In the basket she'd brought with her, the one that held items she was to use to help her own wounded, she found her bone needle and silk thread. She also found a long pair of tweezers used to clean out wounds. She could see debris in the wound, so she used the tweezers to pick out what she could. It was slow going, and surely must have been excruciating, but the knight never made a sound. She wasn't even sure if he was conscious.

Hurriedly, she removed anything she could see, doused the injury with the wine she carried in the basket used to clean wounds, and stitched it up as quickly and as tightly as she could. When she was finished with that, she found the wound on the back of his left knee, which was very difficult because of the mail trousers he wore, and managed to clean that up and bandage it tightly. She couldn't get to it because of the mail, so she hoped the bandage was enough.

She wasn't sure if she'd done any good at all, but at least her conscience was clear.

When she was finished, she put her things back in her basket, leaning over the knight to see if he was even conscious. His eyes were closed and he was deathly pale, so she assumed he was either dead or asleep. It was difficult to tell. As she stood up, she heard his low, rumbling voice.

Like thunder rolling.

"What is your name, lass?" he asked.

She paused. "Annaleigh."

He didn't say anything for a moment. "I told you not to help me, Annaleigh," he muttered. "But you were gracious to do so. I cannot repay you for this."

Annaleigh was surprised that he thanked her. She was certain he would tell her how angry he was that she'd ignored his wishes. "Ye can the next time ye see battle against the Scots," she said. "Mayhap ye'll remember a Scotswoman who showed ye mercy. Mayhap ye'll show some of the same."

"Doubtful," he mumbled. "But I thank you, anyway."

"Will ye tell me yer name?"

"War."

"Yer *name* is War?"

He drew in a long, slow breath. "Ironic, is it not?" he muttered. "But that is my given name."

"Heavens," she said, more to herself. "Did yer parents hate ye, then?"

She said it before she even thought about what she was saying, which was a bad habit with her. But to her surprise, the knight snorted softly. "You will be astonished to know that they loved me very much," he said. "My full name is Warwick. But I have gone by War my entire life."

"'Twas a prophesy, yer name."

"Are you a mystic, then?"

"Nay," she said softly. "I canna divine the future. Sometimes I wish I could."

"As do I, Annaleigh. As do I."

There was something wistful in his tone. Perhaps even regretful. There were volumes of unspoken words in that short comment, perhaps referring to a life that had been hard earned and hard fought, a man with impeccable skills and breeding, now possibly to be cut short.

All because of her.

The guilt returned. Annaleigh came around the front of him, looking at him as he lay on the cold, damp earth. The way he was laying certainly couldn't have been comfortable. His head in particular was on wet earth, mud in his hair and on the side of his face. Setting her basket down, she went around the back of him again and knelt by his head. Pulling off the shawl that was tied around her shoulders, a piece of soft lamb's wool that she'd embroidered herself, she balled it up and gently lifted his head, slipping it underneath so he had something comfortable to rest his head on.

"There," she murmured. "I canna do any more for ye, War, but mayhap that will help a little."

He closed his eyes, feeling the softness and warmth against his cold and dirty cheek. "Once again, I am grateful for your kindness," he muttered. "You did not have to."

"I know. And that is why I did it."

"I shall not forget it."

Annaleigh was prevented from answering because she could hear men's voices in the distance. Scot voices. They were coming closer. She knew enough about warfare to know that if they came into the thicket and found the English knight, they would kill him and, somehow, she didn't want that to happen. Perhaps because she'd tried to help him, perhaps because she had caused all of this, she wasn't certain her reasons.

All she knew was that she had to make sure they didn't find him.

Grasping her basket, she trudged up the banks of the thicket, out into the meadow that was warming under the new morning sun. Immediately, she could see a group of Scotsmen, mostly looking at the dead around them, but when they saw her coming out of the trees, they shouted.

"Annie!" It was her brother, Robbie. "Where'd ye come from?"

Annaleigh gestured to the trees behind her. "Back there," she said. "Ma told me tae look for wounded."

She held up her basket, showing them that she was carrying bandages and such to tend to the Scots injured, and the men started heading in her direction.

"Did ye find any in there?" Robbie asked.

Annaleigh shook her head. "Nay," she lied. "No one. We saw fighting near the river, but no bodies. Did the English carry their dead away, then?"

Robert Scott came to a halt, eyeing his petite younger sister. She was a stunning creature with big, green eyes and curly, red hair that tumbled to her knees in an unruly and glistening mass. She was also well-loved, which was why they'd summoned an army to punish those who had accosted her. It had been costly, but no one would complain. If that's what they had to do to avenge their womenfolk against the English, they'd do it happily.

"The English dunna want their wounded tae fall victim tae the scavengers." He lifted a hand up to shield the bright morning sun from his eyes. "I suppose ye can tend the wounded out here. There are enough tae go around."

The men with Robbie started to wander away, picking through the dead, trying to figure out where to start with collecting the bodies, but Annaleigh reached out and grasped her brother's arm before he could get away.

"Come with me," she said. "Ye can help me. Are men coming with litters tae carry off the wounded?"

Robbie nodded, glancing to the north where the remains of their army was gathered. "They'll come," he said. Then, he sighed heavily as he looked around. "The lads fought valiantly. I was proud tae be at their side."

Annaleigh looked around, too. All she saw was carnage that she had caused. "So many... lads dead or dying," she murmured, blinking away the tears. "Oh, Robbie, why did ye have tae do it? I dinna want this, all of these lads dying because of what happened. Their deaths are on me."

Robbie's jaw ticked faintly, trying to remain stoic while his sister wept. "Their deaths are on the English, not ye," he said steadily. "We canna allow what they did tae go unpunished."

"And all of these dead men are worth the price?"

"I'd kill a thousand Sassenach myself tae keep ye safe," he said with deadly conviction. But he looked at his sister and saw that the entire situation had upset her sensitive soul deeply. She was such a caring creature. He grasped her wrist and gave her a tug. "Come on, *cearc*. Let's find those proud lads in need."

Cearc. It meant "chicken" in Gaelic, something he'd called her since they were children. Robbie was a good older brother, a little reckless at times, but loyal to the bone. He also hated the English with a passion so it was a good thing they were heading away from the thicket. If he discovered his sweet little sister had lied to him, things would not go well for her.

Annaleigh knew that very well.

As the morning deepened, she followed her brother into the fields of the dead and dying Scots, leaving a dying English knight somewhere back in the trees. Even though Annaleigh was focused on helping her own people, still, her mind was lingering back with the big, bloodied Sassenach. There was nothing more she could do for him other than make sure her kin didn't find him still alive.

At least let the man die in peace.

Truly, she hoped it would be enough.

CHAPTER ONE

Eight months later
Thropton Castle, Northumberland
Thirty miles southwest of Bamburgh

"**H**AVE YOU SEEN him?"

"Who?"

"Herringthorpe."

William de Wolfe's brow narrowed in puzzlement. His best friend and leader of an allied army, Paris de Norville, was asking him the question rather breathlessly. Given that they were in the middle of a battle, the exhaustion and excitement was understandable.

But this was different.

Paris had an odd look to his eyes.

"You mean the Angel of Death?" William asked.

"Aye."

"I've seen him in battle," William said, keeping an eye on the action around them. "I saw him cut down three men not fifteen minutes ago, men that were seasoned and skilled. Why do you ask? You know I've not seen him before today. This is the first battle we've supported Bamburgh in since Her-ringthorpe took command."

Paris merely nodded, a pensive and pregnant pause. There was much more he had to say on the subject but bit his tongue. For the moment, anyway. Clad in expensive and well-used protection, he commanded the armies from the House of de Longley, the Earls of Teviot. The red, black, and gold standards were distinctive in the north, announcing the mighty bastion of Northwood Castle. Being one of the biggest castles in the north with thousands of men on active duty, Northwood Castle was a force to be reckoned with.

But, then again, so was de Wolfe.

If the Earls of Teviot were imposing, the House of de Wolfe was twice that and more. Led by the man who was known as the Wolfe of the Border, William de Wolfe commanded five times what Northwood carried and more men than anyone in the north with the exception of possibly Alnwick Castle, another massive fortress in the north. But de Wolfe, once the captain of the army at Northwood Castle, had earned himself much during his service for Henry III, the man they were currently supporting at the moment. He'd earned titles and castles, and had at least six castles and royal garrisons he was responsible for. There was no one in the north more respected or revered than William de Wolfe.

But the man still answered the call to battle, personally.

Every time.

That's where he found himself now. William and his allies were currently doing battle at Thropton Castle because Henry had declared that they should. Bamburgh Castle was an enormous royal garrison and William and his allies were in support of Bamburgh's actions against Thropton. A certain

Hugh de Whitton, Lord of Thropton, had been a big supporter of Simon de Montfort. He'd even been at the Battle of Evesham where de Montfort had lost his life. When that had happened, he'd retreated back to Thropton and kept to himself, refusing missives from the king until Henry finally sent his royal garrison after him.

And that's where they found themselves.

De Montfort supporters had been allowed to keep their property if they swore allegiance to Henry, but that allegiance came with hefty fines. Close friends of William's, the House of de Shera, had managed to hold on to their properties but it had drained their coffers drastically. All over England, great warlords who had supported Simon de Montfort's rise to power were going broke. But de Whitton hadn't gone broke, nor had he communicated any allegiance to Henry.

He'd simply hunkered down and ignored the world.

But no longer.

Leading Bamburgh's mighty royal force was a knight who had earned a reputation at a young age. William had heard the name but he'd never met the man. These days, he didn't get to London because he had an empire of his own that took all of his time, so he'd only heard the name Warwick Herringthorpe. The knight they called War had risen amongst Henry's ranks during his battle against de Montfort, so much so that he'd risen to the king's personal bodyguard until Henry sent him to the north to man Bamburgh. Probably at Herringthorpe's request because any young knight worth his weight wanted to fight. He didn't want to be the king's nursemaid.

By all accounts, Herringthorpe was a hell of a fighting man.

William had seen the evidence.

But Paris' question sounded queer. Even now, the battle for

Thropton had reached the turning point because the gatehouse has been partially destroyed thanks to William's eldest sons. Thropton troops were pouring out through the gap, not a wise tactic considering there were about five thousand men waiting for them, but they'd begun to take the offensive. When that began to happen, the battle wasn't long for the taking. It was only a matter of time before the castle itself was secured and de Whitton along with it.

But meanwhile, it was a nasty fight.

"Well?" William said when Paris didn't respond to his question. "What about Herringthorpe?"

Paris turned to him, opening his mouth to reply, when they caught sight of a bright red warhorse heading in their direction. The horse was made brighter by the fact that his right shoulder had been sliced by a blade and blood streamed. The knight upon him was the most enormous knight in the north, with shoulders as wide as a tree trunk and strength that rivaled Samson.

Sir Kieran Hage had made an appearance.

"Kieran?" William called out to him. "Are you well?"

Kieran reined his horse to an unsteady halt, dismounting deftly and immediately focusing on the slice to the horse's leg.

"Aye," he said, grumbling. "They couldn't get to me, so they tried to disable my horse. 'Tis a deep gash."

William and Paris converged on Kieran, watching his back as he inspected his wounded horse. He'd brought another one with him, as most seasoned knights had a horse in reserve should something happen to their first choice, but Kieran treated his horse like it was a member of the family.

He didn't like it when his family was wounded.

"Bastards," Paris muttered. "Take him back to the camp and

collect a fresh horse. The gates have been breached and you will be needed."

Kieran nodded, grumbling as he took the reins and mounted the horse. "At least he will not bleed to death, but the wound must be stitched." He was about to leave when he suddenly looked at William. "Have you seen Herringthorpe?"

William shook his head. "Nay," he said. "At least, not face to face. The battle had started by the time we arrived and I've not yet spoken to the man. *Why*? Paris asked me the same thing."

Kieran flipped up his visor, of the latest style, and fixed William with his dark, intense eyes. "You do not have a brother you have never met running around, do you?"

William snorted. "Knowing my father, it is possible," he said. "Why?"

"Because Herringthorpe looks just like you."

William frowned. "But I am much more handsome, I am sure."

"Of course," Kieran said. "But Herringthorpe bears a strong resemblance to you in your youth."

William shrugged. "Hopefully he will not realize it and then expect something from the de Wolfe coffers."

Kieran grinned. "If he does, I would just give it to him. The man is terrifying."

William snorted. "I shall determine that for myself."

Paris leaned forward on his saddle. "He's not, mayhap, *your* bastard, is he?"

William shook his head. "I am not aware that I have any."

Paris pressed him because the man never knew when to shut up. "You were not celibate before you met your wife," he said. "Herringthorpe looks enough like you that I should be suspicious. You must find out who his mother is."

The humor of the conversation was running thin and William gave him an impatient look. "Enough," he muttered. "I would have known by now if I had any little de Wolfe bastards running around, so cease your innuendos. You are being ridiculous."

"Herringthorpe is not little," Kieran said quietly. "I'm not saying he's your son, of course, but he has to have some de Wolfe blood in him. The resemblance is uncanny. Mayhap a distant cousin?"

William simply shrugged. "Possibly," he said, disinterested. "There are enough de Wolfe relations throughout England, so it's possible."

The subject wasn't worth speaking on any longer, so they let it drop, mostly because William was growing irritated and Paris wouldn't press him so much that William would take a swing at him. That had happened before. Therefore, Kieran headed back to the encampment to tend to his horse while William and Paris headed towards the castle where the gatehouse was smoldering and heavy fighting was going on. William unsheathed his broadsword, followed by Paris, and charged into the battle where he noticed that two of his sons were fighting in a pocket of angry de Whitton soldiers.

The Wolfe was on the hunt.

Near the gatehouse entry, the portcullis had been heated by a bonfire and then chains were used, tied to horses, that partially pulled the portcullis away from the opening. It was a twisted mess, but men were still able to get in and out. He could see his eldest sons, twins Scott and Troy, and his third son, Patrick. Atty, as the family called him, was more than a head taller than any man around him. Patrick had inherited the height from some towering ancestor so in a fight, he was never difficult to find.

William headed towards his sons.

The Wolfe began to swing his sword, clipping men who were foolish enough to be in his way. Those who turned to fight were summarily dispatched, but the closer they drew to the gate, the thicker the fighting. William found himself not only fighting with his sword, but kicking men in the face only to have them fall to the ground and be trampled by his horse. The truth was that his horse was as much a weapon as his broadsword. The beast could kill a man easily. He could feel the concussion of bodies crunching beneath his horse's hooves as he rode up to his eldest three sons, watching Scott dispatch a man bearing de Whitton colors who tried to take his arm off.

"Where is James?" William bellowed above the noise of battle.

Three hands pointed north and William found himself looking up to the battlements of the castle where heavy fighting was going on. He could see that there was a great deal of activity – swords flashing, men battling, and he could see his son, James, in the thick of it. The man was bellowing like a barbarian, tossing men aside, gutting others, in a fighting frenzy beyond compare. Sweet, humorous James was a madman in battle. William could also see Kieran's sons, Alec and Christian, as they wrestled with de Whitton men who simply didn't want to surrender.

The army from Bamburgh, along with de Wolfe and his allies, had managed to divide the de Whitton army, but a hundred men or more had run up to the battlements, which was where the worst of the fighting seemed to be taking place. As it was, the gate was more or less secured and the gatehouse seemed to have surrendered in general. William pushed through the twisted gate to get a better look at the fighting on the battlements from the inside but the moment he entered the vast bailey, there was a new wave of de Whitton men and he, along with Paris, found themselves being pushed back the way they'd come.

The de Wolfe sword was swinging.

Truth be told, William was more at home in a fight than most. Even missing his left eye, which had been lost to a Welsh archer many years ago, he had better sight than most full-sighted men. He was joined by many de Wolfe soldiers as well as Patrick, who had shoved his bulk in through the opening, and they methodically began to cut down the de Whitton tide.

But then, William noticed something.

He saw why the rush of de Whitton soldiers had pushed towards him because on the other side of the group of men, he could see Bamburgh's royal troops pushing them towards the gate. Leading the troops was none other than Herringthorpe himself and William only knew that because the man wasn't wearing the crimson and gold of the royal army. From what William had been told, he never did. The enormous knight was wearing the latest and greatest protection money could buy and swinging a sword that was the height and weight of a seven-year-old child.

Most impressive, indeed.

What was even more impressive was the fact that the man had been badly wounded in a skirmish at Etal Castle about eight months before. It had been his first major skirmish since taking command of Bamburgh and William remembered hearing the story. He'd lain by the river's edge for three days before a scouting party from Etal finally found him and rumor had it that he'd lingered near death for several days before he finally started to improve.

One couldn't tell that by looking at him now.

The man moved like a force of nature.

Herringthorpe was pushing the troops in William's direction and he knew why – so de Wolfe and his men could cut them down or beat them down enough so they would surrender. Sandwiched between Bamburgh and de Wolfe, the remaining de Whitton troops had little choice but to surrender.

There was really no choice at all.

It was the classic collapse of an army.

When James, Alec and Christian began throwing men from the battlements into the crowd below, William knew that the skirmish was lost for de Whitton. Rather than back off and let his men subdue the enemy, William took pride in leading by example. He'd never been one to let his men do the dirty work, so he involved himself in the blood and gore of a defeated army. He kicked men down, shouting at them to stay on their knees while his soldiers moved in to restrain them, but when one of de Whitton's knights surrendered to him personally, he showed the man respect.

De Wolfe might have been hell in battle, but he was not without honor.

On and on it went until the sun began to set and the de Whitton army was nothing more than a broken mess of defeated men. James, Alec and Christian came off the battlements and, at that point, William backed off. He let the younger knights do their duty while he and Paris slipped out of the gate only to find Kieran and several other senior knights from Northwood Castle ensuring that any troops on the exterior of the castle had also been subdued and restrained.

William found himself looking at Michael de Bocage and Deinwald Ellsrod, two older and seasoned knights that had once been sworn to him when he'd been captain of Northwood's army, long ago. Now, they mostly supervised the younger knights because Michael had an affliction of the joints that made holding a sword painful and Deinwald had become the trainer of men when Northwood's former trainer, Ranulf Kluge, had passed away a few years earlier. Deinwald was the one mostly shouting at the troops and junior knights, making sure things were done the way they were supposed to be done. If they weren't, he wasn't beyond thumping on a helm.

In truth, it did William good to see such things.

He liked it when the world he knew, including grumpy Deinwald, didn't change much.

"Most of the de Whitton army is secure," Michael said with a slight stutter in his speech. "We are moving them to a holding area next to our encampment. Do you know what is to be done with them from there?"

William lifted his visor, wiping the sweat on his brow. "Nay," he said. "We are here in support of Bamburgh, so whatever Herringthorpe wants, we shall do."

Michael nodded, watching as Deinwald kicked over one of the enemy soldiers because the man was trying to stand up when he'd been told to stay on his knees. Herringthorpe and his men were now coming through the gap from the bailey of Thropton, seeing that de Wolfe and Northwood had the situation under control. It was Michael who lifted a hand to Herringthorpe, catching the man's attention.

"We are moving the de Whitton men to a holding area next to our encampment," he said, shouting over the noise of the men. "What would you have us do from there?"

Herringthorpe reined his distinctive warhorse over to William and the knights. His horse was a big, hairy beast with black and white coloring all over, making him quite unique. There was no mistaking Herringthorpe, which could be both a good and a bad thing in battle. Men could aim for him more easily.

They could also run from him more easily.

Lifting his visor, Herringthorpe looked at the collection of seasoned knights in front of him.

"I've not yet had the opportunity to thank you for your assistance," he said in a deep, rumbling voice. "I've only been at Bamburgh since the first of the new year and I've not yet had a chance to make my social rounds. May I know your names?"

It was a polite request and Michael replied.

"I am Michael de Bocage of Northwood Castle," he said. Then, he started pointing in order. "That brute over there is Deinwald Ellsrod and these men are Kieran Hage and Paris de Norville, the captain of Northwood's army. The knight at the very end is Baron Kilham, William –"

Herringthorpe cut him off, his gaze fixed on William. "De Wolfe," he finished. They could only really see his eyes and nose with the lifted visor and the hazel eyes glittering in the sunset were intense. "Everyone in England knows that name. I know you do not recall, my lord, but I saw you many years ago when you visited London. I was quite young, but I remember the awe with which your name was spoken. Henry himself spoke of you with great respect and adoration. It is an honor to finally meet you."

William nodded to the polite words of respect. "And you," he said. "I've heard tremendous things about you, Herringthorpe."

Sir Warwick "War" Herringthorpe gazed at men who were

legends in the north of England. De Bocage had introduced them so humbly that when War realized who he was facing, he was slightly intimidated, unusual for a man who was usually the most confident and powerful in a room of confident and powerful men.

But War was different.

He'd achieved much in his young life, though age was relative. He was younger than the men he was facing but at twenty years and seven, he was in his prime. An enormous man of height and breadth, he'd been a large child and, as such, entered training at an early age. He was big, agile, and smart, and that had equated into being trained by the best trainers England had to offer.

He'd been trained by the Blackchurch Guild.

A Blackchurch knight wasn't an ordinary warrior. He, or even she in rare cases, was the best trained warrior in the world. War had fostered in a regular household until he'd been twelve years of age and as tall as most of the men around him when his father paid a handsome sum of money to the Blackchurch Guild, which admitted War into its training program.

And what a program it was.

Warriors accepted into the guild trained for years. There were several "trainers" at the guild, each man specializing in something – fighting tactics, military strategy, interrogation, weapons. The list went on. Warriors spent months and even years with some trainers, learning from the best, and one unique aspect of the training was that of a monk from the Song Mountains of Henan. He taught a manner of fighting that required no weapons. Warriors learned to fight with their hands and feet, a brutal and powerful form of combat that made Blackchurch knights unique in the world of fighting.

War had learned that particular skill well.

Therefore, he was more highly trained than almost anyone on the battlefield, present company included. William de Wolfe and his knights and comrades had survived decades in the north and they were the best England had to offer.

But so was War.

He was a different breed of knight.

"Then mayhap we can convene the Mutual Admiration Society at some later date," he said, a twinkle in his eye. "I warn you, however, that my praise comes at a cost."

"Oh?" William said, amused. "What would that be?"

"You must feed me well."

William chuckled, glancing at Paris, who was smirking at the humor. The knight had a very personable sense about him. "That can be arranged," he said. "Bamburgh is not terribly far from my seat of Castle Questing. In fact, it is one of the few castles in the north that I do not control."

War grinned. "Nor will you ever if I have anything to say about it," he said. "Leave some castles for the rest of us, my lord. We have ambitions, too."

It was a jest, lightening the mood a little, endearing War to a band of men he'd grown up admiring. But also envying. He was a respectful man by nature, but he was also an honest one. He would never admit it, but they'd give him something to strive for. The knights of Northwood and, subsequently, the de Wolfe Pack knights were something all men looked up to.

But War wanted more.

He'd worked all of his life for it.

"I am certain that you do," William said. "Now that Thropton has been subdued, mayhap Henry will confiscate it and put you in command. I will personally tell him how well you managed this siege."

War dipped his head in gratitude. "You have my thanks, my lord," he said. "That is high praise coming from the Wolfe of the Border."

William's gaze lingered on him for a moment. He couldn't help but see that, indeed, there was some de Wolfe resemblance in just the few features he could see. The eye color, the shape of the brow. He was coming to think that he was looking at a cousin, but those questions would have to wait. There would undoubtedly be a feast at the end of this battle and William would do his interrogation then.

This fine young knight who seemed head and shoulders above other men.

"You have earned it," he said. "I will head back to the encampment, but I am leaving my sons and several other knights here. Tell them what you wish of them and they will make it happen."

"Thank you, my lord."

With that, William turned his steed around and headed off with Kieran at his side while Paris remained behind because Northwood's army was taking charge of prisoners by Michael's command. As Kieran was William's second in command, Michael was his. He watched Michael and Deinwald as they plunged in and began to move prisoners and, satisfied all would be tended well, he turned his attention to War.

The knight was speaking to a couple of Bamburgh knights bearing the royal crimson and gold. Paris reined his horse closer.

"Herringthorpe," he said. "I can send more men into the bailey to corral prisoners if you wish. We seem to have a few hundred out here."

War turned to him. "I have men inside as well," he said. "I will have them drive the men to you and you and your men can put them in irons. What I must do now is find Hugh de Whitton."

"You've not located him yet?"

War shook his head. "Not yet," he said. "I'll find a couple of men to interrogate and they can tell me where the man is."

"Would you like some company?"

War cocked his head. "You?"

"Indeed."

"It would be a pleasure."

With that, they headed off to the inner bailey where James, Alec, and Christian had come off the battlements, joining Paris' sons Hector and Apollo. A couple of senior de Whitton men were located and Paris, James, Alec, Christian, Hector, and Apollo had the privilege of watching a Blackchurch knight's interrogation technique.

It was truly something to behold.

Then again, so was Warwick Herringthorpe.

When the men finally broke, it took little time to find Lord de Whitton hiding in the dungeons dressed as a maid. The man had been positively terrified and rather than punish him once he was located, de Wolfe took control over the situation.

His lesson in benevolence had been an interesting one for the younger knights, War included.

Whereas War had used rather unsavory interrogation techniques against the de Whitton men, de Wolfe had changed tactics once they located de Whitton himself. He hadn't been vindictive or cruel, but simply sat de Whitton down and spoke to the man with respect. It hadn't been long before de Whitton broke down completely and wept, convinced that everything he'd ever worked for had been destroyed. He'd truly believed in de Montfort and what the man had been trying to achieve. He believed that every nobleman should have a voice in his own country. De Wolfe had convinced him that England needed lords who wanted a better future.

That kind of counsel had been something to witness.

Not strangely, War had new respect for de Wolfe after that. The man had not only managed to calm a hysterical lord, but he'd convinced the man to travel to London and beg Henry's forgiveness. De Wolfe even offered to send him with a letter for Henry, asking for clemency. De Whitton hadn't sided with de Montfort out of spite or greed, but out of a genuine belief that the country should be managed by the people for the people. It was a radical ideal that had yet to see its day, but his motives were true.

William saw that even if no one else did.

In spite of himself, War came to see it, too. That had been his introduction to William de Wolfe and what the man stood for.

As War suspected, the first of many lessons to come.

CHAPTER TWO

B Y EVENING, THE rains had moved in.

Thropton Castle sat in a vale with steeply pitched sides and as the rains rolled in, so did the runoff from the mountains. There was a burn, or brook, that ran alongside the castle, which was elevated on a small rise, but as the rain pounded down, the burn became a raging river.

The burn also formed part of the moat, which had been filled with debris when the siege began, so much so that it had been a simple thing for the Bamburgh and de Wolfe armies to practically walk over it and straight to the walls. But with the rains, the moat had filled up and the debris had been partially washed away, flooding into the small vale.

Fortunately, the army encampment was also on a rise, so the swiftly flowing water wasn't an issue, but the rain itself was. Everything was soaked, both man and beast, but the bonfires were too big to be so quickly doused. Heavy oak logs had been soaked with flammable liquid, and the core of the logs burned deep, meaning they would burn through almost anything.

William could smell the heavy smoke all over the encampment. He and Kieran had just left the main de Wolfe tent after having removed most of their mail and protection. The squires, including William's son, Edward, and Kieran's son, Kevin, had gone to work rubbing out the rust and repairing what they could. Edward and Kevin were in that awkward age where they weren't quite children but weren't quite adults even though they were both big, strong lads, so they mostly supervised the other squires. Kevin was a little heavy-handed while Edward was very much the diplomat when it came to communicating.

William could hear them bickering even as he walked away.

Adjacent to the main tent was a long stretch of oiled canvas, which had been propped up with big poles. It was literally just a roof to keep the rain off, with the sides wide open, and the men were gathering beneath it to eat their evening meal.

Overhead, thunder rolled as William entered the shelter, looking for Paris and Michael and the others. The cooks were bringing out big, iron cauldrons of beans and salted pork, which had been simmered together with carrots and greens, making a rich and hearty stew. William spied Paris and the others near the center of the tent and he and Kieran made their way to them.

As soon as he reached the group, someone was handing him a cup of warmed, watered wine, which he took gratefully. He could see that Paris and the de Wolfe allies were clustered with Herringthorpe and his men, and he noted that Paris and War were in some manner of lively conversation. At least, Paris was being lively. The man's free hand was flying all over the place for emphasis as he spoke.

William walked up to the pair.

"Whatever story he is telling you, it is a lie," William said, a glimmer of mirth in his eye. "Do not believe a word of it."

They turned to him, Paris scowling and War grinning. "Is

that so?" War said. "He was telling me a story of your valor, my lord."

"Then it was all true."

They started to laugh, with Paris rolling his eyes. "You cannot have it both ways, William," he said. "Either I am a liar all of the time or none of the time."

William smirked. "What story were you telling him?"

Paris tilted his head in a general northerly direction. "I was speaking of the siege of Langton Castle from many years ago," he said. "You know that we found de Whitton in tunnels beneath Thropton. I was speaking of the tunnels and dungeons beneath Langton during that battle."

"It is a pity Langton was so badly damaged," War said. "It sounds like a magnificent place."

"It was," William said. "It has been rebuilt since that time, but it is not the same. Part of Langton was built by the Romans so many years ago and that craftsmanship was lost with the rebuild. The Scots simply put blocks together to make a wall, but the Romans did something special to them."

"Oh?" War seemed interested. "What did they do?"

"Shaped them," William said, using a hand to indicate a rounded corner. "They built columns into walls and other features. But I am sure that does not interest you overly, speaking on a damaged Scots castle. I hope Paris was not boring you."

"I was *not*," Paris said flatly. He gestured to War. "The man is Blackchurch trained and that included study on ancient buildings to understand their resilience over time. He knows his architecture, William."

William's eyebrows lifted as he looked at War. "I had heard you were Blackchurch trained," he said. "That is quite an accomplishment, Herringthorpe. You must be very proud."

War shrugged. "Some men foster with the master knights of Kenilworth," he said, which was exactly what William and Paris had done. "Some foster with the cutthroats, assassins, spies, and mercenaries of the Blackchurch Guild. Both are prestigious but I will say that Blackchurch has given me a broader perspective of the world."

"I have heard it is very difficult."

"It is," War said. "Not all finish the training term."

"There is a term?"

"Nine years."

"And part of your training was inspecting ancient buildings?"

War nodded. "When one trains at Blackchurch, the training is done in segments," he said. "You spend one year with each trainer. One trains in the history of ancient warfare, one trains in hand-to-hand combat using different methods, and so on. Some training is constant, like weapons and tactics. Practice is daily. But my year with the trainer of ancient warfare took us all over the known world, studying buildings that have withstood the test of time. That is what I mean when I said I received a broader perspective of the world. I have seen a great deal. I have come to understand how men think."

William was listening intently to the well-spoken, articulate man who was clearly quite intelligent. "That can only help you understand better why they do what they do," he said. "That should be particularly useful when dealing with foolish lords who dress as women and try to hide from their enemies."

He was referring to de Whitton and War smiled thinly. "I think that is where you could educate all of us," he said. "I watched you deal with de Whitton today, my lord. One of the things Blackchurch did not teach us was compassion. It is a very stark way to live, not knowing compassion for a man and why he does what he does. We are taught to understand a man's motives, but not to sympathize with them. My father taught me compassion, however, something the trainers at Blackchurch could not erase. What I saw today from you was great compassion and mercy when it came to Lord de Whitton. That was admirable."

William shrugged modestly. "All of the education in the world cannot teach a man mercy," he said. "That is an inherent quality. Either you have it or you do not. Not everything is clear-cut. Every man must learn that for himself."

"Indeed," War agreed. But his gaze seemed to be lingering on William as if Paris wasn't still standing there. "My lord… may I ask you something?"

"Of course."

War started to speak but couldn't seem to say what he wanted to say. He finally broke down in an embarrassed grin. "I suppose I have never met a legend before," he said. "But I have always wanted to ask a man who has achieved such greatness if he is satisfied with his life. What I mean is that even though you have so much in life, things that are well-earned, has that stopped you from wanting more?"

William snorted softly. "I am not a legend," he said. "Although I appreciate your saying so, I am a man like any other. I have lived a good life, a life of service to king and country, but I will not go down in the annals of history as anyone noteworthy. There are thousands of such men who will never be noted as great men or men who shaped a country and that is what I prefer – to be a man who moves this country towards a better future without all of the pomp and circumstance that can accompany such a position. Actions, to me, speak much louder than a man's words."

War thought on that. "But some men like to be recognized."

"And I am one of them," William said. "Do not misunderstand me. I do expect to be rewarded for my service. But it is simply that I like to speak loudly by action, as I said. A man must do what he says he is going to do or his words mean nothing. But this does not answer your question. You have asked me if I am ever satisfied with what I have or do I have an inherent need for more."

"Aye, my lord."

William glanced at Paris, who had a sort of approving smirk on his face. In fact, it was Paris who answered for him.

"There is always more, Herringthorpe," he said quietly. "Any man who is satisfied with what he has is either dead or stupid."

War chuckled. "Fortunately, I am neither."

"Then always keep that hunger. It will keep you alive."

"I intend to," he assured them. "But I am grateful for the advice."

Paris wondered if that was true. If the knight had trained at Blackchurch, then perhaps they could use advice from him also. "I will give you more when you come to Castle Questing, as William suggested," he said. "You *will* come, won't you?"

War looked to William. "I would be honored."

William had just taken a long drink of the warmed wine. "Come soon," he said. "There are men you must meet and there are things we should discuss. It is time you become one of the Northerners, Herringthorpe."

War wanted nothing more at this point in his career. To be mentored and allied with the most powerful men in the north was a garrison commander's dream. As he pondered the possibilities, they were joined by the older sons of both William and Paris.

War found himself introduced to Scott de Wolfe, Troy de Wolfe, Patrick de Wolfe, Hector de Norville, and Apollo de Norville. He'd seen them in the battle earlier in the day, though he had not been formally introduced to them. They were all fine, young, strapping knights, somewhat wearied and bloodied from the intense battle that had taken place, but like all young warriors, they were energized from it.

"Papa," Scott said as he turned to William when the introductions were finished. "De Whitton is asking for you. I do not know if you wish to be bothered by the man, but he has asked that you come to him. He says that he has something to say to you."

William didn't particularly want to go. He hadn't eaten yet and was hungry, but he'd also established a rapport with de Whitton earlier in the day, so he didn't want to minimize that. He'd established it for a reason, to perhaps make an ally out of the man in the long run, something he was quite good at.

He set his wine cup down.

"Very well," he said. "Herringthorpe, will you attend me? He is your prisoner, after all."

War immediately set his cup down, following William from the shelter and out into the rain as his sons remained behind to eat the food their father had yet the opportunity to taste.

Once outside, they were met by the rain again. Around them, the men were hunkered down under shelters and trees, eating and drinking and singing as they tried to stay warm and dry. The smell of smoke was quite heavy due to the canopy of trees and the low clouds, but the atmosphere was relaxed after three solid days of battle as they made their way to the area where the prisoners were being held, including de Whitton.

"I hope the Thropton men do not float away," War said, noting the brook that had become an angry river. "I'm not exactly sure how I would explain that to Henry."

William snorted softly. "If he thought that he could use the army, he would be unforgiving," he said. "But if the men refuse to fight for him, he'll wash them out to sea himself. This is a very delicate situation, as you know."

"You have known the king a long time?"

"A very long time," William said. "My father knew Henry when he was a boy. In fact, my father knew Henry's father, John, as well as Richard the Lionheart."

"That was a long time ago," War said. "My own father was a knight for Henry, but he served John for a short time. When he was young."

"Who is your father?"

"Edmund Herringthorpe."

"Where is his home?"

"Suffolk."

"Is that where you were born?"

"Aye, though my mother was from Northumberland."

William glanced at him. "Oh?" he said. "What is her family name?"

"William!"

The shout caught his attention. William could see Kieran coming in his direction rather quickly, moving swiftly through the rain. There were so many bonfires going on around them, hissing and smoking and crackling in the rain, that Kieran was fully illuminated as he closed in.

William went out to meet him.

"What's wrong?" he asked.

Kieran turned around and began walking back the way he came. "De Whitton," he said. "Christian and Alec were on watch when the man had his food brought to him."

William wasn't sure where this was leading, but he didn't like the sound of it already. "And?"

"And the man took the knife he was given for his food, stabbed Christian with it, and then turned it on himself," Kieran said, sounding strained and unhappy. "It happened quickly, William. Too quickly. We had no idea that de Whitton intended to harm himself."

William could only feel disappointment and shock as he and Kieran and War ended up at the tent where they'd been housing de Whitton. Christian, tall and blond with his father's dark eyes, was in the process of wrapping a bloody wound on his left forearm as de Whitton lay on the ground, a knife in his throat.

It was a damned bloody mess all the way around.

"Christ," William muttered, seeing the carnage. "Did he say anything to you, Christian?"

Christian paused in his bandaging, so much so that his father went to take over. "Aye," he said in his soft, deep voice. "He asked me to forgive him and then he stabbed me, throwing me off guard so I could not stop him from stabbing himself."

William's jaw began to tick faintly. "I see," he said. "Nothing more?"

"Nothing more, Uncle William."

The room fell silent for a moment as War stepped forward, crouching down a few feet away from de Whitton's body, inspecting the scene.

"I do not understand," he said, bewildered. "The man had

been told he would not lose his property if he went to Henry and pleaded for forgiveness. The worst that would have happened is that he came away with a fine. He was not going to be hurt or imprisoned. Why do this?"

William's gaze moved from de Whitton to War, who seemed both baffled and disgusted by the whole thing.

"His dignity would not allow it," he said quietly. "I have seen this before. He told us what we wanted to hear and then waited until he had a weapon, in this case a knife for his meal, before ending his life."

"He has been planning this all along," Kieran said, tying off his son's bandage.

"Exactly," William agreed. "I should have seen it. The hysterical tears, the lack of courage to surrender… he would rather die than surrender."

"Why?" War looked up at him. "His pride?"

William shrugged. "Not really," he said. "It has more to do with ideals, not arrogance. I suspect had de Whitton found the strength not to kill himself, he might have made it to London, begged forgiveness from Henry, but then resume some underground movement against the king to carry on de Montfort's work."

War stood up. "As a rebel?"

William nodded. "Mayhap," he said. "But not a rebel for rebellion's sake. De Whitton is an old man. In speaking to him today, he seemed like an idealist. He would be rebelling for the sake of that idea."

"De Montfort's idea of government?"

William half-shrugged, half-nodded. "Mayhap it is better that he did this so we would not return here in three years when Henry catches wind of his subversion again," he said. "Sometimes men, especially old men, simply cannot change their ways."

War cocked his head. "Then if you suspected this, why be so lenient on him?" he said. "Why not tie him up and restrain him with the rest of his men?"

There might have been an accusation in that. It was enough of a curious tone that Kieran looked up from Christian's arm.

"Because men like de Whitton do not deserve to be restrained like a common soldier," Kieran said. "By giving the man his dignity, the hope is to show him that men he considers his enemy are not as barbaric as he would believe. It is that show of trust and humanity that sometimes can turn the tides of a man's beliefs."

"Or the course of a country," War said softly.

Kieran nodded, conceding the point. "Or the course of the world," he said. "You cannot blame William that de Whitton took his own life. In fact… William gave him the dignity of that choice. Don't you see that?"

War did. "I think so," he said. "By putting de Whitton in his own tent, providing him with shelter and food and respect, it was up to de Whitton what to do with it. He was captured. His castle had fallen. He was facing a life that might or might not have been one he wanted to live. A world with no de Montfort, no high ideas of the people ruling the people."

Kieran nodded. "Exactly," he said. "Now you are coming to understand why de Whitton was given this choice. If you were in the same position, wouldn't you hope for that kind of respect to decide your future and the way you would want to live it?"

War sighed faintly. "Aye," he said. "But now I must tell Henry that Lord de Whitton has taken his own life. I am not certain that is what Henry wanted."

"Tell Henry that de Whitton made his own choice," William said quietly. "You gave him that opportunity and he made his decision. Henry will understand that."

"Will he?"

"I promise he will."

War wasn't so sure. The king he knew saw things in black or white, not the gray area in between, but he didn't argue with the senior knights. He wasn't so arrogant that he didn't know that they might somehow know better than he in such matters.

And they were old friends of an old king.

War lingered on their words, their advice, coming to think that the Blackchurch trainers could learn something about human nature from those two. War had compassion but he was still working on empathy. That was the hard part. As he watched Christian and Alec summon soldiers to wrap up de Whitton's body, he was coming to think that this venture to Thropton Castle hadn't been a wasted effort. The castle had been claimed and, surprisingly, War had learned a little something along the way.

From a living legend, he'd learned a little something about humanity.

Perhaps the seizure of Thropton Castle had been a success, after all.

CHAPTER THREE

Castle Questing

A CHILD WAS screaming.

Not just screaming – hysterically screaming. Annaleigh could hear her from the vast bailey of Castle Questing, which had been her home now for the past three months. Her cousin was the Lady of Questing, Lady Jordan Scott de Wolfe, wife of the greatest English knight on the border.

A man she'd found kind and gentle in spite of his deadly reputation.

And he'd welcomed her into his home and into his family. From the very first day she'd arrived at her father's request, William had never made her feel like an outsider. His children had welcomed her, as well, and he had eight of them. There were the older boys – Scott, Troy and Patrick, and then James and Katheryn, the twins, who were Annaleigh's age. Evelyn, Edward, Thomas, and Penelope rounded out the younger de Wolfes and at this moment, it was Penelope who was screaming her lungs out.

After three months, Annaleigh had learned that sound.

She followed the noise.

The day was bright as she headed towards the stable block where she'd seen some of the younger children playing – Penelope and Thomas, and also Kieran and Jemma Hage's younger children, Rose and Nathaniel. Lastly, Cassiopeia de Norville was with them, also, though she was quite a prim young lady at nine years of age and didn't often go for the rough games that the children would play.

But this game had Penelope in fits.

As she entered the stable yard, she could see Penelope sitting on her bottom in the dirt, crying her eyes out. Her brother, Thomas, was standing over her, frowning at her. Penelope didn't need and want his comfort because she was waiting for one of her older brothers – mostly Patrick – to come and save her, but Patrick was away with the other older sons at a castle to the south in some kind of battle. At least, that was what Annaleigh had understood. They'd been gone almost a month and a missive had been received that morning indicating the army was finally returning home by evening.

But that wouldn't be soon enough for Penelope.

Annaleigh stepped in.

"Lass," she said as she knelt down beside the weeping child, using her sleeve to wipe the girl's face. "Come now, sweetheart. What is it? Have the dogs of hell been nipping at yer feet?"

At four years of age, Penelope de Wolfe was a brilliant, sweet, but highly spoiled child. If the slightest thing didn't go her way, she would make sure everyone at Castle Questing knew about it.

"T-Tommy pushed me!" she spat.

Annaleigh looked at Thomas for his reaction, which wasn't long in coming. The boy with the long, dark hair looked both defiant and terrified at the same time.

"I did *not* push her!" he said. "She wants my sword and she cannot have it!"

He sounded desperate as he held up the offending toy, mostly because he knew what happened to those who upset little Penelope. His father doted on his youngest daughter and would often take her side in things because he couldn't resist the pixie face and crocodile tears, so Thomas and his siblings had often been on the receiving end of fatherly punishment when it came to Penelope.

And Penelope knew it.

So did Annaleigh.

She'd been at Castle Questing long enough to see who ruled the roost and it wasn't the warlord named William de Wolfe. It was a tiny slip of a girl named Penelope.

"What do ye want that dirty sword for?" she asked, lifting Penelope out of the dirt and brushing her off. "I have better things for ye. Come and play with me. We'll go and find the kittens. Eh?"

The lure of a new litter of kittens was great. Penelope knew she couldn't hold them yet, but she longed to touch them. She loved all of the animals that lived in the barns; cats and dogs and even mice included.

"I-I want to pet one," she sniffled, wiping her eyes with a dirty hand.

Annaleigh wiped her face again to keep the dirt from getting into her eyes. "We'll find one ye can pet," she said. "Leave Tommy and Eddie tae their dirty swords. We'll find ye better things tae play with."

She didn't give Penelope a chance to think about it. She simply took her by the hand and led her back towards the stables where the grooms were beginning to parcel out the grain for the evening meal. It wasn't sunset yet, but that time would swiftly approach. They'd have to hunt cats before it became too dark to do so.

"Lady Annaleigh?"

Annaleigh was just entering the stables when a polite address stopped her. She paused to see Sir Talus du Reims coming up behind her and she forced a smile at the gloriously handsome young knight from a very fine family. Talus was a son of the Earl of East Anglia and also related to the House of de Lohr, which made him more elite than most.

And he knew it.

He was also young and impetuous, and when William was selecting knights to go on campaign south to Thropton, he made the younger knights draw lots to see who went and who remained behind to protect Castle Questing.

But there was the rub.

Talus made sure he drew the short stick because he knew Annaleigh would be at Castle Questing while a competitor for her affections, Sir Anthony d'Vant, would be going with de Wolfe. The pair had been competing for Annaleigh's attention ever since she had arrived from Clan Scott's seat of Langton Castle, but she hadn't shown them any particular interest. However, Anthony, realizing Talus would be left behind and perhaps gain an advantage on him, persuaded Christian Hage that he should go on campaign and leave Anthony in command of Castle Questing in his stead.

Christian, who had been charged with command with the army away, agreed.

Therefore, it had been an entire month of Talus and Anthony pursuing the blindingly beautiful Annaleigh Scott with her long, red hair that gleamed like molten metal and a face that was female perfection personified. From her long-lashed eyes to her pert nose to her rosebud mouth and dimpled cheeks, she had most of the unmarried men at Castle Questing passing her a second glance.

Even men who were her distant cousins.

She was far enough removed from de Wolfe and Hage and even de Norville relations, as all three of her father's second cousins had married those great border knights, that she could be considered a marital prospect for them, but she genuinely had no interest. The truth was that she wanted to return home, and return home badly, but her father thought it would be better for her to stay away from her clan for a while, at least until the events of eight months ago and the battle with Etal Castle had blown over.

The problem, once believed solved, had only grown worse.

But she tried not to think about that now, about people she'd known all her life blaming her for the death of loved ones in a battle that had been completely preventable. Perhaps she was a stranger at Castle Questing, and to England in general, but at least they weren't blaming her for something that had been out of her control.

Talus du Reims included.

Even now, as she looked at the powerful young knight, she could see the hope and interest in his eyes. It was the same expression she'd seen from the start.

But she simply wasn't interested.

"Good day tae ye, Sir Talus," she said after a moment, forcing herself to be polite to a man who had been most persistent. "How may I be of service?"

Talus smiled, dimples carving into each cheek. He had the

du Reims curly hair, tumbling to his shoulders, giving him a rather barbaric and romantic look.

"I heard screaming," he said, looking straight at Penelope. "I came to see if you needed help."

Annaleigh looked at Penelope, too, who was gazing innocently at the big knight. "I think I have the situation under control," Annaleigh said. "These things pass quickly with the little lass."

"As I've seen."

"We are on the hunt for kittens."

Talus took it as an invitation. "Ah," he said, walking past them and entering the stables. "It is the time of year when many are born. When I was young, I used to have a cat all my own."

"You did?" Penelope was quite intrigued as she followed him. "Did your mother let you have him?"

Talus nodded. "She did," he said. "My father did not think a cat was a suitable pet for a lad, but I loved that cat. Do you know what his name was?"

"What?"

"William."

Penelope grinned, displaying little, white baby teeth. "That's my papa's name!"

Talus laughed softly. "I know," he said. "But I swear that was his name. William was my favorite cat."

"Where did you live?"

"At a great and mighty castle called Thunderbey. It is far to the south."

"Do you miss your home?"

Talus lifted his gaze to Annaleigh, fixing her in the eyes. "Sometimes," he said. "But there is much in the north to keep me here."

He meant Annaleigh and she knew it immediately. It was a game he'd been playing with her almost since the day they'd met and he was becoming bolder about it, which annoyed her. Without giving him a hint of any reaction one way or the other, she took Penelope by the hand, pulling the girl over to the ladder that led up to the loft.

"Up there," she said, pointing overhead. "I think there are some kittens. Mayhap Sir Talus will climb up the ladder and look for us."

Talus was already to the ladder, preparing to climb, but Penelope began to fuss.

"I want to climb!" she said, pointing to it. "Can I not climb?"

Truthfully, the ladder wasn't very tall. Perhaps only slightly taller than Talus, who was a fairly tall man. He crooked his finger at Penelope, who rushed over to him. He lifted her up by the hips, just high enough so she could get a good look at the loft. After a few moments, she began to crow.

"I see them!" she said excitedly. "I see the cat and her kittens!"

She was starting to squirm, trying to climb into the loft, and Talus had to hold tight so she wouldn't get away.

"How many do ye see?" Annaleigh called to her.

"Many!" Penelope said. She didn't really know how to count, for she was too young to have been taught her sums, but she excitedly held up a hand with splayed fingers. "This many!"

She was squirming so much that Talus had to quickly lower her because she was in danger of falling out of his grip. Once her feet hit the ground, she rushed to Annaleigh and tugged on her hand.

"Please, Annie," she said. "I want to see the kittens!"

Annaleigh squeezed her hand. "We must ask yer mother if it is all right for ye to go intae the loft," she said, pointing up to the slats, which were about six inches apart. "'Tis dangerous for a wee lass, so let us ask her first."

Penelope wasn't happy with that response. "What if she says we cannot?"

Annaleigh was already turning for the stables' exit. "Then we shall go intae the kitchens, find the sweets, and eat them all."

That was an idea that Penelope could agree with, even more than the lure of the kittens. She pulled from Annaleigh's grip and began to run, no doubt running to Castle Questing's enormous keep in search of her mother. Annaleigh laughed softly as she watched her go.

"She is either going tae ask Cousin Jordan if she can go intae the loft or she is simply running straight tae the kitchens tae feed," she said. "'Tis difficult tae know with that one."

Shaking her head with mirth, she started to follow Penelope but Talus caught up to her. They walked out of the stables together.

"I think that is a trait most women share," he said.

"What's that?"

"They are difficult to predict."

"God made us that way, lad."

Talus snorted. "God is a cruel jester sometimes," he said, but quickly sobered. "May I ask you something, my lady?"

"Of course."

"Would you allow me to sit with you at the feast this evening?"

He'd asked that before and Annaleigh had given him permission, but with the caveat that it was simply to be friendly. There was no romance involved. Talus understood it; she knew he understood it. But that still didn't prevent him from asking again and again, hoping that, at some point, she would change her mind. But she never had.

She never would.

She sighed faintly.

"Talus," she said quietly, pausing to look at him. "I dunna mind if ye sit next tae me at the evening's feast, but I've told ye many times before that I'm not looking for a husband. If ye wish tae sit next tae me so we can speak as friends, then I welcome it. But if ye have a mind tae woo me, I canna have ye impose upon me when ye know I am not interested. Do we understand one another?"

The warm expression faded from his face. "Unfortunately," he said. His jaw ticked faintly as he struggled for courage to say what he wanted to say. "May… may I ask if you find something unappealing about me? Something you simply do not like? I can change, my lady. I can change whatever it is you do not seem to care for."

She put up her hands to stop his rambling. "There is nothing about ye that I would change," she said. "I simply dunna want a husband right now."

"But someday?"

"Of course," she said. "I want a husband and family, like all lasses."

"But not now."

"Not now."

"And that goes for Anthony as well?"

"It goes for every man."

He wasn't happy about it, but he didn't want to be unchivalrous. It was obvious that he'd been hoping for a different answer. However, he took comfort in the fact that it wasn't only him – it applied to everyone.

Especially his archrival, Anthony.

"I suppose I cannot fault you for your conviction," he said after a moment. "But I simply do not understand a woman of your age that does not want to marry. I could understand if you faulted me the fact that I am English and you are Scots, but I'm starting to think there is something wrong with me."

He believed that, too. Annaleigh could see it in his eyes. Sighing heavily, she reached out and looped her arm through his, tugging him along with her as she resumed her walk towards the keep.

"Talus, there is nothing wrong with ye," she said. "Ye're a fine young knight."

"From a good family, do not forget."

She laughed softly. "From a fine family," she said. "Yer father is the Earl of East Anglia."

"He is."

"And that's another thing," she said, looking at him. "How do ye think the man would react tae ye marrying a Scots lass? He'd want ye tae marry a fine English lass with lots of money."

Talus was greatly enjoying the feel of her arm through his, this astonishing creature that seemed to radiate her own special kind of light. He was torn between being greatly disappointed in her rejection yet again but wholly excited that she was moving beyond the formalities and addressing him more informally. More than that, she was holding his arm.

That had never happened before.

"He would understand once he met you," he said, trying not to sound adoring. "You are a very special woman, my lady. Surely you know that."

Annaleigh's smile faded. "It would be purely arrogant tae

assume so," she said. "And ye dunna know where I came from, Talus. Ye dunna know what my own people even think of me, so much so that my da sent me tae Castle Questing tae get me away from those… things."

"What things?"

She shrugged. "People can be bitter sometimes, even towards those who dunna deserve it. They like tae cast blame when there is a tragedy."

He paused, looking at her seriously as her hand came away from his elbow. "I've not heard why you came here," he said. "I never asked anyone because it was none of my business, but since you've brought it up, did something happen in Scotland? Is that why you were sent here?"

The wind was beginning to pick up now that the afternoon was waning and Annaleigh brushed the wind-blown hair from her eyes. She debated whether or not to say anything about it, because she was a private person by nature, but she'd already touched on it. Perhaps if he knew she had left some trouble behind, he might not look at her as such a pristine marital prospect.

"My clan has a name for me, lad," she said quietly.

"What?"

"*Fear-dèanamh trioblaid.*"

He frowned. "What does that mean?"

She didn't want to translate those words aloud. *Trouble-maker.* "Do ye not know the Gaelic?"

He shook his head. "I was raised in Suffolk and fostered in the south," he said. "I never learned."

"But ye've been with de Wolfe for a few years now."

He lifted his big shoulders. "I know two phrases," he said. "*Càite bheil an taigh-òsta* and *Tha mi a' dol a mharbhadh thu.*"

Annaleigh burst out laughing. "Do ye know what they mean?"

"I think so."

She wasn't so sure. "Ye said 'Where is the tavern' and 'I'm going tae kill ye'," she said. "Is that what ye meant tae say?"

He fought off a grin. "Not exactly," he said. "Patrick and James told me that it means *you're a beautiful woman* and *I'm an English knight.*"

Annaleigh nearly doubled over with laughter. "God's Bones," she gasped. "I'm surprised ye havena gotten yerself killed with those phrases. They played a terrible trick on ye, Talus."

He grunted, though he did see the humor in it. "I am not surprised," he said. "That is the story of my entire life since I have arrived at Castle Questing. Women who do not wish to be married and knights tricking me into starting a war with Scotland. I should go home to Thunderbey Castle and stay there."

He was feeling sorry for himself, but in a humorous way. She was coming to like Talus, but still not in the romantic sense. He would have made a fine brother. She genuinely hoped they could be friends someday.

"Nay," she said, leaning in the direction of the keep. "Dunna go home. Sit with me at the feast tonight and I'll teach ye enough Gaelic that ye'll be turning the tables on that pair. Atty and James are terrible jokesters."

The allure of sitting with her was too good to pass up, even if she didn't want anything romantic to do with him. "I would be in your debt," he said. "In fact, the army is supposed to…"

He was cut off by a shout from the massive walls of Castle Questing. Looking to the sand-colored walls that reached into the blue expanse of sky, he shielded his eyes from the sun to see what the excitement was about. It didn't take him long to figure out that the sentries were excited about something in the distance and since the de Wolfe armies were set to return today, he had an idea what it was.

He began to head towards the walls.

"You may want to tell Lady de Wolfe that I suspect her husband's army has been sighted," he said. Then, he came to an abrupt pause. "And I thank you very kindly for the conversation. I hope… I hope it will be the first of many, my lady."

Annaleigh smiled, revealing lovely, white teeth. "I would be honored."

He smiled in a way that suggested he was pleased if that was all he could get from her at the moment and, with a dip of his head, trotted off towards the gatehouse.

Annaleigh watched him go for a moment, her smile fading. They'd had a few varied conversations like this one in the past, though not so deep, so she knew he'd forget about it the next time he saw her. Perhaps not forget about it so much as ignore it. The man had a sharp mind and not a bad memory.

He was simply choosing to ignore her wishes.

But she wouldn't change her mind.

Turning on her heel, Annaleigh headed towards the keep to tell her cousin that her husband, the great Wolfe of the Border, was on her doorstep.

CHAPTER FOUR

Bamburgh Castle

EVEN THOUGH HE wasn't the legal owner and the castle didn't belong to him in the least, there was still a satisfaction when the mighty fortress of Bamburgh came into view. In spite of everything, it was *his* castle.

War breathed a sigh of satisfaction.

At the head of the Bamburgh army, about one thousand of them including fifty-one wounded, one of his lieutenants sent a runner ahead to inform the castle that the army was nearly home. Not that they couldn't see it for themselves, but it was good manners to announce it. The battle at Thropton was over for good, with de Whitton buried and the castle left with a small contingent to repair and protect it until Henry could decide what was to be done with it.

The imposing bastion of stone and mortar sat on a promontory overlooking the sea, a sea that had been filled with Northmen for many centuries. A sea that was a murky gray-green, with silt churning up from the heavy currents near the shore. But on a clear day, the view was breathtaking.

War had quickly learned to love it.

The gulls were crying overhead, scouting the land for a meal, perhaps hoping for something from the incoming army. To War, it was as if they were welcoming him home. He'd only been at the castle a short amount of time, but already, it was home to him. God and the king willing, he'd be here for many years to come. In his opinion, it was one of the only fortresses in England worthy of his magnificence.

"Well?" a voice came from his right. "What's next, War? Are we able to relax a little now? There's much we need to do with this army, you know. We have many new recruits that need proper guidance. That was apparent during the battle at Thropton."

War turned slightly, seeing his second in command riding near him. "Who is to the rear?" he asked. "You are supposed to be covering our retreat."

Sir Montmorency "Monty" Vandergriff simply lifted his blond eyebrows, looking off to the meadow of seagrass to the south. "Alexei is to the rear," he said. "You know the men are always vigilant when he is around. They're terrified of the knight from Vilnius, so you've nothing to worry over."

War grunted. "Except I told *you* to cover the rear."

Monty didn't particularly care about that. He gestured towards Bamburgh. "We are almost home," he said. "I suppose I am simply eager to be done with this hellish traveling and warfare. We've had too much of it since we arrived at Bamburgh."

"It was not exactly calm before you arrived." Another knight spoke up, one who had been at Bamburgh and in royal service for several years. He possessed the unlikely name of Clement de Hemmet, which caused no end of jokes at his expense, something he wasn't exactly keen about. "Bamburgh has been active for centuries, so do not think you'll rest here, safe and sound. We must always be vigilant."

War wasn't unaware that Clement had wanted the very position that he currently held. The knight with the odd name had made no secret of the fact that he felt slighted over the king's choice to put War in command of Bamburgh when he had served at his post for so many years. Because of that, Monty and Alexei had watched War's back during the several skirmishes they'd had since they'd come to Bamburgh and, so far, Clement hadn't made a move for War. He'd been completely loyal in all situations.

But they still didn't trust him.

"I think Monty meant that it would be nice to spend an extended amount of time at Bamburgh," War said steadily. "We've had four instances since my arrival when the army has been called out and…"

Clement cut him off. "And after the very first one, you spent months recovering from your wounds," he said. When Monty shot him a withering look, Clement realized he must have sounded condescending. "I mean no disrespect, my lord. The wounds you sustained were substantial. Had we not found you when we did…"

"There is no need to revisit that subject," War interrupted him firmly. "I am sorry if my survival has disappointed you, de Hemmet, but I am perfectly well and fully in command of Bamburgh. If that is something that displeases you, then I am certain you can be sent elsewhere. We do not want you to remain if you are unhappy."

"I am not unhappy," Clement said quickly. "I have been at Bamburgh for several years. My wife was born in the village.

She would not wish to leave."

"Then show Herringthorpe the respect he has earned," Monty growled. "I grow weary of your veiled aggression, de Hemmet."

War held up a hand before the conversation veered out of control. "I do not care what you say to each other in private, but in front of the men, we are united," he said. "The moment it seems that we are not united is the moment I send you away, de Hemmet. Is that understood?"

"Perfectly, my lord."

"Good."

Monty was still glaring daggers at Clement, who was trying not to let his frustration show. He wanted to be a good knight and do his duty. He thought he'd been doing an excellent job of it until War had been sent to assume a command he had expected. But even he knew that War was more than qualified. In fact, he was surprised a Blackchurch-trained knight of Herringthorpe's caliber should even want a remote command like Bamburgh. A man like War needed to be in the heart of the action, in London with the men who would make or break the country. That was where he belonged.

But instead, he was in the wilds of the north, battling the Scots and disloyal neighbors.

It made little sense to him.

"War," Monty said, satisfied that his nasty glares had put Clement in his place. "When are we going to pay a visit to Castle Questing? You said that de Wolfe invited you. That kind of invitation does not come frequently or easily. The man is a god in the north."

The conversation was shifting from Clement's coveting to the Wolfe of the Border. War had to admit that he was looking forward to spending more time with de Wolfe, learning from him and working with him. Usually, War was the most seasoned and well-educated man in the room, but not when de Wolfe and his allies were around. The captain from Northwood, de Norville, and de Wolfe's second, Hage, were all part of this great group of experienced knights like nothing War had ever seen before.

That was saying a lot.

Montmorency was correct about one thing – an invitation to Castle Questing was a coveted one. Bamburgh was allied with de Wolfe and his garrisons – Berwick, Wark, and Roxburgh included – so War saw the trip to Castle Questing as a valuable opportunity.

One he intended to take advantage of.

"I suppose it would be wise to leave as soon as possible," he said after a moment. "De Wolfe asked me to. I need to build a relationship with him, so the sooner, the better."

Monty agreed. "If you do not move swiftly, he may take it as an insult."

"Agreed."

"Then we depart within the week?"

War nodded. "I would say in the next few days," he said. "Let us reach Bamburgh and settle the men, see what the damage is to our stores and weapons, and once we've a plan in place to replace and repair what we spent on campaign, we can depart for Castle Questing."

Monty nodded. "Who will go with you?"

War glanced at Monty before turning further to look at Clement. "All of the knights," he said loudly enough for Clement to hear. There was no chance of him leaving the knight behind to possibly engage in insurrection against him. "We can leave the senior sergeants in charge while we are away. They know what to do better than we do. And my father will not come with us, so they can seek his counsel if needed."

Monty turned to look at the castle looming closer. "Are you sure he will not come with us?" he said. "Edmund Herringthorpe has spoken of de Wolfe with great reverence in the past. He might challenge you to a fight if you deny him the opportunity to meet the man."

War smiled weakly. "If my father had the strength to challenge me, I would gladly concede," he said. "But… I do not think he will. Even he knows a journey like that, as mild as it will probably be, will be too taxing on his health."

He sobered greatly as the conversation turned to his father, a man who had been quite ill for a few years with a weakened heart. It had grown steadily worse since War had taken command of Bamburgh, but Edmund would not be left behind in Suffolk with his son taking a glorious position for King Henry. The man had traveled north and it had nearly killed him, but he was at Bamburgh, reveling in the pride he had for his magnificent son. Knowing he was more than likely not long for this world, he didn't want to miss a moment of War's triumph.

"Mayhap that is true, but you should at least give him the opportunity to refuse," Monty said, knowing that the subject of War's father was a touchy one. "Give the man his dignity in the matter."

"You are right."

Bamburgh loomed ever closer. War found himself looking at the walls, the keep that towered above the outer walls, and the general imposing presence before him. He'd seen many castles in his life but never one as magnificent as Bamburgh. He found that he was most eager to return home and he had the knights pick up the pace with the army, closing in on the last few hundred yards quickly.

It seemed that everyone was eager to go home.

The road to Bamburgh wound up the promontory and through an enormous gatehouse, opening into the outer ward. Already, there were men waiting to take horses and move the men towards the troophouses as War dismounted his black and white stallion. He had to slap a muzzle on the beast before the grooms could even take him away and he grabbed his saddlebags as two of them wrestled his horse towards the stables. The inner ward was busy with the bustle of the returning army and he inhaled that smell – one of victory and hard work, of warfare and leather. All of it filling his nostrils. There was a satisfaction to it.

Slinging his saddlebags over his shoulder, he headed for the keep.

The inner ward was almost as vast as the outer ward, with kitchens and more stables and outbuildings filling the space. The ground was wet, indicative of recent rains, as War made his way to the keep.

Unlike many keeps of the time, the enormous keep at Bamburgh had an entry on the ground level. It was a massive oak door surrounded by a heavy Norman arch and War stepped through, immediately into a low-ceilinged entry chamber. Word of the returning army had reached the keep and before he could take the stairs, he was met by the physic he'd brought with him from London to tend to his father's every need. The man was coming down the spiral stairs just as War put an enormous boot on the bottom step.

They very nearly collided with each other.

"My lord," the physic said. He was a small man with pitted skin who wore the robes of a priest even though he was not of the clergy. "Thanks to God that you have returned safe."

War nodded wearily, removing his helm because of the low ceiling and wiping a hand over his brow. "Aye, I've returned safe," he said. "How is my father?"

The physic's pale gaze was intense. "I have spent the past month convincing him that you would return," he said. "He feared another circumstance like the one at Etal. He was afraid you were laying in a field again, dying."

War shook his head. "I do not have a scratch upon me," he said. "And my father worries too much. What happened at Etal was unusual. It shall not happen again."

"But you have suffered no ill effects?"

War frowned. "I am completely healed," he said. "You told me that yourself. I feel fine."

The physic nodded quickly, not wanting to upset the massive knight. "'Tis only that you lost a good deal of blood those months ago," he said. "Sometimes it takes months or even years to recover from something like that. I have asked you the same question after every battle since."

War scratched his neck irritably. "And I have told you every time that I feel quite well," he said again. "But you've not told me how my father is, Fulke. How is he?"

The physic sighed faintly. "Not well, I am afraid."

War stopped scratching. "Why do you say that?" he said, concerned. "What is wrong?"

Fulke wasn't keen to deliver the news but he had little choice. "His condition has worsened, my lord," he said quietly. "In fact, had you not returned home today, I was going to send you word that you must hurry home. I fear your father is not long for this world. I am very sorry."

War stared at him a moment as if he didn't understand his words. "What do you mean?" he said. "What has changed since I have been away?"

Fulke shrugged. "His breathing is more labored," he said. "His heart struggles for every beat. He is weakening greatly. All I can tell you is that the signs are there that he will not survive much longer. We knew this day would come and, now, it is here."

War gazed at him a moment longer before bolting past him, up the narrow stairs and to the master's chamber on the top floor. He'd given his father the best chamber the day they'd settled in Bamburgh, a chamber with views on all sides.

He'd wanted his father to have the very best.

Bursting through the chamber door, he startled his father, who was semi-propped up with pillows. When War crashed through the door, the old man's arms flailed in surprise.

"Christ, War," he muttered. "If ever a father had a raging bull for a son, it is me."

War glanced at the door; he'd nearly ripped it off the hinges. "Sorry, Papa," he said. "I only just returned and Fulke said… how are you feeling?"

"I have a better question. Are you uninjured?"

War went to his father's bedside, feeling anxious as he looked at the man. "I am," he said. "But you… the physic says you are feeling worse."

Edmund Herringthorpe, pale and tall and rail-thin, gazed at his eldest child. He had two other sons, both younger, both of them still in London and serving the king. Sterling and Callum Herringthorpe were excellent knights and he was very proud of them, but War… War was his pride and his joy.

He'd always had a soft spot for his gloriously talented heir.

"Sit," Edmund said softly. "I want to look at you."

He was patting the bed beside him and War grunted in frustration. He didn't like that his father wasn't elaborating on what Fulke had already said, but he dutifully dropped the saddlebags.

"If I sit, I will collapse the bed," he muttered. "I weigh too much for that bed. Papa, tell me the truth. Are you feeling worse?"

Edmund took a deep breath, one of many he took every hour because his heart and lungs were not working properly these days. "Mayhap I am," he said after a moment. "This is not an easy thing for me to admit."

War studied him a moment, dreading his next question. "How bad?"

"Bad enough, lad."

"The physic said that you were not long for this world."

A glimmer came to Edmund's eyes. "If that is true, then it is a blessing," he said. "Your dear mother has been waiting for me all these years. I have missed her, War."

"I know."

"I fear it is time that we must speak."

"About what?"

Edmund patted the bed again. "Sit down."

"I told you that I will collapse the bed."

"Then we shall both end up on the floor together."

War didn't want to dump his father out onto the cold floor, so he looked around the chamber, spying a heavy oak chair near the hearth. Grabbing it, he carried it back over to his father's bedside and sat down.

"There," he said. "I would prefer not to break your bed if I can at all help it. Now, what is so important that we must speak now? You must rest. Whatever you have on your mind can wait."

Reaching out, Edmund took his hand. That simple gesture weakened War's composure a little because, suddenly, he was a little boy again with his father holding his hand. The initial shock of his father's worsening condition faded and the grief began to come. All he could do was stare at that big, strong hand.

The hand that had always been there for him.

"I am afraid it cannot wait," Edmund said after a moment. "I have waited an entire month for you to return from Thropton. Were you successful?"

"We were."

"Good," Edmund said. "But I have been waiting all that time for you to return. I did not want to miss my last moments with you."

War began to realize that this was serious, indeed. Not that he didn't know this moment would come, because he did. His father's heart was very weak. Even so, he wasn't prepared for it and certainly not at this moment. As the weight of the situation began to bear down on him, he sighed heavily and hung his head.

"God," he muttered. "Is this truly the end, Papa? Is this truly it?"

Edmund squeezed his hand. "Possibly," he said. "Or, possibly it will be next week. Or next month. Or even tonight. I do not know. All I know is that I am weary, War. I want to go home. But before I go, I must tell you something."

Still looking at the floor, War shook his head. "What?" he said. "That you love me? I know you do. I know you love

Sterling and Cal, too. I will tell them of your love for them. You needn't worry."

"Nay," Edmund said, squeezing his hand again to get his attention. "It is not that. It is something… else."

"What else?"

Edmund took another deep breath. "War, I am not sure this is the right time, but with little time left, I have no choice," he said. "You've only just returned from battle and I am certain you have duties to attend to, but none more important than this right now."

He was right. War had duties to attend to with his army, but there was nothing more important at this moment.

He braced himself.

"I am listening, Papa."

Edmund's dark eyes glittered faintly as he looked at the lowered head of his son. "It seems that your mother and I have had a secret all of these years," he said. "I had always promised her that I would tell you when the time was right, but it just never seemed… right. If I do not tell you now, you will never know and that seems wholly unfair to you."

War's head came up, his brow furrowed. "Secret?" he repeated. "What secret?"

"About you."

"What about me?"

Edmund didn't reply right away. Perhaps he was resolved to tell him, but he didn't seem entirely willing to do it. In fact, he still seemed quite hesitant.

War leaned closer to him.

"What secret, Papa?"

Edmund couldn't seem to look at him. "About you," he said. "War, I have loved you since the moment you were born. I will love you until the end of time, as my son. That will never change."

"Of course it won't. Why would you say that?"

"Because your mother was pregnant when I married her."

War's eyebrows lifted in surprise. "Ah," he said, thinking that was all there was to the secret. "I see. Well, it does not matter. You loved Mother and she loved you. There is no shame in conceiving a child before you were married because you demonstrated that love."

Edmund shook his head. "Nay, lad," he whispered. "You misunderstand."

"What do I misunderstand?"

"I was not the one who impregnated her."

That wasn't what War had expected to hear. Not in the least. It took him a moment to realize what Edmund was saying and when it finally sank in, his eyes widened and he dropped the old man's hand.

"*What*?" he hissed, bolting to his feet. "What are you telling me?"

Edmund's eyes were full of sorrow. "I am telling you that although you are my son, I did not father you," he said. "You are my son in name and in my heart and soul, but you are not the son of my body."

War's mouth popped open in utter shock. He could hardly believe what he was hearing. "Who... who told you this?" he said in disbelief. "Did Mother tell you this?"

"She did."

"She was wrong!"

Edmund shook his head. "Nay, lad, she was *not* wrong," he said quietly. "You see, she loved another man before me, very much. She wanted to marry him but her father would not permit it. Your mother was a de Percy; you know this. The House of de Percy is an important house in the north and your mother was expected to marry well. She was not expected, nor was she permitted, to marry a man of her choosing. That is not the way such families do things, as you know."

War put a hand over his mouth as if to hold back the shock but, sadly, what his father said made perfect sense. Families like his mother's did not let emotions rule the day when it came to a proper marriage. As it all began to sink in, he lowered himself back to the chair.

"My God," he muttered. "So Mother was in love with another man before she married you?"

Edmund nodded faintly. "Aye," he said. "You must not blame her, War. Your mother was a loving and giving woman. She loved you very much."

War nodded quickly. "I know," he said. "You do not have to defend my mother's character to me. But this man…?"

"He was your father."

There it was. The confirmation yet again. War let out a long, painful breath. "I do not even know what to say," he said. "This is all so… astonishing."

Edmund wasn't unsympathetic. "I know," he said quietly. "Your mother was not permitted to marry the man of her choosing and your grandfather immediately sought out a betrothal with me. As Baron Herringthorpe, I had more to offer her than a mere knight."

"A knight was her lover?"

"He was the man she wanted to marry."

"Did you know she was pregnant when you married her?"

Edmund shook his head. "Nay," he said. "I thought you were mine until you were born six months into our marriage, an enormous and healthy child. At that point, she had no choice but to confess because you were not an early birth."

War stared at the man. "And you did not spurn me?" he said, incredulous. "You could have sent me to a foundling home at the very least, or you could have smashed my head on the wall. But you did not do that."

Edmund waved him off. "Of course not," he said. "I loved your mother. I loved you, too, the moment I saw you. What happened with your mother... it was not her fault. She was in love. And I loved her, so there was never any question that I would claim you as my son because you were. You still are."

Now that the initial shock was wearing off, War felt weak and drained. And so very, very distraught. He sank back against the chair, struggling to come to terms with what his father had told him.

"But you were tricked into marriage," he finally said. "By Mother and by Grandfather. They tricked you into marrying her, knowing she was pregnant with another man's child."

Edmund shrugged. "It was of little consequence," he said. "I got what I wanted – your mother, three healthy sons, and an excellent dowry. Your grandfather made me very rich when I married your mother though I thought it was an excessive dowry at the time."

"And you found out why."

"I did, indeed."

Edmund seemed at peace with the entire circumstance and after twenty-seven years, it had been time enough to reconcile himself to everything. War studied the man, watching his pale face, thinking that his father was a great man, indeed, for what he'd done. He'd never treated War any differently than his brothers. In fact, he'd always favored War. Edmund Herringthorpe had been generous beyond measure with his wife's bastard and War began to see the man through new eyes. His respect for him, already great, grew by leaps and bounds.

But he still had unanswered questions.

"The man who fathered me," he said after a moment. "Did he know about me?"

Edmund shook his head. "He never knew your mother was pregnant," he said. "Your mother never told him so you cannot become angry with the man. I want to make that clear."

War understood, but he didn't like the idea of a nameless, faceless man taking advantage of his mother. "But he still bedded her," he said. "Planting his seed was always a possibility."

Edmund looked squarely at him. "And you have bedded women before, too," he said frankly. "Did you ever consider that you might plant your seed, also?"

War cleared his throat softly and averted his gaze. "We are not speaking of me."

"Nay, we are not, but you have bedded women yourself, so you cannot throw stones," Edmund said. "Simply because you bed a woman does not mean you disrespected her or took advantage of her. Every couple has a story and there are a million stories between men and women, so you cannot blame this man, War. I have told you that. It is not his fault that your mother never told him she had conceived. I forbid you to become angry or vengeful about this."

He was growing agitated and War held up a hand to ease him. "I will not become angry or vengeful," he said. "It's simply that this is a lot to take in. When I awoke this morning, I was Edmund Herringthorpe's son. Now I discover that I am not."

"You *are*," Edmund emphasized. "I have told you that."

"But not by blood."

"Nay."

"Do you know who my father is?"

"I do."

"Who is he?"

Edmund hesitated. "The man does not know about you, War," he said. "Even if I were to tell you, what would you do with the information? Confront him and demand to take your place as his son? Or would you curse him for impregnating your mother? I am not certain any good can come out of you knowing who your father is."

War sighed heavily. "When you die, you take that knowledge with you," he said, sorrow in his eyes. "I do not know what I will do with the information, but now that you have told me the truth of my birth, something inside of me is desperate to know more. Even if it's a simple knight who never made anything of himself, I still want to know. It is not fair not to tell me of the man who fathered me. I have a right to know, for my own peace of mind."

Edmund still wasn't sure. "Do you swear to me that you will not cause him trouble?"

"I swear."

"Then know this," Edmund said softly. "He is a man with a family. He is a great, great man, mayhap one of the greatest men England has ever known. It would not be fair to him for you to disrupt his life over a choice your mother made long ago."

War's eyebrows lifted. "A great man?" he said. "Who is it?"

Edmund sighed faintly and closed his eyes, turning away. "I met him once, long ago," he said. "He was kind to me and he did not even know me."

"Who, Papa?"

Edmund's eyes opened and he stared off into the chamber before finally turning to focus on War.

"You will be as great as he is. Greater, mayhap."

"*Who?*"

"You are a de Wolfe, lad."

War gazed at him for a moment before his eyes began to widen. His shock started in his hands and feet, stiffening his entire body until it came to his head. Then, his mouth went slack and his eyes bulged.

His astonishment was overwhelming.

"A de Wolfe?" he managed to hiss. "*Who* is it?"

"William de Wolfe."

War didn't remember leaving his seat. Suddenly, he was across the chamber, hand over his mouth as weird gasps of shock were hissing through his splayed fingers. He found himself looking from the window that faced out to sea before turning back to his father as the man lay upon the bed.

"The Wolfe of the Border?" he said in an oddly strangled voice. "*That* William de Wolfe?"

"There is only one."

"And Mother told you this?"

Edmund nodded slowly. "She did," he said. "Lad, you look just like him. I told you that I have met him before and you look just like him. There is no mistake."

War had to make a conscious effort to breathe. Everything was coming out as strange gasps. "I just faced battle with him," he said, feeling as if he were about to lose all semblance of control. "The man brought his armies down from the north and he was at my side as we captured Thropton Castle. I met the man in battle and we spoke afterwards. We had conversations that… Christ, we had conversations!"

"What did you think of him?"

War threw up his hands. "What did I *think* of him?" he said, astounded. "He's the greatest knight who has ever lived. He is a legend. And now you are telling me that I am his son?"

"That is exactly what I am telling you."

War went pale. He could feel it. Suddenly, he was looking around the chamber for something. "Oh, God," he muttered. "Oh, God. I need something to drink. What do you have to drink?"

He answered his own question when he spied a pitcher of wine on the table near the door. He staggered over to it and picked it up, drinking straight from the neck and draining the entire thing in four swallows.

Edmund was watching him carefully.

"You would be his eldest son, to be exact," he said. "I have heard that de Wolfe has several sons, but you are older than they are. He was not married when he and your mother had their love affair. Were the sons at the battle, too?"

War was dazed. "Aye," he said. "I met four of them."

"Were they polite to you?"

War nodded, blinking rapidly as the alcohol in his empty belly began to spread some warmth. "Aye," he said. "I spoke to the eldest two – Scott and Troy – but only briefly. One of his sons is a head taller than I am. A mountain of a man. And the fourth one… he was blond. He fought ferociously."

"They are your half-brothers," Edmund said quietly, pointing out what War probably hadn't realized yet. "If they are anything like their father, then I am certain they are good men."

War closed his eyes, feeling the wine warm his belly. A belly that was in turmoil at the moment.

"I… I must think on all of this," he finally said, turning away from the table and looking at his father. "You cannot expect me to accept everything immediately. I must have time to… think."

Edmund wasn't without sympathy. "I understand," he said. "But I want you to look in my big chest. That one, over there."

He lifted a hand to point to an enormous wooden chest against the wall, painted with stags and the Herringthorpe crest. Dutifully, and wearily, War went to it and opened the lid.

"Near the bottom, against the right side," Edmund continued. "There is a box down there. It is bound with red ribbon. Do you see it?"

War's mind was frazzled. He was shuffling through the chest woodenly, looking for a box with a red ribbon until he finally spied it. He removed it carefully.

"Bring it here," Edmund said.

War returned to his father, putting the box on the old man's lap. Edmund removed the ribbon and opened the heavy lid. War should have been curious about the contents but he wasn't. He was so damned overwhelmed with everything he'd been told that he couldn't spare the energy for whatever Edmund was doing. He simply stood there, wrapped up in his own thoughts, thinking of that living legend he'd spent time with back at Thropton, a man he'd grown to admire, when Edmund finally spoke.

"Here it is," he said, pulling forth a yellowed and brittle piece of parchment. "Your mother wanted you to give this to de Wolfe should you ever tell him what I have told you."

Distracted from his thoughts, War looked at the man, almost recoiling from him, as he held up the carefully folded parchment.

"What is it?" he asked.

"A missive to William de Wolfe telling him of the son he never knew," Edmund said, extending it to War. "Take it. It is up to you whether or not you tell the man what you know. But if you do, give him this. Your mother wanted you to."

War's gaze moved from Edmund's face to the object in his hand. Slowly, he lifted his hand and accepted the parchment, seeing that it was sealed with his mother's personal crest. But the red wax was very old and brittle.

He simply stared at it.

"And she never thought to tell me any of this herself?" he said, bewildered. "As important as all of this is, she never thought to tell me herself?"

Edmund was prepared for the question. "I suppose she was ashamed," he said. "'Tis a very personal thing to discuss and she simply couldn't bring herself to do it. Mayhap she did not wish to see disappointment in your eyes. Disappointment in her. I really do not know the reason, War, but she couldn't tell you. She asked me to do it and I have."

War digested that, thinking on his father, his mother, and William de Wolfe. It seemed positively surreal, but he also realized that his shock was wearing off. What replaced it was something sorrowful and mystifying.

"Papa, I appreciate that you have told me this," he said after a moment. "I appreciate that you feel that this is something important to me but, at the moment, I do not want to speak on it any longer. Not until I have had a chance to truly think it through."

Edmund understood. "You wanted to know," he said quietly. "I told you. What you do with the information is your business from this point forward, but now you know."

War nodded faintly. "Aye," he said. "I know now. But beyond this initial conversation, I do not want to spare it any thought because I do not want our last moments together to be filled with talk of an old family secret. I do not want our last moments together to be focused on William de Wolfe. I want to focus on you. On us. I do not know what I am going to do without you when you are gone and that is all I want to think about."

Edmund smiled faintly. "You will do what you were born to do, War," he said. "My passing will not change your destiny. I have done my job. I have ensured you had the finest training and the most affection I could offer. You are my shining star, lad. Nothing will ever change that."

War looked at him. *Really* looked at him. To realize that he wasn't the man's son by blood was almost more painful and shocking than realizing he was someone else's bastard. He felt as if he were grieving the loss of something he never even had, something that was an illusion. It was difficult for him to put it into words but he didn't want to burden Edmund with it.

The man was dying.

He could tell just by looking at him. His lips were an odd shade of purple, his skin pale, but the words he spoke were those of beauty and family and love. War hadn't wept since he'd been a child but, at the moment, he felt very much like weeping. He honestly didn't know what he was going to do without Edmund.

He sat down next to the bed again.

"I am comforted," he said, though it wasn't the truth. "What can I say to you that will make this moment meaningful? I am afraid to leave this room for fear you will die while I am off doing something mundane, yet I do not know what to say to you that will be meaningful, something I will look back upon and be satisfied that I told you everything I needed to tell you. I suppose I could start by saying that my gratitude towards you is endless. Endless and deep. Without you, I do not know if I would be where I am today. How does one find the words to express something like that?"

Edmund's eyes glimmered dully. "You just did."

"Everything I am is because of you, Papa."

Edmund reached out to squeeze his hand. "Nay, lad," he said. "The brilliance was already there. You achieved everything through hard work and study and practice. Do not diminish what you have done. I was simply there to guide you."

War was looking at Edmund's hand as it held his gloved one. He hadn't even taken his gloves off, not throughout the entire conversation. Gently, he disengaged his hand and yanked his gauntlets off, tossing them to the ground. When he reclaimed Edmund's hand, it was with both of his.

Flesh to flesh.

The tears began to come.

"Will you do something for me, Papa?" he asked tightly.

Edmund could see how hard he was trying to hold back his emotions. "What do you wish, my son?"

War blinked and tears fell onto their hands as they gripped one another. "You just did it."

"What did I do?"

"You called me your son."

"You are, War. I told you that will never change."

"I suppose I just needed to hear it again."

Edmund gripped his hand tightly. "Shall I say it again?"

War shook his head, tears spilling over down his cheeks as he quickly moved to wipe them away. "Nay," he said. "But there is something else you can do for me."

"What is that?"

War sniffled, wiping at his eyes. "When I was a small boy, you used to tell me a story about a whale and a sea sprite," he said. "Do you remember the tale?"

Edmund chuckled softly. "Of course I do," he said. "I had hoped to tell it to your children."

"Would you tell it to me again?"

It was a sweet and poignant moment, from father to son. Edmund could hear four-year-old War asking for stories in that deeply rumbled request, but it didn't matter. His son was asking for a story and no matter how breathless he felt, he was honored to deliver. Thoughts of death and battles and bastard children were gone for the moment as Edmund began the tale of the whale and the mermaid and the pirates who chased them to try and steal their gold.

War had never spent a better moment in his life.

When Edmund finally slept, War openly wept.

CHAPTER FIVE

S HE KNEW HE was just around the corner.

Annaleigh had seen Anthony d'Vant when she'd emerged from the keep into the kitchen yard. Jordan had put her in charge of the morning meal and anything midday that the children wanted, so after the morning meal was completed, she had come to the kitchens to speak to the cook.

The cook, one of William's old quartermasters, had been in the chicken coop. In a day and age when it was usual for household cooks to be women, an old soldier with a great talent for food was something of an anomaly. He was old and gruff and tended to push people around, but William and Jordan liked him a great deal.

His bark was worse than his bite.

That was why none of the de Wolfe children feared him, including Annaleigh. Even though she was clearly Scots and he was clearly English, she and Baker, as he was called, got along splendidly. She let him think he was in control and he let her.

It worked out well for all.

It was a day that had dawned clear and bright, with summer in full bloom, and the day promised to be warm. Clad in a dress of linen, which was light and comfortable, Annaleigh was feeling as bright as the day. She'd been at Castle Questing for a few months now and she was starting to feel more settled. People were kind to her here. They spoke to her kindly and with friendship. She was accepted for the most part. And her cousin was giving her regular duties to perform so she felt productive, as if she were earning her keep.

There was no one to tell her that the death of a loved one was her fault.

"Annie!"

Annaleigh paused, turning to see Penelope running from the keep. She waited for the little girl to catch up to her, taking her hand.

"What are ye doing out here?" she asked. "Does yer mother know where ye are?"

It wasn't unusual for Jordan not to know where Penelope was, mostly because the little girl was like a moth. She flitted everywhere, darting about, until no one could keep track of her. Fortunately, there were many people in and around the keep and castle that kept an eye out for her so she never came to any harm, but Penelope was a slippery little creature.

They loved her that way.

"Mama knows I am with you," Penelope said. "She told me to find you. I am to stay with you."

Annaleigh lifted a dubious eyebrow. "I see," she said. "But the question is – will ye?"

Penelope grinned. "I will if you give me sweets."

"But it is early in the morning, lass!"

"I want sweets!"

Annaleigh shook her head and resumed walking. "Not so early," she said. "Ye'll be running like a madwoman all around the castle in little time if I give ye sweets now. Ye shall have some later."

"*Now.*"

"*Later!*"

Penelope proceeded to tell her just how wrong she was, but Annaleigh wasn't listening. She had suddenly spied Anthony in the stable yard next to the kitchens and she knew that if he saw her, he'd corner her. He'd become more aggressive lately because Talus was becoming more aggressive and, like a good competitor, he wasn't going to lose out. Annaleigh was fair game as far as he was concerned, and most of the eligible men at Castle Questing were concerned, so she didn't want him to see her.

She darted towards the buttery, taking Penelope with her.

"Where are we going?" Penelope demanded as Annaleigh dragged her along.

Annaleigh didn't answer right away. She'd made it to the wall where there were several outbuildings and several places to hide.

"If Anthony comes looking for me, tell him ye've not seen me," she said, letting go of Penelope's hand and pointing to the knight who was just starting to head in the direction of the kitchens. "Please, Penny! Tell him ye've not seen me!"

With that, she left Penelope standing near the buttery while she slipped inside. It was a cold, cramped stone building built into the outer wall and Annaleigh leaned against the heavy door, listening for voices.

They weren't long in coming.

"Greetings, my lady," Anthony said to Penelope, a child he had genuine affection for. "What brings you to the kitchen yard?"

Penelope peered up at him, squinting in the bright morning sunlight. "Sweets."

"Oh?" Anthony said. "I do not see any out here."

"Annie was going to get them for me."

There was a pause as Anthony looked around the yard. "I do not see Annie anywhere. Is she here?"

Penelope remembered very well what Annaleigh had told her, but she was a smart child. She was also manipulative.

And a little spiteful.

"Aye," she said, pointing towards the buttery. "In there."

Annaleigh heard those words and she silently cursed that nasty little girl. She stepped away from the door just as Anthony opened it. He smiled brightly while she gasped, startled.

"So you are here," he said. Then, his brow furrowed. "What are you doing?"

Hiding from ye, she thought. "I… I'm taking stock of the milk," she said, gesturing towards the earthenware containers on the floor. "Lady Jordan has given me charge of the morning meal so I must check the stores."

Anthony believed her, although he probably shouldn't have. Much like Talus, he was coming to sense that she was avoiding him at times, which she was. All of Castle Questing was laughing at the two knights pursuing the young woman who had no real interest in either one of them.

"Do you require any assistance?" he asked politely. "I am at your service."

Annaleigh moved to the door and he stepped back so she could exit. "Nay," she said. "I'm finished now."

"May I accompany you on your rounds?"

Annaleigh sighed. She could tell that she was going to have to speak frankly to him the same way she'd done to Talus, only with Anthony, it was more difficult because he was a genuinely nice man. He was handsome, too, as the d'Vants usually were. He was big and blond, well-built, and had no shortage of female admirers, only he seemed to shun them all in favor of a woman who had no real interest in him.

Annaleigh was coming to think it was simply the thrill of the chase.

"I think not," she said, turning to face him. "I am minding Penelope and we have many things to do this morning, though I thank ye for yer offer. Good day tae ye, Sir Anthony."

She turned away, eyeing Penelope and thinking that the lass needed a swift beating for betraying her, but Anthony spoke up before she could get away.

"My lady," he said. "Will you be busy with tasks all day?"

Annaleigh came to a pause, holding out her hand to Penelope as the little girl took it. "Mostly," she said. "It is difficult tae say. Lady Jordan has given me some responsibility at Castle Questing and I dunna intend tae shirk it."

"I did not mean to suggest that you would," he said. "It's simply that I must run an errand into Wooler later today and thought you might like to come along. It is a fine day and would make for a pleasant ride."

Annaleigh found herself sighing again, looking at Penelope, who was smiling up at her. *That little goat knows what's going on*, she thought. Penelope may have only been four years of age, but she was very sharp. She listened and she observed. Perhaps she knew that Anthony had been trying to woo Annaleigh because she'd heard people talking about it. Perhaps she thought she was helping by making sure Anthony found her, but Annaleigh didn't really believe that. She had a feeling Penelope's betrayal had something to do with the sweets she'd been denied.

And Annaleigh wanted to spank her right on the bottom for it.

"Thank ye, but nay," Annaleigh said. Then, she dropped Penelope's hand and closed the gap between her and Anthony. "Sir Anthony, I dunna mean tae be cruel, but I must make it clear that I'm not interested in a suitor. *Any* suitor. If ye simply mean tae be friendly with yer offer, then I appreciate it and mayhap I will go another time, but if ye mean anything more than that, then I must refuse ye."

The warmth in Anthony's eyes faded a little. "Well," he said, a smirk on his lips. "I suppose that was plain enough."

"I am sorry if it offends ye."

"It doesn't. But you cannot fault a man for trying."

There was some humor as he realized she was clearly rejecting his advances and Annaleigh smiled weakly. "Nay, I canna fault ye," she said. "But I dunna want tae give ye any hope where none exists. And before ye ask me, I dunna find anything wanting in ye. I simply dunna wish tae be courted right now. I've much happening with my family and in my life, and a suitor wouldna be welcome. It would be a… complication."

Anthony smiled weakly in return. "I've heard," he said softly.

"What have ye heard?"

"That your clan blames you for the battle at Etal months back."

Annaleigh nodded with some sorrow and also some shame. "'Tis true."

"I am not entirely sure how they can justify that kind of blame," he said. "From what I heard, the Etal men were completely to blame."

It was nice to hear of his support, something Annaleigh hadn't seen much of since that fateful event. "I think so," she said. "I know I dinna do anything tae invite being attacked by two Etal soldiers. But there are those who think I did."

His smile faded. "Will you tell me the names of these men?"

It was a surprising question, but not so surprising considering Anthony's character. He was very chivalrous, very loyal, even to a cousin of his liege.

It was rather sweet, actually.

"Nay," she said, impulsively putting a hand on his arm in a show of gratitude. "I dunna know their names. They dinna do more than tear my sleeve and frighten me, though they did steal my sheep. I tried tae tell my da of this, but he was bent on punishing the men who did it. When Etal Castle would not turn the men over to him, he decided tae attack. He said that if he dinna, the Sassenach would think him weak."

Anthony nodded in understanding. That was the most he'd ever heard about the situation and straight from the horse's mouth, no less. It also made him angry against those who had accosted her and her clan, who apparently blamed her for her father's decision to punish those who had wronged her. Anthony was a man of deep feeling, of a strong sense of right and wrong, and he didn't like it when others were treated poorly.

Especially Lady Annaleigh.

"He is not wrong," he said, sorry when she removed her hand from his arm. "The English here at the border are always suspicious against the Scots, always trying to test them. And the Scots test the English plenty as well. I suppose he did what he felt was right."

Annaleigh nodded. "I know he did," she said. "I only wish

he had not. Men died because of his decision and, truthfully, because of what happened tae me. That is what some of my clan canna forgive. That is why my da sent me tae Castle Questing. He says it will all go away if I am not there as a target for their anger."

Anthony lifted his eyebrows in resignation. "It makes sense," he said. "People are usually quick to anger, quick to forget. But I am sorry you have had to endure the situation. It cannot be pleasant."

Annaleigh shrugged. "It has given me the opportunity to come to Castle Questing," she said, watching Penelope fidget as she waited for her. "It has given me the chance to know a bonny lass with a big mouth and devious mind."

They were both looking at Penelope now and Anthony grinned at the sight of the squirmy child. "I have known her since birth," he said. "The day she was born was the day command of Castle Questing shifted from William to her. I shudder to think how she'll be when she becomes a woman. God help her husband."

Annaleigh laughed softly. "Agreed," she said. But her attention returned to him. "But for now… please understand I mean ye no disrespect, Sir Anthony. Ye seem tae be a fine man. But I'm simply not ready for anything as important as a suitor right now."

Anthony didn't like it, but he didn't fight her on it. At least, not now. "I hope we can still be friends."

"I hope so, too."

"The next time I go into Wooler, I would still be honored if you would like to ride along."

"I just might."

As the two of them engaged in idle conversation that had

nothing to do with suitors or battle, in the keep high above, they were being watched.

Two older women were focused on them.

One of them was blonde, with wide green eyes and an angelic face while the other was shorter, with dark hair and green eyes. They watched the pair in the kitchen yard while Penelope began to kick at the dirt and turn circles impatiently.

The dark-haired woman grunted.

"I dunna suppose he's finally managed tae break through," she said. "At least she's smiling. What do ye think, Jordie?"

Jordan de Wolfe, Lady Kilham, was watching through analytical eyes. "I think she's being polite as she tells him tae leave her be," she said. "I also think she'd better pay some attention tae Penny before the lass runs wild."

Jemma, Lady Hage, folded her arms beneath her rather ample bosom as she watched. "She's my own brother's child," she said. "I told Ian I'd watch her well and I dunna think that includes letting English knights hound her."

Jordan cast her a long look. "Anthony d'Vant hasna hounded anything in his life," she said, turning away from the window. "He's a nice lad and, truth be told, between Talus and Anthony, I'd pick Anthony. He's a kind man, while Talus…"

"Talus wants a meek and obedient wife," Jemma said flatly. "He'd be good tae her, but he'd also be demanding."

"Anthony wouldna be."

"Nay," Jemma said. "But I still dunna think my brother would like a Sassenach for a son."

Jordan looked at her. "He has a Sassenach for a brother when ye married Kieran," she pointed out. "But it's of little matter, truthfully, because she's never going back tae Langton. If she goes back, there's no knowing what will happen tae her."

Jemma shook her head sadly. "Who knew the lass would be safer in England than with her own kin?" she said. "Robbie never told her about those who wanted tae kill her, those angry enough over losing a son or a father that they wanted a pound of her flesh. He simply told her some people were angry about the battle at Etal. But not *how* angry."

Jordan sighed faintly as she took a seat, picking up the sewing she'd been working on. It was a new tunic for Penelope with flowers and dragonflies on it.

"She'll never hear it from me," she said. "But I'll never let her go back, either. The question is what tae tell her if she asks. And she will ask."

Jemma was still standing by the window. "Kieran says we must find her a husband," she said. "If she has an English husband, mayhap she'll not want tae return home, but if she does, she'll have a knight by her side tae protect her."

"Then our choices are Talus and Anthony? What about Gregory Payton-Forrester?"

Jemma turned to her. "The lad from Beverley Castle?" she said. "I like him. He's a good friend of Alec's."

Jordan nodded. "And Scott and Troy," she said. "That's why I thought of him. He's a good man and he's kind tae his mother."

Jemma pointed at her as if she had the best idea yet. "I like a man who's good tae his mother," she said. "I'll ask Kieran what he thinks."

"Ask me what?"

Kieran picked that moment to enter the solar, hearing his name. William was rolling in just behind him, both of them having come to the women's solar because they knew there would be food there. It was mid-morning and, finished with their duties and having not broken their fast yet, they were looking for food. They would never think of raiding the kitchens but they weren't beyond raiding the women's solar.

"We were speaking of Annaleigh," Jemma said, watching her husband move to the table that still had some food from the morning meal left on it. "The lass needs a husband."

Kieran grunted as he collected a pitcher, half-full of tepid wine. "Talus and Anthony have been trying without any luck," he said. "She simply isn't interested."

"What about Gregory Payton-Forrester?"

That drew a reaction from William. "There is no opportunity there," he said. "The man is already pledged."

"He is *not*," Jordan countered as if he'd just said something ridiculous. "There's a lady who has been pursuing him, but no contract."

William frowned. "There will be," he said. "And I'm not getting in the middle of that. The lady comes from the Lancaster family of Kendal Castle and it would not do well to snatch a marital prospect out from under their noses. They might march on Castle Questing and then we'd all be sorry."

Jordan snorted. "The Lancasters are all mad and everyone knows it."

William wagged a finger at her. "As I said, I am not putting myself in the middle of that situation, not when we have a du Reims and a d'Vant in our own home," he said. "Moreover, this is something her own father should be engaging in. This is not our responsibility."

"It is our responsibility if she is never returning tae Langton," Jordan said, looking up from her sewing. "We know what Robbie said about the kin who want her head on a pike. I'll not let her go back tae such a place where she's not safe. That means she stays with us."

William wasn't in disagreement, but it was more complex than his wife made it out to be. "Isn't that Robbie's decision?" he said quietly. "She's a lovely girl, Jordan, and I would be happy to have her here, but that decision must come from her father."

"I'll write tae him," Jordan said, returning her focus to her sewing. "I will ask him if she can stay here permanently. It will be tae her advantage, especially in marriage. There are many fine and wealthy knights who would vie for her hand. What more could her father want?"

"A Scottish husband," Kieran muttered.

William fought off a grin at Kieran's honest remark but he knew it was a subject that could deteriorate into an argument, so he sought to change the subject.

"Speaking of fine knights," he said. "I just received a missive from Bamburgh Castle. I came to tell you that we are to have visitors from Bamburgh, very soon."

"Oh?" Jordan said, interested. "Who is coming?"

"Sir Warwick Herringthorpe," William said. "He's the new commander of Bamburgh Castle, appointed by Henry. I invited him to Castle Questing in order to introduce him to some of the local warlords. I will take him to Northwood Castle and to Roxburgh. Possibly even to Berwick."

Jordan paused mid-stitch. "Bamburgh," she said thoughtfully. "Werena they part of the battle at Etal around the first of the new year?"

William nodded. "They were."

"The battle ye sat out."

"I could not take sides," he told her what she already knew. "It was the Scotts against Etal and I was not going to take sides in it. I had no choice but to abstain and my garrisons and allies with me."

Jordan nodded as she remembered that particular battle. "Northwood abstained also," she said as she resumed her stitching. "With Paris married tae Callie, he couldna command a battle against her kin."

William took a big slab of bread and cheese, extended to him by Kieran, who was still picking over the food on the table. "That's the complication when we marry Scots," he said, taking a big bite and chewing. "Now, you want to marry Annie to another English knight? If we keep this up, we'll have every fortress on the border related to the Clan Scott and we'll never be able to participate in a battle ever again."

Jordan grinned. "It would be one way to guarantee peace," she said. Then, she looked at him as if a great idea had just occurred to her. "What about this Herringthorpe? Is he married?"

William knew exactly what she was driving at and he put up a hand to stop her in her tracks. "I do not know and it is none of our affair," he said. "I am not going to shake the man's hand in greeting and then in the next breath, ask if him if he would like to court your cousin. I will not do it."

"I dinna ask ye tae," Jordan said, putting her head down to continue sewing. "Jemma and I will."

She said it almost under her breath, but not quite. William looked at Kieran in exasperation, who simply shook his head in resignation.

"If you do that, I will bundle you up and send you back to Langton Castle," William said. "I'll send you back where you came from."

Jordan was struggling not to laugh. "Ye canna send me

back," she said. "We've had eight children together."

"I'll find another wife."

"Who would tolerate ye, ye stubborn man?"

"She has a point," Kieran said. "No one else would want you, so you'd better not send her away."

William rolled his eye before finishing his bread and cheese as the women continued to sew. When he was finished, he downed some of the watered wine before turning to his wife.

"I beg you not to embarrass me in front of Herringthorpe," he said seriously. "All jesting aside, it would be most humiliating for you to approach the man about Annie, so please don't do it. This is Henry's most prestigious knight, a young man rising to power and a young man I would like to form a good relationship with. The last thing I need is my wife embarrassing me in any fashion."

Jordan stopped sewing. "Enough with ye," she said. "When have I ever embarrassed ye? Of course I willna say anything. But that doesna mean I willna look the man over if he's unmarried. Why would it be so terrible tae marry Annie tae the commander of Bamburgh? It would create an unbreakable alliance."

William nodded wearily. "I realize that, but if that is a possibility – and I say *if* – it will be far in the future," he said. "I've barely met Herringthorpe. I do not even know what kind of character the man has, so let me make my own judgment about him before we even speak of this again."

Jordan waved him off and continued with her sewing. Now that the food was gone, William and Kieran no longer had any reason to be in the women's solar so they bid their wives farewell and quit the chamber. As their boots could be heard descending the steps, Jemma turned to Jordan.

"Ye're going tae do it, are ye not?" she muttered.

Jordan never missed a stitch. "Of course I am."

"If William finds out…"

"He willna," Jordan said confidently. "I willna be obvious with Herringthorpe. Whatever I do or say, it will be subtle. But Annie needs a husband and if Talus and Anthony dunna catch her fancy, then mayhap another knight will."

Jemma lifted her eyebrows. "Ye'd better see what Herringthorpe looks like before ye say anything tae him," she said. "If the man looks like a troll and is missing all his teeth, we dunna want him for Annie."

Jordan sighed. "If that's the case, then I'll forget the entire thing."

Somehow, Jemma wasn't sure that was going to happen. Once Jordan was on the scent of something, she rarely let go. A prestigious knight in command of Bamburgh might look like a troll, but if he was well-connected and wealthy, certain things could be overlooked.

Fine marriages were made in such ways.

And they had a fine marriage to make.

CHAPTER SIX

THERE WERE THOSE wondering if this was such a good idea.

The day after War buried Edmund in the churchyard overlooking the sea, they were on the road for Castle Questing.

It possibly wasn't the best course of action.

War was in pain. Grief lined his face, his jaw was hard and set, but he was riding ramrod straight and fixed on the road ahead. He hadn't said a word since departing Bamburgh, leaving Monty and Alexei and Clement riding behind him, watching him, wondering when the man was going to expend his grief. So far, he'd not shed a tear. He'd simply gone on with business as usual.

That wasn't a particularly good sign.

As it turned out, Bamburgh was shockingly close to Castle Questing, so the trip would take about a day. They departed just before dawn and, if the weather held, they would be at Castle Questing before nightfall. War had sent a messenger to Castle Questing the day before, the day Edmund was buried, so they had word of the impending arrival of guests. War only brought his knights and about fifty men-at-arms simply because he didn't want to be caught without some line of protection this far north. As Edmund had once said, it was a wise man who knew when to be safe – and when to be cautious.

On this trip to Castle Questing, War intended to be both.

But it was a silent and uncomfortable ride with War perched like a statue upon his black and white stallion. Surprisingly, Clement kept his mouth shut from his usual passive-aggressive conversation, mostly because he knew Monty and Alexei would throttle him if he harassed War on this day of all days. But they didn't quite trust him so as midday approached, Monty kept an eye on Clement while Alexei rode up beside War.

"My lord," he said in his heavy accent. "Will you pause to rest for a moment? Mayhap your horse could use a rest? We have made good time this morning."

War turned to the tall, very blond, and very big warrior who was from the east. The man had been born in Vilnius, but he'd spent most of his professional life fighting in Slavic states, including the fall of Kiev against the Mongols who came from the mysterious lands in the Far East. He had experienced things that knights from England could only dream of, which was why War had befriended him. As an intensely curious man who was always interested in learning, he and Alexei had formed a fast friendship when Alexei had come to the court of Henry to swear his fealty.

And Alexei was loyal to the bone to War.

"Are you telling me that you are weary, Nevsky?" he said, smiling weakly. "I never knew such a thing was possible."

Alexei returned his smile. "Not only possible, but probable," he said. "We will make Castle Questing well before nightfall. Why not let me rest for a few moments before we continue along our way? I am not as strong as you."

War broke down in soft laughter, the only laughter from the man since they'd returned home from Thropton.

Since then, he'd had nothing to smile about.

"Very well," he said, looking around. "Find a suitable spot and call the men to a halt."

Fighting off a grin, Alexei nodded and immediately turned for the column, calling a halt at that very moment. They were traveling beside a burn with a stream that ran through it so it was an appropriate place as far as Alexei was concerned. The men moved off the road and into the thick, green growth, followed by the knights.

There was plenty of laying in the grass and drinking from the brook as the men from Bamburgh took a quick rest. Even Monty found a tree and sat down beneath it, with Clement standing a few feet away, watching the men. War was about a dozen feet away, gazing out over the meadow beyond the burn as his horse, next to him, drank from the stream. Alexei, having pulled a bladder of watered wine out of his saddlebags, approached War and handed him the bladder.

"I grew up in Suffolk," War said, bladder in his hand as he looked out over the rolling landscape. "It is flat ground."

"You like this better?" Alexei asked.

War shrugged. "My father did," he said. "He liked dramatic landscape. I think that is one of the reasons that he was so eager to come to Bamburgh with me. He loved the sea."

Alexei looked at him, hearing the sorrow in his voice as he spoke of Edmund. There was no use in avoiding the subject. "I have not had the opportunity to express my sympathy for your father's passing," he said. "Edmund was one of the only men I ever met who did not look at me suspiciously, as if I'd come to England to invade it."

"That was my father."

"He was very accepting."

War looked at him, a dull gleam in his eyes. "And he hounded you mercilessly with questions about your homeland."

Alexei chuckled. "He did," he said. "There were times when I would try to hide from him but he would always find me. He wanted to know everything."

War smiled weakly. "He did to the point of annoyance," he said. "You were always gracious to him, Alexei. I never thanked you for that."

"There is no need. It was an honor."

War's smile faded as he returned his attention to the landscape. "I know you think we should not be traveling to Castle Questing right now," he said. "But I have my reasons. My father would not have wanted me to sit around and grieve him. He would have wanted me to continue my life as normal."

"Your reasons for traveling to Castle Questing are not in question, my lord," he said. "But we are concerned for you. We know you and your father were close. It is never easy to lose a parent."

"Is your father still alive, Alexei?"

Alexei shook his head. "He died when I was newly knighted," he said. "We attended a battle together and he fell right in front of me. I held him as he breathed his last."

War closed his eyes for a moment as if to ward off that horrible thought. "I did not know," he said softly. "I am sorry, Alexei. Very sorry. But how… how did you overcome it?"

"His death?"

"Aye."

"It was difficult at first," Alexei admitted. "But I drew upon our affection for one another. If you remember the good times, sometimes it eases the sting of the loss. My father told great stories, you see. For example, if a man had a nice sword, then my father once had a nicer one. That is what he would say. If a man traveled to a faraway land, then my father had always gone further. According to him, he saw everything and he had done everything. I once joked that my father had done everything except childbirth."

War laughed softly. "He sounds like quite a man."

"He was. And not only in his own mind, but in mine."

"And remembering his stories gives you comfort."

"Aye," Alexei said, putting an affectionate hand on War's shoulder. "In time, it will be the same for you."

War's smile faded. He and Alexei were close and he considered the man his one and true closest friend. He always had. He knew that Alexei was trustworthy, but more than that, he trusted the man's opinion.

There was something more eating away at him that Alexei didn't know.

William de Wolfe.

Perhaps that was what had War the most unbalanced in all of this. He was grieving the loss of the man who raised him, the man he thought was his father until Edmund's deathbed revelations. Part of him was angry at Edmund for doing that to him, for waiting until the end of his life before divulging such shocking information. Surely Edmund would know what turmoil it would bring him, now on top of losing the only father he'd ever known.

But another part of him was angry with de Wolfe.

He'd promised Edmund no vengeance, no rage. Having thought the circumstances of his conception over, he was coming to see that de Wolfe wasn't at fault other than the obvious. He'd lain with a woman who loved him and wanted to marry him, but that marriage never happened. It had been Jane de Percy who had withheld the information from him and also from Edmund when she married him, so his mother, whom he loved dearly, was really at fault in all of this.

It wasn't de Wolfe and it certainly wasn't Edmund.

But both were affected by her secret.

Still, War found that he needed an impartial opinion in all of this. Alexei was a mature man, a man of the world, who had seen and done many things in his lifetime. Monty would simply side with whatever War felt and Clement wasn't a candidate in the least.

Perhaps Alexei could help him see the situation clearly.

"There's… something more in all of this," War finally said. "Something more than grieving my father. Something that is troubling me greatly."

Alexei looked at him with both interest and concern. "What is it?"

War was having a difficult time looking at him. "You must never repeat this."

"I will take it to my grave."

"If you do not, a great many people may be affected, including me."

"You have my word."

War sighed heavily. "It seems that my father had a deathbed confession to make," he said quietly. "He told me that although he married my mother and I was born within the tenure of that marriage, he is not the man who fathered me."

Alexei tried to keep the surprise off his face. "Your… your mother had a lover other than your father?"

"Before the marriage," War said. "She was pregnant when

she married my father."

"And he did not know?"

"Nay."

Alexei cleared his throat softly, understanding the implications of deception, among others. "I see," he said quietly. "And Edmund saw it necessary to tell you all of this before he died?"

"Aye."

"Then I would imagine he felt it very important," Alexei said, trying to be of some comfort to what surely must have been startling news to War. "Your father treated you as if you were his blood, War. In fact, he favored you over your brothers. We could all see that. He never loved you less. In fact, I believe he loved you more."

War could see that Alexei was trying to reassure him that it didn't matter that he wasn't from Edmund's loins, but that wasn't the real issue. He held up his hand to silence the man.

"I know," War said, his voice soft because Monty and Clement were nearby and he didn't want them to hear him. "I know my father loved me. And he *is* my father, Alexei. No matter what the truth is, Edmund is the man who raised me. He is my father."

Alexei heaved a sigh of relief that War saw it that way. "Indeed, he is," he said. "But that surely must have been a shock to you."

War nodded. "Shock?" he mused softly. "It was. Shock is a gentle term for what I felt. More importantly, it is *who* my real father is that shocks me the most."

Alexei's features flickered with concern. "Edmund knew who it was?"

"He told me."

"Who?"

"William de Wolfe."

Alexei could no longer keep the shock or concern or anything else off his face. His eyes widened. "De Wolfe?" he hissed. "The man we just saw in battle?"

"The same."

"But how –?" Alexei stammered. "How did he… does he know you are his son?"

War shook his head. "He does not know," he said. "As Edmund told me, my mother loved de Wolfe before she ever met my father. She wanted very much to marry him, but her father would not permit her to marry a mere knight, which was what de Wolfe was back then. He was simply a young knight with no property, no titles yet. She was pregnant with the man's child and unable to marry him because my grandfather betrothed her to Edmund, who had a title and was a slightly better prospect. According to my father, de Wolfe never knew about the pregnancy. He never knew a thing."

Alexei was filled with shock at the astonishing revelation, but he quickly saw the situation for what it was. "And now you must reconcile yourself to the fact that not only was Edmund not your father, but a legendary knight is," he said, reading War's mind. "Forgive me, War, but it was not fair of Edmund to tell you this, at least not on his deathbed. He should have told you sooner. You both could have reconciled this together."

War sighed heavily. "I know," he said. "But it is done. Now, my dilemma is this – my mother wrote de Wolfe a missive to be given to him, explaining about me. Edmund gave me the letter. He cautioned me against seeking any kind of vengeance or retribution against de Wolfe since the man did not know my mother was pregnant and I must say that I agree. But I feel as if I should tell him. If I do not, then I am as bad as my mother and

Edmund for having withheld such a secret. If you were de Wolfe, would you want to know?"

Alexei scratched his head. "I think so," he said. "I think I would want to know if I had any bastards about. Not to claim them as my son, but simply to know them, as my flesh and blood. To help them if they needed and wanted it. But de Wolfe has many sons – we met them."

War nodded. "I am older than the two eldest sons."

Alexei was watching him carefully. "Do you think to challenge them for your due?" he asked tentatively. "You cannot do that, War. They were born within a legal marriage and you were not."

War held up a hand to silence him. "I realize that completely," he said. "Nay, I do not wish to challenge them. But de Wolfe… I do not want another father, but I suppose it is his right to know."

"I believe that is the right thing to do."

War knew that. He just wanted to hear it from someone he trusted. Still, the entire situation had him in turmoil.

"I just lost the man I believed was my father by blood, a man I loved very much," he said. "Now, he is gone and I feel as if I have lost… something. Mayhap it was only an illusion, but I feel as if I have lost what I thought was my life. My *entire* life. I feel that Edmund's confession has tainted every memory I ever had with him and certainly with my mother. They withheld something from me that they should have told me when I became of age. What else did they not tell me, Alexei? What other truths did they withhold?"

"You've lost your trust," Alexei said quietly. "That seems normal enough to me, but I do not believe they withheld anything else from you. Edmund did not have to tell you what he did, War. Remember that. I cannot imagine it was easy for him."

"Nay, I'm sure it wasn't."

"You will regain your trust in him," Alexei said. "You must give yourself time. And you must learn to forgive both of your parents."

"Forgiveness? Is that what I need to do?"

"Aye," Alexei said, almost gently. "Until you do that, you will always feel… lost."

They were wise words. War was well aware of it. After a moment, he looked at Alexei and forced a smile, nodding his head. Alexei smiled in return before turning to the group as a whole and bellowing orders to return to the road.

They had a journey to complete.

❧

BAMBURGH'S CONTINGENT HAD been sighted.

Castle Questing was abuzz with news that a small contingent from Bamburgh had been sighted within its territory. William had constant patrols all over his lands so that any invasion would be quickly seen, so the messenger that had delivered the Bamburgh news was breathless because he'd ridden so hard and so fast to convey the information. William thanked him and sent him to rest. Then he put the fortress on alert and notified his wife.

Guests are imminent.

Even now, Jordan was overseeing the preparation of the room that Herringthorpe would stay in while Jemma and Annaleigh were in the hall and kitchens, respectively. Annaleigh was seeing to the refreshments for Herringthorpe and his men upon arrival while Jemma was making sure the hall was properly cleaned. If she didn't like the way the servants were cleaning it, then she'd snatch a broom and sweep it herself.

There was a flurry of activity going on.

Of course, Annaleigh had no idea that having her greet the travelers in William's solar was all part of Jordan and Jemma's plan to introduce her to Herringthorpe. They didn't even know if the man was married or spoken for, but if not, they wanted him to get a good look at Annaleigh. William was oblivious to their plans, though he shouldn't have been given the conversation they'd had earlier. While he was in the bailey with Kieran as the men made housing preparations for the small escort, Jordan and Jemma were putting their scheme into action.

Perhaps Annaleigh should have wondered why Jordan asked her to put on a pretty frock, but she didn't. She put on one of her best garments, assuming Jordan wanted her to dress nicely for their prestigious guest, who was a high-caliber knight named Herringthorpe. Annaleigh heard all about how Herringthorpe was trained at Blackchurch before swearing fealty to the king himself. He'd evidently earned a name for himself before being granted the position of garrison commander of Bamburgh Castle, a massive fortress in Northumberland. Jordan told Annaleigh everything she knew about the man and Annaleigh never dreamed it was because Jordan was trying to create a sense of awe before the man even appeared.

It worked.

By the time Bamburgh's contingent arrived, Annaleigh was suitably nervous.

The refreshments were laid out in William's solar with artistic precision. There were several pitchers of fine wine and the food dishes upon the table were things warmed over by the cook, but also leftover meals that had been repurposed. There were small beef and egg pies that had prunes and dates in them, along with stuffed eggs, baked apples, copious amounts of bread with fruit and butter. Annaleigh had sliced the cheese herself, creating suns and other patterns out of them as they were placed upon wooden platters. It was quite decorative and she was proud of it.

Then the guests arrived.

She could hear the commotion in the bailey as the contingent from Bamburgh came through the gates. William, Kieran, Talus, Anthony, and William's son, Troy, were there to greet them. Troy, usually stationed at Wark Castle, had been at Castle Questing to speak with his father about a situation in the nearby village of Coldstream when news of Bamburgh's approach had been announced so he decided to remain. Annaleigh made her way to the keep entry, straining to see what she could about the new arrivals, when she caught a glimpse of something out of the corner of her eye.

Penelope was heading for the bailey.

And she was armed.

Curious, Annaleigh came out of the keep and headed in Penelope's direction, but she could see that Penelope was being followed by little Rose Hage, her little brother, Nathaniel, and finally her own brother, Thomas. They were all following her, telling her to come away. Nathaniel began to cry because they were all heading for the bailey and they knew that they weren't allowed out there. The last time he'd set foot in the bailey without permission, his mother, Jemma, had smacked his bottom. He didn't like being smacked. So he began to cry, causing Rose to stop to comfort her little brother. Then, it was up to Thomas to do what evidently needed to be done.

Stop Penelope.

He did by grabbing her arm and yanking the sword from her hand. She began to scream as only Penelope was capable of screaming, which brought Annaleigh on the run. By the time she got there, Penelope was in a furious tug-of-war with Thomas and the sword.

"Here, here," Annaleigh said, separating the two by pulling Penelope away. "Yer father has an important guest and ye're causing a ruckus. Go back tae the kitchen yard immediately!"

Penelope was wailing. "I want the sword!"

Annaleigh didn't argue with her. She swooped down and picked her up, carrying her back towards the kitchen yard and away from the important visitors. But Penelope ended up kicking and screaming, so much so that Annaleigh put her hand over the child's mouth to keep her quiet. By the time they reached the kitchen yard, Penelope chomped down and bit Annaleigh on the hand. Dropping the little girl to her feet, Annaleigh drew back a swift hand and spanked her, open palmed, right on the buttocks.

Shocked that someone should actually punish her, Penelope looked at Annaleigh with great surprise before dropping into the dirt and sobbing.

"And ye'll get more where that came from if ye bite me again," Annaleigh said, shaking her finger at the child. "That was very naughty, Penelope. I'm going tae tell yer mother what ye did."

"She took my sword," Thomas said solemnly. When Annaleigh looked at him, he turned to her with great seriousness. "She took my sword. She said she wanted to fight whoever was coming to Castle Questing."

"Why?"

"Because she said it was her castle and she didn't invite

them."

Annaleigh sighed heavily, looking at the child still sobbing in the dirt. "'Tis not yer castle, Penny," she said. "This is yer father's castle and those people are his guests. Would ye embarrass him so?"

"What happened?"

Annaleigh looked up to see Jordan coming up behind her, but the woman was looking at her daughter with some concern.

"Why is she crying?" Jordan asked.

Annaleigh knew how Penelope was treated around Castle Questing so she hoped she wasn't about to become Public Enemy Number One. "I saw her going out tae the bailey with a sword," she said. "Thomas said she stole it from him and she was planning on challenging Lord William's guest."

Jordan frowned. "Challenge him?" she repeated, looking at her daughter. "Why in the world would ye do that, lass?"

"Annie hit me!" Penelope wailed, pointing a finger at Annaleigh.

Annaleigh quickly found herself on the defensive. "When I picked her up tae bring her tae the kitchen yard, she bit me," she explained, holding up her hand to show Jordan the welt. "I spanked her."

Penelope was on her feet, rushing to her mother and throwing her arms around the woman's legs. "Annie hit me, Mama," she said. "She hurt me."

Jordan may have been a soft touch for her daughter, but she was better than her husband was. She knew when she was being manipulated. Reaching down, she grasped the little girl by the arms.

"Is that true?" she demanded. "Did ye bite her?"

Penelope wasn't expecting her mother not to blindly believe

her. "I… I… she *hit* me!"

"*After* ye bit her," Jordan said accusingly. "Dunna lie tae me, lass. If ye do, it'll go worse for ye."

Penelope simply began crying again, loudly, because she knew she'd done something wrong. It was as good as a confession as far as Jordan was concerned. She swatted her naughty daughter on the behind for good measure and she cried louder. But just as quickly, Jordan picked the child up, hugged her, and turned for the keep.

"Tell William I've had tae tend Penny," she said. "Annie, greet his visitors in my place and make sure they have everything they need. Go, now. They've arrived."

As Jordan disappeared into the keep with Penelope and Thomas, Annaleigh brushed the dust from the front of her dress and quickly headed out into the bailey where William's visitors had just dismounted their steeds. She could see men gathered around, including William, and she quickly made her way over to them.

"Annie!"

Edward de Wolfe came running up beside her. Dark and handsome, even at his young age, he was quite articulate and well-spoken. He'd seen eleven summers but he had the maturity of someone older. Annaleigh reached out and grasped his hand.

"Come with me," she said. "I'm tae greet yer father's guests in yer mother's stead."

"Where's Mother?"

"She took Penny away."

Edward lifted a disapproving eyebrow. "What's she done this time?"

"Hush," Annaleigh squeezed his hand and let it go. "We've guests tae greet, so no talk. Be polite and listen."

She came to a halt behind Kieran, standing a few feet away, as the men chatted amiably. She could hear several voices but because they were so tall, and she so petite, she could only stand back and listen. But soon enough, the crowd backed away and William appeared, heading towards the keep.

His gaze fell on Annaleigh and she could see the puzzlement.

"Jordan had something tae tend tae in the keep," she said quickly. "She asked me tae help ye with yer guests."

William didn't seem too happy, probably because it occurred to him, finally, that this might be a ploy for Annaleigh to meet War. At least, he thought so. If he knew his wife well, and he did, she wasn't beyond such things if she truly believed she was in the right.

"What is happening in the keep that she cannot greet my guests?" he asked.

Annaleigh was reluctant. "Well…" she said uncomfortably. "It's Penny."

"What *about* Penny?"

"She's been naughty."

William didn't need to be told more than that. Maybe it wasn't a ploy, after all, considering any situation with Penelope was quite plausible. William turned to speak to the group of men behind him.

"My wife is unavoidably detained at the moment," he said. "Let us continue this conversation inside where food and drink await."

The men began to move and Annaleigh stood back as the group began to pass her by. She would follow them indoors and quietly monitor the situation just in case they needed something. Three men she didn't recognize moved past her, and a few she did recognize in Troy and Talus and Anthony, but William was still speaking to the man she hadn't seen yet.

But then he moved aside.

A man was standing there, positively enormous in breadth and height, and he was looking up at the impressive keep of Castle Questing. Just for a moment. But then his eyes moved to the bailey, to things around him, and finally to her, standing just a few feet away.

Those eyes.

Annaleigh looked at the man and he looked at her. She'd seen those eyes before. William was with the other men, heading towards the keep, briefly leaving the man alone as he inspected his surroundings. He took two steps before suddenly noticing her and, for a moment, they simply stared at one another. Recognition was in the air as they both began to realize they knew one another or, at least, they'd seen each other before. Perhaps eight months ago in a thicket of trees next to the River Till.

Realization hit Annaleigh like a battering ram.

"*Ye,*" her eyes widened. "It… it's *ye!*"

His eyes lit up, beautiful eyes she'd remembered from those months ago. "Annaleigh?" he said, incredulous. "My God. Is it really you?"

She couldn't even answer his question. She was so overwhelmed at the sight of him that she couldn't even answer him. A shout from William got his attention and he suddenly turned away, rushing to catch up with the group and leaving Annaleigh standing there in shock.

But it was more than shock.

It was horror.

Horror that a reminder of the worst event in her young life

had been standing in front of her. Horror that the man had actually survived because she had given him aid. Not only had she caused the event, but she'd aided the enemy. At the time, guilt had forced her to. Guilt that the knight had been injured because of her. She hadn't really believed the man would survive his wounds, but he did.

And he was here at Castle Questing.

A reminder of everything she was trying to forget.

But, God… he was so handsome. In the dark thicket, covered with mud and gore, she'd never gotten a good look at him other than his eyes and those had been beautiful. Recognizable. But now, she'd just caught a glimpse of the rest of him and to stay he was magnificent… well, there wasn't a word invented that could describe all that he was. He was a god among men, a paragon of masculinity who had just stepped from the lofty heights of Olympus.

And he was here.

Stiffly, Annaleigh began to follow the men into the keep, lagging behind because she didn't want to get any closer. She was only following them because she'd told Jordan she would, but she was struggling to regain her composure. It occurred to her that all she'd ever heard about the visitors were that they were from Bamburgh Castle, someone named Herringthorpe who was a powerful new garrison commander, sent by King Henry himself. In fact, she'd built up a healthy sense of awe about him. Even now, she still had it. But it further occurred to her that when she'd seen the man in that thicket, he'd only told her his first name –

War.

Was he the Herringthorpe everyone was talking about?

She was about to find out.

CHAPTER SEVEN

I T WAS HIS angel of mercy.

At least, he'd called her that once. She'd helped him after the battle at Etal when he hadn't wanted her help and was utterly ungracious, but she'd ignored him and she'd saved his life. That's what the surgeon said after he'd been found three days later.

Who stitched you up, War?

All he'd been able to say was that it had been an angel of mercy.

And it had.

War was preoccupied as he and his men entered William's lavish solar, the one with hide rugs and a hearth that could fit six men in it comfortably. He pretended to be interested in what de Wolfe said, but the truth was that he was reeling with surprise to have seen his angel of mercy in the bailey of Castle Questing when he was positive he'd never see her again. She was Scots, after all. She should be back in Scotland with her kin, the same kin who had attacked Etal.

But she wasn't.

She was here.

And, oh so beautiful.

The lass had hair that glimmered like the metal forged by the blacksmiths – red and gold, shimmering with liquid light. She had skin like cream and big, wide eyes. A fine beauty if ever there was one, even more beautiful in the sunlight. Standing there in a fine but simple yellow garment, she'd been positively radiant.

He wanted to know why she was here.

Who *was* Annaleigh?

But in the same breath, he was struck by the fact that he was in the same room with the man who impregnated his mother, the man who made his birth possible. He was technically his father by blood and his fascination with William de Wolfe was stronger, at the moment, than his fascination with Annaleigh.

He had a powerful need to know the man his mother had been so in love with.

The man whose blood flowed through his veins.

"You offered to introduce me to the warlords in this area and I am greatly appreciative, but I'm curious," he said to William. "You've kept peace along the border for many years, so surely you have some Scottish allies in all of this. I heard that was the reason you abstained from the battle between Etal Castle and Clan Scott those months ago."

William nodded, bringing him a cup of wine. "My wife is a Scott," he said. "Kieran's wife is also a Scott. My ties to Clan Scott go back to the day I married my wife, so when they had trouble with Etal, I had no choice but to abstain. I was sorry to hear you were injured in the battle."

War sipped at his wine. "It was my own fault," he said. "I'd been at Bamburgh barely a month when we went to Etal and I suppose I was trying to establish my dominance."

"What happened?"

War rolled his eyes. "Something very stupid," he said. "I followed a group of Scots I felt were commanding the Scottish troops into a glen by the river's edge. I was caught off guard by a pike."

William grunted. "The Scots do not fight like the English do," he said. "That is the first thing you must learn about them. I realize you are Blackchurch trained, but Blackchurch doesn't teach you how the Scots think. They'll do anything they can to win a battle, including trickery and underhanded tactics. We've all learned that one way or the other."

War took another sip of wine. "Blackchurch does indeed teach about underhanded tactics," he said. "However, this was simply my own arrogance."

"You got in your own way, did you?"

War laughed softly. "I did," he said. "We've all done it."

"We surely have."

War looked at William. "I'm curious – if you are so strongly allied with Clan Scott, how do you pick and choose your battles here on the borders?"

William shrugged. "Anything that involves Clan Scott against other Scots usually involves me," he said. "Anything that involves them against other English does not involve me."

"Including Etal."

"Including them."

"They were not happy that you did not side with them."

"I know. And I do not care. They need me far more than I need them."

War grinned. "I hope to have that same attitude myself when it comes to Bamburgh," he said. "Everyone needs me far more than I need them."

"Everyone is watching Bamburgh now that they know War Herringthorpe is in command," Kieran spoke up, watching War's smile grow. "Where are you from, Herringthorpe?"

War faced the enormous, dark-eyed knight. "Suffolk," he said. "I was born there."

"And your family?"

"My parents are gone," he said. "I have two younger brothers who serve Henry."

"Did your father serve Henry?" Kieran asked. "I do not seem to remember a knight named Herringthorpe."

War shook his head. "My father was never at court," he said. "He preferred the quiet life of the countryside, though he had endless ambition for his sons. That is how I ended up at Blackchurch."

"Did your brothers?"

"One did, one did not."

Kieran nodded in understanding. "And your mother?" he said. "Was she born in Suffolk, too?"

War shook his head. "Northumberland," he said. "She was part of the de Percy family."

William spoke up. "You mentioned she was from Northumberland but I did not have the chance to ask you her family name," he said. "De Percy, is it? I know the family well. Mayhap I knew her."

You knew her intimately well, War thought. He also realized that if he gave William his mother's name, William might begin to suspect that War wasn't simply a new ally. He might suspect that he was much more than that. That information could do one of two things – it could either put William on his guard, given the fact that War undeniably looked like him, or it might make him immensely curious to discover the truth.

Perhaps War didn't need to tell William anything at all.

Perhaps the man would figure it out for himself.

It was a chance, he found, that he had to take.

There was some part of him that wanted to be acknowledged.

"Her name was Jane," he said, looking William in the eye. "Jane de Percy."

William didn't react but Kieran did. "I knew Jane," he said, surprise in his voice. "We all knew Jane. A lovely woman. I'm very sorry to hear that she has passed on."

War nodded, tearing his eyes away from William to look at Kieran. "Thank you," he said. "It has only been a few years. I do miss her, though I fear she might be angry that I buried my father at Bamburgh and not in Suffolk with her."

"Then you must bring her north," William said. "She was from Northumberland, after all. She deserves to be buried where she was born."

"True," War said. "You… you knew her, also?"

It was a leading question, but William didn't hesitate. "I did," he said. "When I first came to Northumberland, I met her at a feast. She was the youngest of three sisters and, as I recall, the loveliest. And her sisters were very protective over her."

War smiled faintly. "I would believe that of Aunt Emelie and Aunt Bridget."

"They were quite adept at chasing away young knights."

War chuckled, as did Kieran and those within ear shot, but there was nothing on William's face that suggested he'd just had a massive revelation that War might be something more to him. In fact, War was studying the man's expression quite intently when Clement suddenly spoke up.

"My lord," he said, addressing William. When everyone

looked at him, his focus turned to War. "Since we are speaking of parentage, it should be noted that Sir Warwick is in mourning. His father passed away at Bamburgh just a few days ago and though he more than likely will not tell you, I will. Sir Edmund was a great man and deserves to be remembered well."

All eyes turned to War with some shock. "Forgive me, War," William said sincerely. "I did not know. You did not have to come to Castle Questing so soon. I would have understood."

War wasn't thrilled that Clement had spoken up and, given the man's envy for Bamburgh's command, he wasn't certain that it wasn't some ploy to make War look weak and emotional in front of these titans of the north. But more than that, War was perturbed that Clement had taken the attention off of Jane de Percy and William's potential memories.

He smiled weakly.

"It is the way of life, my lord," War said. "My father had been ill for some time, so it was not unexpected. But... I will miss him."

William smiled faintly. "Of course you will," he said. "Are you sure you would not rather return to Bamburgh and then come back when the time is better?"

"I am here now, my lord. My father would have wanted this."

"Then a toast to your father and the fine son he raised. Godspeed to him."

Everyone lifted their cup, drinking to Edmund's memory, which made War feel a little better. He drew strange comfort from it. But he was still grossly unhappy with Clement, who didn't flinch or react when War shot him a long look. Next to Clement, Monty looked as if he wanted to throttle the man.

There was tension there.

"My lord," Alexei spoke up, trying to distract their new allies from whatever was happening between Clement and War. "I am interested to know how far your lands are from one end to the other. I am told you have a large portion of this corner of Northumberland."

William wasn't oblivious to whatever tension was happening between War and his knights, but he couldn't put his finger on it. He knew Kieran would, however. The man was a master at reading men and that was often how they went into a conference. William would speak while Kieran would observe and then they would discuss it afterwards. They'd been able to assess, and sometimes avert, many serious situations that way.

He wondered if this would be one of them.

"You are the knight from Vilnius?" he said.

Alexei nodded. "Aye, my lord," he said. "I am Alexei."

"I have only met a few men from that far to the east," William said. "I find it fascinating that men should be so well-traveled, having come all the way to England."

Alexei smiled. "A man has but one life, my lord," he said. "I have lived many lifetimes within mine."

"And now you serve Bamburgh?"

"I serve Herringthorpe."

It was a definitive declaration of loyalty, something William both approved of and appreciated. "If there is time, I hope you will tell me about your homeland," he said. "It is a rare opportunity to learn such things. Northumberland tends to be either Scots or England. There is nothing else unless a Northman or two shows his face."

"I have heard that has happened quite a bit in the past, my lord."

"It happens still, but not as much as it used to," William

said, looking at War. "They do seem to favor Bamburgh, so if no one has told you to be on your guard from the sea, then I will tell you. If you see longships on the horizon, send word to Berwick and to me immediately. Do not wait."

He said it seriously and War took it seriously. "When I first came to Berwick, some of the old soldiers spoke of seeing the Northmen when they were younger," he said. "I'm told that no one has seen them in twenty years, so let us hope that trend continues."

William couldn't disagree. "Absolutely," he said. "But vigilance is key. At Berwick, where my son, Patrick, is the garrison commander, the mouth of the River Tweed is wide enough for a longship. They are always vigilant there."

"I shall be also," War assured him. "Aside from the occasional Northmen, is Northumberland quiet for the most part? The Scots are not too terribly active these days?"

William shook his head. "Not these days," he said. "Except, of course, the attack on Etal, but that was the first activity in quite some time on a larger scale. We have occasional raids into Coldstream or other villages, but those are usually reivers. Not organized clan attacks."

"Then I have come at a quiet time."

"Be careful, Herringthorpe. You do not want to rue the day you spoke those words."

War grinned but as he went to drink from his cup, he caught sight of brilliant red-gold hair at the entry to the solar. He was still drinking when he looked over to see Annaleigh standing there, looking for all the world as if an angel had just walked into their midst. He lowered the cup, staring at her because he couldn't seem to look at anything else.

William, catching sight of her also, motioned her in.

"Come in, Annaleigh," he said. "Let me introduce you to Castle Questing's newest allies. These are the men from Bamburgh Castle you've heard us speak of. The man to my left is Sir Warwick Herringthorpe, the garrison commander. War, this is my wife's cousin, Lady Annaleigh Scott. She is the daughter of the current chief of Clan Scott."

Now, War had a surname to go with that lovely first name. In those few brief words, he learned exactly who she was and her relationship to de Wolfe. Not only was she related to the great Wolfe of the Border, but she was a clan chief's daughter. Honestly, he could expect no less from so magnificent a woman.

But now they were at a tricky moment. They had both acknowledged that they recognized one another and had met before under less than desirable circumstances. But was she willing to admit it in front of witnesses?

Was he?

"My lady," he greeted politely. "It is an honor to know you."

Annaleigh was gazing up at him with her big, green eyes. "And ye, m'lord," she said in her sweet lilt. He could have listened to it all day, but she sounded a bit nervous. "I've come tae make sure ye have all ye need. Is there anything else that's wanting?"

Her last sentence was directed at William, who shook his head. "Nay," he said. "We have all that we need, thank you."

As Annaleigh dipped her head politely and quickly turned to leave the room, War set his cup down. "Wait," he said. "Would it be possible to direct me to your facilities?"

Annaleigh cocked her head curiously. "M'lord?"

It was clear she had no idea what he meant, so he looked at William. "We have been riding since before dawn," he said.

"And now with this drink…"

He trailed off, but the hint was obvious. William immediately set his cup down, too. "I will show you."

"Nay," War said. "You are the lord of the castle. It is not your duty to show me where to go to… well, where to go, and you have guests here to attend to. I am certain Lady Annaleigh can direct me quite capably. A finger in the right direction will do."

William conceded the point as he looked to any number of men in the room who could show the man where to empty his bladder. He wasn't sure it was proper for a young lady to do so, but everyone seemed engaged in conversation, so he relented just this once.

He turned to Annaleigh.

"The garderobe, lass," he said. "Show him."

Annaleigh nodded quickly and scurried to the door. "This way, m'lord."

War followed.

The keep of Castle Questing was quite vast. It had been built two centuries before as a single building but somehow, over the years, it grew in scope. Another wing was added and at some point, a third and fourth floor were added. The result was an enormous keep with forty or more rooms, chambers, and alcoves. Given that two families had raised their children there – the de Wolfe and Hage families – it had served a greater purpose.

But War was positive he was about to become lost.

"How do you know where you're going?" he asked Annaleigh. "I've never seen such a vast place."

"'Tis not far, I promise."

"I lied."

She didn't stop walking. "M'lord?"

"I lied. I do not need a moment of privacy."

They'd crossed over into an area where there was a large common room, seemingly a small hall of some kind, and Annaleigh came to a halt and turned to him.

"You dunna need a moment of –?"

He shook his head, his eyes glimmering in the light of the torches on the walls. "Are we going to continue to pretend that we have never met before?" he asked softly. "I do not need you to show me to the garderobe. I simply wanted to speak with you alone."

Her expression was guarded. "Why?"

He could see that she had no interest in speaking with him alone, and probably anything else, and he immediately felt embarrassed. Ridiculous, even. He didn't even know why he wanted to speak with her alone, only that something was compelling him to.

There was one thing he very much wanted to say to her.

"Because I wanted to thank you for saving my life those months ago," he said, rather formally. "The physic told me that if you had not stitched me up, I would have either died of blood loss or of poison. Whatever you did saved my life and I am grateful. That is all I wanted to say."

With that, he dipped his head at her politely to beg his leave and turned away, heading back the direction they had come. He hadn't taken three steps when she called to him.

"Wait," she said, watching him stop and turn to her. This time, he was guarded and she struggled for words. "I… I dunna even know what tae say. I never expected tae see ye here. I dinna expect tae ever see ye again."

He nodded. "I know," he said. "The same can be said for

me. I am glad that I was able to thank you for what you did."

"Ye dinna want me touching ye at the time."

He grunted in agreement. "I was wounded," he said. "I was not thinking clearly."

Her eyes trailed up and down his enormous body. "But ye survived," she said. "No ill effects?"

He shook his head. "Other than a couple of thick scars, there is nothing."

"Then ye were fortunate."

"I had a guardian angel."

"Ye know that for a fact?"

He smiled weakly. "I meant you," he said. "You were my angel that night."

She began to look extremely uncomfortable, averting her gaze, folding her arms over her torso in a rather protective gesture.

"I… I dunna know how William will react if he knows that I was on the field of battle that night," she said. "I would be grateful if ye dinna tell him."

War shook his head faintly. "I won't," he said. "But why should he be concerned with it?"

She sighed heavily. "Because my clan… we're allied with the English," she said. "Yet I was there that night… I was told tae take valuables from the dead."

"The dead English?"

She nodded, unable to even speak the word. He wasn't surprised but, somehow, he was disappointed. However, she looked upset. Terrified, even. Not at all like she had enjoyed it or had been committed to her duty.

"Did you?" he asked quietly.

She shook her head, her eyes welling. "Nay," she whispered.

"I couldna do it. I came across ye and helped ye instead of killing ye. I think I was expected tae kill ye, but I couldna. My own brother… if he knew I dinna kill a wounded knight on that day, he'd never forgive me. If William knows what I did and he tells him…"

War understood. "I'll not mention it."

"'Tis not that I'm ashamed of what I did," she said as if trying desperately to explain her position. "I'm not ashamed I helped ye, but some would look at it as treachery. We lost many of our lads that day and 'twas all my fault. Tae help an English knight would be salt in the wound."

He cocked his head curiously. "Why was it your fault? You did not start the battle."

She blinked as if shocked he should say such a thing. "Do ye not know how the whole situation happened?"

He thought back to that incident. Truthfully, he didn't remember much from that period in time because he'd been weak with his wound. Much of it was a blur.

"We received a call from Etal because the Scots were attacking," he said. "We were asked to help and we did."

She closed her eyes, briefly, as if greatly pained by his answer. Or perhaps it was because she was greatly pained by what she knew and he didn't.

"But there was a reason behind it," she said softly. "There's always a reason behind a conflict. Do ye know why I tended ye on that day? Because… because I felt guilty."

"For what?"

"Because the battle wouldna have happened had it not been for me."

His brow furrowed. "What did you have to do with it?"

She sighed heavily. "Ye may as well know," she said. "Ye

may not want tae thank me for tending tae ye after ye hear, but the truth is that everything happened because of me. I was tending a flock of new lambs and English soldiers from Etal came upon me. I thought they were sick but they were drunk. They tore my dress and bruised my arms, but I managed tae get away. They stole my lambs. When I told my da, he was so angry that he gathered the clans tae march on Etal. And that's why ye were there."

If War had been told any of that beforehand, he hadn't remembered. In looking at that delicate, beautiful woman, he couldn't imagine anyone attacking her, but he wasn't surprised. Men could to dastardly things. Drunken English soldiers who thought to strip the petals off the fair Scottish flower. The mere idea stirred the flames of anger deep in his chest.

His jaw ticked faintly.

"Had I known that, I would have killed those soldiers myself," he said quietly. "And I would not have answered Etal's call for help. I am sorry that happened, my lady. Your clan had every right to be outraged."

She looked at him in surprise. "Ye... ye wouldna have...?"

"Nay."

Voices came from the direction of the solar as men began to emerge, out into the foyer, and Annaleigh startled at the sound. The spell between them was broken and she suddenly darted off before War could stop her. But it didn't matter.

She may have been gone, but the memory of her lingered.

So did an inkling of interest.

CHAPTER EIGHT

S HE WAS SUPPOSED to be asleep, but she couldn't seem to manage it.

The stars were bright tonight, so bright that they formed an iridescent blanket across the night sky. Annaleigh was watching them from the window of her bower, feeling the gentle night breeze caress her face, remembering that her mother had told her, once, that each star was the soul of a dead warrior. Over the centuries, there had been thousands. Perhaps even millions.

It was a sky awash with the dead.

She didn't know why she should think of that other than the fact that War Herringthorpe could have very easily been among those stars had she not helped him in his moment of need. He'd thanked her for it, which was surprising. That wasn't something she had expected out of his mouth. And the way he had looked at her…

Her stomach still trembled to think of it.

But she'd run from him like a fool. Overwhelmed with seeing him again, overwhelmed with the secret they shared, she'd spouted off at the mouth and then she'd run from him. She'd run straight up to her chamber, which was where she was now.

She didn't even attend the feast that night, though she could hear it from her bedchamber. The noise from the great hall carried. She hoped – and assumed – that Jordan and Jemma were too busy with the guests to worry over her, perhaps each assuming the other one knew where she was or what she was doing.

But no one knew.

She didn't even know.

Annaleigh sat in the built-in window seat of the large window overlooking the entry, four stories below, pondering this particular moment in her life. The great hall was a separate structure, built into the wall of the inner ward, and she had been hearing voices and singing all night. Smoke from the two enormous hearths drifted into her window. But still, she sat, thinking on War Herringthorpe's unexpected appearance and how she had reacted.

How *he* had reacted.

He seemed as surprised as she had been.

A knock on the door startled her from her sleepless thoughts. She was dressed in a sleeping shift, a white woolen garment that tied around the neck with long sleeves. Climbing off the window seat, she quickly collected her shawl, pulling it around her shoulders for modesty as she went to the door.

"Who comes?" she whispered loudly.

"Open the door, Annie."

It was Jordan. Annaleigh threw the bolt and yanked the sticky door open to reveal Jordan dressed in a fine blue garment, her hair artfully arranged and a proper veil woven into her hair that defined her as a wealthy noblewoman. She had dressed well for the feast that night, but her expression was one of concern as she fixed on her young cousin.

"What's amiss, lass?" Jordan said, pushing into the chamber. "No one has seen ye all night. Are ye ill?"

Annaleigh didn't want to tell her the truth. "Aye," she said, her hand first to her head, then quickly on her belly. "I… I've had a bellyache since earlier in the day. I dinna want tae trouble ye with it."

Jordan put a hand on her forehead, feeling for a fever. "Ye're not warm," she said. "Did ye eat something that dinna agree with ye?"

Annaleigh nodded. "I must have," she said. "I'm very sorry tae have disappointed ye today. I wanted tae keep tae my duties, but I… couldna."

Jordan put her arm around her shoulders and shepherded her back over to the bed. "Ye must sleep," she said. "Get intae bed and try tae sleep. If yer belly still hurts by morning, I'll send for the physic."

"Nay," Annaleigh said quickly. "'Tis not necessary. I'm sure I'll be fine in the morning."

"We'll see."

"Did William's guests settle in?"

"Aye," Jordan said, forcing her into bed and pulling up the coverlet. "Those who are not in the hall are already in bed."

"Did ye put Sir Warwick in the keep?"

Jordan nodded, tucking her in tightly. "He's in the young men's wing."

The young men's wing was a section of the east wing, the ground level, where unmarried, visiting men were housed if they were anything more than a knight. The door leading into the keep could be bolted from the outside, meaning no unmarried young man could wander into the keep where there were unmarried young ladies. Usually, knights were kept to the aptly named knights' quarters in the outer ward, but Herringthorpe had warranted enough respect and honor that Jordan had put him in the house.

Exactly three stories below Annaleigh's bed.

She rolled onto her side as Jordan fussed with the coverlet at the bottom of the mattress, watching the flicker of the taper next to her bed and thinking on War. Truthfully, she couldn't stop thinking of him and she wasn't quite sure why. Something about the man had her attention, but it was more than that. She felt an odd kinship with him because she shared something with him that she'd never shared with anyone – an event in battle, a moment where she helped save his life. Until today, she'd put that moment out of her mind because she'd been certain the knight she'd helped in the thicket had not survived.

But he had.

Oddly, she felt responsible for him in some fashion.

"Did ye meet Herringthorpe?" she asked.

Jordan grunted as she tugged on an uncooperative coverlet corner. "Aye," she said. "A very big man."

"Did ye speak with him?"

Jordan tucked the corner in. "Aye," she said. Then, she looked up at Annaleigh. "Did ye?"

"Aye," Annaleigh said. "I'm not ashamed tae admit that I find the man handsome. Do ye?"

Up until this moment, the chatter from Annaleigh had been meaningless. But now, Jordan was starting to pay attention to it. The lass found War Herringthorpe handsome, did she?

That was a good sign.

"I suppose," Jordan said, trying not to display her joy that Annaleigh was actually showing interest in a man. "Did ye have a proper conversation with him, then?"

Annaleigh shook her head. "Nay," she said. "William introduced us and he needed direction tae the garderobe, so we spoke a little when I showed him where it was. But nothing much beyond that."

It was true, most of it. She had the intention of showing him where the garderobe was and they did speak, but there was much more to it. Much more that she couldn't tell her cousin. While she was keeping secrets, she had no idea that Jordan had planned for her to meet War, hoping there might be some kind of attraction.

It seemed they both had secrets from each other.

"He's an important man," Jordan said, going to the head of the bed and laying her hand on Annaleigh's forehead in a maternal gesture. "William says that he's a Blackchurch-trained knight who is the king's favored warrior right now. That means wealth and prestige. It means he has a bright future ahead of him."

Annaleigh didn't need any help when it came to her interest in War because she had quite enough of it without Jordan telling her how great the man was.

"What's a Blackchurch?" she asked.

Jordan smiled faintly. "It's where the best knights in the world train," she said. "William says the Lords of Exmoor are in charge and they only take the best warriors tae train them. They teach them things that normal knights never learn."

"Like what?"

"Ye'll have tae ask Sir Warwick."

With that, she winked at her and blew the taper out, leaving the chamber and quietly shutting the door. Annaleigh lay there, watching the low flames flickering in the hearth, thinking on

Blackchurch now where it pertained to War. Was the man so great that he went to a special training guild?

That only served to feed her increasing interest.

Sounds of the great hall were still floating upon the night air. She could hear the laughter and buzz of distant conversation.

Perhaps War was still there.

Like a siren's call, the mere thought propelled her out of bed.

CB

"I THOUGHT YOU'D gone to bed."

War heard the voice behind him, turning to see Alexei walking up behind him with a cup of something steaming in his hand. They were in a garden that was built into the side of the keep, with high walls but a gate that faced the south wall of the great hall. The distance was about twelve feet between the gate and the wall, but the entry doors to the hall were facing into the bailey, so one had to actually walk around to the south side of the hall to see the garden gate.

And that's what Alexei had done.

War smiled wearily.

"That was my intention," he said. "I wandered out of the hall and saw the gate. One thing led to another and here I am, in this magnificent garden."

It was dark, with a sliver moon, but there were enough torches in and around Castle Questing to light up half of London. There were even torches in a garden that wasn't being used in the dead of night. It was enough light to look around and see the foxgloves and rosemary, lavender and roses, among others. There was even a fishpond.

It was quite the cultivated garden.

"Very nice," Alexei said, looking around. "But I've never known you to be an admirer of flowers."

War snorted softly. "I am not," he said. "But it is peaceful here. I am indeed an admirer of peace."

"For a man that fights as if blood and gore is the very air he breathes, some might find that statement shocking."

War continued to chuckle. "I realize that," he said. "But at the moment, I found I needed the tranquility. It helps me think."

Alexei wasn't stupid. He knew why. "De Wolfe?" he ventured.

War nodded. "Aye," he said. "He's a great man, Alexei. A man to be admired. He has built this spectacular empire all by himself and I keep going back to something my father said."

"What was that?"

"Essentially, he told me not to ruin anything for de Wolfe."

"And you feel as if by telling him the truth, it might ruin things?"

War drew in a deep, thoughtful breath. "I am not entirely certain," he said. "The man has a perfect life. Who am I to ruin it with secrets from his younger days?"

Alexei could see his point. "Possibly," he said. "But I will repeat what I said to you earlier today. If I had a son, I would want to know."

"True enough." War paused, still looking over the garden. "But there is something else."

"What else?"

War looked at him, a lopsided grin on his face. "It seems that you are my father confessor today," he said. "I have yet another secret. It is not as earth-shattering as de Wolfe, but a secret nonetheless."

Alexei looked at him with interest. "Speak."

"You saw de Wolfe's wife's cousin today. The lass with the long, red hair."

Alexei nodded. "She's quite lovely."

War scratched his head and returned his focus to the garden. "When I was wounded at Etal, I was able to crawl off into a hiding place beneath the stump of a tree," he said. "You know the Scots like to send people through a field in the aftermath of a battle, killing their wounded enemies, and I did not want to suffer that same ignoble fate, so I hid myself as much as I was able."

"Understandable."

"Annaleigh found me."

Alexei's eyebrows lifted. "She did?" he said, surprised. "And she did not try to kill you?"

"She stitched my wound and saved my life."

That drew a stronger reaction from Alexei. "So that's what happened?" he said. "The physic said that whoever tended your wounds saved your life. It was her?"

"It was her."

It was clear that Alexei was astonished. "God's Bones," he muttered as he pondered that revelation. "So the lass didn't kill you, but healed you? Remarkable."

War nodded. "Indeed," he said. "But there was a reason behind it, as she told me."

"What reason?"

"Evidently, the entire battle was because of something that happened to her," War said. "She was accosted by two Etal soldiers and her father launched the attack. A revenge attack. That was what we found ourselves caught up in."

Alexei's brow furrowed. "I hadn't heard that," he said. "All we knew was that we were answering a call from Etal against Scottish aggression. Did you know this was a matter of revenge at the time?"

War shook his head. "I did not," he said. "Not until she told me. So, in a sense, she tended me because it wasn't my battle to fight. It seems to me that she still carries a terrible amount of guilt from the entire incident."

"Still?"

"Still."

Alexei fell silent for a moment. "Then mayhap that is why she is here."

War looked at him. "What do you mean?"

Alexei shrugged. "I am not certain," he said. "But if my entire clan attacked an English castle because of me and men died on my behalf, I suspect there are some who would be angry at me for it."

War hadn't thought of that, but it made some sense. "So she came to Castle Questing to escape her angry clan?" he said, watching Alexei nod. "Or it is just as possible that she's simply here to visit."

"True," Alexei said. But he wasn't looking at War. He was looking outside the garden gate, into the torch-lit darkness. "If you care curious, why not ask her?"

War had no idea what he meant until he looked over to see what had Alexei's attention. Standing across from the gate, peering around the corner of the great hall where the entry was located, stood a woman with long, red hair, dressed in a dark gown and possibly a shawl. He could see it around her shoulders. Her attention was turned away from them as she watched people come and go through the hall entry.

Curious, he and Alexei looked at each other in puzzlement before they headed in that direction.

"My lady?" War said as soon as they reached the garden gate.

Annaleigh turned to him with such speed and surprise that she smacked into the wall behind her. Eyes wide, she clutched her shawl tightly against her body.

"My… m'lord," she said. Then, she patted her chest to ease her racing heart. "Ye startled me. What are ye doing in the garden?"

A smile tugged on War's lips. "And I could ask you what you're doing out here in the bailey?" he said. "Are you looking for someone?"

Annaleigh's gaze moved from War to Alexei and then back to War. "Nay," she said. "I… well, I help Lady Jordan with her duties and I came tae see if all was well. If she needed my help. But I can see that everything is as it should be. Good eve tae ye."

She started to dash away but War stopped her. "Wait," he said. "Do not leave. This is my knight, Alexei, by the way. I do not think you have been properly introduced."

Annaleigh paused unsteadily, looking to the very tall, very blond warrior. "M'lord," she greeted politely. "'Tis an honor."

Alexei smiled pleasantly at the extraordinarily beautiful young lady. "The honor is mine, my lady," he said. Then, he looked at War and was struck by the expression on the man's face as he looked at Annaleigh. It occurred to him that his presence, at the moment, was not wanted. "I will see to the men, my lord. Good evening to you."

With that, he slipped away, but War hardly noticed.

He was still staring at Annaleigh.

"He speaks strangely," Annaleigh said, watching Alexei as

War watched her. "Where is he from?"

"Vilnius," War said. "Do you know where that is?"

Annaleigh shook her head. "Nay," she said. "Where?"

War gestured in an easterly direction. "That way," he said. "Many months and even years of travel. There is a great empire there."

"Oh?" Annaleigh cocked her head curiously. "People like us?"

"People like us," War confirmed. Realizing that he really didn't want her to get away, he gestured to the garden. "Would you like to come into this magnificent garden? I'm sure you have seen it many times, but I haven't. There are no gardens at Bamburgh."

Annaleigh hesitated a moment before stepping in. War watched every move, every expression. She was clad in a dark blue gown, long sleeves and form-fitting, and he could see that she had an exquisite curvy figure. Even with the shawl around her, there was no mistaking that she was a tasty morsel and, frankly, if she were his wife or daughter, he wouldn't let her wear such clothing. He'd never seen Scottish lasses wear what she had on, so he could only imagine that she must have gotten it from her English relatives.

But… God's Bones, she looked good enough to eat.

"Jordan spends much of her time in the gardens," Annaleigh said, distracting him from what were clearly lustful thoughts. "She forces her younger children tae tend the gardens with her. She says that working in the dirt builds character and she'll not have her bairns raised like spoiled Sassenach children."

A smile tugged on War's lips. "That sounds like a Scotswoman," he said. "They are some of the most industrious people I know."

"And ye know many?"

He shook his head. "Not too many," he said. "But the ones I do know are very hard working. Very pragmatic people."

Annaleigh thought that was a nice compliment. "Then ye dunna hate the Scots?"

"Should I?"

"Ye're an English knight. That's reason enough, I should think."

"Do you know many English knights?"

She shrugged, looking over to one of the many stone benches in the garden and moving to take a seat. "I have many cousins who are English knights," she said. "They have friends who are English knights. And there are English knights here at Castle Questing. Tae be truthful, when I first came here, I was afraid of them. I thought they would hate me simply because I'm Scots."

"Did they?"

"It's difficult tae hate a woman who is the cousin of England's greatest knight."

He snorted. "That is true," he said. "But hate is a strong word, my lady. I would not say English knights hate Scots as something inherent, like it was there when they were born. That's something that develops over time, as it does with any enemy. One must be wronged, usually, in order to have an aversion against a race of people."

She watched him in the torchlight as he stood over her, a positively enormous man. His biceps were as big in circumference as her waist, she thought, but in spite of his size and obvious strength, she was coming to see that the curt, rude man she'd met upon the field of battle wasn't curt or rude at all.

There was a wisdom about him.

And a gentleness.

"Ye *were* wronged by my clan," she said quietly. "In the battle at Etal, ye were badly wounded."

"True."

"And that is not enough for ye tae hate?"

He held up a finger to get her attention. "But I was also saved by a Scots," he said. "You saved my life, my lady. I am forever in your debt."

She smiled weakly. "There are things about me that are not necessarily true tae a Scots way of thinking," she said. "As a people, we fight tae survive. The land is harsh, invaders are harsh… 'tis the way of thinking we all have, but there are things I dunna agree with. Killing the wounded enemy on the field of battle is one of those things but if my family ever knew what I did, that I saved yer life, they'd never welcome me home again. As it is, I more than likely willna go back."

"Why not?"

She sighed faintly, pulling her shawl around her more tightly in a gesture of self-protection. "I told ye that the battle at Etal was because of me," she said quietly. "But what I dinna tell ye, and the entire reason I'm at Castle Questing, is because my clan began tae blame me for the deaths of sons and fathers. Those who perished in the fight at Etal. They began tae point fingers and whisper. They began tae say terrible things tae me. It was my father's decision tae attack Etal, not mine, but I'm still a target for their anger. That's why my da sent me here. So I would be safe from my own clan. 'Tis a difficult way tae live, knowing yer family hates ye and ye're safe only in the land of yer enemies."

He shifted on his enormous legs, folding his big arms across his chest. "But it was not your fault."

"I know. And so do they. But people in pain need something tae lash out at."

"And that is you."

"Aye."

He thought on that a moment. "I am not entirely sure that is fair to you," he said. "What does de Wolfe say about it?"

"William?"

"Aye."

She shrugged. "Nothing, at least not tae me," she said. "But Jordan says I'm never going back. She says I need tae remain here and marry an English knight."

"Is that what you want?"

She struggled not to grin, lowering her gaze but he swore he could see a flush to her cheeks. "There are those who seem tae *think* it is what I want."

He thought her blush was rather charming and he sat down beside her on the bench, though he was several inches away. It wouldn't do to get too close to her because, quite honestly, the more he saw of her, the more he liked. She was sweet and delicious and gentle, everything that made a woman irresistible in his eyes. Moreover, she had a figure that he just knew would feel good pressed against him.

With his arms around her...

He shook himself from increasingly passionate thoughts.

"Do I sense lads who need a sound thrashing?" he said, a glimmer of mirth in his eyes. "Tell me immediately, my lady. Who is harassing you?"

Her blush deepened. "They're not harassing me."

"Annoying?"

"Nay."

"Frustrating?"

"*Nay.*"

She was giggling now and War found himself caught up in a game he rarely played – the art of the gentle flirt.

With a Scots, no less.

"You must tell me who is menacing you," he demanded, though it was done in fun. "It has been a while since I have beat a man soundly and if I do not have a victim soon, I might do something regretful."

She covered her mouth because she was giggling so. "Like what?"

He cocked his head thoughtfully. "I might have to harass you," he said. "And annoy you. And menace you."

"Ye wouldna!"

"Then tell me immediately who is making demands of you so I have something to focus my appetite to pummel on."

She burst out laughing. "Appetite to pummel?" she repeated slowly. "God's Bones, that sounds painful."

He was enjoying her laughter greatly. "It is," he said. "For *them*. My lady, you do not seem to understand."

"What do I not understand?"

A smile spread across his lips as he looked at her. "You saved my life," he said, suddenly dropping the tone of his voice. "That means I have a debt to repay, any way I can."

Her hand came away from her mouth. "So that's why ye want tae champion me? Because ye'll repay a debt?"

That wasn't what he wanted her to think, not in the least. The lightness of the conversation transitioned into something else at that moment, something warm and curious. Gone was the jesting.

Attraction had made an obvious appearance.

"Nay," he said quietly. "That is not why. It is because I want to and any debt, imagined or otherwise, has nothing to do with it. You are a lady worth defending, even by someone as unworthy as me."

Annaleigh could see the light of warmth in his eyes and it made her heart quiver like nothing she'd ever experienced. She simply didn't think it was possible that he should think as highly of her as she thought of him, but his words said otherwise.

Surely it is only obligation he feels!

"Ye jest with me," she said, her cheeks flushing again. "And other than my English cousins, ye're the worthiest knight I've ever heard of. By the way, what's a Blackchurch?"

His smile grew. "It's simply Blackchurch," he said. "Or, the Blackchurch Guild. It is a training guild where one learns to become the best knight in the world."

"Is it difficult?"

"If you truly wish to know, I'd be happy to tell you sometime."

"Why not now?"

He looked around. "Because it is dark and it is cold," he said. "All proper young ladies should be in bed."

"Yet I'm not," Annaleigh said. "I'm here with ye. If ye send me back tae bed now, I'll spend all night wondering what a Blackchurch is. Ye wouldna do that tae me, would ye?"

He flashed his teeth as he laughed softly. "Nay, I would not do that to you intentionally," he said. "Where shall I begin?"

Annaleigh knew that she had him in her power now. She could see it in his eyes. He was willing to do whatever she asked and she realized it was a frightening amount of power. But he was doing it so willingly, so kindly. Surely tomorrow would see her power ended, but while she had it, she was going to enjoy it.

And him.

She pulled the shawl tighter against the night air.

"From the beginning," she said. "Tell me where ye were born and where ye lived as a lad. Then ye can tell me how ye came tae the Blackchurch and everything about it."

His eyebrows lifted. "You want my entire life story?"

She averted her gaze and looked away. "'Tis too much tae ask," she said. "I'm very sorry. I was simply enjoying the conversation."

She started to stand up but he put an enormous hand on her arm, stopping her. "I did not mean it that way," he said quickly. "I am simply in awe that such a fine lady should be curious about me."

Annaleigh was a smart girl. She knew how to flirt, and how to bend a man to her will, when the mood struck her. She didn't use those charms very often, if at all, but they seemed to come naturally with War. And, like a weakling, he succumbed. Fighting off a grin, she sat back down.

"Of course I am," she said. "Ye're the commander of Bamburgh Castle, a knight sent by Henry himself. Ye must have dozens of ladies throwing themselves at yer feet, wanting tae know yer life story."

A smile played on his lips as he looked at her. "Are you one of them?"

"I asked ye, didna I?"

His grin broke through. "Mostly, I ignore those women," he said. "But you… I will not ignore you."

She smiled because he was. Maybe he understood what she was doing, just a little, and he was more than willing to go along with it.

More than willing.

"Good," she said. "Then tell me from the beginning. Where were ye born and why were ye named Warwick?"

He settled in for a long and hopefully meaningful conversation. "I was born in Suffolk and named for Warwick Castle," he said. "My father fostered there as a child and had fond memories of the place."

"Where did ye grow up?"

He told her.

It was Jordan who came looking for her young cousin about an hour later. She'd gone to check on Annaleigh to see how her bellyache was faring and when she found her bed empty, her first destination was the great hall. In order to get to the hall, however, she had to pass by the walled garden. Glancing through the gate was simply a habit, as she always did that, but in this case, it paid off.

She found her wayward cousin.

And with the very knight she'd hoped there might be an attraction for.

Jordan watched for a few moments, out of sight, knowing she should break up whatever conversation was going on and escort Annaleigh back to her bedchamber, but she couldn't seem to manage it. The two of them were sitting a proper distance apart, beneath the glow of the torches, but whatever War was saying had Annaleigh in gales of laughter. When Jordan realized that, she couldn't keep the smile off her face, either.

Perhaps her matchmaking was going to pay off, after all.

Turning for the keep, she left Annaleigh and War to their conversation.

CHAPTER NINE

I T WAS EARLY morning over the softly rolling hills of the Scots border. The land, at this time of year, was green for the most part, with fields of grain waving golden in the wind. William employed a good many farmers on his lands, men he fairly treated, as they worked the land and gave him a cut of the profits. That went for the agriculture as well as the sheep herders, and there were many this far north. He'd lost track of the herds he had, though Kieran knew. The man wasn't only his second in command, but he kept control of all of William's properties. Because of that, William cut Kieran in for some of those profits, as well, making Kieran a very wealthy man.

On this morning, William had been up before dawn because he'd had a shipment of yew saplings. William had about two hundred archers and the yew wood was for new bows that his men had asked for. The older bows were becoming brittle and in order to keep his archers well-armed, William had ordered the wood. He and Kieran were at the gates in the morning as the wagons of wood began rolling in, brought specifically from a man down in Yorkshire who grew groves of such saplings.

When the last wagon rolled through the gates, William ordered the portcullis lowered as Kieran checked in the last of the wagon loads. Anthony helped him, given that he had a head for numbers, while Talus remained on the walls, vigilant. Troy had returned to Wark before dawn, a journey that took less than an hour, leaving William to continue hosting Herringthorpe.

In fact, Herringthorpe had been heavy on William's mind.

He was probably just being foolish, but something War said the day before had stuck with him no matter how hard he tried to shake him. He kept telling himself that he was being ridiculous, but that didn't seem to settle him down.

Something to do with War's mother.

Jane de Percy.

There was more than just an acquaintance there. Many years ago, before William had met his wife, he'd known, and been fond of, Jane de Percy.

When War had spoken her name, it had shocked him.

But the shock was wearing off.

Jane had been a lovely woman with dark hair, dark eyes, and a big smile. She'd been the youngest daughter of one of the great de Percy families. In this case, from the allied castle of Sedgefield in North Yorkshire. Jane's father and John de Longley, the Earl of Teviot and William's liege at the time, had been undergoing some negotiations, so Geoffrey de Percy had brought his family with him for a nice, long visit.

And William had come to know sweet Jane.

He had to admit that he was indecisive as to whether Jane was marriage material and he further had to admit that Jane was far fonder of him than he was of her. She was fun and vivacious and he liked that, but he never looked at her as someone he could love deeply. It wasn't that she was terribly lacking in any way other than the fact that she was very much a little girl who had never grown up. It was endearing for a while until it became annoying.

But that hadn't stopped him when the woman seduced him.

He knew Jane was madly in love with him. She'd told him enough. She hung on his every word, chased away any other woman who seemed to be interested in him, and generally acted possessively of him for the time she was at Northwood Castle, seat of de Longley. He was amused by her at first and didn't give her infatuation much consideration, mostly because she was immature and he figured that she'd forget about him soon enough. But one night, she'd found him in the stables tending a lame horse.

That was where the intimate involvement had started.

The hour had been late. At the time, William didn't know how she knew he'd be there, alone, but he found out later that she'd paid a servant to report to her on his movements. As he'd taken care of the horse, she appeared in the dim stables, dressed in a heavy cloak. Their conversation had been light, as it usually was, and Jane was always quick to smile or compliment him. But this time, it was different. She wanted to talk in private, she said, someplace where they could not be interrupted. He agreed, though he didn't know why, and they'd gone to the rear of the stall and sat in the straw. No sooner had he sat down when Jane dropped to her knees and tossed off the cloak.

She wasn't wearing a thing underneath.

Truthfully, William wasn't repulsed by her. She had a sweetly rounded little body with big breasts and, being human, he'd succumbed to her seduction. He let her push him back on the straw and unfasten his breeches. He let her put her mouth on his manhood, which sprung to life when she touched him. He let her straddle him, rubbing her wet heat upon him and when he could stand no more, he lay her back on the straw and took her innocence as she wept for joy beneath him.

That went on for the next two weeks.

Jane was the aggressor in all instances. She would catch him in the stables or send him a note asking him to meet her in the alcoves of Northwood's great hall. He could have refused her but he didn't. He would meet her and she would put her mouth all over him before he positioned her against a wall or lay her on a floor and drove his throbbing member into her wet and willing body. For Jane, it was all about the love she felt for him but for William, it was all about her responsive body and his natural male urges and nothing more.

She loved him and he let her.

Perhaps it made him a cad, perhaps not. Jane got what she wanted and he took his pleasure with her. But it all came to a halt one evening when William happened to be in the guest corridor of Northwood's vast keep. He heard Jane and her father arguing, how Jane wanted to marry William but her father wouldn't hear of it. No de Percy was going to marry a mere knight, even if he was a rising star among the knights on the Scottish border. Even when William intervened and offered for her hand because it was the right thing to do given that he'd already marked the woman, Geoffrey stood firm.

No marriage to a de Wolfe.

The next morning, Geoffrey, his wife and daughters, and the two hundred soldiers he brought with him abruptly left for Yorkshire, leaving de Longley puzzled until William told him what had happened. It made more sense then and de Longley wasn't particularly peeved at William for driving out de Percy, but he had hoped for an alliance.

What he ended up getting was polite coldness whenever he sent missives.

That was the end of the Northwood-Sedgefield bond.

William hadn't thought about the whole situation in almost thirty years. Not since it happened. Truthfully, Geoffrey's refusal had been a relief, so he'd never been heartbroken about it. But when War mentioned who his mother was and William estimated how old War was, it didn't take a genius to figure out that War was old enough to have been born the year after William bedded Jane. At least, William thought he might be old enough. He really wasn't sure. But it was that preoccupation that finally had Kieran snapping his fingers in William's ear as the man stared off across the outer bailey without actually seeing anything.

He was far gone with thought.

"Did you hear me?" Kieran said. "William?"

William snapped out of his trance. "I heard you," he said. "What did you say?"

Kieran snorted. "If you heard me, then you would know what I said," he said. "I said that I'm going to have the archers put aside any bolts and bows that may not make it through the next engagement. We can decide what to do with them at that point."

"Fine," William said. "Do as you wish."

Kieran nodded, but he was still staring at William. "What are you thinking of that has you so distracted?"

William almost denied him. It would have been easy to brush him off even though Kieran wouldn't have believed him if he did. Kieran and William had been together for many years and they knew each other quite well, better than almost anyone else save Paris. William knew that Kieran wouldn't believe him if he told him nothing was amiss.

Therefore, he didn't try.

They were intuitive to each other that way.

"I've been thinking about something that Herringthorpe said last night," he said quietly. "Are you done with inventory?"

"Aye."

"Then walk with me."

Kieran did. He and William headed off towards the trade area of the outer bailey, where the smithies and other tradesmen were beginning their work for the day. William seemed lost in thought again until Kieran spoke up.

"What is it?" he asked curiously. "What did Herringthorpe say last night that has you so distracted?"

William sighed faintly, lifting his gaze to the walls where the night shift was just coming off duty.

"He spoke of his mother," he said. "Kieran, you know that she wanted to marry me those years ago. Remember?"

"I do," Kieran said. "I remember that entire incident with her father. How he told you that you were not nearly good enough for his daughter."

William wriggled his eyebrows. "I do not know if I told you at the time, but I was not distressed by his refusal," he said. "Jane was an attractive girl and I liked her very much, but marriage… honestly, I did not want to marry her."

Kieran shook his head. "You never told me that," he said. "I assumed you did, but we never spoke of it after that."

They'd come to the old armory, a tower on the northeast corner of the wall that was still used to store weapons, but only the older ones. Other than being part of the castle defenses and the wall walk on the floor above, the tower wasn't used much.

William paused, leaning against the old granite stones.

"There didn't seem to be a need to discuss it," he finally said. "I haven't thought of that period in my life in quite some time, but I will tell you why I am so distracted. Do you remember when you told me that Herringthorpe looked like me in my younger years?"

"Aye."

"There is a reason for that."

"Why?"

"Because he may be my son."

Kieran wasn't expecting to hear that. The man was perpetually cool in all things but hearing those word come forth from William's mouth had his eyes widening and his jaw dropping.

Quite an unusual expression from the man.

"What's this?" he hissed. "Why would you say such a thing?"

William could see how shocked he was. "Because the reason I offered to marry Jane de Percy was because I had bedded the woman for weeks prior to the incident with her father," he said. "I wasn't in love with her, but she was sweet and quite adventurous when it came to activities in the bedchamber, shall we say. She seduced me and I let her, repeatedly, while I tried to decide if I wanted to marry her. The only reason I offered was because I'd bedded her several times, so I thought… well, I thought I would do the honorable thing and marry her. But her father would have nothing to do with me."

Kieran's mouth was still hanging open. "So you think…?" he began. Then he came to a halt and closed his mouth, thinking on War Herringthorpe as a de Wolfe son. "My God… William, he does look just like you as a younger man. I wasn't the only one commenting on it. Paris did and…"

William lifted a hand to silence him. "I know," he said quickly. "I know Paris did and he was right. At least, there is a possibility that he was right. Herringthorpe was raised by Jane's husband, Edmund, but I do not know when they were married and I do not know how old Herringthorpe really is. I can only guess on the timing of his birth and my guess tells me that he was conceived, possibly, during the time his mother and I had our affair."

Kieran exhaled a long, thoughtful breath as the explosive news sank in. "What do you want to do?"

William shrugged. "I do not know," he said. "Clearly, I cannot tell the man what my suspicions are. They are not even confirmed, so I could just be imagining things. Even if I am his father, I am certain he does not know. He was raised by his mother and Edmund Herringthorpe. Surely they would not tell him. Mayhap Edmund didn't even know."

Kieran thought on that, long and hard. As he was looking off across the outer bailey, lost in thought, he caught sight of his son, Christian, as the man came off the wall from the night watch. Tall, blond and handsome, Christian was also the most cunning man he knew. The man could extract a secret from a corpse, as people would fondly say of him. He had the makings of a great knight and perhaps an even greater spy.

That gave Kieran an idea.

"Let me see what I can do," he said to William. "Mayhap I can find some answers for you."

William looked at him. "How?" he demanded. "Christ, Kieran, do not ask the man outright if that is what you are thinking."

Kieran shook his head. "Not me," he said. "I will not involve myself. Trust me, William. You always have before. But it seems that this question might needs some answers."

William geared up to retort but he knew it was true. He trusted Kieran with his life. He'd trust the man to help him seek answers, answers he never really knew he needed until now.

But he was still nervous.

"He may not even know, Kieran," William said quietly.

Kieran nodded in understanding. "I realize that," he said. "He will not hear it from me or from anything I do. I swear it."

"Think of my wife," William said, a hint of emotion in his tone. "I am certain Jordan will not hold a youthful indiscretion against me, but information like that must come from me. It would be devastating if she heard it elsewhere."

Kieran simply nodded, reached out to squeeze William's arm in mute support, and then left him standing there against the armory wall while he went in pursuit of Christian.

Half of William was terrified of the possibilities.

But the other half wanted to know the truth.

CHAPTER TEN

"WILL YOU CHASE me?"

Penelope was sweaty and flushed from having run around the kitchen yard a few times, but she was still game for anything.

On a bright morning, Annaleigh had been standing with the cook, discussing the evening's meal, when Penelope ran up and grabbed her by the hand. She was playing with Thomas, Rose, Edward, and little Nathaniel, all of them running and tagging each other around the kitchen yard. Nathaniel was too little to really be much of a threat and kept getting "tagged", or touched, and put into an imaginary cage. By the fourth time, he began to wail and Jemma came out into the yard to drag her tired, grumpy four year old into the keep so he could nap.

That left Penelope and her endless energy focused on Annaleigh.

"I'm busy right now, lassie," Annaleigh said as Penelope tugged on her. "Play with Thomas and Rose. I'll join ye when I'm finished."

"Please!" Penelope begged, dragging out the word. "Chase me!"

"Not now. Later."

That left Penelope grossly unhappy. Truth be told, Annaleigh couldn't have chased a one-legged man at that point, even if it was guaranteed that she could catch him. She was completely exhausted from what little sleep she did get the night before, but it had been worth it.

Very worth it.

She didn't even know what time she went to bed because it seemed as if she and War had talked all night long. They talked for several hours at the very least and only stopped talking when the great hall grew silent and the servants began dousing the tapers because everyone had gone to sleep. War had escorted her out of the garden and to the door of the keep but he would go no further, thanking her for a "most pleasant evening" before making sure she went inside and shut the door.

Annaleigh didn't get an abundance of sleep after that.

The entire evening with War kept rolling through her mind as she tried to force herself to sleep. He was a gentle giant of a man who had earned a prestigious reputation as one of the greatest young knights in England. The king loved him, so much so that he gave him an esteemed post at Bamburgh. Everyone who was anyone in the warring circles of England knew the name of War Herringthorpe.

The man named War.

She could easily see what had everyone so enamored.

He had a quiet way about him, self-depreciating at times, but arrogant in others. He knew his worth. God knows, the man knew his worth. He was the most talented man in the room and he knew it, but when he was in the room with William or Kieran, he also knew his place in the hierarchy. They were on top, he was working his way up. He was humorous – very humorous – but he also spoke with a wisdom and seriousness beyond his years. He was brilliant, interesting, and kind. At least, he was with her.

He was perfect.

Did she fancy the man? After last night, she did, but that was something no one could ever know. She was Scots; he was English. A great English knight. He would be expected to marry a lord's daughter, or an heiress or a countess or even a princess. A man like that needed to marry well.

Not a clan chief's daughter.

Even Annaleigh knew that.

It was a sad and disappointing realization.

But that still didn't mean she wanted to entertain Talus or Anthony. Perhaps she should just return to Scotland and forget all about War Herringthorpe. The sooner, the better, because as it was, one more long conversation with the man and she'd probably be madly in love with him.

"Annie!" Penelope cut into her thoughts, tugging on her hand again. "Please chase me! Just a little?"

Annaleigh sighed heavily, glancing at the cook only to see the man smirk. Everyone knew that Penelope's wishes would be obeyed. Therefore, Annaleigh surrendered to the inevitable. As the cook walked away, Annaleigh growled like a bear and Penelope screamed in delight. As she ran off, Annaleigh went in pursuit.

All of the children were screaming happily as Annaleigh pretended to be a vicious animal. She growled and made claw-like gestures with her fingers, giddily terrifying the children. She finally caught Rose, who managed to slip away from her and bump into Penelope, sending her to the ground. It was enough for Annaleigh to capture Penelope.

More screaming.

Penelope, however, didn't want to play the game the correct way. She refused to go into the cage, which was really just a box drawn in the dirt. Annaleigh insisted she go to the cage if she wanted her to continue playing the game, so Penelope flopped on her back in the box and cried angrily.

Annaleigh stood over her, hands on hips, shaking her head.

"It seems to me that someone has done Lady Penelope wrong," Talus said, walking up behind her. "I cannot imagine what that could be."

Annaleigh turned to look at him as he entered the kitchen yard from the stables. "Can't ye, now?" she said, smirking. "Lady Penny has been playing a game and quite imperiously consigning young Nathaniel tae this cage, but when she herself is put in it, she refuses tae comply."

Talus' eyebrows lifted in understanding. "I see," he said. "Well, every hive must have a queen. She is clearly the queen and the rules do not apply."

Annaleigh rolled her eyes at him. "Ye are far too lenient, Talus," she said. "Even Penny needs tae learn tae play by the rules. Life is full of rules."

"I suppose," he said. Then he leaned over Penelope as she cried in the dirt. "May I help you to your feet, my lady?"

Penelope's face was streaked with dirt where she wiped her snot and tears. "Nay!" she said. "I want out of the cage!"

"I am offering to help you."

"Will you give me your sword?"

"Regretfully, I will not."

"But I must fight my way out."

Talus shook his head. "Not with my sword, my lady," he said. "You must find another way to escape."

Penelope sat up and started wailing again. Talus looked stricken, as if he'd done something wrong, but Annaleigh shook her head at him.

"Not tae worry," she said. "Ye did the right thing."

Talus shrugged but was prevented from replying when William came through the kitchen gate, straight for his screaming daughter. The man could hear her anywhere, anytime, and would gravitate in her direction. His older sons would do it, too, and Penelope knew that if she cried long enough and loud enough, it would bring reinforcements.

She was right.

"Why the screaming?" William asked, spying his daughter in the dirt. "What happened?"

Annaleigh had been at Castle Questing long enough to know how William reacted to his youngest child and how Jordan did. While Jordan was firm, William was the soft touch. Had it not been so ridiculous, it would have been laughable.

"Lady Penny made a new game," Annaleigh said. "She made the rules. But she doesna want tae play by her own rules."

William's brow furrowed in understanding. "Penny," he said, going to stand over her. "Stop weeping, lass. Get out of the dirt."

Penelope looked at her father, lower lip trembling. "I'm in a cage, Papa," she said. "Help me."

She sounded incredibly pathetic and Annaleigh rolled her eyes, catching a glimpse of Talus, who was trying to sneak out of the kitchen yard before he was caught up any further in Penelope's web. She, too, turned away as William reached down and picked his child up, holding her tightly as she wrapped her little body around him.

So much for the game.

As William carried Penelope back towards the keep, Thomas and Rose came out of their hiding places, watching the enormous knight cart away the littlest tyrant. With Penelope gone, they ran off somewhere else, leaving Annaleigh to return to the cook. But not before Talus backtracked on leaving the kitchen yard.

He came up behind her.

"I did not see you at the feast last night," he said. "Were you feeling ill?"

Annaleigh paused, turning to him. She sensed he was probing her, which was normal with him. Even though they'd had the conversation about remaining cordial with no romance involved, as he usually did, he forgot about it.

It was becoming annoying.

"I am well enough," she said evenly. "Ye needna worry."

She turned to walk away but he continued to follow. "You missed quite a conversation with Herringthorpe," he asked. "The man is very accomplished. He regaled us with several stories last night. A pity you missed them."

I dinna, she thought, but somehow she knew that Talus must have seen her and War speaking in the garden. With a gate facing the great hall, it was very possible he caught sight of them at some point in the evening, which annoyed her greatly. Was he trying to catch her in a lie? Was he trying to force her to confess?

Her patience with him was growing thin.

"I've spoken tae him," she said as evenly as she could. "He does seem quite accomplished, I agree. Now, I must go about my duties, as I suspect ye must as well."

She forced a smile at him before turning away and walking quickly towards the cook, who was in the process of having a side of beef brought out of the larder. Annaleigh wasn't usually keen on watching meat butchered, but it was better than continuing the awkward conversation with Talus.

At least an hour passed as she watched the cook cut up the beef he was going to make a stew from. Beef, carrots, peas, turnips and other vegetables went into the pot which was then filled with water and herbs and salt. The cook also poured two big pitchers of red wine into the pot, for flavor he told her, and the entire pot had a big fire started beneath it.

All the while, Annaleigh was keeping an eye out for Talus or even Anthony, as she didn't want to get sucked into a conversation with either of them. Truth be told, War was the only one she wanted to get sucked into a conversation with but she had no idea where the man was. Surely he had to be around somewhere.

Perhaps she could stumble upon him, somewhere.

Leaving the cook, she went on the hunt.

CB

"FROM WHAT I understand, she has several suitors," Alexei was saying. "Not the least of which are two of de Wolfe's knights. You met them yesterday – du Reims and d'Vant. Evidently, she's been stirring the blood of every unmarried male from Carlisle to Berwick. English males, I mean. Is that what you wished to know?"

Sitting in his borrowed chamber in the keep of Castle Questing, War was listening to Alexei's report on Annaleigh with a discouraged expression on his face.

"Of course she's stirred their blood," he said. "Just look at her. She looks like an angel. As if heaven's door opened up and she stepped forth. She's positively enchanting."

Alexei was watching War closely. The man had been brooding since last night, since he spent a few stolen hours in the garden with Lady Annaleigh. It was a mood that Alexei had never seen before, so he was trying to decipher what it meant. Either War was unhappy or he was very happy. It was difficult to tell. He was evidently interested in a woman who had saved his life and perhaps wasn't sure how he felt about that.

It was an interesting situation, to be sure.

"You would know more than I," Alexei said after a moment. "Whether or not she is enchanting, I mean. But I have eyes. I can see how beautiful she is."

War lounged back on the bed, leaning against the headboard. It was a moody sort of pose. "She is," he muttered. "But seeing her here… speaking to her… mayhap my father's death has affected me more than I thought. Mayhap I am looking for something to stir my emotions, to distract me from my grief. Do you think that is all this is? That I am looking for a distraction?"

Alexei lifted a blond eyebrow. "If you are, let it not be a cousin to de Wolfe," he said. "You do not want to sour the man on you if you only intend to use the lady and cast her aside."

War shook his head. "Nay," he said. "I do not intend to do that. I do not know what I intend to do. All I know… all I know is that the conversation with her last night made me feel light of heart. Happy. That's not something I feel, not ever."

Alexei was fairly shocked at what he was hearing. Joy coming from War's lips wasn't a normal occurrence. "Your father had been begging you to marry for years," he said. "Is it possible you might consider it with Lady Annaleigh?"

War held up a hand. "Slow yourself," he said. "I only said I enjoyed the lady's company. I did not say I wished to marry her."

"Then why did you ask me to find out what I could about her?"

War shot him a withering look. "Because I wanted to know," he said. "It is not because I want to marry the girl."

"Then you do not mind if she is pursued by others?"

"Is she interested in any of them?"

Alexei shook his head, a smile tugging at his mouth when he heard the insecure squire in War's tone. "From what I've been able to find out, the young knights make arses of themselves and she has no interest," he said. "Were you to pursue her, I do not think there is any competition."

War stood up from the bed, going to the small window that overlooked the inner bailey. "Where are Monty and Clement?" he asked.

Alexei was well aware that he was changing the subject. "Monty will not let Clement out of his sight," he said with some irony. "He is convinced the man is going to corner de Wolfe and tell him that you do not deserve Bamburgh."

War grunted. "Clement is disgruntled, but not suicidal," he said. "If he does something stupid, then there are three knights who could easily cut him to pieces. But he does talk."

"I know," Alexei said with regret. "He walks the fine line between loyalty and subversion."

"I have never trusted him."

"Nor have I," Alexei agreed. "Would it mayhap be wise to speak to de Wolfe about him? Mayhap de Wolfe would like to take on another knight. Clement is a good warrior."

War looked at him. "Leave him here at Castle Questing?"

Alexei shrugged in a way that suggested that was exactly what he meant and War thought on that seriously.

"Mayhap I will," he said after a moment. "He's not a talent-less knight, but I simply do not want him with me. I do not want to be looking over my shoulder for the rest of my tenure at Bamburgh. I will think on it. Meanwhile, I will go and check on my horse. He had a strange gait yesterday. I want to make sure he has not turned up lame."

"Keep an eye out for Lady Annaleigh while you're out there."

"Shut your lips, you bastard."

Alexei burst into laughter, like a naughty boy, and it was difficult for War to keep the smile off his face as well. He kicked Alexei in the shin as he moved past him, causing the knight to double over and trip on the bed.

But he was still laughing.

"Wait," he said, pushing himself off the bed. "Before you go, you have not told me what you intend to do with de Wolfe and the letter from your mother. Do you plan to tell the man while we are here?"

War paused by the door, his smile fading. "I don't know," he said. "I will think about that later. There is too much on my mind, Alexei. Give me time."

Alexei let him go. War quit the knights' quarters, heading out into the bright morning. As soon as he came out of the knights' quarters, he could hear screaming. Children screaming. No one seemed to be in a panic about it, as everyone he could see was going about their business as if there weren't piercing screams filling the air. The closer he drew to the stables, the louder the screaming became.

He was just entering the stable yard when he saw William coming through the gate with a four year old clinging to him. William saw him and, with a smile of greeting, headed in his direction.

"Good morn to you, Herringthorpe," he said. "I'm glad I found you. I would like to take you on a tour of my property, at least those within a few hours' ride, to give you a sense of the borders. We can make a visit to Wark Castle in an hour or so. It would be a start."

War's gaze was on the child in the man's arms. *My sister*, he thought to himself. It was a very strange feeling, he had to admit. His gaze moved from the child to William, feeling such odd familiarity with the man's features because in many ways, they mirrored his own. After his arrival yesterday, and sleeping on thoughts torn between William and Annaleigh, he was quickly coming to the conclusion that he wasn't entirely sure how he felt about any of it. About William, about the letter he had from his mother for William… any of it.

The truth was that his thoughts seemed to be leaning towards Annaleigh.

But he nodded to William's statement.

"Whatever you wish to do, my lord," he said. "And good morn to you, as well."

The child in William's arms suddenly turned around and looked at him. A little lass with long, dark hair and big, green eyes that were red from weeping, but she looked very much like William. Which meant she looked like War. War smiled politely and she frowned.

"This is my youngest child, Lady Penelope," William said. "Penelope is going to go about a few duties with me before you and I head out. Penny, this is Sir War Herringthorpe. Please greet him politely."

Penelope was still frowning. "You look like my dada."

War grinned but, deep down, he was feeling a jolt of shock.

Could even the child see the resemblance? "Is that so?" he said. "It is an honor to meet you, Lady Penelope."

Penelope's response was to wipe her nose with her hand.

"Penny thinks that every man with dark hair looks like me," William said with a chuckle. "Do not be too offended by it."

"I am not," War said, trying to sound neutral. "I'm flattered she would think so."

Penelope began squirming and William put her to her feet. When she took off running, William returned his attention to War.

"Troy has returned to Wark Castle this morning and he will greet us later today when we conduct our tour, but I have also sent word to Northwood Castle and to Berwick," he said. "We can easily make it to Northwood this afternoon after we visit Wark and spend the night there before continuing to Berwick in the morning, if you are agreeable."

War nodded. "I am," he said. "That is why I came. I am grateful that you should take the time to introduce me to your allies."

William smiled weakly. "You are an important new figure in the north," he said. "It is important to see and be seen. Everyone will want to know your name and look you in the eyes, so be aware. Some may be more annoying than others."

War cracked a smile. "I hope I can tactfully deal with them."

"I think you can," William said. His gaze lingered on War for a moment before continuing. "I will go and make the preparations for our departure. Be ready to depart in an hour."

"Will we be returning to Castle Questing, my lord?"

"Probably not."

That told War what he needed to know. He nodded in response and William headed off across the stables, moving for the outer bailey. War watched him go, studying the size and shape of the man who was his father. But as he watched him go, it occurred to him that if he left in an hour and would not be returning, he would not be seeing Annaleigh again.

That realization didn't sit well with him.

He had to pack his saddlebags, but he wanted to at least bid Annaleigh farewell. He had no idea where she was but he knew he had to find her. He'd told Alexei he had no designs on marrying the woman, but that didn't mean he had completely discounted it. He felt like everything was being rushed now, like he had to make a rushed decision where she was concerned. But when he thought on it, it really wasn't a rushed decision at all.

This would *not* be the last time he ever saw her.

That was one thing he'd made up his mind about.

Turning around, he spied the keep and the wall of the kitchen yard. He knew that she helped Lady de Wolfe around the castle, so it might be logical to look for her in the kitchen yard. If not the yard, then perhaps the walled garden. He wasn't exactly sure what he was going to say to her when he found her, but he would think of something.

As he stood there and pondered where to begin his hunt, he could see one of the de Wolfe knights out of the corner of his eye. The man was heading in his direction. When he turned to look at him, he could see that it was one of the sons of Kieran Hage. He couldn't remember the man's name, but he'd met him briefly at Thropton and then again when he'd arrived at Castle Questing. As he watched the man approach, he could see that the knight was focused on him. The man smiled and lifted his hand in greeting as he drew near.

"My lord," the knight said. "I am Christian Hage. You've met so many new faces here, so forgive me if you knew that. I thought to introduce myself again to be sure."

War forced a smile. "I will admit that names have never been my strength," he said. "I usually have to meet men a few times to remember who they are and where they came from or I'll end up calling them 'that tall dolt' or 'that short bastard'. I've been known to do that."

Christian laughed softly, displaying a smile that looked just like his father's. In fact, he had Kieran's face but his mother's eyes, green in color, but he was far taller than his father. He was rather long and sinewy, in great contrast to his father's bulk.

"I'm glad to hear I am not the only one who does that," he said. "But in truth, I come on a mission from Lady de Wolfe."

"Oh?" War said. "What is that?"

Christian pretended to be quite formal in his delivery. "The Lady of Questing would like to know if you slept well," he said. "She has also sent me to discover if you and your men would like some food to break your fast."

War nodded. "You may tell Lady de Wolfe that I slept quite comfortably," he said. "I visited the knights' quarters, where my men were, and their accommodations were quite satisfactory. In fact, I was just going to find my men. It seems that we are to leave for Wark Castle within the hour."

"Ah," Christian said. "The grand tour?"

"So it would seem."

"Then you must find your men and tell them to prepare," Christian said. "May I walk with you?"

"Please."

The two of them began to head off in the direction of the knights' quarters. Christian glanced up in the sky, shielding his eyes from the sun.

"At least the weather will hold for you," he said. "It can be quite unpredictable this far north, or have you discovered that for yourself yet?"

War glanced up into the clear, blue sky. "It has seemed a little erratic at times," he said. "Mist seems to favor Bamburgh."

"Indeed," Christian said. "The entire coast can be covered with it. Berwick, especially."

"Where your cousin is?"

"Aye," Christian said. "Actually, my eldest brother is there, too. Alec. I believe you met him."

"The man who looks so much like your father?"

Christian grinned. "He acts like him, too," he said. "I have two younger brothers, also."

War looked around. "I believe I saw them," he said. "Young boys?"

"Nathaniel is four years of age and Kevin has seen about twelve years," Christian said. "I heard that you have younger brothers, also."

"I do," War said. "Sterling and Callum are in London, serving in the royal household."

"They will not come north to serve with you?"

War shook his head firmly. "All I would want to do is box their ears or kick them in the arse," he said, watching Christian snort. "They are thorns in my side, but I would kill or die for them."

"No truer words were spoken about any brothers," Christian said. He paused a moment before continuing. "I heard you came from Suffolk?"

War nodded. "I was born there."

"But I heard you say that your mother was from the north."

Again, War nodded. "Her family is from Yorkshire."

"Ah," Christian said in understanding. "Mine is from Scotland. She is a cousin to Lady de Wolfe."

"So you're all related?"

"We are a clan unto ourselves," Christian said, grinning. "In fact, in speaking of cousins, I've been wanting to ask you a question. May I?"

"Go ahead."

Christian scratched his head thoughtfully. "I've heard a few people comment on how much you look like William," he said. "I was wondering if you might be a cousin? Most of the de Wolfes are big and dark like you are and, God knows, there are enough de Wolfe relations running around the north. Half of Wolverhampton contains de Wolfe cousins and relations. Mayhap somewhere back in your family line?"

War didn't like the question. In truth, he was caught off guard by it. He didn't get the sense that he was being probed and the reality was that it was simply in the course of conversation. There would be no possible way Christian Hage could know anything about him or his relationship to William, but Christian had pointed out something that War hadn't noticed until he'd come to Castle Questing – the reality was that he did, in fact, look like William. He was surprised it had taken someone this long to point that out.

He supposed the question had to come sometime.

They were just entering the area where the knights' quarters were located and War spied Alexei and Monty outside of the stone building. They looked to be working on a saddle between them. War came to a pause, turning to Christian.

"I suppose anything is possible," he said steadily. "But I do not have any relatives from Wolverhampton, so I could not tell you for certain."

Christian shrugged. "I was simply curious," he said, perhaps sensing that War had other things to do now. "It has been a pleasure speaking with you, Herringthorpe. I hope this will not be the last time we see you at Castle Questing."

"It won't," War said before he could stop himself because he was solely thinking of Annaleigh. "I hope that this is the first visit of many to come."

Christian smiled. "I'm sure it will be," he said. "I look forward to seeing you the next time."

"Won't you be coming to Wark?"

Christian shook his head. "When Uncle William and my father leave Castle Questing, I remain behind in command," he said. "Someone has to keep Lady Penelope from leading a rebellion and taking over the castle. I am the only thing that stands between Uncle William and Penelope's reign of terror."

War chuckled. "I've not been around the lass much, but I've heard tell."

Christian laughed softly. "I'm sure you have," he said. "I will send a servant out here with food for you and your men for your journey."

"I would be grateful."

Christian turned around and headed back towards the keep. He would do what he told War he would do and send his men some food for their journey. He would also make sure to tell Jordan that War's accommodations were comfortable and that he was grateful for her hospitality even though she'd never asked Christian to see to the man's comfort.

That had been all Christian's idea.

When he was done with the food and his Aunt Jordan, he fully intended to find his father and tell him of the conversation.

But something told him that War wasn't being completely truthful.

He could see it in his eyes.

De Wolfe eyes.

CHAPTER ELEVEN

Langton Castle
Seat of Clan Scott

T HE HIERARCHY OF Clan Scott had changed a few times over the years.

A long time ago, Lady Jordan de Wolfe's father, Thomas Scott, had been the clan chief. He'd only had one child, daughter Jordan, so when his time came, his second brother, Matthew, had assumed the role. But Matthew didn't long survive his eldest brother and when he passed away about a year after Thomas, the leadership of the clan passed to Ian, Matthew's eldest living son.

Many years before in a massive clan war against Dunbar McKenna and others, Matthew had lost two of his sons, Donald and Malcolm, so his two remaining sons, Ian and Cord, essentially took charge of the clan. There was another cousin from that generation, Robert, who had been Nathaniel Scott's eldest son. Nathaniel had been the youngest brother of Thomas and Matthew, also killed in the massive clan war.

Clan Scott was no stranger to tension between clans.

Clan Scott was also a large clan, with the main branch located near Edinburgh. The Thomas Scott branch, a lesser offshoot, was often referred to as the Langton Clan because of the enormous castle that sat near the Scottish border. Some even referred to it as the Nest of Adders, a not-so-subtle reference to the infighting but also to the Whiteadder River that ran next to the castle. But whatever it was called, it was a powerful branch of Clan Scott, allied with the most powerful English knight in Northumberland in William de Wolfe.

But there were those who were increasingly unhappy about the English relations.

Cord Scott, the youngest son of Matthew and younger brother to the current chief, was one of those. He'd always been a mild-mannered man and he had established his own relationship with his English cousins, but the man had two sons who were most decidedly not friendly with the English.

Argyle and Brendan Scott hated the English with a passion.

That was where the problems had been for quite some time. Argyle and Brendan had started within the clan a decidedly anti-English movement. They didn't like the fact that they'd been allied with powerful English warlords because in the eyes of some of their allies, that lessened them as true Scots. That was at the heart of their issues – that they weren't "true Scots" as some allied clans had suggested – and that had fed both their rage and indignity. No one was more Scottish than they were, as they bore the name of the country they lived in.

And they very much wanted to prove it.

It was an undercurrent in the clan that had been going on for several years, ever since Argyle and Brendan had grown old enough to be called men. Some of the older clan members thought they'd outgrow the rabble-rousing, the incitement they so often liked to do and tried to keep it secret, but it had only gotten worse as they'd gotten older. They'd become more clever about it, more subversive, but their faction in national pride was a growing issue.

When Annaleigh Scott had been assaulted, that had given them the opening they needed.

And that was where Ian Scott, chief of Clan Scott, found himself.

He knew the chatter that had been going on ever since his only daughter had been attacked by the English soldiers. At first, Argyle and Brendan and even his own son, Robbie, had been working the clan into a frenzy against the English. That was all well and good because Ian intended to avenge his daughter and the younger men whipped the warriors of the clan into a sort of madness, mad enough to charge into England and attack a fully manned English castle. Not just any English castle, but a big one by the name of Etal. Ian had sent word to his English allies asking for their help, but the request was politely declined.

That declination hadn't gone well in Ian's favor.

Nor had the battle itself.

Out of nearly six hundred men, they'd lost forty-seven and had over one hundred wounded, which was a big ratio for such a number. The English had out-fought, out-chased, and essentially overrun them, chasing them back across the border carrying their dead and wounded. Ian had expected the anti-English sentiment to grow but what he hadn't expected was for his clansmen to turn on his daughter, the very reason for the battle itself.

Clansmen that had been divided by Argyle and Brendan.

Robbie, his own son, staunchly defended his sister, as he

should, but Argyle and Brendan began to speak against her. Usually, their efforts to undermine Ian were at least somewhat discreet, but they made no such effort when discussing Annaleigh and how her brazen ways had lured the entire clan into tragedy… and how it would undoubtedly happen again.

Robbie had been furious but Ian had told him not to respond, as it would only add fuel to the fire. But the fire kept burning and, finally, Robbie had snapped, taken his close circle of friends, and had beat Argyle and Brendan severely. Argyle even lost two teeth in the brawl. But all that beating had succeeded in doing was rousing the anger of those who listened to Argyle and Brendan, those who had lost fathers or sons or brothers in the skirmish at Etal.

Those people began to talk.

Even after Ian sent Annaleigh to Castle Questing where his cousin, Jordan, was the Lady of the Castle, people still whispered about her. There were threats. Things were said that should not have been said about an innocent young woman. The months passed, tongues wagged, and the clan grew more divided. There were those that sided with Ian and those that sided with Argyle and Brendan. Ian even pleaded with their father, Cord, to stop the madness, but Cord was torn. He loved his sons, but he also loved his brother, which resulted in inaction at best. Cowardice at worst.

And now, it had come to this.

In the hall of Langton Castle, which had been rebuilt over several years, Ian and Robbie were facing off against Argyle, Brendan, and several senior clan members who had lost sons or brothers or fathers in the skirmish at Etal. They were still fresh from that jarring event when a few rebels from Clan Kerr, a rival clan, raided a couple of farms on the edge of their adjacent lands and a woman had been killed as a result.

There was blood in the air… again.

Ian could see that things were about to come to a head as Argyle, a big man with two missing front teeth and a nasty temper, paced the floor to present a case as to why they needed to seek vengeance against Clan Kerr for their offense. The man shouted and stomped, straw from the compact earth floor sticking to his boots and dogs darting out of his way as his movements became rather violent. As Argyle called for action, Robbie had been watching his cousin also. Much like his father, he could see where this conversation was going and it wasn't going to end well. He glanced at his father before stepping forward, into Argyle's path.

"Argyle," he said firmly, slowly. "For all of yer rage and demands, ye've not yet mentioned the obvious."

Argyle came to a halt, his nostrils flaring with anger. "What do ye mean?"

Robbie lifted a dark eyebrow. "That Clan Kerr outnumbers us two tae one," he said. "Tae attack their stronghold would be foolish. There are too many of them. In this case, it was two men who raided our lands and killed old Miriam. It would be better if my da speaks tae Donal Kerr about this incident. We'll be satisfied if he punishes the men responsible."

Argyle's jaw was flexing beneath his bearded cheek. "Ah," he said, looking to the men around him. "Ye'll resolve it with talk when it comes tae Kerr. But when it involved the Sasse-nach, ye took the whole bloody army of warriors with ye tae avenge yer sister. And she wasna even harmed!"

Robbie knew this would come up, but he was hoping it wouldn't come up so quickly. He was a big man and quite capable of doing serious damage to Argyle, so he didn't back down. The man had been a thorn in his side ever since the battle at Etal and his patience was at an end.

"Ye know we sent word tae Etal," he pointed out. "Or did too much drink and whoring cause ye tae forget? Are the whores sucking yer brains out through yer manhood, then?"

The room erupted in chuckles because it was well known that Argyle visited taverns and brothels because no decent woman would go near him. The more he visited those places, the more the good women stayed away, so it was a self-fulfilling prophesy. But Argyle didn't take the insult well.

His eyes narrowed dangerously.

"At least I've got someone sucking my cock, Robbie," he growled.

"I could have those women suck mine, too, if I paid for it."

Argyle's body began to tense for a fight. "I'll not have the likes of ye lecture me," he said. "What the Kerr committed against us is greater than the sins the English committed, yet ye summoned the entire clan tae seek punishment for the wrongs against yer sister. If they even *were* wrongs. Yet ye'll not summon the lads tae punish the Kerr?"

Robbie's fists began to work, which was never a good sign. Ian, sitting in his customary chair near the hearth, could see his son's body language and he knew what was coming. With effort, he stood up and made his way to his son, putting a meaty hand on the man's shoulder.

"Argyle, I'll not have ye stirring up trouble where there is none," he said. "Ye've been trying tae do it since the battle at Etal and I've ignored ye, but I'll ignore ye no more. Ye're young and stupid and ye dunna know what ye're talking about, yet ye and yer brother spout off as if ye know everything. Ye know nothing."

Argyle glanced at Brendan, who was standing a few feet away. Brendan usually let Argyle lead for the simple fact that he didn't want to be the one viewed as the rebellious one even though everyone knew he was the brains. He simply nodded to his brother, almost imperceptibly, and Argyle faced his uncle.

"I know enough tae know that we should have never gone tae Etal, yet ye willna do the same for old Miriam," he said. "I know enough tae know that ye'll protect yer own daughter, but ye willna protect an old woman."

Ian made a sharp hissing sound, loud enough that it was quite startling. In fact, Argyle instinctively tilted away from his uncle as the man held up a hand to him as if he wanted to slap him. Had he been any closer, he probably would have.

"Shut yer yap, ye foolish child," Ian said between clenched teeth. "Did ye not hear what Robbie said? The Kerr outnumber us two tae one. We were outnumbered at Etal, but we dinna know it until the last. We only knew once we were in battle. If we march on the Kerr now, we know that death and injury will be great. We know there are more of them than us. Tae walk intae a battle with them would be stupid."

"But –!"

"Is that what ye're trying tae do, Argyle? Kill more of our men?"

It was a brilliant move on Ian's part, turning the responsibility for death back on his nephew because the rest of the senior clansmen were looking at Argyle in question now. Sensing that only made Argyle more combative.

"Ye favored yer daughter and men died because of it," he shot back. "Now, I want tae seek vengeance for the death of an old woman and ye willna do it. 'Tis cowardice!"

"Shut yer mouth before I rip yer tongue out," Robbie hissed, moving between Argyle and his father. "My father is the bravest man among us. Where is yer own father, Argyle? Brendan? Hiding in his cottage, drinking ale until he falls down and sleeps in the dirt? Ye've got a drunken fool for a father!"

Argyle flinched, moving towards Robbie, but Brendan grabbed him. Ian took hold of Robbie so he wouldn't break his cousin's neck.

"Enough," Ian said, turning Robbie away from his cousin. "Arguing doesna solve the problem. Argyle, if ye canna be helpful, then ye will leave. I'll not have ye confusing the issue."

Argyle pulled himself from his brother's grip. "There *is* no confusion," he said. "The Kerr killed one of our people. We must punish them."

Ian sighed heavily. "So we send an army of warriors to their stronghold?" he said. "Lad, if the casualties at Etal upset ye, then the casualties against Kerr will be far worse. Do ye not under-stand that?"

Argyle was pale with anger and perhaps some shame. "I understand that our clan has a chief that only values his daughter's life," he said. "A chief should be fair and just, which is something ye're not. We need a man we can trust."

Robbie heard him and swung around. "What are ye say-ing?" he demanded. "That yer drunken father be clan chief? That's a bloody jest and ye know it. Ye only want him tae be chief so ye can rule in his stead, Argyle. Yer ambition is showing, Cousin."

Argyle was losing ground. Robbie wasn't afraid to expose him and, worst of all, Robbie knew exactly what was happening. He was making sure everyone else did, too. Infuriated, Argyle struggled to keep calm.

"If I was ambitious, ye'd already be dead and buried," he

snarled. "Since Uncle Ian willna do right by the clan and punish the Kerr, I seem tae be the only one willing tae point that out. Beware, Cousin – someday, the men of our clan will wake up and realize that they need another man tae lead them."

With that, he turned on his heel and stormed out of the hall. Brendan, without looking at either Ian or Robbie, followed him. Both brothers marched from the hall, shoving dogs aside in their haste to leave. By the time they reached the bailey outside, Brendan grabbed his brother by the arm.

"What's the meaning of that?" Brendan hissed, yanking his brother to a halt. "If ye intend tae rise up and take control, then ye just let Uncle Ian and Robbie know that. It was stupid!"

Argyle didn't like being yanked around by his brother and jerked his arm from the man's grip. "It's time, Brendan," he said, running an angry hand through his mop of dark hair. "It's time tae make plans. Uncle Ian should no longer be our leader, the man we trust. He'll avenge his daughter, but not a dead woman?"

Brendan sighed sharply. "I know," he said. "So do the others. Well, some of them. But now ye've put the man on his guard. We'll never be able tae wrest power from him now."

Argyle knew that but he didn't want to admit it. He kept raking his fingers through his hair.

"She did this," he muttered. "Annie. She's the one who started it."

Brendan shook his head. "This started long before Annie," he said quietly. "It started when she rejected yer advances those years ago when she first became a woman. Ye've never forgiven her and that makes the battle at Etal worse."

Argyle was looking at the ground, his jaw flexing as he ground his teeth. "Why do ye say that?"

Brendan knew his brother well. "Because ye should have been the one tae avenge her," he said. "As her husband, that would have been yer right. Instead… instead, Ian drove the men tae Etal and then sent Annie tae Castle Questing when ye started tae turn men against her. Their deaths, ye said, were her fault."

"They were," Argyle said firmly. "And now she's in England with the Sassenach kin. And now…"

He suddenly paused, causing Brendan to peer at him strangely. "Now what?"

Argyle lifted his head. His jaw had stopped flexing and an odd, wide-eyed expression crossed his features.

"Brendan," he said slowly. Then he looked at his brother and grabbed him by the arm. "Brendan, we dunna have tae wrest power from Uncle Ian. I know a way he'll gladly give it tae us. Tae me."

Brendan cocked his head. "How?"

"With Annie," Argyle said simply. "I'll go tae Castle Questing and take Annie. Nay… *not* take her. I'll need her tae come with me willingly. I'll go tae Castle Questing and tell her that her da has taken ill. Nay… *nay*… that Robbie is ill and needs her. She'll come home for Robbie."

Brendan was starting to catch on. "She'd come without question," he said. "But once ye have her, then what?"

Argyle looked at him as if the answer were the simplest thing in the world. "Then I lock her away somewhere until Uncle Ian willingly surrenders the power of the clan tae me," he said. "I'll tell him Annie is safe so long as I'm clan chief. But if he denies me…"

"Then ye'll tell him she's dead."

"Aye."

"But ye willna kill her, will ye?"

Argyle shook his head. "Nay," he said. "But I will marry her. The lass has denied me long enough. 'Tis time I feasted on her flesh."

Brendan nodded, coming to terms with the plan. "Then we'll go," he said. "I'll go with ye. She may not trust ye alone, but if I go, she'll feel safe enough."

"Agreed."

"What will ye tell da?"

Argyle snorted. "He'll be so drunk that he'll never know we've left," he said. "Besides, the man is loyal to his brother. If we tell him anything, he might tell Uncle Ian."

That was true. Cord was a drunk, and he loved his sons, but Argyle and Brendan had always had far more ambition in them than their father ever had and, in a sense, Cord could relate to them well. He was entrenched in the old hierarchy, when the chief was always the chief. There was no room for uprising or rebellion.

Argyle and Brendan didn't live in that world.

"Then we leave before dawn," Brendan said. "We'll make it tae Castle Questing by nightfall."

Argyle could only nod because his mind was working furiously. All he had to do was get his hands on his beautiful cousin, the daughter of the clan chief, and his troubles would be over.

Or, so he thought.

For Argyle Scott, his troubles were just beginning.

CHAPTER TWELVE

Castle Questing

S HE'D SEEN HIM across the bailey.

Annaleigh spied War as he was in conversation with Christian, a man who was amiable and strangely chatty in a world where knights seemed to be more action than words. But not Christian; he could talk the ear off a magpie. Between him and James de Wolfe, they were quite entertaining at evening meals when everyone was gathered. James would sing, Christian would sing but also tell stories, and they were usually great fun until they'd had too much to drink and resorted to dirty songs and dirty stories.

That had happened more than once.

But Annaleigh liked Christian a great deal. In fact, as she saw him and War speaking, she thought it would be the perfect excuse to talk to War. All she had to do was pretend she was looking for Christian because Uncle William wanted to speak to him and off Christian would go.

Leaving her alone with War.

She thought it was a rather convenient plan.

Therefore, she headed in their direction as they entered the small yard where the knights' quarters and a few other outbuildings were located. War couldn't see her from the way he was standing and Christian seemed to be intently focused on him because the conversation seemed serious. That made her question whether she should interrupt at all so she slowed her pace, moving into the shadows of the keep and watching the pair converse.

But they didn't converse for much longer.

Suddenly, Christian was moving away from War, heading off towards the kitchens. Still in the shadows of the keep, Annaleigh watched him until he went into the kitchen yard before returning her attention to War. He was still standing there, only this time his back was to her as he spoke to the knight from Vilnius. No longer with the excuse she was hunting for Christian, Annaleigh debated what to do. Could she simply walk in there and greet the man?

A smile tugged at her lips.

She knew what to do.

The knight from Vilnius was the first one to catch sight of her. He said something to War, who quickly turned around to see Annaleigh on the approach. Their eyes met and, for a moment, she swore she saw a look of pleasure cross his face. Or perhaps she was imagining it. Where War was concerned, it was easy to imagine things she wanted to see.

"Good day, m'lord," she greeted pleasantly.

War smiled, an expression that seemed to come quite easily. "Good day, my lady," he said. "It is a fine day today, made finer by your appearance."

Annaleigh was already feeling giddy, basking in the man's presence as if he were the sun and she a mere worshipper. So completely unworthy of him. But she gave him a coy expression.

"Flattery, m'lord?" she teased. "If ye say much more like that, my head will be too swollen tae enter the keep."

War chuckled and even Alexei grinned. "Not to worry, my lady," War said. "A couple of hammers and we can widen the door. There is no need to cease the flattery."

Annaleigh giggled. "I think William might have something tae say about a man taking a hammer tae his door."

"Then we'll figure out another way."

Annaleigh's cheeks were beginning to flush. "I appreciate yer willingness tae help me," she said. "But I came for another reason."

"What is that?"

"Lady de Wolfe's request tae see if ye required anything. Did ye sleep well?"

War nodded. "Very well," he said. "God's Bones, Castle Questing is the most hospitable place I've ever stayed at."

"What do ye mean?"

"Because Christian was sent by Lady de Wolfe also," he said. "He asked me the same questions."

Annaleigh immediately felt as if she'd been caught in her lie. Her eagerness to speak to the man was coming back to haunt her. Before she could reply, however, someone caught Alexei's attention and he politely excused himself. Leaving War and Annaleigh alone now, Annaleigh didn't want to look like a fool in front of War. Perhaps he was already figuring out that something was strangely off with both Christian and Annaleigh inquiring on his health and sleep habits.

She was making them all look like idiots.

"I have a confession," she said with some hesitance.

He cocked his head with interest. "Oh?"

She nodded. "Lady de Wolfe dinna send me here."

"She didn't?"

Annaleigh sighed heavily. "Ye may as well know that I'm a liar of the worst sort," she said. "I told ye that Lady de Wolfe sent me because I thought it might look forward of me tae greet ye without a reason. If ye want tae laugh at me, go ahead. I deserve it."

He chuckled and she hung her head. But he quickly realized he'd hurt her feelings so he reached out and took her hand in his, gently.

"I wasn't laughing at you, I promise," he said, holding her soft, warm hand in his callused mitt. "I laughed because… well, that is about the nicest thing anyone has ever said to me. No one goes out of their way to bid me a good morn. But you did. I cannot tell you how honored I am."

She dared to glance up at him. "Truly?"

"Truly."

"Then good morn tae ye," she said, her eyes twinkling with mirth. "And I have no reason tae come here, where ye're clearly busy, other than to bid ye a good morn."

He grinned, his eyes glittering at her. "Good morn, my lady," he said in his soft, deep voice. "Has your morning been pleasant so far?"

Annaleigh thought she was going to sweat right through her dress. War's expression set her senses on fire, as if everything about him was searing her and she was melting before the flame. He was the sun god again and she was before him, humbly, but oh-so-gratefully basking in his glory.

And he was holding her hand.

It was the most amazing moment she'd ever experienced.

"I've had tae contend with Penny the Tyrant," she said. "The lass tries tae turn her da against me if she doesna get her way, but William is a sensible man. He doesna believe a four year old."

War's brow furrowed. "Then I must avenge you," he said. "Where is that little tormentor?"

Annaleigh giggled. "With her father, the last I saw," she said. "Ye'll have tae fight William tae get tae her and I dunna think ye want tae do that."

He released her hand with a smile. "Probably not."

She continued to giggle. "Then it is best tae forget yer vengeance for now." Annaleigh noticed that, behind him, Monty and Clement were pulling out possessions and weaponry and beginning to organize them. She pointed. "Are yer men leaving?"

War glanced at them before returning his attention to her. "We all are," he said. "De Wolfe wants to take us to Wark Castle and then on to Northwood Castle. I am here on a tour, after all, so it is time to start touring."

Annaleigh couldn't help it; her face fell. "I see," she said. "When are ye leaving?"

It was a gesture not missed by War. His eyes glimmered dully as he cocked his head, trying to get a better look at her lowered face. "Within the hour," he said. "I could ask de Wolfe to delay it until tomorrow."

She was starting to feel vastly disappointed and embarrassed that he probably sensed that. "Why would ye?" she asked. "There's no need for ye tae remain at Castle Questing. Ye must get on with yer business."

"I can think of a good reason to stay."

"What's that?"

It was his turn to be coy. He scratched his neck, seemingly awkward for the first time since Annaleigh had known him.

"I'm not entirely sure I should say," he said. "You see, I'm not entirely certain she feels the same way and I do not wish to embarrass myself. Or her."

Annaleigh looked at him, then, thinking she understood what he had implied. "There is someone here that…?" Realization dawned, or at least she thought it did, and her disappointment returned tenfold. "Then ye should ask her, of course. I willna take anymore of yer time, m'lord. I'm sure ye have tae…"

She was starting to back up and he reached out, quickly taking her hand and preventing her from getting away.

"You have no idea who I mean, do you?" he asked.

Annaleigh was trying to pull her hand away but she didn't want to yank. "'Tis none of my affair," she said. "I wouldna pry. But I wish ye well. I…"

He cut her off again, though it was gently done. "I meant you," he said quietly. "Did you truly not know that?"

She paused, her eyes wide. "Me?"

He nodded, a smile tugging at his lips as he dropped her hand again. "May I return to Castle Questing to call upon you?"

"*Me*?" she said, astonished.

"That is not an answer."

"But… *why*?"

"Isn't it obvious?"

"If it was, I wouldna ask ye."

He snorted. "I suppose you wouldn't," he said. Then, he took a deep breath as he summoned his courage. "Let me be clear – I would like to return to Castle Questing to call upon you. That means I would like to come here just to visit you.

When you found me near the river those months ago and healed me, that bound us together in a way that is difficult to understand if you've not faced death before. You saved my life, Annaleigh. That means something to me."

She was starting to overcome her shock, listening seriously to what he had to say. "Is that why ye want tae return?" she said. "Because ye feel some obligation tae me? Because if that is the only reason, it's not a good one. It should have nothing tae do with ye wanting tae call upon me."

He was nodding even before she finished speaking. "I know," he said. "I did not mean I feel obligation. It has nothing to do with that and everything to do with a bond I feel with the woman who saved my life. You did not have to do what you did, but you risked much to do it. That speaks of bravery and selflessness that few people have. You're warm and humorous and beautiful… you're a rare woman, Annaleigh. That is why I want to return to call upon you. I want to see you again."

Annaleigh could hardly believe what she was hearing. Months of dealing with Talus and Anthony, of discouraging them, came rolling back in her mind as she realized this was the one man she *didn't* want to discourage. But she was at a loss as to why the man should be interested in her.

Yet… he was.

"Then I must ask ye a question and I want ye tae be honest with me," she finally said. "Will ye do that?"

"I will always be honest with you. I know of no other way."

His sincerity was soft but unmistakable. She believed him immediately. "Then tell me *why* ye want tae call on me," she asked softly. "Do ye have a purpose in mind? Because I dunna want a friend in ye. That wouldna be proper if we are both unmarried."

"You want to know my intent?"

"Aye."

"Must I be plain so soon?"

"If ye want tae return tae here specifically tae see me, then ye must. I think I have a right."

He sighed. "My intent would be to come to know you," he said. "If you are as remarkable as I think you are, then it would be a natural progression."

"What progression?"

"Marriage, of course."

That made her suck her breath in sharply, purely out of surprise. Although she had an idea that was what he might say, to hear him verbalize it was something else altogether. Suddenly, all she could think of was their differences, things she'd thought of before that had driven her to great disappointment. War was a great knight.

She wasn't anything to speak of, at least not in her mind.

Didna he know that?

"But I'm a clan chief's daughter," she finally said. "I'm Scots."

"I am aware."

"But ye're Henry's favored knight." She pointed out the obvious as if he'd gone mad. "Men like ye dunna marry Scots with no money, no title, no property. Ye marry a woman who can give ye all those things that I canna."

His eyes were glimmering again. "If I met a woman with courage, warmth, and beauty and she was rich and titled, then I would consider her," he said evenly. "But if I meet a woman with courage, warmth, and beauty who is a clan chief's daughter, I will consider her, too. My lady, I do not make this decision lightly. I do not choose a woman based on the size of her purse. I choose a woman based on the size of her heart."

It was the most beautiful thing Annaleigh had ever heard. She truly had nothing to say about it because he'd explained himself quite clearly. She understood him implicitly.

But she still couldn't believe it.

"Ye're certain of this?" she asked, incredulous.

"I am."

He wasn't wavering. Any more doubt on her part and he might forget the whole thing, so she struggled to come to grips with it.

To accept it.

"Then if ye're certain, I would be agreeable tae having ye call," she said. "But ye must ask William first. I'm his ward, so ye must ask his permission."

War was trying to keep the smile of victory off his lips as she agreed to his proposal but he couldn't quite manage it.

"But what of your father?" he said. "Shouldn't I ask him?"

Annaleigh shook her head. "My da sent me tae Castle Questing," she said. "He sent me tae stay, I believe. I dunna think he wants me tae return, so ye must ask William."

That made things easier for War, to be sure. "I will," he said. "May I ask him today?"

"Ye may ask him whenever ye feel the time is right."

"I think the time is right now."

Annaleigh laughed softly. "There's no rush, ye know," she said. "'Tis not as if I've got a horde of men lining up tae marry me."

War cocked an eyebrow. "Nay, but you have two knights who are particularly interested in you," he said, his gaze moving to the walls. "I will have to find them and tell them that you are not to be harassed any longer or my wrath will be swift."

Annaleigh thought of Talus and Anthony and how they were going to take such news, but she couldn't manage to feel sorry for them. She was too busy feeling thrilled for herself. But it occurred to her that War knew.

"And how would ye know that?" she asked.

His determined expression wavered slightly. "I heard such things," he said. Then he hesitated. "That is not exactly true. I had one of my men ask around to see if you were betrothed or married. I was told about the two de Wolfe knights who have intentions towards you."

A smile played on her lips as she realized he'd been asking around about her. "Did ye find out everything ye wanted tae know?"

"Not everything."

"What more is there?"

He bit his lip to keep from grinning. "That will come in due time between us, my lady," he said. "Now, back to those two knights. I intend to have a word with them both."

Annaleigh shook her head. "Mayhap ye should let me tell them," she said. "A woman will be gentler. Ye might only succeed in creating hard feelings and ye dunna want that. Not if ye ever face battle with these men. Ye dunna want them looking at ye and feeling resentment. Not if yer life depends on their allegiance."

She was right to a certain extent, but he wasn't so certain. "I've never had to face this situation before, you know," he admitted. "I feel as if I should tell them personally."

"Ye dunna even know them. I do."

"Point taken."

They stood there and looked at each other for a moment, each of them feeling such glee, such delight. It was such an unexpected moment and, truth be told, War had never intended to ask her if he could return to see her. To court her. God help him, he'd even mentioned marriage. But it had all come about so naturally that he'd never doubted it for a moment. No regrets, no second-guesses.

This was what he wanted.

Nothing had ever seemed so right.

"May I kiss your hand before I go?" he said softly. "I want to find William before we depart."

But Annaleigh shook her head. "Of course ye may not," she said. "What if someone saw? The gossip would spread quickly and we dunna want that."

She was right. He sighed in resignation. "You are correct," he said. "I would not wish to put you in that position. Letting a man kiss your hand who is not your betrothed or your husband."

She could see that he was disappointed and she found it quite sweet. "If it matters, it doesna make me happy tae deny ye," she said. "But for now…"

He conceded. "I know," he said, putting up a hand to silence her. "You are right. But I look forward to the day when it is my right to take you in my arms and kiss you."

"As do I."

A smile spread across his lips. "Do you truly?"

"I do."

That was good enough for him. "Then I will take my leave for the moment," he said. "If I stand here and look at you any longer, I may forget myself. In fact, I…"

He was abruptly cut off by shouts from the wall. There was a great deal of activity at the gatehouse and both War and Annaleigh turned to watch a group of men on horseback racing in through the gatehouse while the sentries on duty scrambled to lower the portcullis.

More men began shouting.

Monty and Clement, who had been dealing with their imminent departure, wandered over next to War as they watched the men of Castle Questing mobilize. Even Christian came bolting out of the keep along with Kieran, heading for the gatehouse, as Talus and Anthony appeared.

Everyone was rushing for the gatehouse.

"What is happening?" Monty asked curiously.

War shook his head. "I'm not sure," he said. But he hadn't forgotten Annaleigh, standing next to him. He turned to her. "Mayhap it is best you go into the keep now, at least until we know what the activity is about."

Annaleigh nodded. She was a little concerned, too, because the soldiers at Castle Questing didn't panic for no reason. She'd been around long enough to know that. Not that they were panicking but, clearly, something was happening. Politely, War took her elbow and walked her out of their small area out into the bailey. He turned her towards the keep as men began shouting again and William emerged from the keep, moving swiftly past Annaleigh on his way to the gatehouse. He was shouting to the gatehouse and the reply was something they all heard.

Reivers.

Annaleigh ran to the keep as War, Monty, and Clement headed for the gatehouse.

The smell of battle was in the air.

CHAPTER THIRTEEN

T HERE WAS A battle going on.

Argyle and Brendan could see it in the distance. It was a clear day and, for some reason, the village of Coldstream was in an uproar. They could see the reflection of shields against the sun and people were fleeing the village. The men paused on a rise to the west, overlooking the village in the distance, and they could see all of it.

"Kerr again," Argyle muttered. "In the daylight, they're raiding Coldstream? They're madmen."

Brendan's gaze was riveted to the distant village. They were far enough away, with a clear field of vision, that they weren't in any immediate danger, but frightened villagers were passing them on the road. Brendan finally reached out and grasped an old man by the arm.

"What's amiss?" he demanded.

The old man was carrying a satchel, helping an old woman and younger girl along. "Reivers," he said, pulling from Brendan's grip. "The Bones. *The Bones!*"

He hurried away, pulling the women with him. But his information had told Brendan and Argyle exactly what they needed to know.

The Bones.

A group of particularly vicious reivers called themselves The Bones, a gang of outlaws that roamed these northern lands and tended to raid larger villages, like Coldstream. They were bold and brazen, so the raid in the daylight made sense because they'd done it before. They called themselves The Bones because once they were finished raiding, that was all they left behind – the bones. The bones of a village, the bones of people, the bones of a once-idyllic life.

It was one of the most feared names on the borders.

"The Bones," Argyle muttered, his gaze on the village in the distance. "I'm not going near that place. We must go around."

Brendan agreed. The men of The Bones fought like mercenaries, so no one wanted to engage them. They left the clans alone for the most part, so the clans left them alone as well, but what they didn't leave alone were villages of any size. If there was a settlement, chances are they'd raided it.

There was no protection, anywhere.

"I've heard they've gone as far north as Edinburgh," Brendan said.

"And Yorkshire tae the south," Argyle said, reining his sturdy pony west, down into the thick growth around the river. "I've heard they've even raided intae Lancaster."

"That would be a long journey," Brendan said, following his brother as they quickly moved into the greenery for cover. "But the lads are bold, I'll give them that. And tae raid Coldstream is madness. Wark Castle is right across the river and Castle Questing not far beyond that. Would they truly take on de Wolfe?"

Argyle reined his horse to a halt and Brendan behind him.

They were beneath the trees now, well hidden from anyone on the road, but they could still see a bit of the village in the distance. If they listened hard enough, they could hear the screams.

"So de Wolfe is distracted," Argyle said thoughtfully. "'Tis better for us. Annie will see how determined we were tae deliver the message of Robbie's illness because we risked trouble with the reivers take make it tae Castle Questing. It will lend truth tae our appearance."

"True," Brendan said. "But one thing we've not discussed is de Wolfe himself."

"What about him?"

Brendan pointed to the village in the distance. "It doesna matter if he's distracted with the reivers," he said. "This willna last forever. He'll be back tae Castle Questing by tonight, when we arrive. If we tell him that Robbie is ill, he'll not let Annie go home without an escort. I'd wager tae say he'll insist, especially if the reivers are in the area."

Argyle frowned as he thought on that statement. It was clear he'd not considered de Wolfe sending an escort with them to return to Langton, so the wheels of thought began to churn. But not for long. After a moment, he nodded his head.

"Then we tell Annie that Robbie doesna want anyone tae know he's ill," he said. "We'll tell her that neither Uncle Ian nor Robbie want de Wolfe tae know, so she'll have tae come with us in secret. She'll leave a message behind for de Wolfe telling him that she decided tae return home but not why. She'll tell him not tae follow. Simple enough, isn't it?"

Brendan simply didn't think so, but Argyle always had an answer for everything. He shrugged and gathered his reins, kicking his shaggy pony onward, towards the east where there was a stone crossing over the river about a mile downstream, near a tiny village called Carham. It was a narrow crossing, but it was their only option at that point.

They had to make it to Castle Questing.

The sense of urgency grew.

CHAPTER FOURTEEN

WAR COULD SEE why William de Wolfe was considered England's greatest living knight.

Even at the man's age, which could be considered elderly by some, he was still the most skilled warrior War had ever seen. When they'd fought at Thropton, War hadn't actually done battle side by side with William, but during the raid at Coldstream, he'd never left the man's side.

It was truly something to behold.

It also did something to War's psyche.

His entire life, he'd been an overachiever. He'd always been the best, the strongest, the smartest in everything he did. Even at Blackchurch, where all of the trainees were the best of the best, he stood out among them. There was nothing deficient about War Herringthorpe, but in fighting next to the Wolfe of the Border, he felt awed. As if he still had more to learn. As if the man who had given him life was everything he'd ever wanted to be.

And he couldn't tell him.

Wouldn't tell him.

At least, not yet.

While William used skill and talent rather than raw power in most instances, War was young and beastly. He sliced off arms and heads and, at one point, ending up in a fist fight because he and William and a few other men had been ambushed by some wily reivers and he'd been dismounted at the time. There was punching and kicking and neck wringing going on and through it all, War found himself watching William when he wasn't fighting for his own life.

Watching the man who fathered him was like watching a mythological god from old.

And War couldn't decide how he felt about it.

He'd wrestled with it all through the battle, which was fortunately short-lived because the reivers were badly outnumbered. When the knights brought up the rear of the army that had been sent to Coldstream and they descended on the reivers in earnest, that was when the fighting began to dwindle. Before that happened, however, the battle was quite vicious.

And quite eye opening.

The Bones.

They'd heard the name of that horrible band of reivers the moment they'd entered the village and they kept hearing it from everyone around them. Even the soldiers were speaking of The Bones, men who dressed in finery that wasn't easily found or cheaply purchased, but men who fought brutally and terribly. They were the most feared outlaws on the border.

Their tactics were barbaric. Men on horseback were in danger of losing their lower legs because rather than try to fight a man who was on a horse, the men of The Bones would go for the legs and feet, trying to disable them. They also went after the horses themselves but, in the case of the knights, they were met with beasts that were as trained as their masters.

War's black and white stallion was particularly brutal against a man in fine silk and expensive leather protection who had tried to go for the horse's legs. The man came away missing part of his hand when the horse snapped at him. After that, the men of The Bones stayed away from the distinct stallion and the powerful knight astride him. War found himself chasing men, beating them away from soldiers on foot who seemed to be targeted more than most. Rather than running away from the men from Castle Questing, The Bones ran in circles, trying to confuse and disorient the English.

But the English held firm.

It wasn't an easy fight to win, however, and it continued for most of the afternoon. When the evening began to set and the sun's last rays disappeared in the west, the men of The Bones decided their time was finished and they began to disappear. The English weren't going to give up Coldstream and although The Bones had done damage, they hadn't really run off with anything substantial. No stores, no valuables.

For The Bones, the incursion into Coldstream had not been successful.

The English garrison from Castle Questing was victorious.

When William realized the enemy had retreated, leaving behind several wounded who were put under restraints and taken back to Wark Castle, he left about three hundred soldiers in Coldstream to guard the village for the night. In the morning, he'd send more men over to help the cleanup. The villagers of Coldstream had been through battles before so they were a hearty bunch, capable of rebuilding, but William's men offered extra protection.

It was protection much appreciated.

War remained in Coldstream with the men while William and Kieran took the rest of the army back to Castle Questing. Troy, who had been stationed at Wark Castle, also remained in Coldstream to command the de Wolfe men and help with the cleanup. But the old knights like William and Kieran headed home. They'd put in their time in the past, as young knights who took posts for the night or helped cleaning up after a battle, but no more. They'd long since proved their worth.

The old men were looking forward to a warm meal and a warm bed.

The de Wolfe army heading for Castle Questing was being led by dozens of torches even though the moon overhead was fairly bright. Castle Questing was less than an hour from Coldstream, so it would be a short journey this night that seemed oddly still after the bedlam of the day. William found himself looking into the night sky, to the dusting of stars that spread across the heavens, when Kieran spoke up beside him.

"You did not have a chance to see Herringthorpe fight at Thropton, did you?" he asked.

William shook his head. "Not really," he said. "There were moments when we were near each other, but I never saw the heavy fighting that I heard tale of. Why do you ask?"

Kieran sighed faintly. "I am going to tell you what you have already heard," he said quietly. "Tonight only confirmed it."

"Confirmed what?"

"The man fights like you," Kieran muttered. "William, I know I told you that Herringthorpe looked like you back at Thropton and we've discussed it since, but I have never been more convinced that the man is related to you than I am tonight. It was like watching you in your younger years. His movements, the way he swings a sword… everything."

William looked at him. "I know," he said with some resignation. "I saw."

"You see it, too?"

William shrugged, looking back to the sky. "It's more a feeling," he said. "I cannot describe it, but it's in his facial expression at times. It's not me he looks like – it's my father. I swear to you, he looks just like Edward de Wolfe."

Kieran grunted softly. "It's not possible that he's your father's bastard," he said. "He died years before Herringthorpe was conceived."

William shook his head. "I wasn't suggesting that," he said. "I am suggesting that it is, indeed, *me*."

"You're convinced?"

"Possibly. Or it could be that we are imagining things that do not exist."

"True."

"A mind can play tricks."

"I would agree in Paris' case, but not in mine. Or yours."

A shadow of a grin crossed William's lips. "Paris will see him when we go to Northwood tomorrow," he said. "He was the first one who really spoke of it back at Thropton. The trick with Paris is to keep the man's mouth shut. He will ask Herringthorpe to his face if he is my bastard and this situation must be handled far more delicately. If there even *is* a situation. We could all be mad for all we know."

Kieran thought he heard something in William's tone and he looked at him, preparing to reply, but he was prevented by Christian's sudden appearance.

Christian rode a big, gray warhorse that was as fat as a holiday goose. He rode up beside his father and uncle, flipping up his visor as he looked at them.

"May I send a rider ahead and tell Castle Questing to be prepared for the wounded?" he asked. "We've got three men with fairly serious injuries and I would like for Aunt Jordan and my mother to be ready for them. We should tell them we have incoming."

William nodded. "Send a rider," he said. "Since we are not sure where The Bones went, you will tell Anthony to be on his guard. I do not want them sneaking up on my castle. Where is Talus?"

Christian threw a thumb towards the rear of the column. "Back there," he said. "He took a serious gash to his left leg. Those bastards tried to cut if off."

"I know," William said. "I saw it. He'll need immediate tending with a wound like that."

Christian agreed. He spurred his horse forward, finding a young soldier astride a jumpy horse and sent the man charging ahead to Castle Questing. They would soon be seeing it in the distance, its ramparts lit up with torches against the dark night, and there was comfort in knowing they weren't far out. Once Christian sent the rider ahead, he returned to his father and uncle.

"I think we can pick up the pace a little," he said to his father. "What say you?"

Kieran agreed. In battle, or on a battle march, as William's second in command, he made most of the logistical and general decisions for the army. William didn't bat an eyelash as Kieran began to give commands to pick up the pace. The men began to move faster, including Talus with his gashed leg, and the warhorses broke into a steady trot.

"How long do you intend to keep men in Coldstream, Uncle William?" Christian asked as the horses bounced along.

William's horse had a smoother trot than most of them, so he was riding easily. "At least for a few days," he said. "I told Troy to send Herringthorpe and his men back to Castle Questing in the morning. It is not his duty to protect one of our villages. Moreover, he did not come for that. He came to meet my allies."

"Did you see the man fight?"

"Of course I did."

"He fights like you, Uncle William." Christian finally looked over at William and his father. "Papa sent me to find out what I could about him. Did he tell you that?"

William looked at Kieran. "You told Christian about my suspicions?" he asked.

Kieran wouldn't look at him. "If anyone could find out about Herringthorpe, it is Christian," he said. "My son has the tongue of a serpent and the mind of a fox. I told you that I would not probe Herringthorpe personally, but I asked Christian to find out what he could. He can do it better than we ever could."

William wasn't pleased, but there was a large part of him that was very curious now. He looked at Christian. "Well?" he said. "What did you discover?"

Christian pulled back on the reins of his horse because the animal was starting to speed up. Once the beast was settled, he answered.

"Nothing out of the ordinary," he said. "We spoke of many things but, mainly, I asked him if he was related to the Wolver-hampton de Wolfes because he has the look of the family in general. I was casual about it, of course, and the question came up naturally in conversation. It was not forced. But he said he did not have any relatives in Wolverhampton."

William didn't know why he was disappointed to hear that. Perhaps he was hoping for a clue of War's familial relations more than he realized, but just as quickly, he told himself that his disappointment was stupid. He shouldn't hope for such things. He had a family he was deeply proud of, including twin sons who were his heirs. Nothing could ever take that away from them, not even a bastard he'd not known about. But given War's reputation and clear talent, he had to admit that it was something he would be proud of, too.

Proud of a lad he never knew he had.

It was a situation that had him torn.

"Although I appreciate you taking the initiative, Christian, please do not ask him anything more," William said after a moment. "As I told your father, whatever I think is purely speculation. There is no proof. Even if the clues point to the probability, it is possible that Herringthorpe knows nothing, so please do not bring it up again. And you will take this information to your grave."

"Aye, Uncle William."

"Swear it to me. Not a word to anyone."

"I swear."

William was satisfied. With that, he reined his horse around, intending to head to the rear to see how Talus was coming along with that leg. Kieran and Christian watched him go, but once he was out of earshot, Christian addressed his father.

"I think Herringthorpe is holding something back," he said quietly. "Something about him… something wasn't right, Papa."

Kieran looked at him with interest. "You think he was lying to you?"

Christian shook his head. "Not exactly," he said. "But there was something in his face when I brought up Wolverhampton and the de Wolfe family. Something in his eyes that told me he knew something. Or mayhap he had heard something. I cannot explain it more than that."

Kieran pondered that for a moment. "You have an excellent instinct when it comes to men," he said. "If you think the man knows something more, I believe you."

"But what do we do about it?"

"Nothing," Kieran said. "William asked you not to and you will obey him. Understood?"

"Aye, Papa."

They let the subject drop but, somehow, Christin knew that wasn't the end of it.

So did Kieran.

ʚɞ

WITH THE ARMY away and the castle buttoned up, there wasn't much more for the inhabitants to do than continue with their regular duties. Soldiers and servants alike went about their usual tasks, focusing on their duties and trying not to think about their army at war.

That included the servants in the keep. Jordan had been with them for the rest of the afternoon, as Penelope and the younger children played in the kitchen yard, watched over by Jemma. Jordan supervised the usual tasks and also tasks she completed while William and Kieran and the men were out of the keep, like washing linens and clothing. She never really did that while they were in residence, mostly because William wasn't fond of the way linen smelled after it had been washed, but there were times it had to be done. At the moment, those tasks were simply busy work to keep her mind off of her husband in battle.

She simply didn't want to think about it.

After the sun set and the castle was lit up against the night sky, the smell of the evening meal could be savored upon the air. Jemma had brought the children in and while they were playing in the upper floors, she went to make sure there was food for the evening. Jordan was still with the house servants, finishing with the linens on all of the beds, guest beds included. Everything had been stripped earlier and the servants were in the process of replacing linens with those that had been freshly washed and dried.

When word had been received that the army would soon be returning, Jordan began to move the servants quickly to ensure everything was completed by the time they returned. In particular, she wanted to make sure that War's chamber was properly swept and prepared for the man's return since he'd been doing her husband a favor by lending his sword to a raid on Coldstream. She'd been in another chamber to make sure a fire in the hearth was lit but hurried down to the unmarried men's wing to make sure the servants were almost done. But her appearance startled one of them, a young woman who had recently come to work at Castle Questing from a nearby village, and as soon as Jordan popped into the doorway, the young maid bumped into War's saddlebags, which had been placed on a wooden bench.

Everything dumped over and scattered.

The girl fell to her knees beside the bags, terrified that Jordan was going to scold her and send her home, but Jordan went to her knees beside her.

"I'll do this," she told the girl. "Go back tae yer duties. I'll put his things back."

Trembling, the girl went back to what she'd been doing, verging on tears, but Jordan assured her that it was nothing to be upset over. The truth was that Jordan didn't want a mere servant touching War's things so, as the Lady of the Keep, she took great care in righting the bags and carefully placing everything back inside.

It was mostly clothing, soap, combs, and personal items. There were a few random daggers, a sewing kit, which was usual for knights, and a writing kit that was carefully and tightly packaged. It contained vellum, sand, ink, wax, and quite possibly a stamp with War's seal on it. Jordan only opened it long enough to make sure the ink hadn't spilled, and it hadn't, as it was in a tightly corked phial.

Carefully, she put it back into the saddlebags on the right.

But a few more things were scattered, not the least of which were letters or documents that had been bound up with leather strips. They'd come loose and were strewn over the floor. Jordan collected each one, including one that had gone underneath the bed. As she picked that one up, the wax seal on it fell off and she lost her grip on it trying to catch the seal.

Putting the other documents she'd collected in a neat stack, she picked up the one that had been dropped twice. In fact, it was completely open on the floor and although she wasn't the nosy kind, nor did she care about Herringthorpe's business, she had to physically look at the document in order to pick it up. As she looked at it, she caught a name she recognized in the fold.

Willaume de Wolfe.

That gave her pause.

Jordan knew she shouldn't read it, but her husband's name, in traditional Norman spelling, was clearly written. What in the world would War Herringthorpe be doing with a letter mentioning William de Wolfe? Curiosity had the better of her.

Nay, not curiosity… *concern.*

Jordan read the letter.

Mother of God… she wished she hadn't.

CHAPTER FIFTEEN

"**W**HERE HAVE YOU been?" William asked. "I've been looking everywhere for you."

Jordan was in the chamber they shared, high above the bailey of Castle Questing. In fact, their chamber had windows that faced the bailey and the north, so she knew exactly when the army had arrived. When William found her, she was sitting in the window seat of one of those windows, gazing off into the night.

Her husband's words didn't change that.

"And so ye've found me," she said.

Dirty and exhausted, William stepped into the chamber. "What are you doing here?" he said. "We returned twenty minutes ago and I've got several wounded that need attention."

"I'll get tae them in due time," Jordan said steadily. "Is Jemma in the hall?"

"Aye," William answered.

"Then they are well tended for now."

Puzzled by his wife's behavior, William stepped further into the chamber. "What's wrong with you? Are you ill?"

Jordan drew in a long, pensive breath. "I'm not ill," she said.

"I've simply been… thinking."

"What about?"

Jordan looked up at the sky. It seemed unusually clear tonight. "Did ye know a lass named Jane?"

William had been in the process of irritably removing his hauberk but his wife's question brought him pause. It was an extremely odd question about something, or someone, quite specific and he wondered why.

He proceeded carefully.

"Jane?" he repeated. "Is there a family name?"

"I'm sure there is, but I dunna know it," Jordan said. "She is related to Herringthorpe."

That brought a measure of shock to William. "Jane Herringthorpe is War's mother," he said evenly. "I knew her long ago as Jane de Percy. Is that the Jane you mean?"

"I suppose it is," Jordan said. "How well did ye know her?"

William shrugged. "Well enough," he said. "De Longley and her father were allies while I served de Longley. Why do you ask? What is this about?"

Jordan leaned back against the cold stone wall. "Did ye know she bore ye a son?"

William froze, his hauberk half-off his head. Suddenly, he could feel something bubbling in his chest, something he couldn't define, but something that felt like… fear? Shock? Astonishment? He wasn't sure what, exactly, he felt only that her question filled him with horror.

"What in the world are you talking about?" he said, yanking the hauberk off and letting it fall to the ground. "Jordan, what is wrong with you? Why do you ask me that question?"

Jordan finally looked at him. For the first time, she held up what looked like a large, folded piece of vellum, hanging open.

William could see it in the weak light.

"Because this is a letter tae ye from a woman named Jane who married Edmund Herringthorpe," she said softly. "I was with the servants when they were cleaning Sir War's chamber and his bags were accidentally knocked over. When I was putting everything back in, this letter was on the floor and it was open. I was putting it back intae his bag when I saw yer name on it. I was naturally curious, so I read it. This letter is from Jane addressed tae ye, telling ye that she was pregnant when her father denied yer request tae marry her."

William had gone cold. It wasn't that he was particularly shocked by the news. In fact, it was confirmation of what they'd all been speculating. What had his blood running cold was the tone of his wife's voice and the expression on her face. He'd told Kieran that something like this wouldn't upset her, or at least she'd be forgiving, but now he was wondering if that was entirely true. It never occurred to him that she wouldn't be.

Jordan, his everything for living, the very blood that pumped through his veins. No man had ever loved a woman more. No man had ever been more dependent upon a woman than he was with her. He thought he knew her as well as he knew himself but he quickly reconsidered that. Perhaps it had been foolhardy to think so. He could be rather calm about it because it was his mistake, but to Jordan… it was evidence that her husband, one she believed perfect, had indeed made a *big* mistake. It meant something different to her than to him. Clearly.

His pulse began to race.

"It is War, isn't it?" he asked hoarsely.

Jordan's answer was to extend the letter to him. Stiffly, he went to her, taking the letter from her, but his gaze never left her face. She was looking at him, those enormous green eyes he knew so well, and it was beginning to make him ill that he couldn't read her emotions in the depths. A wall had gone up.

Tearing his gaze away from her, he read the letter.

My Dearest Willaume,

I've tried to write this letter to you a thousand times and a thousand times, I burned it when I was finished. But this letter, I've not burned, my dearest love. You must know what happened when you left me that cold November day last year.

Our days and nights of passion took root and even as my father denied our marriage, your son grew in my belly. I told my father, hoping he would change his mind and allow us to marry, but he became enraged. He wrote to his old friend, Edmund Herringthorpe, and told the man he would make him very rich if he agreed to marry me immediately. Since Edmund had a good name but no money, he did. Your son was not born a bastard, but the son of a good and kind man my father tricked into marrying me.

Even as I write this letter, I am watching your son sleep in his cradle by the fire. He looks like you, my dearest love. He has your hair, your eyes. I look at him and I see you, and I am content. If I could not have you as my husband, then at least I can have your son. I regret to say that he shall be raised as a Herringthorpe, but Edmund loves him very much and will be good to him. You can rest assured that your son will be properly educated, but it is with sorrow that I tell you he will know nothing of his de Wolfe roots. Out of respect to Edmund while he is still alive, I will not tell him.

It is my wish that our son, Warwick, know of his true heritage upon my death, or upon the death of Edmund, and it is my wish that Warwick be given this letter to give to you as explanation of who, and what, he is. He is your son, my beloved, the proud first son of Willaume de Wolfe. I am so sorry we could not raise him together, but I hope you are not angry with me for not telling you sooner. I am sure you understand that I could not risk it.

Pray, be good to our son. Treat him fairly.

That is all I can ask.

All my love,
Jane

It had her seal on the bottom of it.

William read it twice. When he was finished, he drew in a long, heavy breath, lowering the letter in his hand and processing the contents. He was feeling very old, very weary, and very despondent. Still seated near the window, Jordan spoke softly.

"Ye dinna know?" she asked.

He shook his head. "Nay," he said hoarsely. "But when we fought at Thropton, Paris and Kieran commented on how much Herringthorpe looked like me. I laughed it off as ridiculous. But when he appeared at Castle Questing, he mentioned that his mother had been Jane de Percy and quite possibly his birth happened after Jane and I… well, after we had our affair. The more I looked at him, the more I wondered."

"Now ye know."

"Indeed, I do."

Silence settled between them and William's anxiety began

to rise. He didn't like the tension between them. He never liked it when they fought and he would always move heaven and earth to soothe her, but this was different. Far different than meaningless arguments they'd had in the past.

This was something soul-shattering.

"What are you thinking, Jordan?" he finally asked softly. "Have I damaged something between us with a youthful indiscretion?"

Jordan pulled her shawl more tightly around her shoulders as the night breeze wafted in through the window, lifting tendrils of her blonde hair.

"I'm not sure," she said after a moment. "I know ye had a life before me. I dunna fault ye that. But something is bothering me."

"What is it?"

She sighed faintly, venturing back into the cobwebs of her memory. "When we first met, do ye recall me asking ye if there had been someone special before me?"

William thought on her question as he moved to the chair next to the window where she was sitting. He lowered himself onto it, wearily, as he tried to figure out what, exactly, she was speaking of.

"I seem to," he said. "It was a long time ago, Jordan."

"What do ye recall?"

He shrugged. "I'm not sure," he said. "Is there a specific instance you are referring to?"

"We were in bed together."

"That happened every day."

"That is true," she said. "But there was a moment when we spoke of the women before me. Ye told me ye only loved yer liege's wife which, at the time, was me."

He nodded slowly as the vague memory returned to him. "I remember," he said. "You asked me of the women I'd had before you."

"Go on."

"What more would you have me say?"

She turned and looked at him, then. "Ye told me that there hadna been anyone before me," she said. "That ye hadna given yer love tae anyone else but me. But clearly, that was not the truth."

He sighed with great regret. "It *was* the truth," he said. "I swear to you upon my oath that it was. Jane… I did not want to marry her. She wanted to marry me."

"But ye had a child with her, English."

English. That was the nickname she'd called him since the day she'd met him, a term of endearment that was like music to his ears. But at the moment, all he could hear in it was her hurt and confusion and it tore at him like nothing he'd ever known before. He could hear in her voice that, somehow, he'd hurt her.

He felt like the most horrible man in the world.

"Jordan," he said, trying to sound as if he weren't pleading with her. "Do you want to know the truth? She seduced me and I let her. You knew I'd been with other women before I knew you. There is no crime in that, but I swear to you upon my father's grave that I never loved any of them."

"But ye offered for her hand."

There was the pain in her tone again. It was like someone was taking a dagger and hacking his heart out. "Aye, I did," he said. "Jane was a nice lass and I enjoyed her company, but I was not in love with her. She, however, was greatly in love with me and like any man, I was fed by flattery at that age. She loved me and I let her. After two weeks of a torrid romance, she wanted to marry me so I approached her father and asked for her hand because I felt it was the right thing to do. I'd just spent two weeks in the woman's bed and I felt as if I'd sullied her for the man she would eventually marry. So, I did what I felt was right and asked for her hand and for no other reason than that, but her father denied me. It seemed that he didn't want a simple knight for his daughter. I did not know she was with child or I would have…"

He stopped himself, unwilling to continue the subject to the logical conclusion because it was too painful and shameful for him to do so. To think of a life without Jordan was no life at all for him.

But Jordan knew. She knew exactly what he was going to say.

"If ye'd known, ye would have demanded a marriage," she finished quietly. "'Tis the noble thing to do and ye're a man of honor."

He nodded weakly, lifting his head to look at her in the dim light. "Aye," he murmured. "I would have done the honorable thing."

Jordan gazed into his tormented eye, but she had enough torment of her own. The story of Jane de Percy was something William had never mentioned, not in all the years they'd been married, and the truth was that she was wounded. Wounded by William's lack of transparency. She felt as if he'd kept something from her, something that perhaps didn't matter at the time but now mattered a great deal.

William's bastard was on their doorstep.

With a sigh, she looked away and gazed out of the window again.

"I canna fault ye a love affair before ye knew me," she said after a moment. "But ye should have told me that ye'd come close tae marriage with another woman. I think it only fair."

He grunted and hung his head. "Would it matter if I had?" he asked. "Would it have changed how you felt about me?"

Jordan shook her head. "Nay," she said. "But at least I would have known that there was once someone else important tae ye. That ye were capable of giving yerself over tae another. In all the years we've been married, ye've made me feel like I was the one and only woman ye've ever given yerself tae. As if ye had no other affairs before me. Ye built a world of illusions around me, English. I dunna know why ye'd do that."

"Because I love you."

Jordan sighed faintly. "Mayhap ye love the illusion of me," she said softly. "Ye've built me up like the Virgin Mary. Ye've made yerself out tae be the congregation that worships me and only me. But that's not true."

"Christ, Jordan, it *is* true."

She didn't respond. He sat there and looked at her, wondering just how much this was going to affect them. Perhaps he had been wrong in not telling her about Jane de Percy because he'd indeed come close to marriage with her and, truth be told, they'd had quite a passionate affair while it lasted. But he really didn't think it mattered and saw no reason to tell her about something that had never mattered to him.

But it evidently mattered to her.

"Jordan," he said, his voice strained with emotion. "Mayhap I really did try to create an illusion around you, an illusion that you were the only woman I had ever looked at, but we both know that wasn't truth. But you *are* the only woman I have ever loved and I will swear that until the day I die. You are my sun, my moon, and the universe around me and nothing is right in this world if you are not in it with me. I am sorry if I hurt you by not telling you about Jane, but it never occurred to me that it mattered to do so. Forgive me if it did matter. I am deeply sorry that you had to find out this way because, surely, it was not the right way for you to know. If I could have spared you, I would have. But you must know I would never, ever intentionally lie to you or hurt you. Surely you *know*."

"I know," she murmured. "I do know that, English."

"Then can you find it in your heart to forgive me?"

She continued to gaze from the window until, very slowly, she turned to look at him. The man was desperate. Repentant and desperate. She could see that in his eye, so terrified that he had ruined something he'd had for so many years, something that was his rock and his anchor. Their love had been the one constant in his life for the past twenty-five years and he'd been grateful for it every day.

But she'd been right and he knew it. He'd made her think that she was the only woman he'd ever held in such regard, the only one he'd ever had a truly passionate affair with. Perhaps that was his way of making her feel special and loved, building her up to be the only true woman in the world for him. But she was coming to see that he had built an illusion around her to make her think that and it hadn't been right. She'd found out the hard way that he hadn't been as transparent with her as he could have been.

But Jordan knew, in the long run, it really didn't matter.

He was still her English.

"In about an hour I will," she said, a hint of mirth in her exhausted face. "Give me an hour and I'll forgive ye. But for now… I just want tae be alone."

The relief William felt was indescribable. He went to his

knees next to the bench, reaching out to take her hand as he placed his big head in her lap.

"I love you more than the sun loves the day," he whispered, his lips against her fingers. "More than the moon loves the night. If I could take your hurt away, I surely would, but know that nothing was ever intentional, Jordan. If I withheld something you think I should have told you, forgive me, love… I simply never thought a silly affair was important compared to the glory of you."

He could feel her free hand in his hair. "God's Bones, English, I canna stay angry with ye when ye put it like that," she said. "And I'm truly not angry. Mayhap a little sad tae think a lass loved ye so much before I did."

He kissed her hand. "She may have loved me, but I loved you," he said. "There is no comparison."

"Swear it?"

"God, yes."

She stroked his hair. "I dinna think I could feel jealousy at my age," she said. Then she chuckled softly. "Mayhap that's all it was. A little jealousy. But I better not hear anything more of bastards about with the de Wolfe name or ye and I are going tae have a serious go-round."

He started to laugh. "I swear to you, none that I know of," he said. "I did not live a chaste life before you, but I lived a careful one."

"Evidently not too careful."

He lifted his head and looked at her. "Sadly true," he said. He kissed her hand again and his smile faded. "But facing this now… the fact that the letter was in War's saddlebags means that he knows he is my son. If he finds the letter missing, he might assume I have it. Or someone stole it and is going to blackmail him. I realize that it is a great deal to ask, but your counsel would be appreciated in the matter, my lady. What do I do?"

Jordan gazed down at her handsome husband, her hand still in his hair. "I am concerned as tae why he had that letter in his bags," she said thoughtfully. "Did he bring it tae give it tae ye? Or has he been carrying it around, building up some sort of rage against ye?'

William pondered that. "Why would he be angry at me?" he said. "I knew nothing about him or about Jane's condition. She never told me anything."

Jordan shrugged. "It may not matter tae him," she said. "If he knew he was yer son, why not come tae ye before now? Why did I have tae find that letter in his bags? He should have told ye when he first arrived."

William lifted his eyebrows. "I am not entirely certain that is something you tell someone you've only just met," he said. "Mayhap he is waiting until the right moment."

"Or mayhap he has come tae harm ye somehow."

William shook his head. "He cannot harm me," he said. "I've never gotten that feeling from him. I'm a fairly good judge of men's characters, Jordan. In my profession, I have to be. I've never felt hostility from him, not ever."

Jordan wasn't going to push the subject, but she couldn't help feeling suspicious of War and his motives. "Then if ye want tae know what tae do, I think that ye must tell him that I found the letter," she said. "If he is looking for the right time, the time would be now. Ye must make it the right time. But tell him *how* I found the letter– that it was by accident. I dunna want the man tae think we were spying on him."

He nodded faintly. "But… what should I say to him?" he

asked. "Do I acknowledge him as my son? He stands to inherit nothing from me; that belongs to Scott and Troy. War has no right to anything, so what do I say to him? What does he expect from me?"

Jordan stroked his hair. "Ask him," she said softly. "Ask him what he wants. Mayhap he only wants tae know that ye know about him and nothing more. Mayhap he only wants tae be yer acquaintance."

"That is all it can ever be, Jordan," he said. "I may acknowledge him, but I will not accept him as my son. I will not do that to the sons I already have."

"And I would hope he would not expect ye tae," Jordan said. "But I'm still concerned that he had that letter in his bags and dinna tell ye about it. Clearly, he knows who ye are. And ye know who he is. Ye must address that so there is no confusion and ye must make sure there are no hard feelings. The man is in command of Bamburgh and is tae be yer ally. Ye dunna want it tae be a relationship fraught with tension."

No, William didn't want that. He went from kneeling in front of Jordan to sitting against her, his back against her legs, his hand still holding hers.

"What about Scott and Troy and the rest of my sons?" he asked, sounding bewildered. "Do I tell them? Do I not? I do not know what to say to them."

Jordan could hear his confusion, his sadness. He didn't want to hurt their sons by telling them that there was a half-brother out there. She gave his hand a squeeze.

"Talk tae War before ye do anything else," she said. "Find out what he wants. Find out how he feels. That will give ye the direction ye need."

She was right. William kissed her hand again, glad they'd

worked out the problem between them but feeling apprehensive at the situation he was facing with War.

There was nothing he could do but get on with it.

"He's in Coldstream until the morning," he said. "I'll address him when he returns."

With that, he stood up wearily, feeling as if he'd aged a hundred years in just a few short minutes. He felt old and weary and sad.

Sad for the son he never knew.

"Where are ye going?" Jordan murmured.

He raked his fingers through his hair. "Down to the hall to see to the wounded," he said. "Will you come with me?"

Jordan stood up from the bench. "Aye," she said. "We'll go together. But once ye've seen tae yer men, I want ye tae come back tae bed with me. Jemma and Annaleigh can tend tae the wounded tonight."

He lifted an eyebrow at her. "Come back to bed with you?" he repeated. "I go to bed with you every night."

She gave him a coy look. "That's not what I meant."

He was trying not to chuckle. "The last time you said that to me, we had Penny."

She fought off a grin. "I've said that tae ye many a time and we've not had a child every time," she said. But her smile faded as she looked up at him. "Tonight, I just want ye tae hold me."

It was a sweet request, one that William was more than willing to honor. With a smile on his lips, he took her hand again, kissed it, and led her from the chamber.

For William and Jordan, tonight belonged to them.

CHAPTER SIXTEEN

TALUS WAS DEMANDING far too much of her attention.

It was true that the man had a nasty, and large, gash on his left leg, one that the physic had to pick mail out of, but Talus was convinced it was the end of his world as he knew it. At least, for Annaleigh he did. The moment the returning army entered the confines of Castle Questing and Talus had been helped into the great hall where Jordan and Jemma had set up a corner to treat the wounded, he asked for Annaleigh and she'd been forced to attend him.

That's where she found herself now.

Truthfully, it was a terrible gash and it had been painful to have it cleaned out and finally stitched, but Talus was determined to milk Annaleigh's sympathy for all it was worth. He groaned and made faces, asking her to hold his hand as the physic dug into his leg, and she'd begrudgingly complied. She wouldn't have done it at all except for the fact that she'd been told that War and his men were still in Coldstream, so there was no immediate chance of War seeing her hold Talus' hand. But the moment the physic was finished stitching, she pulled her hand from his sweaty grip. He'd tried to reclaim it, but she'd moved far enough away that he couldn't.

Talus groaned and grunted as Annaleigh calmly told him that there were other wounded men that needed her attention. He didn't argue with her but it was clear he hoped that all of his moaning might convince her that he needed her most of all. But she was immune to it, helping the physic collect his things as they moved on to the next badly wounded man, who had been gored in the leg.

Eventually, Talus fell into a fitful sleep, bringing relief to Annaleigh. Until he passed out from sheer exhaustion, she could hear his grunts and sighs all across the hall. Anthony even came in at one point to see to the wounded and showed genuine concern for Talus. He and Talus may have been love rivals, but there was still a bond between them, as most knights who served together had. Annaleigh assured Anthony that Talus would recover and he seemed relieved.

But then he began to follow her around the hall.

Under the guise of being concerned for the wounded, Anthony stuck to Annaleigh as she moved from man to man and she couldn't shake him. While she was bandaging arms and legs and hands, he was holding the limbs steady for her. She didn't need him, but he seemed to want to be helpful. Still, Annaleigh knew it was more than that. He kept brushing a hand against hers or smiling at her when she looked at him. That went on for quite some time until Kieran, exhausted from having been up all night and on the wall because no one knew where Anthony had gone, entered the hall and chastised the knight in front of Annaleigh for leaving his post.

Humiliated, Anthony fled back to the battlements.

Kieran was usually such a cool and collected man that Annaleigh had been surprised that he'd been nasty with Anthony.

He even threatened the knight with something called the Helm of Shame, which Annaleigh had never heard of but sounded awful. It was enough to send Anthony fleeing from the hall. Annaleigh hoped she would never be threatened with such a thing.

The night eventually passed into morning.

Annaleigh was sitting next to a man who had been gored in the abdomen because the physic felt he was the most seriously wounded when she heard the faint cry of the sentries on the wall. The morning's light was barely peeking over the eastern horizon as she wearily stood up from her post, making her way to the entry to the great hall, gazing out over the cold and purple bailey and listening to the soldiers on the walls.

Men had been sighted and that's all she knew. She hoped it was War returning but she wasn't certain until the gates opened and knights came pouring in, including a massive warrior astride a black and white stallion. Annaleigh was fairly certain it was War simply by the size of the man but she couldn't be sure. She stood there and watched until the knight dismounted and then she was certain he'd returned home.

And he was uninjured.

She murmured a brief prayer of thanks and returned to her wounded man.

But she wasn't alone for long.

Knights entered the great hall, clamoring for food and drink and sending the sleepy servants running. Annaleigh looked up from her gravely wounded patient to see War crossing the floor in her direction.

And he was looking at her.

She smiled wearily at the man and he smiled in return, but the closer he drew, the more she could see that he was spattered in gore. Blood had dried on his tunic and mail, hands, and seemingly everything else, and she stood up, looking at him in horror.

"God's Bones, man," she said, pointing to the mess. "Is any of this blood yers?"

He was still smiling wearily. "Nay," he said. "I am quite well. Have you been up all night?"

Annaleigh was relieved to hear he was in one piece, uninjured and unpunctured. She nodded to his question. "Aye," she said. "There are many wounded. This man took a blade tae the belly. The physic isna sure he'll survive."

War looked at the man, an old soldier who was pasty in pallor, but his attention quickly returned to Annaleigh.

"You are brave and compassionate to tend the wounded, my lady," he said softly. "But do you think you could spend a few moments away from them?"

She cocked her head. "What do ye mean?"

"So you can sit with me while I eat something."

There was something warm and promising in that sweet invitation and a smile spread across her lips.

"Of course," she murmured. "I can spare a few moments."

With a grin, War turned around, back towards the feasting tables where food was being delivered, and Annaleigh followed behind him. She hadn't taken five or six steps, however, when she heard her name being called weakly. Pausing, she turned to see Talus over near the wall, lifting a hand to her. He was summoning her.

Frustrated that her plans with War were being delayed, she came to a halt with War beside her.

"He took a bad cut tae his leg," Annaleigh said. "Let me see tae him. I'll join ye in a moment."

War cocked an eyebrow, immediately suspicious of Talus' motives. "I'll come with you," he said.

War followed her over to Talus, who immediately grasped Annaleigh's sleeve when she came near.

"My lady," he said hoarsely. "May I have some water?"

He seemed terribly pale. Unusually so. Frustration turning to concern, Annaleigh put a hand on his forehead and emitted a hiss.

"He's burning with fever," she said, suddenly filled with a sense of urgency. "War, will ye find the physic and send him tae me? Quickly, please."

War didn't seem so annoyed, either, as he realized something was seriously wrong with Talus. He quickly set off to find the old physic that had been tending men, women, and children at Castle Questing for several years. As he rushed away, Annaleigh called to the nearest servant for water and rags.

She had to get the man's fever down.

"When did ye start feeling so poorly, Talus?" she asked, pulling the covers off him. He was dressed in a sweat-stained tunic and linen breeches that had been torn to shreds because of his thigh wound. "I was sitting on the other side of the hearth and ye slept soundly all night. I could see ye."

Talus sighed heavily, closing his eyes as Annaleigh began to remove his tunic. "I do not know," he said weakly. "I dreamed of fire. When I awoke, my eyeballs felt as if they were ablaze, yet I am both hot and cold."

Annaleigh managed to get the tunic off of him. "'Tis the fever making ye feel like that," she said as the servant brought over a bucket of water and the requested rags. "We must cool ye down."

With that, she dunked the rags into the cold water, wrung

them out, and began bathing Talus' head and neck. The servant also took a rag and began to do the same thing with the man's arms and chest. They were hard at work when the physic appeared, a man by the name of Collingwood.

Oddly enough, Collingwood was a sickly man himself. He had a disease of the lungs and, sometimes, he could hardly breathe, but he was an excellent physic and William had learned to trust him. More than likely, he wasn't going to live much longer, but that didn't stop him from working very hard when there was the need for a physic. William kept him on because the man had nowhere else to go, but also because he needed a physic for a castle this size.

Even if the physic was a patient himself.

"The poison is in his veins," Collingwood said after a quick assessment of Talus' fever and the color of his eyeballs. "You are doing the right thing, Annie. Cool him down. I must fetch the rotten brew I've been steeping since last eve."

Annaleigh looked at him queerly. "*Rotten* brew?"

Collingwood nodded. "It is made from rotten bread, but only bread that has turned blue," he said. "I've no time to explain. Keep doing what you are doing and I will return shortly."

Annaleigh nodded quickly and the man fled.

Talus was quickly sliding in and out of consciousness. Sweat had formed on his upper lip and forehead. Annaleigh and the servant bathed him steadily, but whatever poison had him in its grip was working swiftly and savagely. As Annaleigh worked over him, trying to bring his fever down, she could see War's shadow over to her right. She paused a moment to look at him.

"I am sorry I canna join ye for yer meal," she said softly. "But he needs help. I hope ye understand."

War did something then that surprised Annaleigh. He moved forward and began taking off Talus' boots, which were still on.

"The man needs a tepid bath," he said. "That is the only way to reduce the fever quickly. Do you have a private room where you can take him?"

Annaleigh nodded. "The corridor where yer chamber is, I suppose," she said. "There are other chambers there, but…"

"Then we take him to my chamber," War said. "Wait here."

He was off again, his enormous bulk moving through the wounded and out into the hall. Annaleigh watched him for a few moments, but he was heading off somewhere so she returned her attention to Talus. The servant had moved to the man's feet to soak them in cold water while Annaleigh put a cold cloth behind his neck, letting it sit until his body heat started to warm it up.

It was warming up quite quickly.

They continued bathing Talus' arms, neck, and feet with cold water. The physic finally returned with a cup of something that smelled awful. Annaleigh was a few feet away from him and even she could smell the rancid scent. But the physic went straight to Talus, trying to rouse the man.

"My lord?" he said, shaking him. But Talus was difficult to rouse, so the physic put his hand behind the man's neck and tried to lift his head. "My lord, you must drink this."

Annaleigh moved to help him. She held Talus' head up, as much as she could, while the physic tried to force that terrible-smelling potion down his throat. Talus sputtered and coughed as he drank it, but he managed to ingest a good deal. That seemed to satisfy the physic. He set the cup down and put his hand to Talus' forehead.

"He must drink that brew every few hours," he said. "I've been steeping it since last night, knowing we would be having wounded, but it is not yet at full strength. Still, I could not wait for it. Sir Talus needs it now."

The physic wiped Talus' mouth and neck where the brew dripped down as Annaleigh picked up the cup that had contained the concoction, sniffing it and feeling her eyes water at the mere scent.

"God's Bones," she muttered. "'Tis a strong brew."

"It is meant to cure."

Annaleigh thought that might be debatable given the pungent smell but she didn't question him. She simply nodded, set the cup down, and resumed bathing Talus' face and arms with the cold water. The physic, unable to do anything more for him than he'd already done, picked up the coverlet on the floor, the one that had been tossed off by Annaleigh when she realized Talus was running a fever. He was in the process of putting it on Talus' legs when War entered the great hall again.

He made his way over to Annaleigh, but he was focused on the physic.

"I have prepared my chamber for this man," he said, yanking the coverlet off of Talus' legs. "I am having the servants fill a tub with cool water."

The physic nodded. The enormous knight was taking charge of the situation, which was interesting considering the knights should be busy with settling the army. But this man was a visitor, a stranger to Castle Questing, yet he was showing genuine concern for a fellow knight.

An interesting situation, to be sure.

"That was to be my next request to Lady de Wolfe," the physic said. "Although he needs to sleep, if we can find him a tub and a bed somewhere out of this hall, it would be best for him."

War gently pulled Annaleigh aside as he reached down to pick up Talus. "I will take him," he said, pulling Talus into a sitting position. "Come along, lad."

With that, he bent over and lifted Talus onto his broad shoulders. Given the fact that Talus wasn't a small man by any means, it was an impressive feat of strength. Annaleigh quickly ordered the bucket and rags to be gathered, following War out of the hall and into the keep as he carried limp Talus. By the time they reached his borrowed chamber, the copper tub that the servants had dragged in was about half-full of lukewarm water, by War's orders.

War dumped Talus into the tub.

He stood back after that, watching Annaleigh and the physic and the servant fuss over Talus as the man lay virtually unconscious. He was so limp that War ended up holding him up by the head as the others bathed him in the tepid water, but the truth was that War was only doing all of this to be close to Annaleigh. It wasn't as if he had any great devotion to Talus, but Annaleigh was doing what she did best – helping and healing – and he simply wanted to be near her.

That was the sole reason he'd done what he did.

He couldn't break his fast with her, nor could he speak to her, really. At least, not a private conversation. She was trying to save a man's life, a man who had designs on her no less but, at the moment, that didn't bother War. Tending Talus was the right thing to do and as he watched her work, he remembered the woman who had tended his wounds after the battle at Etal. The woman who, despite being Scots, was determined to do the right thing and help a man in need.

She was still determined to do the right thing.

Her bravery and sense of compassion impressed him. It had since the beginning of their association, only now there was something more to it. There was pride – he was *proud* of her, proud of her good character – and there was admiration. *Great* admiration. Every moment that he spent with her deepened his appreciation for her and her genuine desire to help and to heal.

She was a rare woman, indeed.

The tending of Talus du Reims went well into the morning. He was unconscious for quite some time before they finally pulled him from the old tub, with War's help, and put him on War's borrowed bed to be vigorously dried off. But he remained in his damp linen breeches while his thigh swelled with poison. The wound itself was red and full of poison, straining against the stitches with the swelling.

But Annaleigh and the physic worked on.

As the early afternoon came, there wasn't much to do with Talus any longer other than wait. They'd tried to give him more of the rotten brew, but he was hardly able to take any because of his unconscious state. They'd pour it in his mouth and he'd choke on it, so they finally stopped trying.

And the waiting began.

At some point, the physic had sent for William, who had been in his chamber with his wife all morning, sleeping after a busy night. But he appeared in the borrowed chamber in the unmarried men's wing, standing in the doorway and realizing that Talus' gash had been far more serious than they'd all thought.

The physic told William that he thought the blade that had cut into Talus had been poisoned, as The Bones had been known to rub poison on their weapons so when they cut into a man's flesh, the poison entered the body and death was more of a potential. William had run into The Bones many times and he'd heard of poison on their blades, but he'd been fortunate to never have actually seen that rumor in action.

Regretfully, their luck had run out. He was seeing it now.

The death watch for Talus du Reims had begun.

News of his impending demise was spreading. Kieran showed up to the vigil, weary from being up all night, saddened by the approaching loss of a fine knight. Christian also came, as did Anthony, who was greatly distressed to see his love rival as well as his friend in such a state. The knights began to gather and as word filtered through the castle, others were showing up to the entry to the keep, soldiers who weren't allowed inside, but they were gathering to show respect for Talus, who was well liked by the men. He was young and fiery, with a sense of humor but a sense of discipline, so he had few enemies.

The mood settling over Castle Questing was a somber one.

Annaleigh hadn't left Talus' side. Perhaps there was some guilt there, as he'd tried so hard to woo her but she'd never given in, so she felt sorry for the young knight who'd been unable to gain the wife he so badly wanted. She sat next to his head, putting cold cloths on it. Sometime mid-afternoon, she went to replace the cloth and his eyes were open.

Talus was staring at the ceiling, his eyes dark against his ashen pallor. Annaleigh leaned over him slightly, to see if he would notice her, and slowly his eyes began to track her.

He smiled.

She smiled.

"My lady," he said weakly. "I… I had a dream."

"Ye did?" she said, trying to show the man some interest in death as she never had in life. "What did ye dream about?"

"Home," he said simply. "I saw my home and the bay it presides over. I saw my mother but she did not see me. I tried to speak to her but she walked away."

Annaleigh replaced the cloth on his head with a cool one. "'Tis only a dream," she said. "Dreams can be strange."

He was watching her, every move she made, in an odd sort of trance. As if nothing else in the world existed around them.

"My mother is waiting for me," he said. "Soon, I will go to her."

Annaleigh forced a smile. "Home?" she said. "I am sure Lord Kilham will send ye home if ye wish. Mayhap ye can recover there, in yer home by the bay. Would ye like that?"

The bright light in Talus' eyes faded. "Nay," he muttered. "Not that home. My mother is dead. She waits for me in the heavenly halls."

It was difficult for Annaleigh to maintain her smile. "Mayhap she does, but ye shallna meet her today," she said, trying to think of things to say. "In fact, Anthony wants tae go tae Wooler. I hear they have a festival there this time of year. We'll all go and eat decadent things, like currant cake and pear tarts and custard. When ye're strong enough, we'll go."

Talus closed his eyes and sighed deeply. "If I take you to Wooler, it will be without Anthony," he said. He paused a moment. "My lady… will you hold my hand?"

Annaleigh didn't hesitate. She didn't even look at War, perhaps to not see his reaction, perhaps to silently convey it meant nothing. She simply took Talus' hand and held it tightly.

"There," she said. "Better?"

He grunted softly. "Much," he said. "I do not want to die alone."

He meant it. Tears stung Annaleigh's eyes as she looked up

at the physic, who was standing on the other side of Talus. The man simply shook his head faintly. *No hope.* Realizing that, Annaleigh swallowed hard, swallowing away the emotion she felt for the life of a friend cut short. Annoying or not, Talus had always been kind to her. She did indeed consider him a friend.

"Ye willna," she said after a moment. "I'll not leave ye."

"That gives me comfort," Talus murmured. "My lady… Annie… I know you told me that you were not in need of a husband, but I must confess something."

"What?"

"I was determined to convince you otherwise."

A smile tugged at Annaleigh's lips. She'd known that from the beginning, when he'd tried to woo her and she would knock him back, and then he'd simply overlook the fact that she wasn't interested in him and try again. That had been their game. But this was the first time that he had admitted it.

"Is that so?" she said, pretending he hadn't been so obvious about it. "We're still friends, Talus. We will always be friends."

He sighed again, heavily, but didn't reply. Collingwood bent over him, putting a hand to his forehead, his cheek, before pulling the hand away. The expression on his face told Annaleigh that nothing had changed with Talus' fever. He'd been running a high fever for several hours, at least, more than likely while he was sleeping during the night. Annaleigh and the physic and even Jemma, who had also been in the hall, had been tending other wounded as Talus had slept peacefully, so they hadn't noticed his temperature rising.

There was really no telling how long he'd been with fever.

Sometimes, fevers could last for days or even a week or two, depending on the severity, but high fevers could be deadly. They would break down the body quickly as the poison infected the lungs and heart and other things needed to survive. Soon, the body would begin shutting down because of too much poison and too high a fever. Everyone in that small chamber had seen something like that happen, now unexpectedly with Talus.

Life was a fragile thing, indeed.

"Annie," Talus said, his eyes rolling open. "Will you do something for me?"

"If I can."

He was fixed on her. "I know that you do not love me," he said. "I know that you do not care for me in a romantic sense, but I want to give something to you."

Annaleigh didn't like the sound of that. "Ye needna give me anything, Talus," she assured him. "Friends dunna expect gifts from one another."

"Please," he said, begging her. "I wish to do this. Please… will you listen?"

She didn't want to, but she reluctantly agreed. "Speak, then."

He swallowed hard, but as he held Annaleigh's hand, she could feel him tremble. His sweaty hands were beginning to quiver. In fact, his entire body was beginning to shake.

"My father, Tobin, is the Earl of East Anglia," he said. "I have an older brother, Tevin, who is Viscount Winterton. He will inherit the title and the property, but I hold the title Lord Rivenhall. My father gave it to me, a landed title, so that I would have some income. Rivenhall has two villages that I collect taxes from. I have some wealth of my own."

His trembling was growing worse and Annaleigh patted his hand. "That's very nice, Talus," she said. "I dinna know that."

He lifted his head, looking at her intently. "I want to give it to you."

She was confused. "Give me what?" she said. "Ye canna give me yer title."

He shook his head. "You misunderstand," he said. "I *can* give you my title. As Lady Rivenhall, the income would become yours when I am gone."

Annaleigh's eyes widened. "Talus, I canna…"

He cut her off. "Please, Annie," he pleaded. "Please, marry me. Let me die a contented man, even if you do not love me. I've never loved anyone but you and I want to give this to you, as I'd always hoped to."

Annaleigh was horrified but she refrained from telling him so. He was still holding her hand, gazing up at her beseechingly, and she felt pressured. Cornered and pressured. She simply couldn't lie to the man or take something that she wasn't entitled to just because he was dying. It occurred to her that War was listening, as she knew he was standing behind her, somewhere, but she didn't take his opinion or even their blossoming relationship into consideration.

The conversation, at the moment, was purely between her and Talus.

"Talus," she said, squeezing his hand. "I dunna need or want yer lands or title. 'Tis something ye must give tae the woman ye choose tae marry, and the woman who chooses ye. That is something special, only for her."

He was disagreeing with her even as she finished. "There will not be another," he said. "My body is wracked with fever. I know that I will not survive the night. Please, Annie… please, marry me. Let me do this for you. Let me die a happy man."

Annaleigh didn't want to do it, not even for a dying man. "I canna," she said, pulling her hand from his grip. "I'm sorry,

Talus, but I canna. It would be a lie. I would be taking something from ye that doesna belong tae me."

"But…"

"Nay," she said firmly. "Dunna ask me again. It wouldna be right. A woman who would take advantage of a sickly man is a woman of great dishonor. Ye canna ask me tae be dishonorable, knowing that ye willna… that I willna… nay, I willna do it. I'm sorry."

He just looked at her, disappointment etched on his face. He dropped his hand without trying to reclaim hers, closing his eyes and turning his face away. Unable to look at him any longer, Annaleigh stood up and turned around only to see that the entire chamber had heard the exchange. Humiliated, she quickly pushed through the group, fleeing the chamber.

Tears filled her eyes as she entered the foyer of Castle Questing and she wiped at them furiously. The more she wiped, the more they fell. She was walking, though she didn't know where. She was simply walking, anything to get away from that horrible and emotional scene in War's borrowed chamber. But the mural stairs that led to the upper chambers were off to her right and she spied them. Like a moth to a flame, she went straight to them and raced up the stairs, up to her chamber high above in Castle Questing's towering keep. She'd just made it to the third floor when she heard a sound behind her.

War was right on her heels.

"God's Bones," she said, nearly tripping on the top step. "Ye startled me."

He smiled faintly. "I did not mean to," he said. "You ran off and I wanted to make sure you were well. What du Reims asked of you in there… he should not have done that, but I understand why he did it."

Annaleigh sniffed, wiping at her eyes. "Do ye?" she said. "Because I dunna. I dunna know how he could expect me tae be so… so shallow. I would marry a dying man simply tae take his money? How can he ask me such a thing?"

"It's more than that," War said quietly. "He wants some part of him to continue. His legacy, as it were. As his wife, you would represent him even though he's gone."

"I will *not* marry him."

War could see that she was standing on principle. She felt very strongly that to grant Talus' request would be taking advantage of him and he had to admire a woman who wasn't greedy or petty. One more thing yet to admire about her.

"Where were you going?" he asked.

She turned and gestured to her chamber. "There," she said. "I need tae… think. Tae breathe."

He came up the stairs and put his hands on her shoulders, turning her for the door. "You need to rest for a few moments," he said. "You've been taking care of wounded all night and you are exhausted. Go into your chamber and rest a while."

She let him push her to the door. It was unlatched, as it always was, and she pushed it open. A young lady's boudoir was revealed beyond. Annaleigh wandered in and sat heavily on the chair near the bed, bending over to remove her shoes, but War stood in the doorway. For propriety's sake, he would go no further. In fact, he was pushing the boundaries as it was by being where he wasn't supposed to be.

"I will return for you in a while," he said. "Sleep if you can."

"Wait," Annaleigh said, shoe in-hand. "Where are ye going?"

He paused, smiling faintly. "Back down where I belong," he said. "If Lady de Wolfe catches me up here, she might take a stick to me."

Annaleigh nodded, though it was with regret. "Possibly," she said. "But I would like for ye tae stay. Ye dunna have tae go further than the doorway, but I would like for ye tae stay. Just for a few moments."

His smile grew. "If I stay, you will not rest," he said. "We will chatter like two magpies."

"I like magpies," she said, grinning. "Ye're preparing tae leave Castle Questing, War. Would ye really relinquish a moment of time like this tae something as mundane as sleep?"

Immediately, he shook his head. "Nay," he said flatly. "But I also do not want to be selfish and inconsiderate. You have been tending wounded all night."

"And ye have been up all night, too, I'd wager."

He conceded the point. "I have."

She put her shoe onto the ground by the bed and went to remove the other one. "Was the battle at Coldstream terrible?"

He shrugged, leaning against the door jamb and crossing his big arms. "Any battle is terrible," he said. "You would know that."

He was referring back to the first time they'd met. "It is never a pleasant thing," she said. "Tell me something. Did ye ever tell anyone that I tended ye back at Etal?"

He shook his head. "Nay," he said. "I simply told my men that it was an angel of mercy. I'm not sure how they would have taken it knowing a Scots, the very people we were fighting, had tended me."

"And I never told anyone for the same reason," she said. "It was bad enough that my kin believed I caused the battle. Had they known I'd tended an English knight, they would have run me through."

He couldn't tell if she was jesting or not. "That seems a little extreme," he said. "They wouldn't have really done that, would they?"

Her warm expression faded. "I would never have believed it before," she said. "But since the battle at Etal, things have… changed."

"How?"

She shrugged, setting her other shoe on the ground. "I told ye that they blamed me for everything," she said quietly. "People who I thought were my friends began shunning me. Men who had been loyal tae my father for years began tae speak of him as if he were no longer the chieftain they trusted. And my father's younger brother's sons began tae speak ill of him, trying tae turn men against him."

War was looking at her seriously. "Did those men try to usurp him?"

"Nay," she said. "Just talk. But bad talk."

"And he sent you here because of it?"

"Aye."

"Does de Wolfe know this?"

She nodded. "Aye," she said. "I told him. He told my father that he would support him in the case of an uprising, but it has been quiet since I left. My father is a good man – I am sure he has been able to overcome those who have mistrusted him."

War wasn't so sure, but he didn't say so. Rebellious factions within clans weren't usually easily pacified because it had more to do with simply one factor, in this case, a clan chief's daughter starting a war. More than likely, whatever movement against her father probably had to do with power or greed or envy.

It could be anything.

All War knew was that she was never going back.

"Let us hope wisdom and reason prevail," he said after a moment. "But you've been happy at Castle Questing?"

"Very happy."

His gaze lingered on her, clearly with something on his mind. "You'll be happier at Bamburgh," he said. "Your time at Castle Questing is only temporary, my lady. When I go on this tour with de Wolfe, I will ask him if I may court you."

"Are ye going tae wait that long?"

He could hear the hope in her voice and it gave him joy because it reflected the hope in his heart, too.

"Mayhap not," he said. "Mayhap I'll ask him tonight, before we depart on our tour. I suppose I do not want to wait that long, either."

Her cheeks flushed a sweet shade of red and that lightened his heart all the more. He still could hardly believe this glorious creature was interested in him. More than interested – *accepting*. Warm, open, and curious. Everything about her connected with him on so many levels. He was coming to think that meeting in the thicket near the river hadn't been coincidence – it had been fate. He was meant to be with her and she with him.

He couldn't wait to start the rest of their lives, together.

"But after ye ask him and after yer tour with the allies, ye must return?" she asked, interrupting his reflections. "For how long?"

"Not long, I hope," he said. "It is true that I must return to Bamburgh for a time once we are finished, but I swear that I will return as soon as I can to Castle Questing. And you."

Annaleigh couldn't help the smile on her lips. "It's strange," she mused softly. "When I first saw ye as ye came tae Castle Questing, I will admit that I was surprised."

"Why?"

"Because I dinna think ye'd survived yer wound," she said. "I tried tae help ye in that terrible hour, but I dinna know if I actually did. So it was surprising tae see ye looking so well. More than well, War. Ye looked glorious as ye rode in through the gates."

He gave her a half-grin and bowed his head graciously. "You have my thanks, my lady," he said. "I am deeply flattered."

"What did ye think when ye saw me?"

"That you were the most beautiful thing I'd ever seen."

She blushed sweetly. "'Tis kind of ye."

"It is the truth," he said. "But I also felt an attraction. I am not a man who becomes attracted to a woman in an instant, but with you, I did. I thought you were lovely the first time I ever saw you."

She snorted. "I wouldna have known," she said. "I believe ye said 'if ye've come tae rob me, I shan't give ye much of a fight'."

He broke down into soft laughter. "You remembered that, did you?"

"Of course I did."

"Then you have an amazing memory."

She shrugged modestly. "I've always been able to remember the smallest thing," she said. "That's why ye must be careful what ye say tae me. I *will* remember."

He rolled his eyes, but there was humor there. "God help me," he said. "Thank you for the warning."

She could tell that he was jesting so she giggled. "Are ye going tae say something tae me that ye'll regret, then?"

His eyes glimmered warmly at her. "Never," he said softly. "Everything I say to you, I mean it from the heart. Every word of it."

Annaleigh could feel the sincerity from the man. The warmth, the genuine interest and concern from him… everything was washing over her, causing her heart to race. It was true that she was weary, wearier still after the situation with Talus, but she couldn't sleep. She didn't want to. She could have talked to War forever.

She was thrilled that she was going to have that chance.

"I believe ye," she said softly. "But it has occurred tae me that ye've not slept all night, either. Ye came intae the hall tae eat and ye were pulled away from that tae help Talus. It was quite compassionate of ye tae do it, but I'd expect no less from ye. Ye're a man of honor."

A smile of appreciation tugged at his lips. "I would like to think so when the situation warrants it."

"Ye must go eat something now."

"Very well. I'll go eat something if you rest."

"Are ye making a bargain with me?"

"I'm trying to."

She chuckled. She knew the man must have been terribly weary, but here he stood, speaking to her as if he had nowhere better to be. For his sake, she knew she should let him go about his business and for her sake, perhaps she *did* need a few minutes of rest before returning to Talus.

That was the reality of things.

"Well," she said, standing up with her shoeless feet against the cold floor. "I'll agree tae it. But only for a few minutes. I must return tae Talus and apologize for running away and becoming angry with him. I suppose ye must understand how the man has tried tae woo me ever since I arrived and, at times, I've even hidden from him just tae avoid him. But mayhap he was truly trying tae do something nice for me. Or mayhap he's still trying tae woo me."

She was moving towards him and War couldn't take his eyes off her. "That is a determined man if he is still trying to woo you from his sick bed," he said. "But mayhap it wasn't that at all. Mayhap he really did mean to leave you with his legacy. That may be how he looks at it."

Annaleigh sighed faintly. "I suppose," she said. She'd come to within a foot or so of him, gazing up into his handsome face. He was more than a foot taller than she was, by far, so she had to crane her neck back. "If the man truly is dying, then I shouldna have run out on him."

"Do you think he is?"

She cocked her head thoughtfully. "I've seen many a man succumb tae a swift and terrible fever with a wound," she said. "But ye dinna. And I think yer wound was worse."

"It was," he said. "But the reivers were using blades dipped in poison. That's what's killing him."

Annaleigh knew that because she'd heard Kieran and Christian speaking of it when they first started bringing the wounded into the hall. She thought of Talus burning with fever brought on by a terrible poison, feeling increasingly guilty that she'd run from him.

But she would make amends.

"Off with ye, my handsome lad," she said, a weary twinkle in her eyes. "Eat and rest. I will see ye after ye've done both."

War smiled at her. She was too close, too tempting. That beautiful face was upturned to him, the eyes glimmering. He knew he should not touch her in any fashion but he simply could not stop his hand from moving to hers. The moment he touched the soft, warm flesh, he knew he had to taste it. Gazing into Annaleigh's eyes, he brought her hand to his lips and kissed it.

"You will most certainly see me after I've done both," he said softly. "You are going to be seeing me, quite frequently, for some time to come."

Annaleigh's voice was caught in her throat. No one had ever kissed her hand so sweetly. In fact, no man had ever shown her such consideration and gentleness, at least a man whose attention she welcomed. She could feel the fire in her cheeks spreading to her belly and her entire body began to tremble.

This was all so new and wonderful and exhilarating.

She wanted to take her hand away. She didn't want to take her hand away. War had been correct; if Jordan saw them, she would probably take a club to him. But his lips were still on her flesh and she could feel the stubble of his face. She could feel his hot breath against her skin. She was so consumed by the sensation that she couldn't manage to move her hand. Awe and fascination were all she could manage to feel.

And War seemed to know it.

He was pleased when she did not pull away. An impulsive gesture on his part had come to mean everything, as if his entire life and future with her hinged on this moment. He didn't know how she would react, but he wouldn't have been surprised if she'd yanked her hand away. It was improper what he'd done.

But she hadn't pulled away.

He could see that she was staring at his mouth and chin, an astonished expression on her face, so he kissed her hand again just to see how she would react.

He heard her sigh raggedly.

"Have you never experienced such a thing, Annie?" he asked softly.

Annaleigh didn't even notice that he called her by her nickname. "Not really," she murmured. "Not from someone that I wanted… that had my attention."

He grinned. "Then I do have your attention?"

"Ye have all of it."

Somehow, he'd pulled her closer and then he was holding both hands. He held them up to his face, her palms on his cheeks, gazing at her as he'd never looked at a woman in his life.

"Tell me again," he whispered.

Annaleigh could hardly breathe. The man's hot, scratchy flesh was against her palms and she found herself fingering his skin. That graduated to stroking his cheeks, acquainting herself with the feel of him.

For Annaleigh and War, the journey had begun.

War felt her caresses and he lost all of his self-control. It was ash, blowing upon the wind, completely vanished. He put his enormous arms around her and pulled her against him, his lips slanting over hers carefully so he wouldn't startle or frighten her. With utter tenderness, his lips claimed her own.

For an instant, Annaleigh was surprised, but that quickly vanished as she collapsed against him. There was nothing in the world but War at that moment, the all-consuming embrace that went beyond delight. Beyond comfort. It was a world where she could lose herself and did quite happily as his lips suckled hers with incredible gentleness. He kissed her mouth, her chin, scratching her face with his stubble. Giddy, warm sensations filled her body, flowing through her veins, and her breath began to come faster and faster.

It was a kiss beyond imagination.

Annaleigh wasn't entirely sure how long they'd been in a heated embrace when they began to hear voices down the stairwell. War's head shot up, his lips red and chaffed, and he quickly released Annaleigh and put his finger to his lips in a silencing gesture, indicating for her to go back into her chamber. He pointed to the bed and she quickly made her way to it as he closed the door. Breathlessly, she climbed into bed and pulled the coverlet up just as she heard voices near the top of the stairwell, louder this time.

It was Jordan as far as she could tell.

Her door swung open.

"Annie?" Jordan said as she scurried into the chamber. "Are ye ill, lass?"

Annaleigh was laying on her side, turned away from the door, and rolled over to face her cousin.

She yawned.

"Not ill," she said. "But I was up most of the night with the wounded and when I became angry with Talus, I thought… I came back tae rest. Is something amiss?"

Jordan nodded, pulling her into a sitting position. "Talus is dying, lass," she said quietly. "Get yer shoes on and come with me. He's asking for ye."

"He is worse?"

Jordan simply nodded again without elaborating, so Annaleigh pulled her shoes on and quickly followed the woman from the chamber. But as she did so, she kept looking around to see where War was. There were other chambers on this level, so he must have slipped into one of them, waiting for Jordan to leave the floor.

She was, with Annaleigh right behind her.

They made their way to the first-floor unmarried men's wing where Talus had slipped into unconsciousness. There were several people still in the chamber but Annaleigh didn't look at any of them as she resumed her seat next to Talus' bed, taking his hand again and apologizing for running away. She made up some excuse, that she was too overwhelmed with his generosity, hoping he could hear her.

But he never awoke.

The hours slipped away.

Sometime near sunset, Talus du Reims' fever-wracked body gave up the fight. As Annaleigh held his hand and William and Kieran stood on the other side of the bed, he simply stopped breathing. Whatever poison The Bones had put on their blades, one that seemed to be affecting other wounded men but not to the extent it had affected Talus, had done its job. A knight with a bright future was now walking the fields of heaven, more than likely wondering how he got there so quickly.

Annaleigh sat with Talus' cooling corpse into the evening as William and Kieran made arrangements for a casket. They had them in the vault, in storage, plain pine boxes to transport bodies in, but Jordan had insisted on something nicer for the son of the Earl of East Anglia, so William had sent men to Coldstream where there was a barber surgeon who was also a woodworker and, later in the evening, the men returned bearing a nice pine casket for Talus. The last Annaleigh saw, Talus was being lifted into the box by William, Kieran, and Anthony.

For her friend, the young knight who had tried so hard to woo her, she'd genuinely wept.

CHAPTER SEVENTEEN

THE BRIDGE THAT was supposed to be about a mile downriver had turned into a day-long odyssey to find another bridge that wasn't completely broken down in order to cross the River Tweed into England.

Argyle and Brendan had given up an entire day of travel because of a destroyed bridge. They'd ended up traveling all the way to Kelso and crossing there before having to travel all the way back to Castle Questing with a horse that had turned up lame just as they'd made the Kelso crossing.

Frustrated, tired, and hungry, they approached the gates of Castle Questing just after sunset, but the gate sentries had no intention of admitting two lone Scots even though Argyle had been clear about their relation to the House of de Wolfe. Even then, the gate sentries were leery until they sent for Jemma, who had been in the great hall overseeing the meal because Jordan, William, and Kieran were dealing with the passing of Talus du Reims. Jemma wasn't happy to be pulled away from the great hall, but at the mention of who was at the gates, morbid curiosity pulled her out of the hall and to the gatehouse where the portcullis was down.

It didn't take her long to recognize her nephews.

The portcullis lifted.

"What in the world are ye doing here?" Jemma demanded as they came through. "And why are ye traveling at night? Have ye no sense, lads?"

Argyle was leading his lame horse while Brendan wearily dismounted his.

"We were caught up in the trouble in Coldstream," Argyle said. "We were going tae cross there, but the village was overrun so we were forced tae cross in Kelso, but my horse hurt his leg. Can I have a servant take him tae the stables and tend him?"

Jemma began barking orders as well as any battle commander and men came running. In fact, it was widely known that she was feared even more than her husband was. Two servants came to take both Argyle and Brendan's horses away and the weary Scotsmen started to head towards the hall, but Jemma didn't move. Because she didn't move, they came to a halt.

"Ye dinna answer me," she said, looking between them. "Why have ye come?"

Argyle glanced at his brother before answering. "We risked trouble with the reivers tae come here, Auntie," he said. "Do ye not think it's serious?"

"That's not an answer."

"It's the only answer I can give ye. I've come tae speak tae Annie directly."

Jemma's eyebrows lifted. "Annie?" she said. "Why? Who has sent ye?"

Argyle shook his head. "I can only tell her," he said. "Where is she?"

Jemma frowned. "Argyle, what's this madness about?" she

said. "Who sent ye with a message for Annie?"

"Robbie."

"What does he want?"

"I can only tell Annie."

The conversation was becoming circular and Jemma eyed her nephews. The sons of her brother, Cord, they'd always been shifty. She'd never much liked them, to be truthful, but they'd clearly braved hazardous travel to get to Castle Questing, so whatever the message was, it must be important.

So they said.

"Then ye go intae the hall and eat," she said. "I'll bring Annie and ye can tell her with a room full of witnesses tae ensure ye dunna do anything stupid."

Argyle was offended. "What would we do?" he said. "We came tae relay a message because Robbie asked us tae. We risked much with The Bones running about. Aye, we heard it was them. And now ye think we're going tae assault Annie? That we've come all the way tae Castle Questing tae do that?"

Jemma didn't back down. She pointed to the hall. "Get in there," she said. "And stay there. Dunna leave the hall. If I come for ye and found ye've left, I'll tell Kieran and he'll have every Sassenach soldier at Castle Questing hunting for ye. I dunna have tae tell ye what will happen when they find ye."

Argyle grunted with frustration, waving a hand at her as if to wave her away, but he and Brendan headed dutifully towards the hall as Jemma headed towards the keep. Neither man turned around until they were very nearly to the hall and, then, it was Brendan who looked over his shoulder.

"Is she still there?" Argyle asked quietly.

Brendan faced the hall entry. "Nay," he said. "She's gone tae find Annie. Or tell Kieran that we've arrived. There's no telling with her."

Argyle could smell the roast mutton and it was making him hungry. "We stay the course," he muttered. "We tell Annie that Robbie is ill and she must come home."

"But she mustna tell anyone."

"They'll never let her leave with us if she does."

The scheme was set and on the brink of being executed. They'd come too far to back away now. With Annaleigh in their possession, they could force Ian Scott to do anything they wanted him to do.

And that's exactly what they intended.

But the key would be getting her out of Castle Questing without anyone knowing. Much would depend on her loyalty to her brother and his wish that his illness be kept secret.

Very shortly, they would know…

One way or the other.

CHAPTER EIGHTEEN

"H AVE YOU GOTTEN any rest at all?"

The question was from William to Kieran as Kieran entered William's solar and landed heavily on a cushioned chair. The enormous knight kicked his feet out as he sank against the back of the chair and put his hands over his face.

"A little," he said. "But there was much to do."

"Like what?"

"Like assess the knights and the status of the army," Kieran said, hands still over his face in an exhausted gesture. "Like assess the wounded. Christ, William, do I really need to go on?"

William was seated at the colossal, heavy table he used to conduct business. It had been brought all the way from Rome, carved from solid oak with scenes from ancient battles. William had seen it a woodworker's shop in York and he'd spent three hours negotiating a price for it. He loved that table.

His wife thought it was hideous.

He was writing something onto a piece of fine vellum, carefully scripting out the letters, but Kieran's snappish reply had him glancing up.

"You do not," he said. "I was simply asking a question. Why not let Christian do those things? He is your second, is he not? He's competent and well-trained."

Kieran took his hands away from his face and reclined his head on the chair back. "He is," he said. "But he has had command of the army with Anthony resting from a day and a night of command. And Talus… that is a big loss, William. He was a fine knight."

William nodded wearily. "I know," he said hoarsely. "I am writing his father now. I will send the missive on ahead, but you will make arrangements for a contingent of de Wolfe men to take him home to Thunderbey Castle. You must do this right away."

"I already have," Kieran said. "They will be ready to depart at dawn."

"Good."

"What are we going to do about The Bones?"

William stopped writing and looked at him. There was fire in his hazel eye as he set the quill down.

"Find them and burn them," he growled. "They have bases around here from where they launch their raids. I want those locations found and I want every man in that bloody band of murderers burned until they are ashes. Then we'll put the ashes in the garderobe and shit upon them every day for the rest of eternity."

A look of approval crossed Kieran's face. "Excellent," he said. "Are you telling Talus' father that?"

William nodded. "I am telling him that and more," he said. "There will be one man we will not burn. I want you to identify the leader of The Bones and that man will be sent, in irons, to Thunderbey for Tobin du Reims to do with as he pleases. I will deliver the man responsible for Talus' death and deliver him with pleasure."

Kieran was more than willing to do all of that. He liked Talus and the young knight's loss weighed heavily on him. It could have just as easily been one of his own sons, like Christian since Christian had been in that battle, too. Honestly, he had no idea how he would go on with life should something happen to Christian.

It was something he tried not to think about.

Kieran had four sons – Alec, Christian, Kevin, and Nathaniel, and he loved his sons as deeply as any man had ever loved his offspring, but there was a pride he took in Christian that was difficult to describe. Probably because he was so unlike Kieran in many ways. Alec and Kevin looked like Kieran and acted like him, and Nathaniel was very much Jemma's son, but Christian was different than all of them. Maybe that's why Kieran was grieving Talus' loss more deeply than he should have; it reminded him that his own sons could have very well have fallen victim, too.

And whoever was responsible was going to pay dearly.

"I will do this and do it gladly," he said after a moment. "Christian and Talus were friends, you know. My son grieves him."

"We all do," William said, returning to his vellum. "This is not a joyful task, composing this letter."

"I imagine not."

William picked up his quill and continued writing out the words, pausing when he was searching for the right phrase, as Kieran closed his eyes and immediately drifted off to sleep. William finished the missive to Kieran's heavy snoring, but that wasn't unusual. He and Kieran had been friends since they'd been young boys and they'd rarely been apart in all that time, so William was well-acquainted with Kieran's snoring. Truthfully, he found it comforting because it was one thing that never changed. Men lived or men died, kings came and went, but Kieran kept right on snoring. William was nearly finished with the missive when Kieran suddenly snored loudly as if startled and his head popped up.

"He does not trust him," he muttered.

William signed the missive and reached for the sand. "Who does not trust him?"

"Christian," Kieran mumbled. "He does not trust him."

William sanded the missive and blew off the excess. "Go back to sleep," he said. "You are dreaming."

But Kieran didn't do as he was told. He rubbed his eyes, becoming more oriented. "I was dreaming of Christian," he said, sounding sleepy and weary. "He spoke with Herringthorpe and he thinks the man is hiding something. He doesn't trust him. I forgot to tell you that with everything that has gone on since yesterday."

William looked at him for a long moment. It was clear that something was going on in his mind. Slowly, he put the missive to East Anglia aside, stood up, and walked around the table. He picked up a small missive right on the edge of the tabletop. It was folded up but he unfolded it and went to Kieran, extending it to the man.

"And with everything that has gone on since yesterday, I forgot to tell you this," he said quietly. "Read it."

Kieran took it from him, looking at it curiously. "What is it?"

"*Read* it."

Kieran did. William wandered back to his table, pausing

only once to see if Kieran had changed expression, but the man's features remained like stone.

Until he read it a second time.

Kieran's brow furrowed as he read it through again, as if his initial shock were over and now he was starting to show some emotion. By this time, William had reclaimed his seat and was carefully rolling the missive to East Anglia. As he heated the wax to create the big de Wolfe seal, Kieran lowered the missive in his hands and rose stiffly from the chair.

"Then we were correct all along," he said quietly. "War really *is* your son."

William nodded. "He is."

"And he gave you this missive?"

"Nay," William shook his head. "Jordan did. She read it before I did. She was cleaning the man's chamber and it fell from his saddlebags. The letter was open, the seal broken, and she saw my name. Naturally, she read it, as it pertained to her husband."

"How did she take the news?"

William was looking at the tabletop, thinking on how to answer. "It did not please her," he finally said. "It was not an ideal way to discover that your husband, whom you thought was perfect, had fathered a bastard. I do believe she was a little jealous, even after all of these years."

Kieran wriggled his eyebrows. "I can well imagine that," he said. "I am certain Jemma would not have taken such news half as well as Jordan did. I'd be missing a certain part of my body right now."

William cracked a smile. "How unfortunate for you," he said. But he quickly sobered. "The point is that Herringthorpe doesn't know I have it. He does not know that *I* know. Clearly, he knows that I am his father, but I have many questions about this."

"What do you mean?"

William lifted a dark eyebrow. "*Why* is he carrying that missive around?" he said. "Jane wanted him to give it to me. Why hasn't he?"

Kieran shook his head. "I do not know," he said. "But the more I think on it, the more I do not like it. There's nothing like a man with a vendetta carrying around something to remind him of that vendetta."

William looked at him curiously. "You think he means to harm me somehow?"

Kieran shrugged. "I do not know," he said. "But the man just lost the only father he'd ever known, and now you find him carrying around a missive from his mother, to you, explaining that you are War's true father. He must be grieved and angry and confused. Wouldn't you be?"

William couldn't disagree. "Jordan has advised me to ask him why he has the letter and why he has not given it to me," he said. "What is your suggestion?"

Kieran opened his mouth to reply but was interrupted by a knock on the solar door. Both Kieran and William turned to see War standing in the doorway.

For a moment, they were both caught off guard. Had he heard their conversation? That was on their minds but until War indicated that he'd heard, neither one of them was going to react in any way. They were seasoned knights who had long learned not to give away what they were thinking.

But the mood, at least for them, was full of uncertainty.

"I am sorry to interrupt," War said, looking between the two. "I was hoping I might have a moment of your time, Lord

Kilham. If this is not a good time, then I shall come back at your convenience."

William passed a glance at Kieran before replying. "Now is a perfect time," he said. "Come in, please. We have been discussing du Reims' death, among other things. I have just finished writing a message to the man's father, which has been one of my unhappier duties."

War stepped into the chamber. "Although I did not know du Reims, I know who his father is," he said. "Tobin du Reims has spent much time in London, as a guest of the king on occasion."

"Have you ever been to Thunderbey Castle?"

War shook his head. "Nay," he said. "But I have heard that it is quite impressive."

"It is," William said. "The Earls of East Anglia and the House of de Wolfe have been friends and allies for decades. Back to the days of my father, in fact, when our alliance formed with the House of de Lohr. De Lohr and du Reims are related."

War nodded. "I knew they were your ally," he said. "Speaking of allies, and not to rush things along, but are you still planning on taking me to Northwood and Berwick, or would you prefer to do that another time? Much has happened since we spoke of it yesterday."

William sat back in his chair. "I must say that I am not as enthusiastic about a journey to Northwood and Berwick now as I was yesterday, but you came here for a reason and that reason was not to sit around and be idle," he said. "We shall go tomorrow morning. And I did not thank you and your men for lending your swords to the raid in Coldstream. It was a privilege to serve beside you, War."

War smiled faintly. "The honor was mine, my lord," he said.

"In fact, I was hoping that we could become even closer allies. That is what I wished to speak to you about."

William thought this might be the moment when War spoke of the secret they all knew. It was that great ghost in the room, hanging over them, and William found that he was eager to know what War was thinking on the subject.

He braced himself.

"I am listening," he said. "Speak freely."

War took a deep breath and cleared his throat, eyeing Kieran. "It is a… personal matter, my lord," he said. "I mean no disrespect to Sir Kieran, but may I have a moment of your time alone?"

Kieran started to move but William stopped him. "You should know that Kieran and I have no secrets," he said. "Kieran has been my second in command for twenty-five years, my best friend since I was a young boy, so even if he is not in the room, chances are he will know of the subject matter at some point. And he is very wise, a neutral and calm voice when the situation is wrought with emotion. I would like him to stay unless you are insistent he leave."

War shook his head without any marked disappointment or irritation. "As you wish," he said. "If you trust him, then I trust him."

William nodded to silently thank him, but he was thinking that War was most definitely leading up to Jane's missive. On the other hand, William knew he didn't have the missive, so why tell William what he knew without the proof? That was the first inkling that it might be something different.

He found out for certain when War opened his mouth.

"I am not entirely sure this is the right time to ask you this, but I find that I do not wish to delay," he said. "Time is short and things happen, like skirmishes in the midst of a peaceful visit. My lord, I would like permission to court Lady Annaleigh."

That brought a reaction from William. He couldn't help the surprise that rippled across his face. Kieran, too. He looked at William to see what the man thought of the request and he realized they both had the same expression.

Astonished.

All William could think of at that moment was of Jordan's plan to matchmake between War and Annaleigh when War had first come to Castle Questing. He'd been irritated with her for her plans but, as it seemed, she'd been right and he'd been wrong.

He'd never hear the end of it.

"Annaleigh?" William finally said. "You wish to court my wife's cousin?"

War nodded. "I do, my lord," he said politely. "But I would like to explain something you are not aware of. This goes back to the battle at Etal Castle several months ago."

William was even more puzzled. "I am listening."

War took a deep breath, focused solely on William as if Kieran weren't in the room. He'd never had to ask a man to court his daughter, or in this case, a ward, and the only indications of nervousness were his hands, clasped behind his back, with white fingers because he was gripping them so tightly.

"As you are aware, I was badly wounded in the battle," War said. "I had crawled into a thicket of trees by the river, trying to hide myself from the marauding Scots who go about stripping the dead of their valuables. I knew I would not be able to defend myself, so I hid. Annaleigh was one of the women roaming the battlefield and she found me. Instead of trying to kill me, she tended me. She saved my life, my lord."

William was even more astounded now. "God's Bones," he muttered. "Is this true? I hadn't heard this, not at all. Annaleigh never told me."

"That is because she kept it to herself," War said. "She was not certain how her kin would react if they knew she saved the life of an English knight, so she hadn't told anyone. You probably should not tell anyone, either. It could jeopardize her because she has told me that her clan blames her for that battle. They might move against her if they knew that she saved the life of an enemy."

William was already shaking his head. "They'll not hear it from me," he said. "The information will not leave this chamber. But the coincidence is uncanny."

"Coincidence, my lord?"

William nodded. "That was exactly how I met my wife," he said. "It was after a border skirmish and I had a nasty leg wound. She found me on the field of battle, stitched my wound, and saved my life."

That seemed to relax War a little. "You're right," he said. "It *is* an uncanny coincidence. It would seem that the women from Clan Scott are brave beyond measure."

William grunted in agreement. "More than you know," he said. "Have you seen her since? Or was your arrival at Castle Questing the first time you'd seen her since the battle?"

War smiled weakly. "It was the first time since the battle," he said. "She told me her name those months ago, but I had no idea where she was from or anything beyond her name. When I arrived at Castle Questing, I had the opportunity to thank her for what she did, but my feelings for her grew from there. I would very much like to court her, my lord. Nay, *more* than that. I would very much like to marry her and I seek your permission."

As his surprise faded, William thought heavily on the question. Before him stood inarguably one of the most powerful knights in England. The man was as glorious as a rising sun, a man among men, who had not yet reached his zenith. He was the commander of a massive castle on the coast, but a man like War Herringthorpe was destined for bigger things.

It was the de Wolfe blood in him.

William liked to think that the skill and talent of War was due to his bloodlines. There was no denying that de Wolfe men were great knights. More than that, War carried the blood of the House of de Percy, a hugely prestigious and powerful family. When those two bloodlines met, the creation was exactly what stood before him –

Powerful.

Courageous.

Intelligent.

Legendary.

And this man wanted to court Annaleigh.

Nay… marry her.

But William didn't feel as if he could feely give his permission, not until a few things were made clear between them. He'd been expecting War to come to him with what he knew, with Jane's letter, yet War came to him instead with a request to court one of William's wards. While he was pleased by the request and had no real objection other than the final word would have to come from Annaleigh's father, he was still wrestling with the fact that War was his son and hadn't yet confronted him with it.

William simply wouldn't wait any longer.

Things had to be out in the open.

"You will allow me time to think on it," he said after a moment. "I must also speak to my wife, given that Annie is her cousin. But first, I wish to speak to you about something else. Will you sit down?"

That wasn't exactly what War had been hoping to hear, but he did as he was asked. He didn't want to do anything contrary to William's wishes considering he was trying to gain his wants from the man. He moved over to the chair William had indicated and sat stiffly, perched on the edge of the chair as if he were going to leap up at any moment. The nervousness was showing again and it was Kieran who finally poured him a measure of wine and handed it to him, simply to relax him. William stood up and leaned against his table, facing War.

For a moment, the two of them simply stared at one another. There was curiosity in the air, perhaps even puzzlement. Neither one of them really understood the other. There were elements at play that ran deep, elements of grief and bewilderment, but open interest and suspicion. There was even… hope.

Aye, perhaps even that.

It was a strange mixture of sensations.

"The only way to bring about this subject is to start from the beginning," William finally said. "My wife's duties, as chatelaine, involve many things. But one of the things she personally manages is the cleaning of the keep. I know it sounds strange to bring that up at this moment, but I have a reason for doing so. She was overseeing the cleaning of the chambers in the area where you are currently lodged and that included your room. The servants were finished sweeping your chamber when one of them bumped your saddlebags, which fell over onto the floor. The contents spilled out. Let me assure you that no servant touched your possessions, but in order to get them back into the bag, my wife did."

War was listening carefully. "It was an accident, I am certain," he said. "I am not distressed. I am pleased that she would take the initiative to do it."

William could see that the man had no idea what he was leading up to, so he simply continued. He didn't want to drag it out.

"As she was putting your things back into the bag and trying to be careful with them, she found something," he said. Then he held his hand out to Kieran, who put the missive in his hand. The entire time, Kieran had been holding it. William turned it over to War. "This was open when she picked it up. She saw my name."

Without another word, he extended it to War, who was looking William straight in the eye when he took it. In fact, he didn't even look at it. He simply took it and kept his gaze on William. Then, he finally glanced at it.

Something in his expression changed.

"I see," he said after a moment. "Did you read it?"

"I did."

War nodded, but it was only an acknowledgement that he understood the sequence of events. Beyond that, it didn't mean anything. Missive in hand, he stood up.

"Then you know," he said.

"I know."

"Did you know before you read this?"

William shook his head. "Nay," he said honestly. "As your mother said, she never told me. I never heard from her after her father told me to go away and leave her alone."

War grunted. It was clear that the formal, polite manner was now wavering with the introduction of a very touchy subject. His jaw began to flex as he faced something he hadn't wanted to face yet.

It was a most unexpected happening.

"And you did?" he said. "You simply went away and left the woman you loved, the woman you had bedded?"

William could feel the tension. He glanced at Kieran, who was watching the situation closely. In truth, he was glad Kieran was there as a witness. He didn't want this to be a private conversation that could potentially turn ugly.

"War, I am going to be completely honest with you," he said evenly. "I realize this is a difficult subject for you and I'm sure you think that I wronged your mother somehow but let me explain what happened before you judge me. You should have all of the facts if you are going to do that."

War looked at him. "I am not judging you," he said. "The truth is that I only found out about this when my father, or at least the man I knew as my father, confessed everything to me on his deathbed. Not only did I have to endure his death, but I had to endure being told that everything I'd believed in my entire life was a lie. If I become emotional about this it is because the man I knew and loved as my father is dead. That is bad enough. But oddly enough, my anger isn't directed at you. It is directed at him. I haven't had much time to think on this situation because so much has happened in the days since his death and, truth be told, I have avoided it all. But now that we are speaking of it, there is some anger. Anger at men who keep secrets that affect others."

William understood that completely. "I know," he said, not unsympathetic. "I can only imagine how you must have felt. I do not know why your mother did not tell you sooner, but I am sure she had her reasons."

"What reasons?" War said, his jaw ticking. Then, he shook his head and turned away. "I am coming to wish my father hadn't told me at all."

There was hurt in his voice. Such hurt. William couldn't help but feel a good deal of sympathy for him.

"Did he give his reasons for telling you?" he asked softly.

War shrugged. "He felt I needed to know," he said. "He told me all he could, from my mother's perspective, but when he told me who my father was… he forbade me to become angry with you."

William watched the tense body language as War twitched, wrapped up in a maelstrom of emotion and bewilderment.

"Do you want to hear of the situation from my perspective?" he asked quietly. "I would be more than willing to tell you."

War considered that. He really did. "I do not know," he said after a moment. "As I said, I've not really thought on all of this since my father told me. Mayhap I simply do not want to think about it right now. I really do not know. But I suppose I do have one question."

"What is it?"

"Did you love my mother?"

William sighed heavily, looking at Kieran, who nodded his head faintly. He was giving William permission to tell the man the truth because to lie to him would only bring about more hurt and more lies.

And he didn't want to lie to him.

He'd been lied to enough.

"Nay," he finally said. "I was not in love with her. But she was in love with me. She wanted to marry me, so I offered for her hand because… well, as you so eloquently put it, I had bedded her. I thought it was the right thing to do. But her father denied me and sent me away quickly. I was told not to return under any circumstances."

War didn't like that answer. He began to rub his big hands together, a nervous gesture, as he processed the conversation.

"*I* loved my mother," he said. "She was a good woman."

"She was, indeed."

"Then tell me you did not take advantage of her, or worse," War snapped. "Tell me everything that happened between you two was because she wanted it to happen. That you both wanted it to happen."

"Everything that happened between us was of our own free will, I swear it." William watched him twitch and wring his hands. "Now, I have a question for you. May I?"

War nodded, distracted. "Ask."

"When were you going to give me your mother's letter?"

War paused in his twitching and wringing. "I am not certain," he said. "When the timing was right, I suppose."

"And what did you hope to gain by it?"

War looked at him sharply. "*Gain* by it?" he said. "I do not want to *gain* anything by it. I do not want anything from you, de Wolfe. Other than an alliance, I want absolutely nothing from you. I was carrying the letter in my bags in case I decided to tell you everything and for no other reason than that. Beg pardon, my lord, but I want to be perfectly clear… do you mean to suggest I was going to try and wrest money from you with it?"

William was surprised the conversation had taken such a bitter, suspicious turn. "Of course not," he said. "But the fact is that you are my son by blood. Everyone around us, at least my own men, could see it if I couldn't. You look like me and you fight like me, so I am undeniably your father. I suppose I should have asked if you had any expectations after giving me the letter."

That didn't help War's sense of insult. "*Expectations?*" he repeated, aghast. "What expectations could I possibly have? I was only going to give you the letter because my mother wanted me to and for no other reason than that. I will repeat the fact that I do not want anything from you. I do not expect anything from you. I was perfectly happy not knowing you were my father and it does not make me happy to know that the man I thought was my father was, in fact, tricked into marriage because my mother was pregnant with me. She was pregnant with *your* child."

He was starting to get agitated so Kieran stepped in. "War," he said steadily. "William was not implying that you wanted something from him and even if he was, he didn't mean monetarily. He meant friendship. A pleasant familial relation-ship. He was simply asking you what your feelings were on the matter and nothing more."

War's jaw was ticking furiously as he looked at Kieran, but his ire had William's ire rising. The young man was hurt and angry and although he said his anger wasn't directed at William, it was quickly heading in that direction. Angry and disgusted… perhaps disgusted that he was the son of William de Wolfe. Perhaps all of William's power and reputation was repugnant to him somehow. It was difficult to tell, but William was rapidly growing offended by the stance. In his opinion, there was no call for it.

But War obviously felt differently.

"Let me be plain on my part," William said as he turned back for his table. "I have six sons. I do not need or want another and if you think I was suggesting that you were here to intimidate me somehow, then you are not as reasonable as I was led to believe. Every word out of my mouth is evidently some kind of slander to you, so it is best if we end this conversation now before we both say something we will regret. Be ready to depart on the morrow to Northwood Castle and I shall bid you a good evening."

War stiffened. "No need, my lord," he said. "I will be returning to Bamburgh Castle on the morrow. I consider my association with you purely professional and I would appreciate the same consideration in return."

"You have it."

"I would also appreciate it if you do not mention our… situation to anyone. I would not want it to get out."

"Nor would I."

The words stung War. So the man didn't want to be associated with him, did he? War had words of his own for the man who had bedded his mother.

He meant them to wound.

"I would not want men thinking that my royal appointments were because I was William de Wolfe's bastard," he rumbled.

There was contempt in his tone. It was a low blow and William had to take a deep breath, struggling not to clap back, but he simply couldn't help it. War's anger had him angry and hurt also.

"You should be so fortunate if they thought so," he muttered. "And let me be perfectly clear about our professional association, Herringthorpe – what you think is immaterial to me so long as you give me your troops when I ask for them. If you do not, I will tell Henry and Henry will remove you from your post. You'll find out the hard way just how powerful I really am."

It was a crushing display of rank and superiority. War knew it was the truth. William had the upper hand on him and there was nothing he could do about it. Nothing he could say about it. But, damn it all to hell, he was seething inside. He wasn't used to being humiliated like that.

But he had been, brutally so.

It never occurred to him that he might have deserved it.

"I am at your disposal, my lord," he said through clenched teeth.

It was the only thing he could say and they all knew it. William glared at him a few moments longer before turning away.

"You may leave now," he said.

It was a sour and devastating ending to a most unexpected conversation. With that, War quit the solar, heading out of the keep as Kieran went to the doorway and watched. He could see War's tall, straight back as he crossed the inner bailey and took a turn to the left, disappearing behind the north wing of the keep.

Kieran sighed heavily.

"Damnation, William," he muttered. "He is *just* like you. Stubborn and proud, both of you."

William was feeling horrible about the situation and how it played out. He pretended to busy himself with other things, struggling not to show how badly it had affected him.

"Put a watch on him and his men," he rumbled. "When dawn comes, make sure he leaves. I would also make sure he has no contact with Annie, at least not until we both calm down. I do not want him saying something to her in anger because that would draw my wrath."

Kieran could feel William's pain. He turned to him, watching him fuss with pieces of vellum on his table, pretending to be occupied with them when the truth was that his mind was on that enormous knight who had just departed the solar. Kieran could read the man's mind even if he didn't know exactly what he was feeling.

"Let his anger cool, William," Kieran said quietly. "In fact, let *your* anger cool. I suspect the death of his father has compounded his confusion and angst about the situation with you. I do not think he is lashing out at you personally. I believe he is lashing out at the situation in general but, somehow, it turned personal. He will come to understand that, with time."

"And if he doesn't?" William said, glancing at Kieran. But then he waved the man off. "I do not care if he doesn't. It is of no consequence to me what he feels or thinks."

Kieran knew it wasn't true but he didn't contradict him. He simply nodded his head.

"I'll tell Christian to keep watch on him," he said. "We'll make sure he departs at dawn. You needn't give him a second thought."

"I won't."

Kieran knew that wasn't true. As he quit the solar and headed out of the keep, he knew most definitely that it wasn't true.

Something told him that the scene in the solar wasn't going to be the end of it tonight.

Not in the least.

CHAPTER NINETEEN

"**A**RGYLE! BRENDAN! WHAT are ye doing here?"

The shocked question came from Annaleigh, who had just walked into the great hall with Jemma, straight to a table next to the entry door where two dirty, tired Scotsmen were stuffing themselves with mutton and carrots. They were so hungry that they didn't even stop eating when Annaleigh came up to the table, her mouth hanging open.

"Annie, lass," Argyle said, chewing. "'Tis been a long time since we've seen ye. Are ye a Sassenach yet?"

Annaleigh frowned at his silly question. "Of course not," she said, standing at the end of the table with her hands on her hips. "*Why* are ye here?"

Argyle took a couple of swallows of ale before looking between Jemma and Annaleigh. "Did Aunt Jemma tell ye?"

Annaleigh looked at Jemma. "Tell me what?"

Jemma scowled. "What am I tae tell her?" she said. "Ye wouldna tell me, so here she is. Give her Robbie's message and be done with it."

Argyle swallowed the bite in his mouth, casting Brendan a long look before answering. "Aunt Jemma, I swore tae Robbie that I would tell Annie in private," he said. "If he wanted ye tae hear, he would have told me tae tell ye."

Jemma was unhappy with their nonsense and she knew for a fact that it was nonsense. But they had come a long way, and there had been some difficulty, so she figured that no harm could come to Annaleigh in full view of the entire hall. Argyle and Brendan had always been shifty, but more than that, they were part of the movement against Annaleigh's father, according to Annaleigh. Perhaps that's what had Jemma most suspicious. Against her better judgment, however, she relented.

"Very well," she said. "I'll go. But ye'll stay here and tell her. Ye'll not leave the hall, do ye hear?"

Argyle and Brendan solemnly nodded and Jemma, moderately satisfied, headed off to the other end of the hall where men were becoming loud and drunk and a fight was breaking out. When the petite woman became lost in the sea of men, Argyle bolted to his feet.

"Ye must come with us right away, Annie," he said. "Robbie is dying. He's asking for ye!"

Annaleigh gasped, her hands flying to her mouth. "What happened?" she said, immediately in tears. "What's wrong with him?"

Argyle was moving around the table, already grasping for her. "He sent us tae tell ye but he doesna want anyone else tae know," he said. "Not even Aunt Jemma or Aunt Jordan. He told us only tae tell ye and tae bring ye home right away."

Startled and frightened with the news about her brother, Annaleigh let Argyle lead her out of the hall in spite of the fact that Jemma had told them to remain. Brendan was behind her, his hands on her shoulders as Argyle took her wrists, all of them herding her out of the hall the moment Jemma's back was turned.

And Annaleigh went right along with it.

"What's the matter?" she wept. "Please tell me. What happened tae my brother?"

Both Argyle and Brendan were keeping an eye out for anyone who might prevent them from doing what needed to be done. They had Annaleigh exactly where they wanted her and they didn't want interference from anyone. Argyle had daggers on him, as did Brendan, and if anyone tried to stop them, a dagger would be pointed straight at Annaleigh. They hadn't expected to have her in their possession so quickly, but here she was.

They had to move and move quickly or all would be lost.

"A fever," Argyle said. "He's been sick for days with it and the physic says he's dying. But he doesna want anyone tae know."

Annaleigh wept with sorrow. "But why?" she said, wiping her face. "Mayhap we could find help for him. We have wounded in the hall from a battle yesterday or I would ask our own physic tae tend him, but he has many wounded. Men are dying. We lost a knight today, a man who was my friend."

Argyle looked at her, brow furrowed. "No knight is a friend of a Scots," he said. "I asked ye if ye were a Sassenach yet. If an English knight is yer friend, then mayhap ye are. Break yer father's heart!"

Annaleigh yanked her hands away from him. "Dunna say such things, Argyle Scott," she said, wiping more tears from her cheeks. "My brother is dying and ye scold me? What about my da? Is he well?"

Argyle grasped her wrist again, pulling her towards the stables, which weren't too far away, fortunately. He pulled her past the walled garden and around the corner where the stable yard was.

"Yer da is well," Argyle said. "But ye must come. When we left, he was showing signs that he might be becoming ill also, so ye must come. But we canna tell anyone."

"But *why*?" Annaleigh begged.

Argyle came to an abrupt halt. "Because if the Sassenach know yer brother is dying, and mayhap yer father is ill, it will weaken the clan," he said. "The death of a chief and his heir will make the clan weak to our enemies, so ye canna tell."

It was a perfectly logical statement if they were dealing with enemy English, but they weren't. Annaleigh was puzzled as well as distraught.

"But William and Jordan are our kin," she said. "They wouldna think us weak. They would help."

"They're English," Argyle hissed at her. "They are not our kin."

"They are!"

Argyle yanked on her. "This is the way Robbie wanted it, so this is the way we're going tae do it."

Annaleigh yelped when he yanked too hard and twisted her wrist. "Argyle!" she snapped. "Let me go!"

They had reached the side entrance to the stables, a small door that the servants used to go in and out, and Argyle let go of Annaleigh's wrist long enough to grab her by the hair. He yanked and pulled her against the wall, out of sight, as Brendan crowded in around them to shield them in the darkness.

"If ye make a sound, they'll stop us," Argyle hissed, his stinking breath in her face. "Is that what ye want? For yer brother tae die without ye by his side?"

Annaleigh was less distraught and more fearful now. Argyle

was hurting her, as if she were his captive or someone to be hated, which told her that something was wrong. She'd foolishly come to the stables with her cousins and now… now, she didn't have a choice any longer. She was here whether or not she wanted to be.

She struggled to calm down.

"Argyle, let go of me," she said steadily. "Ye're hurting me."

Argyle loosened his grip, but he didn't let her go. "Annie, I've no time tae argue," he said. "We must collect horses and leave. My own horse is lame, so I canna ride him. Do ye have a horse of yer own?"

"Nay."

"Then I'll steal one."

Annaleigh was trying to loosen his grip further. "Ye dunna have tae hurt me," she said, trying to pull her hair free. "I told ye I'd go. I want tae see my brother. But I want tae collect my things before we go."

Argyle still wouldn't release her. "Ye canna," he said. "Those Sassenach bastards may stop ye. Ye want tae see Robbie before he dies, dinna ye?"

Annaleigh stopped struggling against him for a moment, her eyes wide with fear. "Is he really dying?" she asked, moving from Argyle to Brendan. "Bren? Is he really dying?"

In situations like this, Brendan was always the follower and never the leader because if anything went wrong, he could always say that Argyle had forced him to participate. Therefore, he didn't answer, but looked to Argyle for his response.

"Do ye think we'd come all the way tae Castle Questing just tae trick ye?" Argyle asked. "Use yer head, lass. Of course we wouldna. Robbie is dying and ye must come. Can it be any simpler than that?"

Annaleigh wasn't unaware of the fact that she was boxed in by her cousins. They weren't about to let her out of their sights, nor were they willing to let her stray in any fashion. They'd spirited her out of the hall and now that she was showing some resistance, Argyle had his hand in her hair. One way or the other, they were going to force her back with them to Langton.

That told Annaleigh that something was off, indeed.

As she'd told Jemma and Jordan and William when she arrived at Castle Questing those months ago, Argyle and Brendan were two of the men in the clan leading an insurrection against her father. They hadn't been obvious about it, but more stirring the embers of discontent. If they stirred enough embers, a blaze would result. They'd spoken against their uncle and against his niece, convincing those who would listen that Annaleigh had been the cause of that terrible battle at Etal. They'd been at the head of the blame against her.

And now they were trying to force her to return home.

She didn't want to go.

Fear clutched at Annaleigh. She wasn't exactly sure how she was going to convince Argyle and Brendan to leave her alone, but she suspected there was no way to discourage them. Therefore, she'd have to be clever about it unless she wanted them to do something drastic.

She had to be compliant.

It was her only hope.

"I believe ye," she said. "But if ye want me tae find ye a horse, ye'll have tae let go of my hair. If anyone sees ye, they'll think ye mean tae do me harm."

That caused Argyle to drop his hand from her hair. He even smoothed at it, pretending he'd never hurt a hair on her head.

"Where are ye going for the horse?" he asked.

Annaleigh pointed through the open door, into the stables that were dark except for the torchlight that was streaming in from the walls.

"In there," she said. "There are palfreys at the other end. I'll go in and ye'll meet me at the front."

"We'll go with ye," Argyle said in a tone that suggested he wasn't about to let her get away from him. "Go on, now. We'll follow."

Annaleigh was feeling increasingly frightened. She just knew they were up to no good. Even when she lived at Langton, her father would never leave her alone with this pair. They were foolish and without restraint, even around their cousin. Her heart began to pound as she ducked her head to go through the doorway.

The moment she stepped through, she knew she had to do something. She simply couldn't be complacent with the two of them because she knew, in the end, it would only contribute to her demise.

And she was certain that's what they had in mind.

As she stepped through the portal, the door itself was open and leaning against the wall to her right. As fast as she could, she leapt clear of the opening and grabbed the door, slamming it back on Argyle's face.

As Argyle yelped and fell back, his nose smashed, Brendan pushed forward and threw his weight against the door. Annaleigh couldn't hold out against it and she stumbled back, but it was enough to give her a head start at running. She screamed as Brendan tore after her, running for the main entry to the stables where surely someone would hear her. At this time of night, most of the servants were eating or in bed, but there was always someone around.

She was counting on that someone to raise an alarm.

But she never had the chance.

Brendan caught up to her and grabbed her from behind. Panicked, Annaleigh struggled against him, throwing her fists and trying to fight him off. But in the process, she didn't look where she was going. She tripped just short of the main stables' entry and pitched forward with Brendan nearly on top of her. It was enough momentum to ram her head right into the side of the stables' entry and the contact was brutal enough that it knocked her unconscious immediately.

Annaleigh went down with Brendan on top of her and no one saw or heard a thing.

Or, so they thought.

Unbeknownst to Argyle and Brendan, the worst was yet to come.

CHAPTER TWENTY

"NAY, I'VE NOT seen him," Jemma said. "Was he supposed tae come tae the hall?"

Kieran was standing near the dais of the great hall where his wife was, but he was looking for War. He could see War's men at the end of the table, near the hearth – the men called Monty, Alexei, and Clement – but no sign of War himself.

"Nay," Kieran said, still looking around. "But I'd hoped he'd come here. I wanted to speak to him."

"Why?"

Kieran looked at her. "Because he and William had words," he said, lowering his voice. "Most of them not pleasant. I was hoping to soothe Herringthorpe somehow."

Jemma was concerned. "God's Bones," she said. "Did they fight?"

"As I said, it wasn't pleasant."

"But why?"

Kieran sighed. "It is a long story and one I will tell you later, so please do not press me right now," he said. "I'd like to find War. I must speak to him."

Jemma was many things, but a pest to her stoic husband

wasn't one of them. At least, not when it mattered and, at this point, she could see by Kieran's expression that it mattered. She'd been married to him long enough to know that.

"As ye wish," she said reluctantly. Since she couldn't ask him more about War, she shifted to the one thing that had been heavy on her mind for the last hour or so. "Did anyone tell ye that Argyle and Brendan have come tae Castle Questing?"

Kieran looked at her sharply. "Cord's sons?"

"Aye."

"What are they doing here?"

Jemma shook her head. "I dunna know," she said. She wagged a finger in her husband's face. "But I dunna trust that pair. Whenever there's trouble or subversion, they're in the middle of it. Annie told me that they were leading the rebellion against Ian. They've been the ones speaking out against him and telling our kin that Annie caused the battle at Etal. They're trouble, I tell ye."

Kieran knew that. "But why did they come?"

Jemma shrugged. "Tae speak tae Annie," she said. "They said that Robbie sent them with a message and they wouldna tell me what it was."

Kieran frowned. "They were speaking out against Annie, yet Robbie sent them with a message for her?" he said. "That does not sound right."

"I'm well aware," Jemma said. "I told them not tae move from the hall. In a room full of witnesses, they dunna dare…"

She suddenly trailed off as her gaze moved to the tables near the open hall door. As short as she was, she leapt up onto a bench so she could see better, but what she saw did not please her. Not in the least.

"Damn those fools," she snapped. "I told them tae stay

there!"

Kieran was trying to see what she saw. "Stay where?" he said. "What is amiss?"

Jemma pointed to the far end of the hall. "*There*," she said. "They were sitting at the table with Annie. But they've gone – and so is Annie."

Kieran and Jemma looked at each other at the same time, with the same expression. It was a moment of both realization and concern. Annaleigh was gone, Argyle and Brendan were gone…

That was not a good sign.

"Find them, Kieran," Jemma hissed, climbing off the bench with her husband's help. "I dunna know where they'd be, but ye must find them."

"How long since you last saw them?"

Jemma was looking around the hall desperately to see if they might be somewhere in the vast group of men and servants.

"Not long," she said. "Mayhap ten minutes or more?"

Kieran simply nodded and headed out of the hall. He'd have to wait to find War because finding Annaleigh with her two unscrupulous cousins was more imperative at the moment. Jemma's timeline gave him a sense of context, as he was certain they couldn't have fled the confines of Castle Questing in that time. But they could get into trouble.

What trouble, he didn't know.

He had to find them.

Christian was just coming in the doorway as his father was walking out. Kieran grasped his son by the arm.

"Have you seen Annie?" he asked.

Christian shook his head. "Nay," he said. "But Argyle and

Brendan are here. One of the sentries told me."

Kieran nodded quickly. "I know," he said. "They told your mother that they had a message to deliver to Annie in private and now they're all missing. Help me find them, Christian. Those men are not to be trusted and especially not with her."

Christian knew that. His manner turned serious.

"But where would they go?" he said, looking around. Then he darted around the side of the hall where the walled garden was. Kieran was on his heels but they could both see the empty garden through the gate. "They're not here. I'll check the keep and you can check the stables."

Kieran nodded. "Hurry, lad," he said, slapping an affectionate hand on his son's shoulder. "If they're not in the stables, I'll head to the knights' quarters."

"Right," Christian said. "What do you want me to do if I find them?"

Kieran cocked an unhappy eyebrow. "Get those two bastards away from Annie and out to the gatehouse," he said. "I do not want that pair running loose until I find out *why* they've come. They would not tell your mother, but by damn, they're going to tell me. Or else."

Christian knew what "or else" meant. His father had very creative ways of interrogation. He was already running off towards the keep as Kieran headed off to the stables.

As usual, the compound of Castle Questing was lit up with dozens of torches against the night sky. William made sure that the entire great wall was lit up as well as the inner wall that divided the small inner ward from the outer ward. That meant light was cast everywhere, almost as bright as daylight sometimes, and Kieran could see the stables in the distance.

The stables had its own yard, tucked up against the north-west wall. At this time of night, it was quiet because the animals had been secured for the night long ago and, usually, there was a servant who kept an eye on them throughout the night. That servant had been known to spend most of the night in the hall, however, only venturing out to the stables on occasion. William kept him on because his knowledge of horses was excellent, so they tolerated his propensity to dally in the hall during the night.

As Kieran approached the stables, he didn't see the servant, but he wasn't surprised. Everything seemed quiet at the stables for the most part, with only one door open of the two big, double doors at the entry. It was for ventilation at this time of year. He was about thirty feet away, just entering the yard, when Annaleigh suddenly appeared in the open door with Brendan on her back. In truth, the man tackled her and she crashed into the door jamb, smacking her head and landing in a heap. Brendan landed on top of her.

Startled, Kieran began to run.

"Release her!" he boomed. "Brendan, let her go immediately!"

Panicked, Brendan looked up to see Kieran barreling into the yard. He grabbed Annaleigh by the arm, yanking her up and against him, as Argyle suddenly appeared and put the blade of a dagger right against her chest.

"Stop or she dies!" he shouted.

Kieran came to a halt so quickly that he skidded in the dirt. He was about ten feet away now, frozen in place, as Brendan hauled Annaleigh up against him and her head rolled back. It was then that Kieran could see the blood all over the left side of her face, dripping down onto the swell of her pale bosom even as he watched.

But Argyle's blade never moved from her chest.

"You'll never leave here alive if you do not release her," Kieran growled. "She's hurt, Argyle. Give her to me."

Argyle had blood dripping from his nose. He was nervous and trapped, a bad combination. He wiped at his nose with his free hand, smearing blood on his face, before daring to look at Annaleigh in his brother's grasp.

The woman had blood all over the left side of her face.

"Nay," he said, wiping at the blood coming out of his nose again. "She's going back with us tae Langton. We came for her and we're going tae take her. Get out of the way."

"I will not."

"Get out of the way or I'll kill her!"

Kieran didn't move. "If you kill her, then I will make sure you are executed in the most painful way possible," he said, his dark eyes glittering. "Make no mistake; you will not leave here alive. I will filet the flesh from your body. I will cut the meat from your ribs and break each rib in turn. You will feel every cut, every stab, every broken bone. And then I will start on your brother. Do you understand what I am telling you?"

Argyle did. He was terrified of the massive English knight and he knew the man meant every word. Men like Kieran Hage had shaped a nation. He'd been present at battles between Scots and English, killing Scots, having no regard for their lives or safety. He'd married a Scotswoman, but that had been long ago. Jemma Hage was English now. Though she was Argyle's aunt, he never considered her Scots.

Like her husband, she was the enemy.

Argyle's grip on the dirk tightened.

"If yer threat is sincere, then I'll cut the lass right now," he said. "I'll cut her in front of ye. I'll make her suffer if ye dunna get out of my way."

Still, Kieran didn't move. "Tell me why you want her."

"What's that?"

"You heard me. Tell me why you want her. What are you going to do with her?"

Argyle snorted. "If ye must know, we're going tae use her," he said. "The sons of Matthew Scott lead Clan Scott, but Ian has grown soft and weak."

"What does Annie have to do with that?"

"How else are we tae convince the man he needs tae stand down?"

"You mean you would use her to coerce Ian to surrender as clan chief?"

"If he wants his daughter tae live, he'll do as we wish."

"So your father is behind this?"

"My da has cunning sons. He'll appreciate us when he's chief. We'll rule alongside him."

Kieran stared at him as the plan, in its entirety, was revealed. After a moment, he shook his head. "Is *this* your plan?" he asked. "All of this chaos with convincing your clan that Annie was responsible for the deaths of their loved ones at Etal was meant to undermine her father?"

"She served a purpose. She will continue to do so."

Kieran sighed sharply. "This is stupid, even for you, Argyle," he said. "Ian has the support of William and other English allies. He is the rightful chief."

"His time is over."

"So you have tried to turn the clan against him? Against his daughter?"

"He's weak!" Argyle shouted.

As he said so, he jerked the blade in his hand and it nicked

Annaleigh on her white shoulder. A thin stream of red blood appeared. Kieran was coming to think that Argyle could very well nick her to pieces right in front of him. It might not kill her, but it would be torturous and painful. She was unconscious now but, at some point, she wouldn't be. And she'd be cut up from Argyle's wicked blade.

Kieran needed help.

He'd sent his son back to the keep where Christian would be searching every nook and alcove for his errant Scottish cousins. He didn't expect to see Christian anytime soon. Therefore, he needed help from the walls. The sentries were on the walls, going about their rounds, but he hadn't seen a soldier pass his way and the ones he could see in his periphery were too far away to notice what was transpiring in the stable yard.

Kieran was going to have to do some fast talking to free Annaleigh from her captors.

In a show of surrender, he put up his hands.

"Very well," he said, trying to stall for time. "I can see that you mean what you say. What do you want from me?"

Argyle was still agitated. "Get out of our way."

Kieran shook his head. "Think, man," he said. "How do you intend to leave? On foot? Dragging an injured woman? Or are you planning on riding out of here? If so, where are your horses? How will you take Annie with you if she cannot ride?"

Argyle frowned, looking at Brendan for the first time as if his brother might have the answer. "I want horses," Argyle said, returning his attention to Kieran. "Give me your horse."

Again, Kieran shook his head. "Not mine," he said. "He responds only to me. He would be useless to you. If you let me enter the stables, I'll find you horses that you can ride."

Argyle's face darkened. "Nay," he said. "Dunna come any

closer."

Kieran grunted in exasperation. "So we are to stand here all night?" he said. Then he waved his hands at Argyle in a sweeping motion. "Back away so I can come in."

Argyle was torn. He didn't want Kieran any closer, but he needed the horses. He had to get out of there. They could slide past Kieran, but they couldn't slide past the entire de Wolfe army and that's what was coming if they didn't move quickly.

They had to get out of there.

"Pick her up," he hissed to his brother. "Pick her up and back away."

Brendan awkwardly picked Annaleigh up, her wounded head dangling over his left arm. Argyle began to back up with him, keeping the distance between him and Kieran.

"Come in and get us two horses," he said. "Brendan and I are going through the postern gate. We'll meet ye around the side. Bring the horses and if ye bring any men with ye, we'll throw Annie down the side of the mountain that Castle Questing is perched upon."

Kieran took a few slow steps towards the stables' entry. "And what do you think will happen to you if you do that?"

"We'll run off. We'll take our chances."

"I'll have a thousand men looking for you. You cannot escape."

"Mayhap not, but Annie will still be dead. Are ye going tae take that chance?"

Kieran never had a chance to answer. The next thing he realized, Argyle's head was flying off his shoulders and blood was spraying everywhere. He saw the flash of a blade and heard Brendan scream.

Help had arrived.

CHAPTER TWENTY-ONE

H E WASN'T QUITE sure how he was going to tell Annaleigh what had happened.

He'd been trying to figure it out ever since leaving de Wolfe's solar. All he could see was the hope in her eyes when he had asked permission to court her. Now, all he could see was the disappointment knowing that he hadn't secured William's blessing.

He was a failure.

That wasn't something he normally experienced. Ever since he'd been a small boy, success and victory had come easily to him. There had been a few setbacks, of course, but nothing catastrophic. He'd always been able to recover.

But this time, it was different.

Not only had he not received permission to court Annaleigh, but the entire situation with de Wolfe had spiraled out of control.

What do you expect to gain?

Those words from de Wolfe were rolling around in his head. He'd been so deeply offended by them that the conversation had immediately turned sour. De Wolfe had tolerated his anger until he became insulting and, then, the man had come back at him. Truth be told, War knew he deserved it, but he had been quite wounded by William's intimation that he expected to "gain" something.

Truthfully, War didn't know what he wanted.

Up until a few days ago, he'd only had one father. He'd been content. Now, he'd lost the only father he'd ever known and de Wolfe didn't seem too keen to having another son. It wasn't as if War expected him to fall at his feet, weeping with joy and gratitude. Or… maybe he had, just a little. Maybe he'd hoped for an embrace and a warm reception with de Wolfe declaring how proud he was that War was his son.

Maybe that's really why he'd been offended in the first place.

Wouldn't *any* man be proud to have War Herringthorpe as a son?

After leaving the solar, he'd gone straight into the kitchen yard because he'd thought Annaleigh might be there. She seemed to spend a good deal of time in the kitchen yard, so he was hoping to find her there, but she was nowhere to be found. The cook was there and his helpers, but no Annaleigh.

War had plopped down on a bench against the kitchen wall and sulked.

Aye, *sulked.*

He thought long and hard about what had happened. He tried to maintain his indignant stance, but the more he reviewed the conversation, the more he could see that he'd needlessly become angry. War had always prided himself on maintaining his composure in any situation, but he'd failed in this case.

Yet one more failure in an accumulating list of them.

He was coming to think that de Wolfe had simply restrained himself from showing joy or surprise or gratitude in the face of such news because he was waiting for War to display how *he* felt. The man wasn't going to lay himself out there if War was unhappy about the whole thing and War hardly blamed him for that, but War had taken that restraint as rejection.

That's what this was all about.

Rejection.

Given the way he'd acted, War didn't blame de Wolfe for behaving the way he had. War had all but said he didn't want anyone to know of his association with William. He didn't even know why he'd said it. His only excuse was that perhaps the truth was that he had expected William to openly embrace him and when he hadn't, that hurt turned to rage.

As he sat and sulked, he was beginning to feel stupid.

Worse than stupid.

Ridiculous.

He could have just kicked himself. He'd gone in there to ask for permission to court Annaleigh and he'd left with absolutely nothing. He could hardly face Annaleigh with what he'd done, but he knew one thing – he had to apologize to de Wolfe. Even if the man didn't accept his apology, at least he would have tried. He did the exact thing that Edmund told him not to do and he hoped he wasn't going to pay the price.

He hoped it wasn't going to cost him Annaleigh.

Taking a deep breath and forcing himself to his feet, he headed from the kitchen yard. He began practicing what he was going to say to de Wolfe, asking for the man's pardon. He didn't even think about bringing up courting Annaleigh again because de Wolfe might think he was only apologizing to gain permission, so that wasn't going to come up. He was just exiting the kitchen yard when he saw Kieran heading towards the stables.

Hage.

De Wolfe's second in command and, by de Wolfe's own admission, his best friend for many years. Kieran had remained calm during the dust up in the solar, trying to defuse the situation. But, at that moment, War would not be defused.

Now was a little different.

Perhaps he needed to speak with Kieran Hage first.

He began to follow Kieran as the man headed to the stables. He picked up the pace to catch up with him when he suddenly saw Kieran bolt, straight for the stable yard. Curious, not to mention concerned, War began to trot after him. He couldn't see the stable yard or the stables itself from his angle but when he came around the corner of the inner wall, he could see everything perfectly.

What he saw had him stopping dead in his tracks.

Kieran was standing a dozen or so feet from the stables' entry, frozen, but War could see clearly what had the man rooted to the spot. In the entry, he could see some man he didn't recognize pulling limp and unconscious Annaleigh with him and another man who had a dagger pointed at her chest.

Annaleigh had blood on her face.

After that, War saw red.

He didn't know who the pair was and he didn't care, but they were dead men. He had no concept of the situation, of what had happened or why Annaleigh was bloodied, but none of that mattered.

The man named War, bred for battle, emerged full-force.

His first instinct was to run past Kieran like a madman and

charge the pair that had Annaleigh, but he was thankfully able to curb the urge. He was seasoned enough to know that doing so would put Annaleigh's life in danger. He couldn't even entertain the thought that she might be already dead. In fact, if there was a dagger pointed at her, then clearly she must be alive. He clung to that belief.

She's alive!

He had to save her.

Kieran was speaking to the pair in even, steady tones but War couldn't hear what was being said. Not that it mattered. He began looking around frantically for a way into the rear of the stable yard, but the area was fairly self-enclosed. He didn't know Castle Questing well enough to know if there were any additional entrances but he assumed so. He ducked away, rushing back along the wall towards the kitchens which, if he remembered correctly, butted up against the stable yard wall.

Perhaps there was a way in that way.

"War!"

He heard his name, turning to see Alexei coming from the hall, waving at him. Other than a few daggers, War wasn't armed, but Alexei was. The knight from Vilnius always wore his broadsword, in every situation. He even slept with it. War rushed the man, reaching out to unsheathe his broadsword when he came within range.

"I need your weapon," he said, extreme urgency in his tone. "Go to the mouth of the stable yard and stay out of sight. I will need you."

Alexei's relaxed expression instantly morphed into one of great concern. "What is happening?"

War didn't have time to explain. "Annaleigh is in trouble," he said. "Go to the mouth of the stable yard and stay out of sight. When I need you, I'll shout."

Alexei was wise enough not to ask any questions. He'd served with War long enough to know that this was a moment to simply follow orders, and he did. As he ran over to the entry to the stable yard, War, with Alexei's broadsword, raced to the rear of the kitchen yard where it joined with the stable yard. As he'd hoped, there was as small gate between the two.

Quietly, War lifted the latch. Unfortunately, the iron gate had a sticky hinge and the gate creaked as he opened it. He paused a couple of times, hoping a break in the noise wouldn't make it sound as if the gate were being opened to those who might be attuned to such a thing. The last thing he wanted to do was tip off whoever held Annaleigh captive, so after a few breaks in the opening of the noisy gate, he slipped into the stable yard.

War was in the shadows, away from the torchlight, so Kieran didn't see him as he continued to converse with the men who held Annaleigh. War couldn't see her from this angle, but as he frantically looked for a way into the stables other than the main entry, he saw a small servants' door cut into the side of the south wall.

With great stealth, War slipped up to the door and opened it with the ultimate care. Fortunately, this door made no noise as it opened and War slid into the stables, his gaze fixed on two men at the entry, facing Kieran.

At this point, he could hear what they were saying. There were demands for a horse. Kieran offered to get them horses, but he had to be allowed to come into the stables. The men began to back up, away from the enormous knight, and the man dragging Annaleigh heaved her into his arms, but he almost dropped her. War found himself wincing as the man held

Annaleigh precariously and awkwardly. He could see her head and left arm flapping uncomfortably.

Moving with extreme care and silence, War crept along in the shadows, dropping to his knees to stay low when those shadows no longer covered his movements. Now, the men were threatening to throw Annaleigh over a mountain. War could hear them. Kieran was telling them how unwise that would be. The men began to back up further, their backs to War, and as Kieran approached the entry cautiously, War knew he had to act now and act swiftly.

The Vilnius sword began to arc.

The first contact he made was with the man who seemed to be doing all of the negotiating. War didn't even go for a simple kill; the skills he'd learned at Blackchurch came into play, the nuances of situations where heavy force was used or light but deadly force. At the moment, it was heavy force, for he sliced through the man's shoulder and neck, completely separating his head from his body.

As the first man's head went sailing into the air before hitting the ground in a burst of blood and tissue, the man holding Annaleigh screamed like a woman, but not for long. War's sword carved into that man as well, only he skillfully took off the top half of the man's head rather than the whole head because he didn't want to chance cutting Annaleigh. The way the man was holding her was too close to his shoulders.

Therefore, half a messy head went sailing into the straw.

Annaleigh and the man hit the ground.

War was on Annaleigh faster than he could draw another breath. He scooped her into his arms and rushed from the stables, still holding Alexei's sword. He was in panic mode at this point because she was in his arms and he was desperate to get her to safety. But he could hear Kieran calling behind him and he slowly came to a halt just shy of the stable yard entry.

Breathing heavily, and protecting his burden, he turned to the big knight.

"War," Kieran said, his features full of concern. "All is well, lad. It was just those two and not an entire army out to get her. She's safe now."

War was struggling to calm down but he wasn't doing a very good job. "She's injured," he said. "I have to find the physic."

Kieran could see that War was terrified. He'd never known the man, a Blackchurch-trained knight, to be anything other than cold and calculating in battle, but this… this was something different.

Emotion was involved.

Blackchurch had never covered things like love.

Kieran could see that, as plain as day. He put both hands on War to steady him before taking a moment to examine Annaleigh. She was still unconscious, with a wound somewhere on her bloody head. He didn't have time to search it out. Turning towards the gatehouse, he began bellowing the alarm. His voice carried all over the compound so men began running in his direction, no questions asked.

One of those men was Alexei.

He charged into the yard, his eyes wide on War with a bloodied lady in his arms and a bloodied sword.

"My God," he hissed. "War, what happened?"

"He saved Annaleigh," Kieran answered for him. "Will you help him into the keep and find the physic for Annie? She needs help."

Alexei nodded, now putting his hands on War to direct him

towards the keep. War was moving stiffly at this point, still wrought with panic but trying very hard to calm. He hadn't taken two steps when men began rushing at him from the keep.

William was among them. One look at War holding a sword and bloodied Annaleigh and William went into battle mode.

"Stop there, Herringthorpe!" he boomed. "Drop the weapon!"

There was great confusion now as William began shouting orders. Hearing this, Kieran rushed to War's side and held out a hand to William, who was ordering the men around him to produce swords in War's direction.

"William, *stop*," Kieran commanded. "This is not how it looks. War just saved Annie's life from Argyle and Brendan. If it was not for him, Annie would be in great jeopardy right now. They did the damage to her – *not* War."

William was still in battle mode, but now confusion was part of the mix. He looked at Kieran with great bewilderment.

"Argyle and Brendan?" he repeated. "What in the hell are you talking about?"

Kieran put his hands on War's broad shoulders to steady him. "Argyle and Brendan arrived here earlier tonight and demanded to speak with Annie," he said loudly and clearly so there would be no mistake. "They told her they had a message from her brother and demanded to deliver it privately, but their plan was to take Annie back to Langton and use her to coerce her father to surrender his position as clan chief. They were the ones who wounded her, William. Not War. He saved her life."

William blinked, stunned at what he was hearing. His gaze moved from Kieran to War, holding a clearly wounded Annaleigh. Processing the turn of events quickly, he stood aside and made a clear path to the keep.

"Then get her inside," he said hoarsely. "Quickly, now. Take her to her chamber immediately. I will send the physic."

War didn't hesitate. He ran past William with Alexei in tow, both of them running as fast as they could. William followed swiftly, shouting to his men to seal up Castle Questing in case there were any more Scots about, perhaps waiting for Argyle and Brendan to emerge with their hostage. As William and Kieran went about securing the castle, War was already up the mural stairs and into Annaleigh's chamber.

William had already sent a soldier to the hall to summon the physic as War placed Annaleigh carefully on her bed. There was a female servant on this level, awakened from her slumber in the alcove as War and Alexei entered. Alexei sent the woman for hot water and as she fled, frightened and confused, Alexei managed to wrest his sword from War, who was still holding it tightly in his left hand.

War let it go.

His focus was on Annaleigh.

With the gentleness of a mother, he smoothed her hair away from her face, trying to get a look at the damage on the left side of her head. He could hear Alexei behind him, leaning over him to get a better look.

"It's difficult to tell where the blood is coming from," War said, his voice trembling. "It's in her hair, so it must be a scalp wound."

"Aye," Alexei said, hearing the fear in War's tone. "Wounds to the head bleed madly. It could be something quite small, in fact."

He was trying to ease the man because he was so worried. War touched the left side of Annaleigh's head tenderly, trying to see where the blood was coming from. Then, he spied it – a fairly long gash just inside of the hairline by her left temple. As the servant rushed back in with a bucket of hot water and linen, Alexei quickly took it from her. Dunking the linen in the water, he wrung it out and handed it over to War.

Carefully, War began to clean the area.

"It is still bleeding a little," he said, inspecting the cut. "It is going to need stitches. Where is that damnable physic?"

"Coming."

War and Alexei turned to see William entering the chamber. The reply had come from him. He made his way over to the bed, peering at his wife's cousin.

"Has she awoken?" he asked.

War shook his head as he returned his attention to Annaleigh. "Nay," he said. "She has a substantial gash and a lump the size of an egg on her head. They must have hit her over the head with something very hard."

"Kieran says had it not been for you, she would more than likely be in a good deal of trouble."

"I was glad to assist, my lord."

William's gaze moved from Annaleigh to War as the man tended to her with the concern of a mother to child.

Or husband to wife.

He watched War for a moment, the man's expression as he looked at Annaleigh, the tender manner in which he cleaned the wound. Had he known absolutely nothing about the man and this was the first time he'd ever met him, he would have thought him to be deeply in love with Annaleigh. It was in everything about him.

Kieran's words came ringing back to him.

I suspect the death of his father has compounded his confu-

sion and angst about the situation with you.

Perhaps that was true. Perhaps that's why things went so badly in the solar between the two of them. William remembered how the death of his own father affected him and he couldn't imagine what would have happened had he been told, at the same time, that he wasn't Edward de Wolfe's offspring. In hindsight, he supposed he didn't blame War for being edgy about the whole thing, especially when William produced a letter that War hadn't been ready to give him yet. The man was still working through his grief with his father when William handed him the letter and demanded answers.

Nay, William hadn't handled that well at all.

Perhaps apologies were in order.

He turned to Alexei.

"Will you leave us, please?" he asked.

Alexei did without hesitation. He quit the chamber, leaving the door open, as William moved to the other side of the bed, across from War. The man was still focused on Annaleigh, as he should be. The fact that William was in the chamber was inconsequential to him.

When in love with a woman, William rather understood that attitude. The world faded when gazing upon the face of the only person who mattered, especially when she was in distress.

"I was wrong, War," William said softly. "I realize this may not be the time or place for this, but I must apologize to you for behaving as I did earlier today. I should not have become angry with you for reasons I do not yet fully understand, but I know it was not right. Even if you do not wish to accept my apology, know that I am sorry all the same."

War put the bloodied linen back into the bowl and looked up at him. "I was going to say the same thing to you," he said quietly. "I was wrong. I behaved horrifically. My only excuse is that I suppose I wasn't yet ready to deal with our relationship. Things have changed so quickly in my life over the past several days that I find that I can hardly comprehend it all."

William held up a hand in an easing gesture. "There is no need for you to apologize," he said. "I am to blame. I should not have told you I had your mother's letter. I should have let you bring it to me when you were ready."

War nodded, digesting that as his gaze moved to Annaleigh. "I have a confession to make, my lord."

"What is that?"

"I am proud to be Edmund Herringthorpe's son," he said. "But the truth is that Edmund was not a very good knight. Adequate, but not great. Now that I've had some time to think about the blood that flows through my veins, I would like to say that I am proud to bear that heritage. De Wolfe heritage. If I could thank you for anything at all, it would be for giving me that part of you. You gave me life and for that, I am grateful."

William smiled faintly. "You do the de Wolfe bloodlines proud, War," he said. "You are a fine tribute to your ancestors. Mayhap it is too soon to bring this up, but for your father, whom you loved very much, mayhap you should consider keeping his name. If you wish to take the de Wolfe name, I will not stop you, but Edmund sounds like a fine man. He raised a fine son."

War looked at him again, his eyes glimmering with unshed tears. But there was a smile on his face. "Thank you," he said quietly. "My father *was* a very fine man. But I am coming to see that you are, as well. I mean no disrespect to you that I shall keep my name as it is."

"Of course not. You *are* a Herringthorpe."

"I am a de Wolfe in Herringthorpe-sheep's clothing."

William chuckled. "That you are, lad," he said. "And there has never been a finer de Wolfe. But to continue to honor your father and his name, I suspect that is something that should only be known between us."

War nodded reluctantly. "That is true," he said. "If my true bloodlines were known, men would call me a de Wolfe regardless of what I wished to be called."

"More than that, it would put your mother in a bad light," William said softly. "I would not want you to shame Jane that way. Keeping Edmund's name is a tribute to her, also."

War nodded. "Agreed," he said. "I could not let men think that my mother was… unchaste by bearing a bastard."

"We do not want to give the gossips any fuel," William said. "And we do not want to damage the name of Lady Jane de Percy."

War smiled in agreement, thinking on his mother and the secret she had kept, of her love for a warrior who would go on to be England's greatest knight.

That brought something to mind.

"Your understanding and generosity does your reputation justice," he said, his attention returning to Annaleigh again. "I am honored by it. But we have an interesting situation here not unlike the one between you and my mother."

William's brow furrowed. "What do you mean?"

"Annaleigh," War said simply. "Although I will make it clear that I've done nothing more than speak to the woman, I fear that my feelings for her are quite strong, as my mother's were for you. In this case, you are my mother's father and I am you when you went to my grandfather to ask for my mother's hand. You have that power over my life and happiness, my lord.

I hope you will not tell me to go away and stay away."

William was prevented from answering when Jemma and the physic arrived in the chamber and War was practically yanked away from the bedside by Jemma, who was desperate to get to her niece. In fact, War ended up stumbling and William had to steady him as Jemma and the physic descended on Annaleigh, followed shortly thereafter by Jordan. With the three of them crowding around her bed, War and William were pushed to the doorway, watching from afar.

Watching anxiously in War's case.

"They will take good care of her," William assured War quietly. "But I will tell you that the two men you killed were Jemma's nephews."

War was resolute. "Though I am sorry for their demise, they left me with no choice," he said. "Any man who would think of touching Annie will face my wrath. I will kill for her, as I have proven. I will also gladly die for her."

William could hear the passion in his voice and he looked at him, studying the man's features. He did indeed look like William's father, Edward. Even more so at close range.

He allowed himself to feel some pride in the man, after all.

"If Annie is what you truly want, then you will have no argument from me," he said softly. "I will speak to her father, Ian, and when I tell him how you saved her life, I am certain you will have no argument from him, either. Given the way you two met, I believe you are destined to be together. I know my wife and I were. It seems that you are to follow in our footsteps in that way."

War looked at William, the anxiety on his features changing into that of joy. Tempered joy, as if he wanted to become excited about it but truly couldn't. Not until he knew Annaleigh was going to be well again. But that didn't stop him from giving William a grateful nod of the head.

"Thank you, my lord," he said sincerely. "Your blessing means a great deal. And if Annie and I could be so fortunate to have the years of happiness between us that you and your lady wife have had, then I will consider us most fortunate, indeed."

Before William could reply, Annaleigh's foot twitched. Both William and War saw it, with War stepping forward to see if he could get a look at Annaleigh's face. He wanted to see if she was awake. William remained back by the door as Kieran came to stand in the doorway, looking with concern at all of the activity.

"How is she?" Kieran asked.

William shook his head. "I do not know," he said. Then, he looked at Kieran. "What did you do with Argyle and Brendan?"

Kieran lifted his eyebrows. "We've collected their body parts and put them in canvas sacks," he said. "War made quick work out of them."

William grunted as he returned his attention back to the bed, where Annaleigh was now moving around a little more. "He is a de Wolfe," he said softly. "I expected nothing less from the man when the woman he loves is threatened."

There was something in his tone that made Kieran peer at him closely. "Have you two spoken again?"

"We have."

"And?"

William wouldn't look at him. "And he and Annie shall be married at some point, I'm certain," he said. He looked at Kieran again, a smile on his lips. "We have made peace and I am glad. He's a worthy man, Kieran. Worthy of my bloodlines. But the world will never know it."

Kieran understood much in those few words. "You will not

tell anyone?"

"Nay," William said. "To honor Edmund Herringthorpe and to honor Jane de Percy, who most certainly would look like a trollop if the truth were revealed, no one will know. If you've told Jemma, you will make sure she doesn't tell a soul."

Kieran nodded. "I will," he said. "You'll not even tell your sons?"

William shook his head. "Why?" he said. "There is no reason to. War is a Herringthorpe and that's all they ever need know. It is better that way."

Kieran understood and he was surprised that two men with such great pride were able to see beyond the situation and how it would affect the legacy of others. Truthfully, he wasn't surprised that William saw it because he knew William as well as he knew himself. He knew that in a situation that really didn't matter in the long run, protecting a man's – and woman's – legacy was more important than feeding his pride in a newly discovered and important son. And War… clearly, he had William's sense of compassion and good judgment.

A Herringthorpe he would remain, as a tribute to the man who raised him.

As William and Kieran contemplated the secret de Wolfe cub, War was completely focused on Annaleigh as she came out of unconsciousness. The physic, along with Jemma, had cleaned up the rather large gash on her head and just as she was coming around, the physic began to stitch it up. Annaleigh winced with pain, disoriented when she opened her eyes. She saw Jordan and Jemma and the physic, her eyes wide with confusion. The physic threw in another stitch and she gasped, her hand flying to her head, but War was next to the physic and managed to grab it before she could touch her wound.

"Annie, you've been injured and the physic is tending your wound," he said softly and steadily as he held her hand. "Just a stitch or two more and he shall be finished. You've been very brave, angel."

Jordan and Jemma looked at him in surprise as he called her a term of endearment, but he did not look at them. He was completely focused on Annaleigh, who fixed on him with her groggy eyes.

"Injured?" she repeated. "What… where am I? What happened?"

"You are in your bedchamber," War said. "Look around but do not move your head. Do you recognize it?"

She blinked, looking around as much as she could but obeying his request not to move her head. "Aye," she said hesitantly, but her eyes abruptly widened and she tried to propel herself off the bed. "Argyle and Brendan! They want tae take me back tae Langton! Where did they go?"

Many hands reached out to still her, including War's. "They are no longer a concern," he said, still holding her hand but also making sure she didn't try to jump up again. "They will never threaten you again, I promise."

Annaleigh winced when the physic quickly put another stitch in her scalp. "They lied tae me," she said. "They told me that Robbie was ill and that I was tae return home tae see him right away. They told me that he was dying."

William heard her and he came up to stand at the end of the bed along with Kieran. "Is that why they came?" he asked her. "To tell you that your brother was dying?"

Annaleigh's gaze moved from War to William. "Aye," she said. "They said my father might be ill, too. But it was all a trick. They took me out tae the stables and wouldna let me leave. I tried tae run but… but I dunna remember what happened."

"You fell and hit your head," Kieran said. "I saw what happened. You were running from Brendan when you fell and hit your head on the stables' door."

The physic finished with the stitches and stepped away from the bed as Jordan and Jemma moved in to bandage up her head. But Annaleigh was still in fight or flight mode, still thinking on the terror she had endured.

"They were awful," she muttered. "They grabbed me and were forcing me tae go home with them so they could use me as a hostage against my father. I always knew them tae be sly and nasty, but they were going tae hurt me just tae gain their wants."

"No more," War said softly. "You're safe now. You do not have to worry about them any longer."

Annaleigh looked to War, still kneeling beside the bed, still holding her hand. She was becoming more lucid now and her eyes glimmered at him when she realized what he meant. She may have been groggy, but she wasn't daft.

She knew.

"Ye punished them, dinna ye?" she asked quietly.

He nodded faintly, lifting her hand up to kiss it. "I would do anything for you."

She smiled at him but it also occurred to her that William was watching. So were Kieran and Jordan and Jemma. Everybody was watching. Embarrassed, and not to get War into any trouble with William, she tried to discreetly remove her hand from his but he wouldn't let go. She couldn't understand why War wasn't more concerned with what everyone was witnessing until William spoke up.

"War is going to remain here with you, Annie, while Kieran

and I go to Langton Castle," he said. "War has asked permission to court you, but the final word must come from your father. Also, I do believe your father could use a show of strength from his allies against those within your clan who might be thinking of usurping him as chief. Kieran and I intend to deliver Argyle and Brendan back to him as a gift from your betrothed."

Annaleigh had no idea what he was talking about. "What gift?" she said, puzzled. "And what betrothed?"

William grinned. "Did you not just hear me?" he said. "War asked permission to marry you. I have given it, but the final word must come from your father."

She blinked. Then, she looked at War, open astonishment on her features. "My… my betrothed?"

War couldn't keep the smile off his face. "If you'll have me."

Realization set in. Now, she knew why he'd refused to let go of her hand and she could hardly believe it. It seemed that a good deal had happened while she lay unconscious so rather than ask an avalanche of questions, she simply accepted it. She accepted her destiny. Aching head and all, she sat up and put her arms around his neck, squeezing the life from him. As Jordan and Jemma, William and Kieran beamed, War squeezed back.

It was the best embrace he'd ever experienced.

"I'll have no other," Annaleigh whispered into his ear. "From now until the end of all things, there will be ye and no other."

They were words to live by.

When William and Kieran returned from Langton Castle almost three weeks later, War received the final approval from Ian, who was more than willing to give it when William and Kieran told him the story of how War saved Annaleigh from

Argyle and Brendan. Furthermore, when William and Kieran came home, it was with Cord Scott in tow. At Ian's request, the man went straight into the vault of Castle Questing for his fate to be determined for his part in his sons' plot.

But that would come at a later date.

The only thing that mattered to War was that he had his Scots angel, the lass who had once saved his life. He'd been able to repay that debt and then some. War Herringthorpe was a man shadowed by the greatness of his bloodlines, but he was also a man who had found his way in life on his own. His own path, his own love, and his own destiny.

Edmund would have been proud.

EPILOGUE

Bamburgh Castle
Six months later

WAR WAS DRUNK.

He was absolute, unashamedly drunk as he sang loudly alongside James de Wolfe and Christian Hage, and another knight he'd met a few months back by the name of Apollo de Norville. Men he'd become close to over the past several months, through dealings with another de Montfort former supporter, and business on the border, including cleaning out The Bones and sending their leader, a one-eyed bastard who called himself Father Moon, back to Tobin du Reims to do with as he pleased in the wake of Talus' death.

Men who could be so cold and deadly in battle, but men who could celebrate and show their joy in life more than anyone War had ever seen. When those three got together in a relaxed or joyous situation, happy chaos ensued.

It all started with a song.

There once was an old whore named Rose,

With a wart on the end of her nose.

When her legs she would spread,

And men lost their heads,

The smell would knock everyone dead!

The corner of the great hall of Bamburgh that had heard the song burst into loud, lewd laughter. Men were cheering and drinking, drinking and cheering, and War was in the middle of it as James and Christian dragged him onto the table where they were all standing. They began shouting for everyone to quiet down, throwing things at those who didn't shut their lips fast enough, as James drunkenly put his arm around War's broad shoulders.

Finally, the crowd quieted down.

"Here before you stands a bridegroom," James said. Then, he pinched War's chin affectionately. "Look at this man's face. Does he not look handsome?"

The crowd cheered.

"Does he not look happy?"

More cheering.

"Then shut yer yaps because the man has something tae say!"

He spoke the last sentence in an exaggerated Scottish accent, like his mother and aunt would say. The cheers grew to enormous proportions and food and bones were being thrown at him, at Christian, and at Apollo, who threw them back. Apollo even leapt off a table and began punching some fool who had hit him in the mouth with a chicken bone.

At War and Annaleigh's wedding feast, they'd served chicken.

It was Annaleigh's favorite.

"Shut up, all of you!" War boomed. "If my wife cannot hear what I have to say, I will slay every one of you and take great pleasure in your suffering. Do you comprehend me?"

He was met with laughter, but the room dutifully subdued. War put his arm around James' shoulder just as James was embracing him, a gesture of the camaraderie that War had developed with his allies. He began pointing to the men around him.

"You," he said, pointing to Christian. "I love you. And you, Apollo. I love you, also."

Christian and Apollo put their hands over their hearts in thanks, a gesture of reciprocation. But War wasn't finished yet.

"To Alexei and Monty, my faithful men, I love you both," he said, loudly so the room could hear him. "I even love Anthony d'Vant, who lost out to me for Annie's affections. He was an honorable loser and a worthy opponent. To Lord Kilham and Sir Kieran, I love them as if they were my very own kin. To Sir Paris… well, I've tried to love you and I am trying still, but you would sorely test God's love, so I'm not entirely sure how I shall endure, but I shall try. You command a mighty army and I want to love you."

William, Kieran, and Paris were standing over by the dais, cups of fine wine in hand, wine provided by the House of de Wolfe on behalf of the bride. William and Kieran looked at Paris, laughing at the man because he really had been a thorn in War's side for the past several months because he kept insisting that there was nothing about Bamburgh that Northwood didn't do better. It was a good-natured rivalry that bordered on slander at times, but that was the way bonds were built sometimes – by one man being an arse and another man letting him know just how big of an arse he was.

Such was War and Paris' relationship.

But Paris wouldn't be publicly called out so. He pointed at War and shouted. "You will love me more than all of these dolts by the time I am finished with you," he said. "And Northwood is still superior to Bamburgh!"

The room rolled with laughter and War balled a fist at him, indicating what he thought of that statement. But War soon held his hand up to the crowd, begging for silence, and the room quieted down.

"To the House of de Wolfe, to whom I owe everything," he said. "My love and gratitude to Scott and Troy, to Patrick and even little Eddie and Tommy. It has been my privilege to know you all. Thank you for being so welcoming and for introducing me to my bride."

Seated at the dais, Scott and Troy, sitting with their wives, as well as Patrick, waved at War, who waved back. In the past six months, War had built tremendous bonds with the older de Wolfe brothers given they were commanding castles and outposts near Bamburgh. It was true that, by blood, they really were War's brothers, but that was a secret that was maintained to this day.

And it always would.

"But most of all," War said, looking at Annaleigh on the dais, seated between Jordan and Ian. "But the very most of all I reserve for my wife, my beautiful Annaleigh. My darling, sweet Annie. May nothing but happiness ever enter our lives, sweet angel. May nothing but love fill our hearts. And may nothing but the goodness of faith and loyalty ever fill our home. To my beloved bride, I drink this toast."

Everyone lifted their cup except for Annaleigh. She smiled adoringly at her husband from across the room, watching as

James broke the spell and poured wine over War's head. That seemed to bring on the loud, raucous celebration again as War shoved James so hard that he fell over backwards into a group of seated men. As everyone laughed at James' expense, War came off the table and made his way through the cavernous great hall of Bamburgh to the dais where his wife awaited.

His wife.

It was their wedding day.

The first thing War did when he came to the table was point to Jordan, who was holding Penelope in her arms. The child was sleeping like the dead and his eyebrows rose.

"She is sleeping through this?" he asked, incredulous.

Jordan smiled at her sleepy girl. "The lass would sleep through the coming of Christ," she said. "But if I put her in her bed where it is nice and quiet, she'll wake up and cry. So… she'll sleep well here in the midst of the noise."

War shook his head at such a child. Edward and Thomas, the younger boys, were sitting politely with their mother and War dug into the purse at his side, a fine purse made of silk, and pulled out two coins. He gave one to each child and they loved him for it. He also gave money to the other children, to Cassiopeia de Norville and Rose and Nathaniel Hage. All of the children loved Uncle War, as they called him, because he was kind and generous.

But none loved him more than Annaleigh did.

The past six months had been something out of a dream for her. She's remained at Castle Questing, permanently, while War came every week to court her. He would bring her flowers or fine fabric he'd purchased in the village of Bamburgh, or pomade that smelled like herbs. Every time he came, he brought her a gift. One time, he'd even brought her brined vegetables in an earthenware jar tied off with a red silk ribbon. The gifts weren't particularly fine or elaborate, merely a token of his admiration for her.

Admiration that soon turned to love.

Ian, with things in his clan settling down with the loss of Cord, Argyle, and Brendan, even came to Castle Questing a few times to become acquainted with this legendary knight who wanted to marry his daughter. He'd come to like the big man with the big voice who could command an army with the wave of his hand, just like God. There had never been a doubt in his mind that granting War permission to marry his daughter had been the right thing to do because, even now, with a wild party going on around them, War and Annaleigh only had eyes for each other.

It did a father's heart good to see it.

"Annie," Ian said, leaning towards her in his chair. "Mayhap it's time for ye and yer husband tae retire while the laddies are occupied with food and wine?"

"He's right," William said, setting his cup down. "While they're distracted. Otherwise, they're going to follow you into the marital chamber and it will be an unhappy night for you both because they'll want to linger and give you instructions. I do not think you want that."

Annaleigh rolled her eyes. "Not from that bunch," she said. Rising from her chair, she bent over to kiss her father on the cheek. "Will ye escort us upstairs?"

Ian shook his head. "As much as I'd love tae, I dunna want tae fight off that group of Sassenach," he said, his eyes twinkling with mirth as he gestured to the young, drunk knights. "Let their fathers do that. I'd only be in the way."

Annaleigh giggled. "Are ye sure?"

"I'm sure," Ian said. "Sleep well, lass."

Annaleigh kissed him again. "I will," she said. Then, she smiled sadly. "I'm sorry Robbie isna here. I'd hoped he would come."

Ian patted her cheek. "He thought it best tae stay at Langton," he said quietly. "There are still some who side with Cord and Argyle, so it is best not tae remove both Robbie and me from Langton just now. We'd return home and find our castle taken."

Annaleigh understood. There was still some discord within Clan Scott, minor though it was. "Then ye'll tell Robbie that I missed him," she said, kissing him on the cheek again. "I'll see ye in the morning."

Ian smiled at his only daughter, pinching her cheek affectionately. "I'll not worry if I dunna see ye," he said. "Ye might have more important things tae do."

Annaleigh knew what he meant and she struggled not to blush. Sticking her tongue out at him, a sassy but loving gesture, she turned to her husband and slipped her hand in his.

"Well?" she said. "Shall we go?"

"I want to go!" Penelope suddenly awoke, mumbling sleepily. She tried to sit up in her mother's arms. "I want to go, too. Where are we going?"

"You are not going anywhere," War said, pushing her down by the forehead so she was cradled in Jordan's arms again. "Go back to sleep."

Penelope started to whine as Jordan explained why she could not go with Annie and War, two of her favorite people in the world, as William and Kieran began to lead them from the hall. But not before William turned to Paris.

"If that mob starts coming, you hold them off," he told him.

"Give us time to get them to their chamber."

Paris was well into his drink. "For Herringthorpe, I would not lift a finger," he said. "But for Annie, I'll hold off the horde. Hurry, now, while they're distracted."

Like a covert operation, William and Kieran took War and Annaleigh quickly from the hall and into the keep of Bamburgh, which was surprisingly small given the size of the castle itself. While Kieran stood guard at the keep door, William took them up to the third floor of the keep, which was one giant chamber. There were windows on every wall, affording a complete view of both the sea and the countryside beyond.

Annaleigh had come to love that room, and that view, deeply.

"You should be safe for tonight," William said, looking around at a chamber that had been cleaned and stocked with wine and fruit and bread. There was a fire burning brightly in the hearth. "Do you require anything before I go?"

Annaleigh shook her head. "I dunna think so," she said. "But I do want tae thank ye, William. Were it not for ye, none of this would have happened. I owe ye my very happiness."

The way she said it made William take a second look at her. Something suggested that she knew the secret that War and William had kept buried and, God willing, always would. William wouldn't have been surprised if War had told her, because that was War's prerogative. Annaleigh was now his wife and, by all rights, should know everything about him. William looked at War, a hint of puzzlement in his expression, and War nodded his head in confirmation.

"She knows, William," he said softly. "I told her."

William looked at Annaleigh, who nodded, smiling. "I will take the secret tae my grave," she said. "For Jane's sake, I wouldna want it tae become gossip. Ye needna worry about me."

William smiled faintly. "I would never worry about you," he said. "You've proven yourself too many times, Annie. You know we consider you part of our family. But just so you are aware, my wife is taking credit for this marriage. She says that she arranged it."

Annaleigh laughed softly. "If that is her wish, then I'll allow her tae believe it," she said. "But know that I'm grateful for everything. Ye've been so kind tae me."

"Does that mean you'll let Penny visit you here at Bamburgh for long periods of time?"

Annaleigh burst out laughing. "Ye'd miss her too much," she said. "Ye can hardly stand tae be away from her even now."

William grinned, conceding the point. "True enough," he said. Then he held up a finger as if he'd just remembered something. "Before I go, I have something for you. War, I was going to give it to you in private but if Annie knows the nature of our relations, then I will present this to you both."

With that, he pulled forth a gold nugget from a pocket in his fine tunic, only it wasn't a nugget at all. It simply gleamed like one. He put it in War's palm, giving both War and Annaleigh a complete view of what it was.

A golden brooch gleamed in the weak light, some kind of flower design, and Annaleigh gasped at the beauty of it. There were fine, yellow stones on it.

It was absolutely magnificent.

"What is this?" she said, plucking it off War's palm. "It looks like a flower."

"It is," William said, watching Annaleigh inspect it closely. "That belonged to my mother, Adalira, and she got it from her own mother. The flower is native to the country she was born in, a sort of thorny bloom. I do believe the brooch is hundreds of years old because my mother's family was quite old, all the way back to the beginning of the world she used to say."

Annaleigh flipped it over, seeing that something was etched on the back of it. "What is this writing?" she asked. "I dunna recognize it."

William watched her examine the brooch. "That is because it is written in a language that is as old as time itself," he said. "You see, my mother's mother was born in the lands beyond The Levant. Very ancient lands. She was Saracen, meaning my mother was half-Saracen. The blood of ancient warriors flows through my veins, and War's veins, because of her. The writing on the back says '*Love is the beginning of forever*'."

"What a lovely sentiment," Annaleigh said. "And what a great and valuable treasure this is."

William nodded. "Sentimentally, it is," he said. "My mother died when I was quite young and that is all I ever had of her. My father gave it to me. He told me that the women in my mother's family passed it from mother to daughter but because my mother only had sons, my father gave it to me and told me to give it to a daughter."

Annaleigh was listening seriously. "But you dinna," she said. "Why not?"

He shrugged. "I'm not sure," he said. "Katheryn and Evelyn received so much on their wedding day that one more token would not have made a difference. They're not shallow women, mind you, but mayhap I simply wanted to save it since it is all I have of my mother. But I want you to have it, Annie. War is my firstborn son and I feel as if it belongs to you now. You will pass it to your daughter."

Annaleigh hugged him fiercely. "Thank ye," she said sincerely. "I shall treasure it always."

He smiled at her. "I know you will, lass," he said. Then he took a deep breath as if to shake off the sentiment that was clinging, something that made him sad when it pertained to his mother. "And with that, I will bid you both a good eve. Do not open this door for any reason unless you want a room full of drunken knights. They'll climb into bed with you and make your lives miserable."

Annaleigh giggled as War shook his head. "Nay, they will *not*," he said. "I will throw them from the windows if they try and it is a long way down."

William fought off a smile. "It is," he agreed. "But they might try regardless. Oh, and do not worry about the posts for the night, War. Kieran and I have seen to it. We will make sure Bamburgh's walls are protected since you are occupied."

War was deeply grateful. "I appreciate it," he said. "And speaking of walls, thank you for keeping Clement at Castle Questing. Not having that man around Bamburgh any longer is a great relief. I was growing weary of looking over my shoulder at every turn."

William's smile broke through. "It was my pleasure to accept his fealty, forced though it was," he said. "The man never had a choice in the matter, though it is good to have him as a replacement for Talus. He has been quite competent so far."

"He is competent, indeed," War said. "Just not here. Not with me. Alexei and Monty are like my brothers, but Clement… he simply never fit in with us."

"I do hope we are able to meet your real brothers one of these days."

War nodded. "They hoped to attend the wedding, but Henry has kept them busy in France," he said. "I am certain they will return home soon. I am anxious for Annie to meet them."

William nodded before giving Annaleigh a kiss on the cheek before opening the chamber door. "And with that, I will take my leave," he said. "Good night to you both. And bolt this door when I've gone."

He slipped through and War shut the door, throwing the bolt. When he turned to look at his wife, they both burst out laughing.

"Will they truly come up here and get in bed with us?" she said, incredulous. "What drunken fools they are."

War snorted. "Fools, indeed," he said. "I am serious when I said I'd throw them out the window. I do not want anything spoiling this night. I've waited six long months for it and nothing is going to interrupt it."

Annaleigh smiled coyly. The past six months had been a lesson in restraint for them both. It wasn't as if they hadn't had the opportunity to fornicate. It was simply that War wanted their first time together to be as husband and wife. It wasn't the act he was desperate to engage in, as he told her, but the opportunity to demonstrate his love to the woman he'd chosen to spend his life with.

Annaleigh couldn't disagree with him.

But now, the time was upon them and War didn't waste any of it. Reaching out, he took her in his arms and kissed her deeply, something he'd done freely over the past several months. She had a beautiful mouth and he loved to kiss it.

Now, the night belonged to them.

The mattress, made with fresh linens, beckoned them and while their mouths were still fused, War picked Annaleigh up and carried her over to the bed. She was clad in a pale blue silk, elegant and beautiful, and he set her to her feet carefully while trying to navigate the ties on the side and back. He was so eager to remove the dress that he ended up breaking a couple of the ties, apologizing profusely, but that didn't stop him from breaking another set of ties trying to get her out of it.

Annaleigh giggled at him in between heated kisses.

To match his passion, she grabbed at the ties on his breeches and gave a big yank. Grunting with the power of her pull, War started laughing as well. He ended up stripping himself and her, all by the light of the fire. Annaleigh had been so focused on undressing the man herself that she hardly realized when he'd stripped her first. Utterly nude, with the firelight dancing off her pale flesh, she didn't feel an ounce of shame as she faced her husband.

War was an enormous man to begin with and his manhood was proportionate to that. Annaleigh could feel it between them, on her belly, as he held her close. He was fully aroused and very hard but, for a moment, they simply held one another, flesh against flesh in the first moment that they'd been able to do so. It was a powerful moment. When War's big hands moved to cup her buttocks, she let him.

She cupped his, too.

War groaned, feeling her hot hands on his buttocks, as he gently caressed hers. His mouth slanted over hers again and, suddenly, they were falling back on the bed, but Annaleigh didn't shy away from him. She wrapped her tight, little body all around him, her legs around his waist, her arms around his neck, indulging in kisses that set her entire body on fire.

He set her body on fire.

She was eager to know him as a wife would know a husband.

War seemed to sense that because he was desperate to join his body with hers. She was holding him so tightly that he had to loosen her legs around his waist and shift his body so their pelvises were against one another. His mouth left hers, blazing a trail down to delicious breasts he'd become very acquainted with over the past six months. Round, firm, and silken, he took a nipple between his lips and suckled her tenderly.

Beneath him, Annaleigh gasped with pleasure.

There were no more words to be spoken, only the anticipation of what was to come, the physical demonstration of their feelings. War had to shift his body again because he was so big against her petite frame but, soon enough, he could feel her wet heat against his manhood and he could wait no longer. He pushed into her slowly, aware of how small she was beneath him, seating himself a tiny bit at a time and giving her time to adjust to his size.

He could feel her body twitch underneath him.

Annaleigh's maidenhead resisted him and he pulled back, coiling his buttocks before plunging into her and pushing through the barrier. Annaleigh gasped with the sting of possession as he seated himself, but it took three more thrusts before he was fully embedded. With each stroke, she groaned with the newness of the sensation, the minor pain such an action brought. But this is what she had wanted, what they had both wanted.

She welcomed the feel of her husband's body into hers.

"Is that all?" she grunted once he was fully seated. "Is there more?"

War lifted his head. "There's more," he murmured. "We have only started. I promise that you will not be disappointed."

Annaleigh trusted him, feeling the raw sting of his initial

possession fade as he began to move gently within her. Her legs wrapped around his hips instinctively, holding him close as the discomfort gave way to pleasure.

Very quickly, she was coming to enjoy it. His thrusts were driving her to the brink of madness. She had no way of knowing how this union would affect her, only knowing that the mere act of it filled something in her she never knew needed to be filled. Every stroke, every thrust seemed to ignite something deep in her belly, creating a hunger that needed to be satisfied.

Something only War could fulfill.

Annaleigh ended up watching him through half-lidded eyes, watching the rippling of his muscles and the expression on his face. It was something between passion and insanity, that dark area when a man's mind was so consumed with the woman he loved that nothing else existed. Her pelvis began moving with his, instinctively, meeting his every thrust as if they'd always done it this way. As if they'd always been together.

As if, over the eons, they'd done this time and time again.

Annaleigh knew him and he knew her.

But that kind of passion could not hold out forever. War's climax came as a guttural rumble in his throat and Annaleigh felt his manhood spasm deep inside her. But he kept moving, his big hand moving between their bodies to stroke her taut bud of pleasure. Annaleigh was quickly propelled into the heavens as she experienced her first release, her nails digging into his back as wave after wave of pleasure rolled over her.

It was bliss without end.

Annaleigh thought she might have actually blacked out because when next she realized, War had shifted his weight off her. Laying beside her, he gathered her in his arms and held her tightly, throwing a big leg over her hips to pull her close against him. Still trying to catch her breath, Annaleigh lay in his arms, feeling more contentment and love than she'd ever felt in her life.

"Well?" he murmured into her hair. "Was it worth the wait?"

Annaleigh lifted her head so that she could look at him. Their faces were very close together and she reached up, putting a gentle hand to his cheek.

"Ye're worth everything," she whispered. "There is nothing about ye that isna worth everything in this whole bloody world."

He closed his eyes as she tenderly touched his face, relishing the feel of it. "You became my world the moment I saw you after the battle of Etal," he murmured. "It is because of you I am here, Annie. God has brought you to me, more than once, so when I look at you, I see my destiny. I see my past, my present, and my future. I just can't believe we haven't always been meant for one another."

Annaleigh smiled, running her fingers over his lips and watching him kiss the tips. "It's as the brooch says," she said. "The one that William gave us. *Love is the beginning of forever.* For us, I canna remember when I've not loved ye. I'll love ye beyond forever, War. In this life or in any other."

He kissed her fingers, her palm. "What I feel goes beyond love," he whispered. "It's worship. I worship you, Annie. I always will and I feel as if I always have. With you, there's no beginning and no ending. Just… love."

With a grin, Annaleigh wrapped her arms around his neck, pulling him to her lips and feasting on him. There wasn't one touch, one word, or one action that didn't convey the deep and abiding love she had for him.

And he for her.

When their first child was born less than a year later after two of the longest days of War's life, the meaning of the brooch struck them even more than it had on their wedding day. As they gazed down at little Liam Herringthorpe, his name being a subtle tribute to War's de Wolfe bloodlines, the words on Adalira's brooch rang more clearly than they ever had.

Love is the beginning of forever.

For War and Annaleigh, nothing could have been more true.

Love *was* their forever.

CB THE END ☙

Children of War and Annie

Liam

Kyle

Taggart "Tag"

Logan

Brody

Jane

Mary

McCall "Mac"

Edmund

HOLDINGS AND TITLES OF THE HOUSE OF DE WOLFE AND CLOSE ALLIES AS OF 1267 A.D.

Sons of William de Wolfe – Earl of Warenton (as of 1267 A.D.)

Scott de Wolfe – Viscount Kilham (as the heir to the earldom)

Troy de Wolfe

Patrick de Wolfe

James de Wolfe

Edward de Wolfe

Thomas de Wolfe

Wark Castle (Wolfe's Eye):

Larger outpost for the Earl of Warenton. Literally sits on the border between England and Scotland.

Berwick Castle (Wolfe's Teeth):

Massive border castle, strategically important, de Wolfe.

Castle Questing (Wolfe's Heart):

Massive fortress, seat of the Earl of Warenton, William de Wolfe.

Rule Water Castle (Wolfe's Lair):

The largest outpost in the de Wolfe empire, known as The Lair. Seat of Scott de Wolfe, Viscount Kilham, heir apparent to the Earldom of Warenton.

Kale Water Castle (Wolfe's Den):

Larger outpost on the England side of the border, strategic.

Roxburgh Castle (Wolfe's Claw – unofficially):

Large royal-held castle near Kelso, formerly manned by knights from Northwood, but awarded to the House of de Wolfe by royal decree for meritorious service to the crown. Volatile location, often attacked by Scots, and is manned by both royal and de Wolfe troops.

Northwood Castle:

Massive border castle, very important and strategic. Belonging to the Earls of Teviot. Not part of the de Wolfe empire, but strongly allied to de Wolfe by marriage and blood. The Earl of Teviot is Adam de Longley, recently married to Cayetana Fernanda Teresita Silva y Fausto, Princess of Aragon.

KATHRYN LE VEQUE NOVELS

Medieval Romance:

De Wolfe Pack Series:
Warwolfe
The Wolfe
Nighthawk
ShadowWolfe
DarkWolfe
A Joyous de Wolfe Christmas
BlackWolfe
Serpent
A Wolfe Among Dragons
Scorpion
StormWolfe
Dark Destroyer
The Lion of the North
Walls of Babylon
The Best Is Yet To Be
BattleWolfe

De Wolfe Pack Generations:
WolfeHeart
WolfeStrike
WolfeSword
WolfeBlade
WolfeLord
WolfeShield

The Executioner Knights:
By the Unholy Hand
The Mountain Dark
Starless
A Time of End

Winter of Solace
Lord of the Sky
Splendid Hour
The Whispering Night
Netherworld
Lord of the Shadows
Of Mortal Fury

The de Russe Legacy:
The Falls of Erith
Lord of War: Black Angel
The Iron Knight
Beast
The Dark One: Dark Knight
The White Lord of Wellesbourne
Dark Moon
Dark Steel
A de Russe Christmas Miracle
Dark Warrior

The de Lohr Dynasty:
While Angels Slept
Rise of the Defender
Steelheart
Shadowmoor
Silversword
Spectre of the Sword
Unending Love
Archangel
A Blessed de Lohr Christmas

The Brothers de Lohr:
The Earl in Winter

Lords of East Anglia:
While Angels Slept
Godspeed
Age of Gods and Mortals

Great Lords of le Bec:
Great Protector

House of de Royans:
Lord of Winter
To the Lady Born
The Centurion

Lords of Eire:
Echoes of Ancient Dreams
Blacksword
The Darkland

Ancient Kings of Anglecynn:
The Whispering Night
Netherworld

Battle Lords of de Velt:
The Dark Lord
Devil's Dominion
Bay of Fear
The Dark Lord's First Christmas
The Dark Spawn
The Dark Conqueror
The Dark Angel

Reign of the House of de Winter:
Lespada
Swords and Shields

De Reyne Domination:
Guardian of Darkness
A Cold Wynter's Knight
With Dreams
The Fallen One
Black Storm

House of d'Vant:
Tender is the Knight (House of d'Vant)
The Red Fury (House of d'Vant)

The Dragonblade Series:
Fragments of Grace
Dragonblade
Island of Glass
The Savage Curtain
The Fallen One

Great Marcher Lords of de Lara
Dragonblade

House of St. Hever
Fragments of Grace
Island of Glass
Queen of Lost Stars

Lords of Pembury:
The Savage Curtain

Lords of Thunder: The de Shera Brotherhood Trilogy
The Thunder Lord
The Thunder Warrior
The Thunder Knight

The Great Knights of de Moray:
Shield of Kronos
The Gorgon

House of De Nerra:
The Promise
The Falls of Erith
Vestiges of Valor
Realm of Angels

Highland Warriors of Munro:
The Red Lion

Deep Into Darkness

The House of de Garr:
Lord of Light
Realm of Angels

Saxon Lords of Hage:
The Crusader
Kingdom Come

High Warriors of Rohan:
High Warrior

The House of Ashbourne:
Upon a Midnight Dream

The House of D'Aurilliac:
Valiant Chaos

The House of De Dere:
Of Love and Legend

St. John and de Gare Clans:
The Warrior Poet

The House of de Bretagne:
The Questing

The House of Summerlin:
The Legend

The Kingdom of Hendocia:
Kingdom by the Sea

Regency Historical Romance:
Sin Like Flynn: A Regency
Historical Romance Duet

Gothic Regency Romance:

Emma

Contemporary Romance:

**Kathlyn Trent/Marcus Burton
Series:**
Valley of the Shadow
The Eden Factor
Canyon of the Sphinx

**The American Heroes Anthology
Series:**
The Lucius Robe
Fires of Autumn
Evenshade
Sea of Dreams
Purgatory

**Other non-connected
Contemporary Romance:**
Lady of Heaven
Darkling, I Listen
In the Dreaming Hour
River's End
The Fountain

Sons of Poseidon:
The Immortal Sea

**Pirates of Britannia Series (with
Eliza Knight):**
Savage of the Sea by Eliza Knight
Leader of Titans by Kathryn Le
Veque
The Sea Devil by Eliza Knight
Sea Wolfe by Kathryn Le Veque

Note: All Kathryn's novels are designed to be read as stand-alones, although many have cross-over characters or cross-over family groups. Novels that are grouped together have related characters or family groups. You will notice that some series have the same books; that is because they are cross-overs. A hero in one book may be the secondary character in another.

There is NO reading order except by chronology, but even in that case, you can still read the books as stand-alones. No novel is connected to another by a cliff hanger, and every book has an HEA.

Series are clearly marked. All series contain the same characters or family groups except the American Heroes Series, which is an anthology with unrelated characters.

For more information, find it in **A Reader's Guide to the Medieval World of Le Veque**.

ABOUT KATHRYN LE VEQUE

Bringing the Medieval to Romance

KATHRYN LE VEQUE is a critically acclaimed, multiple USA TODAY Bestselling author, an Indie Reader bestseller, a charter Amazon All-Star author, and a #1 bestselling, award-winning, multi-published author in Medieval Historical Romance with over 100 published novels.

Kathryn is a multiple award nominee and winner, including the winner of Uncaged Book Reviews Magazine 2017 and 2018 "Raven Award" for Favorite Medieval Romance. Kathryn is also a multiple RONE nominee (InD'Tale Magazine), holding a record for the number of nominations. In 2018, her novel WARWOLFE was the winner in the Romance category of the Book Excellence Award and in 2019, her novel A WOLFE AMONG DRAGONS won the prestigious RONE award for best pre-16th century romance.

Kathryn is considered one of the top Indie authors in the world with over 2M copies in circulation, and her novels have been translated into several languages. Kathryn recently signed with Sourcebooks Casablanca for a Medieval Fight Club series, first published in 2020.

In addition to her own published works, Kathryn is also the President/CEO of Dragonblade Publishing, a boutique publishing house specializing in Historical Romance. Dragonblade's success has seen it rise in the ranks to become Amazon's #1 e-book publisher of Historical Romance (K-Lytics report July 2020).

Kathryn loves to hear from her readers. Please find Kathryn on Facebook at Kathryn Le Veque, Author, or join her on Twitter @kathrynleveque. Sign up for Kathryn's blog at www.kathrynleveque.com for the latest news and sales.